*This book is dedicated to Nick, Ellie &
Matt with all my love.*

Chapter 1

Far below, the bends in the river Thames were outlined by the lights of the city, shimmering and winking through the thinning clouds like elusive diamonds. Siena's fingers clutched the armrest as the knots in her stomach tightened.

'You OK?' asked the older woman next to her in a soft drawl of an American accent. 'Nervous flyer?'

Ever since they'd left Charles de Gaulle airport, Siena had been convinced her next seat neighbour was Mary Steenburgen but it wouldn't have been cool to initiate conversation with a celebrity if you let on you knew who they were.

'Nervous,' Siena laughed, the pitch a little too high. She was absolutely bloody terrified, but it had nothing to do with the flight. 'No. This is hardly a flight is it?' She put on her best twinkly, smiley face. 'Straight up. Straight down.' She had enough air miles to get to the moon and back. Her third set of Louis Vuitton luggage was looking positively shabby these days.

'Been to London before?'

That gentle voice. This woman had to be her.

'Once or twice.'

'Sorry you're British. Stupid question. I can tell from your accent. You going home for Christmas?'

Stoopid, as 'perhaps Mary' pronounced it, wasn't so stupid.

Officially, Siena was as British as Marmite and Twinings tea which Maman insisted on having for breakfast every day, but she'd lived most of her life in France. She thought she felt French but then how would she know if what she felt was French or English? Sometimes, quite often really, she had no idea what she should feel about a lot of things.

'No I'm going to stay with my sister. I have to be back in France for Christmas,' she blurted out. Back at the Chateau for Harry's sixtieth birthday party on the twenty-third. She looked at her watch and worried at her lip. They'd have missed her by now. The dinner reservation was for eight thirty. Yves, her almost fiancé, would be cross, her mother furious and Harry, her stepfather, disappointed perhaps.

'How lovely, dear.' Mary's face dimpled with a gentle smile. 'I love spending time with my sister.'

Siena flushed. Mary would think she was a terrible sister. She hadn't seen Laurie for two years despite the open invitation. Resolutely ignoring that chain of thought, she focused on her possibly celebrity neighbour. Had she read somewhere that Mary Steenburgen had a sister? Siena did know she was married to that guy from Cheers and CSI. There'd been pictures of them out walking their dogs in *Hello* or *Grazia*.

'She older or younger than you?'

'Sorry? What?'

'Your sister, older or younger?'

'Older. Eight years older.'

'You close?'

Siena swallowed. 'We text. Facebook a bit.' That sounded rubbish. With a sigh she added, 'It's a bit complicated. A lot complicated actually. My parents split up when we were young. I lived with my mother in France. Laurie stayed with my father in England. I only met her properly for the first time two years ago.' So no, not close at all.

'Oh, my!' America's perfect mom actress, if it was her, looked horrified. 'That's an unusual arrangement.' Then with a sympathy laden smile she added, 'How lovely that you're going to see her. Will you be staying long?'

That was the million dollar question. Siena crossed and uncrossed her legs, staring down at her recent manicure, admiring her Santa Scarlet glossy nails. The text she'd sent Laurie asked if she could stay for the weekend. The note she'd left her mother said she'd be back in a month. Neither was quite true.

'I don't know yet. Until I'm ready to go home, I guess. Spur of the moment thing, you know.'

That sounded better. Spontaneous. Fun. Not a desperate and pathetic escape. Sisters hanging out. Spending quality time together. Not arriving completely out of the blue with only five hours' notice.

'You gotta stay for Christmas. I love London at this time of year. The stores. Hyde Park. The lights.' Mary gave a self-deprecating laugh. 'What am I talking about? You come from Paris. Now there's a city at Christmas.'

Siena closed her eyes at the quick punch to her heart. Galeries Lafayette's exterior, encrusted with the brilliance of thousands of sparkling lights and of course, the tree. The fir lined Champs-Élysées lit up and glittering, refracting diamond shards of white into the night. That swoosh of skates on ice at the Eiffel Tower and the breathless bump when you hit the sides. Tartiflette, hot and warming, from the Christmas Markets at Notre-Dame and the Trocadéro.

She loved the build-up, but somehow every year when Christmas finally arrived, the sparkle had burnt itself out. The actual holiday itself never seemed that enjoyable.

So why had she stupidly promised in her note to go back in time for Christmas when she could be lonely anywhere?

In the meantime she had a few weeks' grace to give herself time to breathe and work things out. Everything seemed to have crowded in on her recently, until she couldn't think straight anymore. Surely her mother would understand.

With the change of air pressure in the cabin, her ears popped. The captain announced they were due to land in ten minutes and the flight was on time. She glanced back down the aisle still fearful a hand might clamp down on her shoulder and someone utter the words, 'You need to come with me, mademoiselle.'

She looked at her watch. It might take a while to get through passport control, it always did at Heathrow but at least she didn't have to wait for baggage. The potential disaster of only having two pairs of boots and a capsule wardrobe was more than outweighed by being able to make a speedy getaway from the airport. Once out of there she'd be home free.

With that consoling thought she gave the American, who probably wasn't Mary at all, a smile and turned back to the copy of *Hello* spread out on her lap. A picture caught her eye and she couldn't help a tut escaping.

'Big mistake,' she shook her head. What had the young movie star been thinking?

'Sorry dear?'

Siena showed her neighbour the double page spread in the magazine.

'I mean seriously, would you? Off the shoulder, one side only. Seriously passé. Although the Dolce & Gabbana shoes are nice, almost save the outfit, even if they are last season's.'

The woman studied the picture with a thoughtful serious gaze.

'Sometimes, dear, you don't get any choice in the matter. There's so much that goes on behind the scenes. Agents. Publicists. Poor girl, her life is probably not her own. Imagine dancing to someone else's tune, all the time.'

Siena didn't need to do any imagining.

'Especially when you're so young. She should be out having a good time. It gets easier when you get older and you can tell them to go hoot.'

Bonté divine, Siena hoped so.

Just as she'd finally decided to ask the woman if she was Mary, the sudden roar of the plane's engines signalled their descent and despite her stockpile of air miles, Siena couldn't help clutching the seat rest, again. In no time at all, the wheels touched down with a bump and a hiss. They'd arrived.

England.

Siena closed her eyes. Here she was. The captain's voice welcomed them to London, announcing that it was eleven o'clock in the evening local time.

Eleven o'clock. Was that all? It seemed a lifetime ago since she'd tiptoed out of the Chateau like a thief in the night clutching her hastily thrown together cabin bag.

Despite the lateness of the hour, Heathrow was rammed. All around, voices jabbered in a multitude of languages.

Her phone beeped. Another text from Orange mobile welcoming her to England, the third since she'd got off the plane. Nothing from Laurie. Then again, it always took a while for your mobile to sync with a new network. Siena might not know her sister that well, but one thing she did know – Laurie was one hundred percent reliable. She'd be here.

In the last two years she'd kept in touch, like she'd promised. During two fleeting days, when they'd met as adults for the first time, Laurie had made the incredibly generous promise that there would always be a room for Siena in her house. Now, Siena was counting on it.

Flicking through the touch screen on her phone, she brought up her favourite picture. The first one Laurie had sent to her. It had been a talisman in recent weeks.

She enlarged the picture with two fingers on the touch screen, bringing the small double bed framed by a brass bedstead into focus. Its pure white duvet looked as soft as a mound of freshly fallen snow, dotted with a pastel palate of scatter cushions in lilac, pale blue and silver grey. Behind the bedhead, the wall had been papered with a pretty toile wallpaper. White painted tables flanked the bed each with a bedside light.

If this picture had been a photograph, it would have been worn thin where she'd touched it, marvelling at the thoughtfulness of the sister she barely knew. She smiled as she looked at the digital image, reducing it in size as if tucking it carefully away. Tonight she'd be sleeping in that bed. Safe. In her own room. If it hadn't been so sad, Siena could have laughed at the fanciful direction of her thoughts. She was hardly little orphan Annie. She had her own room in several houses in France, one in Mustique and one in New York.

This one was different. Her sister hadn't had to do that for her. Laurie owed her nothing, not really, despite what Maman always said.

'Passport, miss,' snapped the uniformed man in the little booth. 'Please put your phone away.'

'Sorry.' She gave him a brilliant smile which surprisingly had no effect at all. Miserable little man. Still smiling, determined to win him over, she pushed her passport under the glass toward him and shoved her phone in her bag.

No point phoning Laurie now, when she'd see her in a few minutes.

With a bored glance, the terse passport officer stared at her, back at her photo and then pushed the passport through a barcode reader. He studied something on the screen for a longer moment. For a brief second, Siena's heart beat faster. Surely nothing would have been flagged up; not this quickly?

He looked at her face, then back at the passport. When he looked at her face again, she tried to keep her face utterly impassive, just like her photo. Her heart thumped uncomfortably hard. Yves' family had contacts throughout the French legal system. Did they extend here?

After the longest thirty seconds in history, the passport was finally pushed back under the glass. Siena almost sagged with relief as she tucked it into her bag and strode without looking back through the Nothing to Declare channel.

Done. Through this point and she was home and dry. Officially in England.

As she neared the double doors, she slowed. Would Laurie look the same? Was her hair any different? Inside her chest, Siena's heart did a little squiggly jump and she pushed through the doors, another smile already lighting up her face as she scanned the waiting faces. A blur of faces peered back at her, eyes anxious and hopeful.

She quickly smoothed her hands down her denim-clad thighs, the palms ever so slightly damp. In her hurried departure, there'd been no time to visit the hairdressers or have a facial. Although her jeans were 7 For All Mankind and her top was Stella McCartney, it was a going shopping outfit rather than a stepping off a first class flight into the international arrival hall at Terminal 4. Thankfully she hadn't seen anyone she knew on the flight and it didn't look as if there were any paparazzi here.

Siena's gaze flitted backwards and forwards with the eagerness of a spectator at the Roland-Garros tennis final. Where was Laurie? It was difficult to see everyone. There were quite a few smartly dressed men, holding up signs with names handwritten in misshapen capitals. How much nicer was it, being met by family? Someone to hug and kiss like they always did in the films. Usually when she arrived anywhere with her parents, they'd have a driver waiting.

Again she scanned the faces. Had she missed Laurie? She looked back.

Maybe her sister was late. Just parking the car. Nearly quarter to twelve. Traffic should be good now, although perhaps not. The Arc de Triomphe at this time on a Saturday night was bedlam. She checked her texts again. Had she given her the right time of the flight landing? Maybe in her rush she'd told Laurie the plane left at eleven instead of landing at eleven. Nope, there it was, the last text she'd sent earlier this afternoon.

Hey Laurie. You know you've been inviting me to come stay, forever, and how I was welcome any time and that you'd come pick me up? Don't faint. I'm coming. My plane lands at 11.00pm tonight. Heathrow. Air France. Flight 1080. Can you pick me up? Can't wait to see you and to finally get to stay in my room.

Where was Laurie?

Even if the number of people hadn't thinned in the last half hour, she would have noticed him straight away. Anger and irritation rolled off him in waves. Like an angry Moses, his strides ate up the floor, people melting out of his path. From the inside pocket of his black leather jacket he pulled out a white piece of paper and held it up, then slumped against a pillar.

Siena almost laughed out loud. This guy needed to learn a thing or two about customer service. His eyebrows had merged into one angry slash across his forehead. With a scowl like that he'd scare his passengers back onto their plane.

His face now held a look of bored resignation, the sheet dangling from his hand as if it was too much trouble to even lift it to chest height like the other drivers did.

She checked her phone again. Still no word from Laurie. It was now ten past twelve.

Siena shifted her bag and her weight from foot to foot.

The movement caught the attention of the dark-haired guy at the barrier as he briefly turned around. How could a grown man pout like that and still look attractive? He should have looked ridiculous but that fuller lower lip was really rather cute. She sneaked another look at his face and he swung around properly to give her a baleful glare. As he did, she caught sight of the name on the sheet he held.

Ah *merde*!

He'd spelt her name wrongly but then most people did, so she could hardly hold that against him. Flashing her best million kilowatt smile, she took a step forward, her head inclining towards her name. He looked down at the name and then back at her, not saying a word. His face didn't warm one iota, if anything he looked even more forbidding.

Like a Mexican standoff, both of them stood waiting for the other to break and say the first word. They stood there as the seconds ticked away, neither saying anything. Clenching her hands to her sides, the tiredness she'd been fighting won. 'I'm Siena. Just one 'n'.'

'How do you know I'm not here to pick up Sienna, two 'n's?' he grumbled.

Damn, that hadn't occurred to her. She shrugged, 'Sorry, my mistake.'

She'd only taken two strides when a hand grabbed her arm.

'I'm guessing you are Laurie's sister?'

'Yes.' Siena observed him with curious eyes. Piercing blue eyes bored into her, the wide mouth with its full lower lip had flattened into a mutinous line. Gorgeous and grumpy, without an ounce of charm.

'I had to pick you up. Laurie isn't around at the moment.'

'Oh.' Siena felt a bit put out. 'Where is she?'

He raised an eyebrow. She hated it when people could do that. 'Where is she? You're asking that?'

'It wasn't a trick question.'

'Seriously? You text at six in the evening. Expect her to drop everything. Pick you up and then you ask, 'Where is she?''

'I don't see what it's got to do with you.' Whoever this man was, he had a cheek.

He stood and considered her for a moment, she felt like a model being sized up to see if the designer's clothes would fit.

'No, I guess you don't. You're right, it has nothing to do with me.' Despite agreeing with her, he still managed to make it sound like an insult. 'She's up in Yorkshire.'

'Yorkshire!' Siena felt a bit stupid echoing his words but she didn't actually know what or where Yorkshire was or why it was up. That sounded decidedly odd, as if it were in space or something, which she was pretty sure she would have heard of, if any part of the world had colonised space.

'Norah had a fall, Laurie's been at the hospital for most of the day. She asked me to pick you up. She can't get a great phone signal there, so couldn't contact you to let you know she wasn't around. I'm to take you back to the house for tonight. Laurie will speak to you in the morning.' He bit out each sentence as if he had a mouthful of tacks he was scared of losing.

Siena vaguely remembered the mention of a Norah from some of Laurie's recent emails.

'I thought Norah worked for Uncle Miles. Wasn't she the housekeeper?' mused Siena out loud which was stupid because the driver was hardly going to know.

Could a scowl get any deeper? 'She still is. He's dead obviously but she's still the housekeeper at the house.'

'OK,' said Siena still doing her best to keep her smile up despite his quelling expression and the confusing information.

Siena felt she'd strayed into very dangerous territory but had no idea what had tipped it over into a fully operational minefield. Any minute now, this rather scary but gorgeous man, might blow. It unnerved her. People were usually nice to her. Most people. It seemed safest to keep smiling and not irritate him further by saying anything. Although her smiles didn't seem to be having much effect on his mood. The silence stretched out between them until eventually with an exasperated huff, he spoke.

'Norah is eighty-six,' he said it slowly followed by a laboured pause, 'Laurie said she couldn't just abandon her.'

'Yes, of course not.' Siena's cheeks were starting to hurt but she persevered.

'So she asked me to pick you up.'

'Ok, well … Hi, I'm – you know who I am. Laurie's sister.'

'I know exactly who you are,' he replied dryly.

Did he have to make it sound as if she were so unsavoury? She was house trained.

'Is that your luggage?' He pointed to her cabin bag and the bulging duty free bag.

She nodded. The cabin bag did look a bit sad on its own but there'd been no time to pack properly. Luckily she'd been able to stock up on all the essentials in duty free.

'Yes, it's not much but I need to buy my spring wardrobe soon anyway, so I figured I might as well do it while I'm here. So, yes that's it, I'm afraid.'

He gave her a dirty look. 'It's not a problem, I promise you.' Without another word he set off, deliberately walking at speed as if to keep a healthy distance between them.

'Er, excuse me?' she called after him. He turned. 'Haven't you forgotten something?' He might be a poor excuse for a driver but he should still do the basics. 'My bags?'

Blue eyes burned bright with indignation and he shook his head, muttering under his breath. He snatched the bags up and marched off. No tip for him then. Oh hell, they used sterling in England didn't they? There were only euros in her purse.

Following, she tried to keep up with his long-legged stride.

Maybe this had been a terrible idea. Her phone buzzed in her pocket and she snatched it up. Laurie? No, Maman. Her diaphragm tensed and for a minute she couldn't breathe. Flash. Flash. Flash. Like a lighthouse, the beam on her iPhone pulsed with urgency. She stopped and stared down, her finger hovering over the screen.

Ahead of her the man had stopped and turned.

'Going to get that? Or just stare at it all night. Some of us have places to be in the morning.'

She sighed and caught up with him. Once they got to the car, he would be driving and she could get in the back and sleep until they got to Laurie's house in Leighton Buzzard. She had no idea what part of London that was or how long it would take to get there but it felt easier not to ask him.

Siena skidded to a halt but didn't dare open her mouth. He had to be kidding. What sort of Mickey Mouse outfit did this guy work for?

'Come on,' he growled over his shoulder as he unlocked the boot of the mud-covered Land Rover. 'It's already after midnight.'

'Seriously?' She stared at the dirty green paintwork, unconsciously echoing his earlier phrase. 'This is your car?'

'Seriously yes. It's my car. But don't worry, there is an alternative.'

'Thank goodness for that.' She looked around the car park and spotted a pristine black Mercedes parked two bays along. 'Where?'

He looked down, his eyes travelling the length of her legs to the floor. She followed his gaze.

'What?'

'You're looking at them.'

She flushed. Tossing her head she crossed to the door of the car, with as much *froideur* as she could manage, opened it and hauled herself in. It was a long way up. Half way, she realised her mistake.

He stood by the door grinning holding a set of keys. 'Missing something.'

She slid back out, refusing to look at him, keeping her face totally impassive and walked around the back of the car to the passenger seat. So, she was used to left hand drive cars, he didn't need to be mean about it.

This horrible thing looked Spartan and uncomfortable. Unlikely she'd be taking a nap. Even climbing up was ungainly and her tight jeans protested, cutting sharply into her thighs. Immediately her feet were buried ankle deep in white paper bags, Coke cans and disposable coffee cups.

A pervading scent of manure and sweaty socks filled the vehicle. You couldn't call it a car; it wasn't civilised enough.

Years of being instilled with impeccable manners didn't prevent her involuntary shudder. His eyes sharpened for a moment and she thought she'd offended him again. Although he seemed pretty easily offended.

'Sorry about the mess. I wasn't expecting passengers today.'

'Were you ever?' The words slipped out before she could stop them.

His head shot round and his dark eyes flashed with the closest thing to approval she'd yet seen. He gave her a rueful smile. 'You got me there. No, this is my work horse.' He patted the dashboard affectionately as he glanced down at her feet which she'd used to push the mass of litter to one side. There was a rustle as a couple of Coke cans tumbled together.

'Ugh,' she clutched her knees in her hand lifting her feet above the mess, 'you haven't got rats in here have you?'

A mischievous glint danced in his eyes and his face lit up with a sudden cheerful smile. 'It's a distinct possibility.' And with that he started the engine, which coughed into life with a noisy, diesel fuelled rumble.

Siena sneaked a surreptitious look at his profile as he concentrated on manoeuvring the beast out of the car park. Now they were in the car his temper seemed to have abated. He seemed a tiny bit more human and, she had to admit, very good-looking in an unpolished way. Not that he was her kind of man. Too scruffy and masculine. Butch. Far too butch. Dark stubble shaded his chin and cheeks, emphasising the strong lines of his face and heavy jawline. Put him in a decent suit and he'd brush up nicely, although his arms and legs seemed rather muscular. Powerful. She tucked her hands under her legs and shrank into her seat.

Yves had a completely different build; slim and slender and of course, much older.

She checked out his clothes. Double denim. A fashion fiasco. She suspected he wouldn't care if she pointed out that some people believed it was an unpardonable offence to wear jeans and a denim jacket unless you were a member of Status Quo.

Clean hair; nice and silky even though it might as well have been cut by a near-sighted trainee with a pair of blunt hedge clippers. Breathing in, she took in his scent, slightly earthy but not unclean. Siena could bet he didn't do aftershave.

'There isn't an exam you know.'

Siena started and blushed. What was wrong with her? This man had caught her sniffing him, or as good as. Her face burned. At home she would have apologised profusely. It was rude to stare and plainly even ruder to overtly smell people but for some reason, maybe being away from home gave her tongue licence to say what she really thought for a change, she said, 'Just checking out my surroundings and getting my orientation.'

'I'm Jason. I'm twenty-nine. That do you?'

'And are you always this *fache*?' she shrugged as she grasped for the proper word. (Cross, that was it.) And then very nearly spoilt things by gasping at her own boldness. She never said things like that to people and she'd certainly learned not to with Yves. That sort of thing did make him cross.

'No, only when I've been up since half past five this morning and I have to be up again in five hours.' He slipped a silver foil packet out of his pocket, easing out a tablet with one hand and popping it into his mouth.

'I guess you're a bit tired then.' No wonder he was knocking back the energy tablets or whatever they were.

He shot her an incredulous look. 'No shit Sherlock.'

Siena snapped her mouth shut. She'd been about to add, that she was grateful for him coming out. These people worked incredibly hard. Was it any wonder he was cranky with those hours? Although it was probably a hazard of the job, early morning airport runs were probably the most lucrative. She wrinkled her nose.

'You know,' she smiled to show she was being helpful rather than rude, 'you might get more customers if you cleaned up in here. Maybe got a better car.'

'I can't see how.'

'You mean your customers don't mind?'

'None of them have complained so far.'

Siena pulled a face to herself in the dark. Maybe British people were less fussy about their taxis.

With an ungainly swerve, the car rocked at speed around a bend taking the slip road. Alain, the family chauffeur, would have been appalled.

Weren't they now going in the opposite direction to the sign-posts for London? Her stomach followed suit and nausea churned in the pit of her stomach.

'Where are we going?' she asked, rather proud that her voice sounded normal. She should have asked this Jason man for some kind of identification. Thierry Deneuve's seventeen-year-old daughter had been kidnapped in Italy last June. Everyone knew he'd paid a hefty ransom demand to get her back, even though the police warned them not to.

'Home?'

'What, your home?' Siena sat up straighter, clutching her bag closer to her chest and eyed the passing lights outside. They were going by pretty quickly now. She probably looked ridiculous but if she had to make a run for it, she had everything she needed in there.

Jason turned his head and gave her a funny look. 'Strictly speaking, I guess it's Laurie's house.'

'I might have just stepped off the plane but I can read.'

'Good for you.'

Did he think she was stupid? 'So why are we headed in the opposite direction?'

Occasionally taxi drivers in Paris took her on a circular route if they heard her speaking English, making the assumption she was a tourist.

'We're not.'

'So why did it say London that way?' She pointed back up the motorway.

'Because. It. Is.'

'So why are we going this way towards Slew?' She pointed to the overhead blue sign, which had handily appeared at exactly that moment. He didn't need to know she didn't have a clue where Slough was.

Jason snorted and said in a strangled voice, 'Where?'

'Slew,' she said her eyes narrowing. Wait 'til she spoke to Laurie; she'd tell her to not to use this cab company again.

Despite his bone-deep tiredness, Jason shook with laughter.

'Oops.' He wrenched the wheel and they veered off the M4 onto the slip road towards the signs for M25 Gatwick and M25 Watford.

'Nearly missed it,' he said still chuckling to himself. How in hell's name was this spoilt brat related in any way to Laurie? It wasn't possible.

'So,' he snorted again, 'where,' another snigger, 'where do you th-think Laurie lives? Not *Slew* obviously.' He wheezed and started slapping the steering wheel trying to regain some equilibrium.

'Leighton Buzzard.' Siena folded her arms across her chest and stuck her chin in the air.

'Good,' he wheezed again, 'because that's where we're headed. And it's pronounced Slough as in bough.'

'I think it's very rude to laugh. How was I supposed to know that? If you were in France, I wouldn't laugh at your pronunciation.'

He gave her a dry look. 'But I'm not French. So why would you? You're English.'

With a pout she folded her arms.

He gave her a closer look. She looked damn good, if you liked that sort of thing. A babe but too high maintenance. Skyscraper, Fifth Avenue, Mayfair type maintenance. He knew the type. Knew them well. Trust fund babies who expected the world to drop everything at their bidding. Incapable of doing anything for themselves. Been there, done that and he wasn't going to be anyone's gravy train again. Stacey, his ex, had boarded that ride and then left him the minute he chose a new route.

And yet, despite all his best intentions, here he was again, knight to the rescue. At six o'clock this morning he'd been in Glasgow. If anyone else had asked him to race to Heathrow he'd have told them where to stick it but he owed Laurie. She let him rent her house at a ridiculously low rate and as she was shacked up with one of his best mates, she couldn't be all bad. Cam had very high standards when it came to women.

'So you thought you'd pop over to see your sister,' he asked, still cross on Laurie's behalf.

'Yes. Fancied spending some time together.' The cheery, shallow smile made him grit his teeth. He wasn't about to enlighten her. Laurie had been quite specific in her instructions. If anyone from her family enquired, he wasn't to mention she'd gone to live in the house she'd inherited from her Uncle Miles. Apparently her mother was very unhappy about the terms of the will. And Jason would not betray Laurie's confidence … especially for his spoiled, snobby – and rather hot – passenger.

Chapter 2

When the noisy Land Rover finally drew to a stop, they could have been anywhere. It was pitch black and Siena only had Jason's word for it that they had arrived at the correct destination.

Jason opened the door, and waited for her, his breath rising into the icy air in a plume of steam. She followed quickly. This was the house she'd grown up in. She lived here until she was six. They'd been a proper family here. A mum, a dad and two sisters. Nails digging in her palms she looked around. A narrow hallway opened up in front of them, with a beautiful wooden staircase leading upstairs.

Siena blinked as he flicked on lights and smiled at the sight of the natural oak spindles on the staircase, which had a striped runner lining the centre of each step with brass stair rods. A large mirror, framed in rustic oak, reflected the antique brass light in the centre of the ceiling. This was lovely and not at all how she'd pictured the house from her mother's dismissive comments. She waited for a moment. Not a shred of recognition. Nothing. Absolutely nothing.

'Lounge. Kitchen.' Jason nodded to closed doors on the right.

'Your room is upstairs at the back. Bathroom in the middle.'

Siena blinked and picked up her bag, back ramrod straight as she held back the sudden inexplicable tears. They had no business here. She needed sleep. That was all. Today had been lots of things, none of which she wanted to tax her brain with at the moment. All she knew was that her eyelids felt heavy, her head felt heavy and her stupid heart heavier still. What had she been expecting? A sense of homecoming? If she didn't get to bed now, she'd never make it up the stairs and she had to see her bedroom.

Rummaging through her bag she pulled out her purse. Euros would have to do.

'Thanks,' she said thrusting a ten euro note into Jason's hand. Without looking back she clattered up the stairs. She heard the front door slam with some force but she was too intent on her room to look back. She took the last four two at a time.

Perhaps it would feel different up here. In her room. The room her older sister had decorated for her. The room she'd slept in every night until she was six and ten-twelfths, before her mother took her to France, leaving Laurie and the father she didn't remember behind.

Stopping at the closed door, she took a deep breath, grasped the handle and stepped into the warm glow cast by one of the bedside lights. Someone had left it on for her. The soft light made her feel welcome, as if she were expected, as did the bed, piled high with cushions with shadowed furrows in the deep feather duvet. It made her want to dive right in. The room looked perfect. She touched the little white painted chest at the foot of the bed as she took in every bit of the English cottage-styled loveliness, from the shiny spars of the brass bed, to the delicate lacy curtains at the window, through to the sanded floorboards and the pretty rug under her feet. The room looked exactly as it had in the photograph. But that was her only sense of recognition.

Panic clutched at her chest.

Once she'd seen a rescue team on the mountainside digging desperately for survivors. She felt like one of them, frantically shovelling through her memories, desperate to find one that confirmed she'd once played with toys, got dressed and slept in this room.

But there was nothing. Bleakness settled on her. Had this been a stupid mistake?

She took a deep breath and pushed her shoulders back. Crazy thinking. So she didn't remember the house. It didn't matter. Tomorrow, Laurie would be here and they'd be sisters together. They could have a proper sister sleepover with wine, chocolate, a chick flick like in real chick flicks and she could forget about Maman. And Yves. And engagements. And weddings. And letting the family down. And everything. She closed her eyes. Maman was bound to have found the note by now.

But she was an adult. She didn't have to ask permission to go away. She'd told Maman she'd be back for Christmas. For Harry's party.

With reluctance she pulled out her phone and looked at the series of missed calls. Ignoring the anxiety spiralling through her chest, she switched it off and buried it deep in her handbag.

The double bed looked so plump and inviting. As she turned back the covers, the feather duvet rustled and shifted with a siren call promising comfort.

Stripping off her clothes and scattering them on the floor, she pushed the pile of cushions aside and slipped between the sheets, immediately sinking into the mattress. Did it feel like coming home? She lay cocooned in the crisp white cotton and listened. Outside, a few cars rumbled past. They sounded very close and so loud. So different from the Chateau.

As her head sank into the pillow and she drifted in that half-awake, half-asleep dream world, she thought she heard footsteps on the stairs but it was too much effort to open her eyes again. Laurie was home. She fought sleep for a minute but it overcame her. They could have breakfast together.

Chapter 3

The bathroom, with its Victorian styled sink and bath, had a damp used-not-so-long-ago taint to it but there was no sign of Laurie.

Siena's eager tour of the downstairs of the house had taken precisely eight minutes. She almost checked the walls to make sure she hadn't missed a secret passageway or a door leading to another wing. Nope. The hallway of the Chateau had more furniture than this whole house.

Where was Laurie though? Siena figured she must have gone out to get some groceries as the fridge was almost bare apart from something called shepherd's pie, although it didn't look like any pie she'd ever come across, and a tiny bit of milk in the oddest glass bottle she'd ever seen.

Conscious of the dryness of her mouth, she squeezed past the pine table big enough to seat four, stopping to take a closer look at the cheerful place mats covered in jaunty chickens in reds, yellows and oranges before switching on the enamel red kettle. The cosy country kitchen made you want to stay awhile, sit at the table and chat. It was easy to picture evenings in here, sitting in the spindle-backed chairs, sipping wine at the table with her sister. She sighed. She couldn't wait to see Laurie. They were going to have so much fun and hopefully she wouldn't mind her staying a bit longer.

Reaching above into the distressed cream-painted wooden

cupboard, she found an assortment of china mugs, each patterned with different flowers. Making herself a cup of tea, she leant against the counter and studied the eclectic collection of china egg cups and pottery jugs which lined the shelves of the wooden dresser on the other side of the room.

Taking her tea, and crossing the terracotta tiled floor which felt cold under her feet, she went through to the tiny, tiny lounge. The whole room was smaller than her dressing room in the Paris apartment but despite that, the cottage style sofa with its floral print purple wisteria trailing across the plump feather-cushioned sofa strewn with perfectly co-ordinated fat cushions in muted colours, was charming. The room even had a proper open cast-iron fireplace with a surround of flower painted ceramic tiles and a clutch of brass fire-tools in a stand beside it. Twists of newspaper piled with coal sat in the grate waiting to be lit. Feeling a little bit like Goldilocks but sure that Laurie wouldn't mind, she picked up the box of matches from the crowded wooden mantle. There were several framed pictures including one of Laurie and her boyfriend Cam laughing their heads off at something out of the shot and a faded black and white photo of an older man. Siena studied it for a moment and put it back hurriedly.

The flames had caught. Nice going on the fire making front. With a happy sigh, she snuggled down and picked up her magazine, one of a collection she'd bought at Charles de Gaulle. It was hardly a taxing prospect, whiling away the time waiting for Laurie by flicking through the pages of party themed sequinned dresses, shimmering eye shadows and gorgeous clutch bags and listening to the snap and crackle of the fire. She turned another page. So, she'd miss Claude's Christmas soirée at the Musée d'Orsay. Possibly the best event in Paris and the only thing she'd miss. With a moue of acceptance she shrugged. No matter. She'd have fun with Laurie.

And as if she conjured her up, her mobile phone vibrated into life.

'Hi Sien … son texted me … picked you up OK.' Laurie's Dalek voice snapped in and out of range.

'I can hardly hear you.' Siena winced at the plaintive whine in her voice. It sounded so pathetic and needy, not the image she wanted to portray. 'Are you still in Yorkshire?'

'Yes. Sorry. Really bad line. At …pital. How's the room? Do you … Can't leave N … hospital at least … Don't worry Jason will—' The signal died leaving a long buzzing tone.

Her heart bumped a little uncomfortably and she worried at her lip. So who had used the bathroom this morning? And when was she going to get the chance to explain properly to Laurie how long she planned to stay? Laurie probably assumed Siena finally had a free weekend and had taken up the invitation originally extended over two years ago.

She winced. That sounded crap. It was crap. One hundred and four weekends that she'd failed to come and see her sister; she should have managed at least one. She glanced back at her phone, now registering all the missed calls and voicemails. She could go through and delete them but keeping them was like keeping a wasp in a jar. Safely contained and fine as long as it stayed in there.

Nestled in her hand the phone felt like a time bomb ticking.

'Time to finish up, Ben.'

As if someone had pulled the plug on the power, Ben dropped the hose he was using to wash down the concrete floor and pulled off his beanie hat, stuffing it into his pocket. The hose flailed wildly for a second, hitting Jason's trousers before Ben managed to get to the tap to switch it off. Jason stared down at the dark wet patch running from crotch to knee. Yup, looked exactly like he'd wet himself. He shook his head and rolled his eyes behind Ben's back. No point bawling the boy out. He only had himself to blame. By now he should know full well that Ben took every-thing quite literally.

Jason sighed out loud. The plus point meant you could be

incredibly direct, the downside was that you had to be extremely careful what you said.

'If you wash out the pipes on the bottling line, then you can finish.' He took a quick look around the small barn area, feeling that familiar sense of pride. The gleaming fermentation tanks, the bottling line and the stores of grain lined up in the old stable area. The high roof of the barn made it a cold, but light and airy environment to work in, one that he had never failed to want to arrive at every morning.

'Good work today. Now that lot's bottled, we can start again next week.'

They'd worked like stink today, so hard neither of them had felt the cold of the barn, until he'd got soaked. Now the cold stung and the chill seeped below his layers. They could wrap up for the day. Today's backbreaking pace had paid off. Back on schedule, all ready to start brewing tomorrow. Ben had managed to fix the miller, so that they could grind down the malt barley and get it together with the water into the mash tun. Brewing was a magical process. It never ceased to amaze him that you could get so many infinite flavours from the simple combination of water and grain

He rolled his stiff neck. A satisfying day, which would be all the better for a long hot shower, an instant meal and bed. All he had to do was finish up in the office, nip over the courtyard to see Will, enjoy a quick post work pint and head home. It was handy having his business partner running the pub next door and of course owning a convenient barn that was perfect for a micro-brewery.

'Jason, what you having? Busman's holiday?' Will slid off the bar stool, lifted the wooden flap and went round to the other side of the bar. Ben was already ensconced comfortably at the bar, halfway down a pint.

'Corona, please.'

'Seriously ...' Will rolled his eyes at Ben. 'Young Ben here is loyal to the cause. Drinking a pint of Chiltern Glory. It's your money. If you buy a pint of your own, it's win win.'

Ben raised his glass. 'Tastes good, boss.'

Jason laughed. 'Go on then.' He had just wanted to neck something cold. 'I'll have a half.'

'Ironed out all the problems?' Will was the perfect business partner, silent when he needed to be and hugely supportive and enthusiastic at all other times. They'd known each other since university when they'd played rugby together but they had more in common than their shared passion for beer. Both of them had lost their fathers in recent years which had strengthened their bond of friendship, although unlike his, Will's relationship with his father had always been strained, which Will put down to the fact that he suspected they weren't actually related by blood at all.

'Yup. One of the tanks sprang a leak but Ben sorted it out.'

'Pretty handy at welding, aren't you Ben? You coming tonight?'

'Yeah.' His brown eyes lit up with enthusiasm. 'You get posh totty in wine bars don't you. They go in for all that malarkey, don't they?'

Will nodded, veiled amusement in his eyes, like an elder statesmen with a young buck.

Jason rocked his head back. 'Oh shit, I'd forgotten about that. I'm knackered. I had to go on bloody rescue mission last night for Laurie.'

'I thought she had a boyfriend for that sort of stuff. Cam's a lazy bastard'

They both laughed. Cam had been at university with them too and neither of them could quite get over the fact that he'd found his soul mate and settled down.

'Laurie's sister decided to pop over for the weekend from Paris. Like you do. No warning or anything. So I had to rush to the frigging airport to collect the spoilt brat.'

'So where is she now?'

'I bloody hope on a flight back to where she came from.'

'That's alright then. So what time will I see you?'

Jason rubbed the back of his neck. 'When I get there.'

'Might be a new customer for the brewery. And I want to check out the competition,' Will grinned, 'and Ben wants to check out the hot chicks.'

Leaning back against the front door, Jason kicked off his wet boots on the large square doormat he'd purposely bought to protect Laurie's carpet and began to peel off his clothes, dropping them onto the floor. He dried out a bit in the pub but invariably he came home dirty and wet, an inescapable aspect of the job. It had become a habit to strip off his outer clothes at the door, less distance to carry them to the washing machine later.

He padded quickly up the stairs, already anticipating the first jet of hot water pouring over his aching shoulders. No doubt about it, showers had to the best invention of the modern world. Along with ice-cold beer drunk straight from the bottle. He'd missed a trick, he should have snagged a bottle before he'd come up.

Thoughts of condensation, dripping bottles and the shock of the cold on his throat were abruptly terminated by an outraged shriek as he took his third step into the room.

Bloody hell fire. Lying completely naked – why wouldn't she be in a bath – was a vision of rosy tipped nipples, magnolia skin, long legs and a narrow strip of strawberry blonde that declared the owner was a natural blonde. He swallowed hard, unable to take his gaze from her pert high breasts, which she was doing her best to cover by crossing her arms.

'Get out, get out!' She flapped her hands at him.

'Shit, what are you doing in here?'

'Taking a bath, you *espèce d'imbécile*? What are you doing?'

Jason tried to avert his gaze to focus on her face. Even at the height of her embarrassment, the flush that outlined her high cheekbones was dainty pink.

'I was hoping to take a shower.'

26

'Turn around. Stop looking.'

He bit his lip and turned around. 'I was trying.' Not as hard as he was trying not to snigger now.

'Try harder,' she snapped.

He heard a slosh of water and the slide of skin on plastic and a thud as she manoeuvred out of the bath.

When he turned round, she had a towel firmly wrapped around her, toga style.

'What are you doing here?'

'What do you mean what am I doing here? What are you still doing here? As Laurie's not here I thought you'd be on the next plane back.'

There was a silence and all he could see was the crown of her head. It gave him a momentary feeling of victory. Then she tipped her head up, her chin thrust upwards.

'I thought I'd stay until she comes back.'

She was in for a very long wait then. He sucked in his cheeks trying to bite back a smirk. 'When did you last speak to her?'

'This afternoon.'

Jason almost laughed out loud as he caught the reflection in the mirror of her quickly crossing her fingers and slipping them behind her back. With her head tilted slightly to one side, her eyes watching him warily, she reminded him of a defiant teenager, except that there was nothing teenage about her body; she was all woman.

'Funny that she didn't mention she'd moved to Yorkshire permanently.' There didn't seem much point trying to hide it any more. Siena would realise soon enough that her sister now lived in the house in Yorkshire.

Her eyes clouded and he could see her weighing up what to say next. He wanted to laugh, but something in her face made him aware for the first time of a slight hint of vulnerability. Not as self-possessed as he'd assumed. It made him pause.

'It was a really bad line,' she tossed her chin in the air, 'but it doesn't answer my question. What are you doing here? You said she'd moved to Yorkshire. So, what? You thought you'd move in?'

She folded her arms, giving him a hard stare before realising it's pretty difficult to hang on to a towel and fold your arms. The towel slipped, revealing one very erect and perky nipple. Desire shot to his groin. He narrowed his eyes and glared at her, trying to quash the unruly thought that he wanted to reach forwards and touch her naked breast. What the—? Where the hell had that come from? He was in danger of embarrassing himself in his boxers.

Flushed from her bath, her chest rising and falling with fast breaths of indignation, her pink, pink mouth pursed in imperious indignation, she looked very cute. The kind of cute he'd long since given up on. The kind of cute that needed a lot of looking after which, as he'd so disastrously proved, he was not capable of.

'If you leave now, I won't report you to the police. I took your registration number down last night, you know.' The way she lifted her chin, trying to hold his gaze, told him she had a nice line in bravado but was making every word up.

'The police will find you. I texted my mother. Go now and I won't tell your company.'

Jason frowned as she carried on talking complete gibberish, taking perverse pleasure in her rising determination to appear in control, which he knew wasn't very nice of him but he didn't want to be nice to this girl. He wanted her out of his house.

Two spots of colour burned fiercely on her cheeks, giving her away.

'Won't tell them what exactly?' He leaned his hip against the sink and folded his arms.

What was she on about? He was the company, Will was a silent partner, so there was him, and Ben, but most of the time Ben was away with the fairies. She obviously meant some other company, although he wasn't sure where that came in.

'That you're,' he could see her struggling to find the word, 'squatting.'

'Squatting?' He spat the word out. No one accused him of not paying his way, especially not these days when money was tight. How many times had he tried to pay Laurie more in rent than the ridiculously low amount she charged? Every time she insisted he was doing her a favour keeping an eye on the house.

'Yes.' She shrugged her wide but fine boned shoulders. 'I bet you used the same key as last night when you let me in.'

'And how did I get that key?'

Her mouth shut with a tight snap. The silence yawned between them and he left it hanging there, stringing out her uncertainty.

Her mouth firmed in a mutinous line and her eyes narrowed.

His mouth quirked as he imagined the Sergio Leone music from *A Fistful of Dollars* and a standoff between two cowboys.

She tossed her head. 'I don't know but I'd like you to leave.'

'For the record, sweet cheeks, I live here. And newsflash, I'm having a shower right now.' He turned his back on her, switched the shower on and pulled his boxers down.

With a startled gasp, she fled from the bathroom and he heard her bedroom door slam.

Jason stomped down the stairs ready to strangle someone. Preferably Siena with one 'n'. No judge in the land would see him go down. The spoilt brat had used every last drop of hot water. He felt chilled to the bone and three seconds of lukewarm water had almost finished him off. She was still hiding in her room and just as bloody well. Hopefully she was packing her bags, although she could organise a taxi herself to the airport this time.

He stormed over to the fridge about to yank open the door, when he did a double take. Surely not. A plastic container sat on the side by the microwave, ringed with what looked suspiciously like the remnants of a shepherd's pie. His stomach rolled, the familiar twinge of acid burning. Bugger, he needed a proper meal. Slowly he opened the fridge door. 'I don't bloody believe it,' he yelled and slammed the door shut. Trust fund Barbie had helped

29

herself to his dinner and to add insult to injury had left the plate, cutlery and packaging on the worktop.

Scrap all previous thoughts, he'd happily drive her to the airport, with her fancy pants designer wheelie bag and stuff her and it on the first plane back to Paris. What time was she leaving?

Was it really only this time yesterday, he'd got Laurie's panicked call? How could he refuse to dash up to Heathrow to pick up her sister, who'd apparently decided upon an impromptu visit? Personally he thought an impromptu visit was bullshit for self-centred and thoughtless visit but hey, what did he know. Laurie sounded thrilled about it, if a little sad that she couldn't get away. Of course she couldn't get away, not with a houseful of builders ripping the place apart, Cam away and now poor Norah rushed into hospital. He'd only met the rather elderly Norah and her husband Eric once but if she'd been hospitalised it had to be serious as she was one tough old bird.

He opened the fridge again and grabbed a beer and stared desolately at the empty shelves. After a knackering day working, he did not want to go to the supermarket but it was preferable to another ulcer. With reluctance he put the beer back. Best not down that on his tender empty stomach and then drive. He needed his driving licence. Grabbing his jacket, he tucked his wallet into his pocket and walked into the hall, as Siena came down the stairs.

'I've got a bone to pick with you.'

'What?'

'You ate my dinner.'

'How was I supposed to know it was yours? I thought it had been left by the housekeeper for me.'

He raised one eyebrow in silent sarcasm.

'Look, there was no one here. I didn't know you lived here, did I? I thought you were a taxi driver and you didn't say anything about it last night.'

OK, he now felt slightly bad because he hadn't done much to disabuse her of that thought.

'That's because I thought you would have gone by the time I got back tonight.'

'I didn't.'

'I can see.' This was becoming slightly farcical and mad as he was about having a cold shower and no supper, his childishness was starting to prick his conscience. This was Laurie's sister and he owed Laurie big time. She'd helped him out when he was starting up the business. He softened his voice and asked more gently, 'So what time are you leaving? Do you need me to help organise a taxi to get you to the airport?'

'That's OK. I don't need a taxi.'

'Right,' he smiled. 'Train? You haven't got a lot of luggage so crossing London shouldn't be too bad. I can give you a lift to the station in the morning if you like.' He shrugged into his jacket.

In a gesture that was fast becoming familiar, she lifted her chin. Warrior Princess Barbie. 'I'm staying for a while.'

His head shot up. That was not part of the plan. He liked living alone. Not being responsible for anyone but himself. It had taken a long time to get here, confident that his mother and sisters were financially secure. As for his ex-girlfriend Stacey, the guilt about her still burned a hole in his stomach.

'A while? I don't think so.'

A mutinous line flattened out her mouth. 'It's not your house.'

'But you can't stay here.'

Up went the chin again. 'Laurie said I could.'

Jason almost growled. 'When did she say that?' It was news to him.

'It doesn't matter when she said it, I have a room here.'

'Yes ... but—'

'I'll stay out of your way.'

Yeah, right.

'So how long's a while? Long weekend?'

She shrugged and he caught her swallow. Not as sure of herself as he'd first thought. 'What about work?' Wouldn't it be nice to just take off for a few days? 'Won't they be expecting you?'

She shook her head, amusement lighting up her face. 'I don't work.'

'Why doesn't that surprise me?' he muttered. In spite of himself he had to ask. 'So what do you do all day if you don't work?'

She drew herself taller. 'I do loads of stuff. Go to fashion shows. Meet my friends. Go out to the theatre, exhibitions, shopping. We go to parties. Ski. I'm really busy. All the time.'

'Nice life if you can get it,' he observed dryly. 'Not so much of that going on in Leighton Buzzard, I'm afraid.' Which guaranteed she'd be bored and on a plane home within the next twenty-four hours.

She gave him a dazzling beam which almost knocked him for six. Christ, she might be bloody annoying but she was one hell of a babe.

'Thanks Jason. You won't know I'm here. I promise.'

He had a feeling, he might.

Taking her to the supermarket had seemed a brilliant idea. Ensure she bought her own meal for the night and stop her nicking his. What he hadn't counted on was how long it took her.

As he stacked a six-pack of Becks in his basket, he looked around. Where had she got to? He was about done. Siena obviously went in for more complicated stuff. He'd left her for dust on the first aisle when she started feeling up peppers. Seriously? He wasn't a complete philistine, he got the concept of five a day but did you need to check them out so carefully? This was supposed to be a smash and grab raid. Pizza. Beer. Pizza. More beer and a couple of ready-made shepherd's pies and spag bols. And a shaving gel and deodorant periodically.

Turning back and re-tracing his route, he spotted her at the far end of the aisle in front of the refrigerated cheese cabinet. Her sodding basket empty. She stood there, looking too cute for her own good, attracting some excited second glances from two young guys who had suddenly developed a strong interest in the yoghurt section next to her.

Completely oblivious, Siena picked up different cheeses and read the labels, her head tilted to one side like an enquiring sparrow.

For crying out loud, why hadn't it occurred to him? She probably couldn't cook. Wouldn't have a clue. This had been a complete waste of time. He strode down glaring at the two guys who suddenly decided that maybe yoghurt wasn't their thing after all.

'What are you doing?' He shook his head. 'Come here,' he grabbed her elbow and firmly escorted her round the corner into the ready meals section. 'Do you like pasta?'

'Wow.' She turned to him, her eyes wide. She looked like fricking Alice in Wonderland. 'Look at all this.' Shaking him off, she wandered along the aisle inspecting the packaging. 'Four cheese sauce? Cannelloni? Barbecue pork noodles? Beef rib in ale?' She turned to him, eyes alight with enthusiasm. 'They've got everything. It's amazing. I didn't know you could buy it all ready-made like this.'

Jason bit back a retort. Probably never been in a supermarket before in her life.

'Yeah, who knew?'

'Gosh, I've never seen this before.' She reached out her hand and picked up a plastic container of bolognese sauce.

He realised that her wonder had turned to amusement. 'Doesn't anyone in England know how to cook?' She raised one eyebrow with a demure smile.

Typical Frog. Always thought they owned cooking. Hadn't she heard of Jamie Oliver or Gordon Ramsay?

Out of the corner of his eye, he thought her saw her mouth twitch. Was she having a laugh? She certainly looked amused but he wasn't, far from it.

'Plenty of people cook, but they might not have time, when they're *working*.' He said it with the emphasis on working. 'Princess, I am starving. You ate my tea, remember? I want to go home

33

and eat. Right now, I don't care whether you live on bread and cheese or rice pudding but pick something to eat. I'm leaving.'

OK, so now he was being a complete bastard, but he was bloody starving and absolutely knackered having had less than five hours sleep in the last twenty-four. He was running on empty, and still had this bloody wine bar opening thing to go to, while madam looked as cool as a cucumber and was quite probably laughing at him. It pushed too many buttons. 'I suggest you get your sweet little arse into gear and get a move on, otherwise I'll leave you here.'

With a cheeky smile, she looked over her shoulder down at her backside. 'Do you think so? Thanks.'

He gritted his teeth. Giving into the overwhelming sense of sheer exasperation he made a deep guttural noise in his throat at her and stomped off, the basket swinging painfully into his shins.

'I growled at her. Physically growled.' He rested his forehead on the edge of the kitchen table. What the hell had got into him? He prided himself on a bit of sophistication, even if he was now, to all intents and purposes, a manual labourer.

'And then I felt guilty. So when she asked what I was doing this evening ...'

Ben sniggered, snorting out some of the lager he'd swigged from the bottle. 'Seriously. You growled. At a chick?'

They were sitting in the kitchen waiting for Siena to come down. He knew as soon as he'd uttered the words, 'You're welcome to come too,' which he hadn't meant at all, that he'd strayed into foolish, downright stupid territory. That's what lack of sleep and lack of food did to your brain. And now they were still waiting for her to emerge from her room. Yup he really, really regretted opening his mouth.

'Chick? Her? She's Barbie to the power of ten. Seriously. It's like she's been beamed down from planet airhead.'

'So how long's she staying with you?'

'She's not staying with *me*. She came to see her sister. She's leaving tomorrow. It won't take long for her to realise Leighton Buzzard can't match the entertainment of Paris.'

Tonight's wine bar opening was possibly the most exciting thing that had happened this year. He realised he was pulling faces.

'Really got under your skin, this one,' observed Ben.

'No. She's just very …' Jason motioned wringing her neck with his fingers, 'irritating.'

'Like that Shakespeare bloke said, you complain too much.'

Jason cocked a very surprised eyebrow. Ben was a great lad and his talents in fixing mechanical faults on the bottling line and washing out pipes couldn't be faulted but it took all of his literacy skills to manage to read *The Sun* as far as page three. Quoting the bard seemed rather out of character.

'The original quote was protest—'

'Perzactly. You're protesting, so it means you fancy her really.'

'How do you figure that?'

'Mate, you haven't stopped talking about her since I got here. You don't even talk about Claire this much and you're shagging her.'

Jason wasn't about to correct Ben's blithe assumptions. He knew he was sleepwalking into a relationship and he ought to nip things in the bud but at least Claire was relatively low maintenance and had her own place. Unfortunately, she seemed very good at engineering things so that from the outside it appeared as if there was more going on than there was. So far it was OK but at some point he was going to have make it clear he wasn't interested in a long-term relationship.

He wanted a nice easy life. Work, come home, eat, go to the pub. Watch a bit of football at the weekend. And that was the way it was going to stay. He was not going to worry about anyone else's problems. Siena was Laurie's problem. Not his. His phone buzzed. A text from Claire. *Where are you? We're here.*

Ben's phone buzzed almost a second later.

'Mate, she'd better get a move on. There's free food there. I don't want to miss out.'

'I thought you'd eaten. Scrub that.' Stupid observation. Ben could eat his body weight in carbs and still go back for seconds. Lean and muscled, which came in handy, he used up a lot of energy, with his regular rugby training and playing for the local team every weekend.

'At la—' the words died in his throat and he heard Ben mutter, 'Holy fuck.'

Siena appeared in the doorway, rippling blonde hair, ten foot long sooty lashes, skin tight jeans which accentuated every inch of her legs that seemed to go on forever and a top that, while it wasn't particularly low cut, certainly made sure you couldn't miss how perfect her boobs were. Which he knew were perfect because he'd seen them for real, not so very long ago. For a minute he thought he'd swallowed his tongue. Jeez she packed a powerful punch, as did the perfume that filled the air around her. His groin threatened to give him away.

On high, high heels, which added a sashay to her walk, she came into the kitchen, a wide smile showing off perfect, Daz-white teeth that any American cheerleader would be proud to own.

Ben had clearly died and gone to heaven and he hadn't even seen her naked. There was absolutely nothing subtle about the unabashed admiration shining in his eyes.

'Siena, this is Ben. He's an idiot. He works with me.' Jason gave him a sharp jab in the ribs.

Ignoring him completely, she stepped forward and with what he felt was unconscious charm, politely held out a petite hand, tipped in some dark purpley colour.

'Hi Ben.' She smiled up at him and he smiled goofily back.

'Hi Siena.' His meaty fingers dwarfed her hand as he shook enthusiastically for at least ten seconds too long. 'Nice to meet you.'

'And you. What do you with Jason? He hasn't told me much.'

She shot him an amused look. In the face of her flawless manners, he felt like some uncouth lout.

'We make beer.' Ben seemed totally hypnotised like some dopey cartoon character. Man, it was pitiful.

'Brew beer,' snapped Jason and then regretted it. Ben might not be the sharpest tool in the box but he was a damn good worker, kind-hearted and mostly harmless. Certainly not someone you'd want getting caught up with the likes of Siena. 'Right. Shall we go?'

They trooped out of the kitchen, Siena in the lead.

'Put your tongue away.' Jason muttered into Ben's ear. The stupid boy turned around and grinned. Jason shook his head. Oh God, she would chew him up and spit him out as a slight aperitif. Ben was a good-looking lad, and as a local rugby hero had plenty of fans of his own, but he was not rich enough for Siena's blood. Any man she went out with would have to have a billionaire bank balance; Ben definitely didn't fall into that category. Neither did Jason, thankfully. But he didn't want her deciding to amuse herself with someone during her brief stay.

Siena would rather have died than admit to anyone how long it had taken her to step out of the bedroom and go downstairs. When she'd heard the two deep voices downstairs, her nerve had almost failed her. She found Jason's grumpy disapproval disconcerting. It seemed as if everything she did annoyed him and she had no idea why.

At home she knew everyone, knew what to expect. For the first time in her life she felt horribly out of depth. What if Jason's friends didn't like her either? What if they were all like him? She'd only said yes to his invitation to the wine bar because she'd been a bit bored today. At home, she could always go down to the kitchens and chat to Agnes or the other members of staff.

Now as they walked into the wine bar, she could let some of the tension go. What a relief that Ben had been so sweet. At least she could talk to him all night, and this bar was lovely. You could almost imagine you were in London or Paris. She didn't like to admit it but what she'd seen of the town so far hadn't lived up to what she'd imagined. Luckily this place was more what she was used to. The décor reminded her of a place in Monaco, although without the presence of Johnny Depp or Cameron Diaz.

'Jay, over here.'

A tall blond guy with a scrubby ponytail hailed them from the bar and Jason led the way over to a fabulous Perspex bar which sparkled with embedded crystals. Fascinated, Siena reached out to touch it, probably Swarovski.

'Isn't it gorge?' The petite girl who had bounded over to give Ben a big hug and greet Jason with a brief kiss on the cheek, all the while managing to studiously ignore the blond man, grinned at Siena.

'It's amazing,' agreed Siena.

'The whole place is amazing. Not very Leighton at all. I love it.'

'Pretentious if you ask me,' said the blond guy, narrowing his eyes as he looked at the other girl.

No tension there then, thought Siena watching the body language between the two of them.

Around her the group exchanged hellos, hugs and kisses until Ben came to her rescue.

'Guys, this is Siena.' Ben put his arm round her and pushed her forward into the group moving away from the bar as he made the announcement. Siena almost giggled, he made it sound as if he'd made some huge discovery. Then as all eyes turned his way, he flushed pink and rattled off a series of names with the speed of a machine gun. 'Lisa. Claire. Will. Katie. Tom.'

'Ben!' admonished the friendly girl. 'Hi Siena. I'm Lisa. This is Claire.' She pointed to a girl in black jeans with a blonde bob, 'Katie.' Siena quickly registered blue jeans, pink silky shirt. 'Tom.' He winked. Clearly Katie's boyfriend from the way his hand casually rested on her hip.

Lisa's mouth tightened fractionally. 'And that's Will.' She inclined her head towards the blond guy who had turned to talk to the barman

'Nice to meet you.' As she said the words, Siena realised that in Lisa's case she actually meant them. The bubbly woman, with her sparkling eyes and wide mouth seemed to want to put Siena at her ease without asking or wanting to know anything more.

'Wow,' Lisa's eyes widened as she looked downwards. 'OMG. If I knew you better I'd be down on my knees kissing those babies. Your boots are awesome. Where did you get them? Oh God, I bet they were really expensive, weren't they?'

'Not really. A couple of hundred euros.' Siena shrugged and smiled. She couldn't actually remember. At home no one ever asked that sort of question. For a second she had that stepping out on ice feeling, wondering whether it would hold up or if cracks would radiate out from where she stood.

'Of course, darling. So you bought two pairs,' drawled Claire.

Siena felt herself blush. She had actually. She particularly liked this pair of Gianvito Rossi two-tone fringed ankle boots, so had bought them in the other colour.

Lisa frowned at Claire. 'They're absolutely lush.'

'Thank you.' Siena smiled back. Compliments she could handle.

'Where did you get them, then if you paid euros? Not that I could afford them. They're so nice.' Lisa stretched out her hand as if she wanted to touch them.

'Paris.' And even saying that had her praying the ice would hold up.

'Paris.' Claire rolled her eyes. 'Gosh, how the other half live. Pop over to buy shoes, do you?'

'I'd love to go to Paris,' said Katie hurriedly and then looked at Tom. 'Not hinting. Definitely not hinting. No need to worry that I'm expecting you to whisk me off for a romantic weekend.'

'We can go to Paris,' said Tom with a cheeky grin. 'Two months' time when England plays France in the Six Nations.'

'Ha, ha.' Katie smiled and Tom pulled her towards him and kissed her neck.

Siena looked away, unused to the display of open, easy, affection.

'So how do you know Ben?' asked Lisa with a friendly smile,

tossing her tawny blonde hair over her shoulder, her eyes guileless.

'I don't really.' The other girl's warmth was irresistible. Siena definitely wasn't in France any more. Normally newbies on the block were circled like prey. Weighed up in whispers as their credentials were checked out. Subjected to a gamut of interrogative conversations full of nuance and ultra-polite queries. Lisa's uncompromising acceptance made her feel warm and funny inside.

'I met him tonight.'

'Quick mover,' Tom chipped in, nudging Ben. 'Nice work mate.'

'She's with Jason,' explained Ben shaking his head and mock punching Tom's arm. He inclined his head towards Jason who had finished talking to Will at the bar and had come to join the group. 'Staying at his place.'

'Really?' The girl called Claire managed to get plenty of loaded inference into the one word.

Jason's lips tightened into the forbidding expression she was rapidly becoming used to. 'Siena is my landlady's sister. She's here for the *weekend*.' He gave Siena a pointed look.

He didn't need to sound quite so pissed off about it. Good job she hadn't told him how long she planned to stay. Laurie was bound to be OK with it. When they'd talked before about Siena's dream of studying fashion design, her sister had been so encouraging.

Will started handing out drinks, obviously ordered before they'd arrived. 'Look there's a table over there, with a couple of stools.' He nodded over the vacant table and the group started to move that way.

'What do you want to drink?' asked Jason, including both Siena and Ben in the question.

'Half a lager, please.'

'I'll get mine thanks,' said Siena reaching into her handbag for her purse and following him to the bar.

'I can stand you a drink.' Jason scowled again.

Really, what was his problem? She'd never met anyone quite

so grumpy.

'I wasn't worried about that.' She smiled ultra-sweetly at him. What would it take to get him to crack a smile once in a while? 'But I'd like champagne.'

'Of course you would.'

She ignored his sarcastic tone. 'And as they probably only sell it by the bottle, I'll pay.'

It gave her a childish satisfaction when the barman responded to her before Jason who had waved first. 'What champagnes do you have?'

After consulting the bar menu, she placed her order and handed over her American Express. Not a great selection, but the Lanson would do. The barman made a great show of filling the ice bucket and removing the foil and wire. With the explosive pop of the cork, he glanced at the machine terminal, his face darkened.

'Sorry madam, your card's been declined.'

Siena looked down at the card machine. 'How annoying. *C'est la vie.* Try this one.'

She leaned on the Perspex bar, tracing the pattern of crystals. It really was very pretty. If it weren't for keeping off the radar she would have put a photo on Snapchat to show her friends in Paris, although half of them had probably gone to Cannes this weekend.

'That's been declined too.'

'Are you sure? That's odd.' She gave him a what-can-one-do smile. He looked a lot less friendly all of a sudden. 'Do you want to try again? It's never happened before.'

'Did you tell your credit card companies you were popping over to England for the weekend? Maybe that's why they're not working,' suggested Jason.

'Don't be silly.' She patted his arm. 'I was in New York last month, Whistler two months before that. I don't need to tell them. I'm always travelling.'

'To have one declined …' His lips twitched.

She shot him a withering look.

'I might be,' she was going to use the word impetuous but paused, 'spontaneous,' that sounded better, 'but I'm not careless. And yes I have read Oscar Wilde.'

Digging into her bag again, she pulled out her Credit Lyonnais debit card. 'How about this?'

'Not an English bank, so do you have your passport?'

How annoying, she'd only taken it out of her handbag five minutes before she left the house, thinking it would be safer left in the bedside drawer.

'You do realise I've opened a seventy quid bottle of fizz that you can't pay for.' Goodbye customer service, hello pissed off barman. His earlier smiling obsequiousness had been replaced with sharp-eyed cynical scepticism.

'Don't be ridiculous.' She shrugged and rolled her eyes at him with a half-laugh. 'Of course I can pay for it. Your card machine can't be working properly. I've travelled all over the world and this has never happened before.'

'It's happened now.'

She opened her purse again. 'Look, I've got euros. You can have those.'

The barman's lip curled. 'Do I look French? Does this place look like we're in Spain? Does it say euros accepted here?' He paused, lifting his chin with a pugnacious sneer. 'No. It does not.'

He didn't have to be quite so mean. 'Look, it's a genuine mistake. I can afford it, easily.' For goodness sake, her stepfather owned a vineyard and estate outside Epernay and her monthly allowance would more than cover the cost of several cases of vintage Dom Perignon.

'Doesn't look like it from here.'

'I've tried to pay. It's not my fault nothing is working and you won't accept euros or my bank card. I really don't know what you expect me to do.' Siena kept her tone low and reasonable, trying to ignore the curious glances and open stares being sent her way.

'Obviously,' the man's voice had got much louder, as if he

deliberately wanted to humiliate her, 'I want you to pay up.' He leaned over the bar towards her, his eyes sparkling with sudden malice. 'Otherwise it's going to have to be a police matter.'

Her heart rate rocketed. Her palms were suddenly clammy. She'd never been in this sort of situation before. His angry face reminded her of Yves when he didn't get his own way.

'Enough.' Jason's voice cut through with strident authority, making her jump. 'She's not exactly a hardened criminal and you are being unnecessarily unpleasant. Stick it on this card and while you're at it, I'll have a large glass of house red and a pint of Becks.'

The barman frowned and took Jason's card, shooting Siena a look of disgust.

'Thank you,' she said letting out a huge breath, she hadn't realised that she'd been holding on to. The relief was almost painful. 'That's really kind of you. I will pay you back. I promise.

'I'm sure you will.' He shook his head. 'Prick.'

'I suppose he had some right to be cross.' Her legs felt slightly shaky.

'He didn't have to be such a dick about it or be so horrible. I hate bullies and I hate men that bully women even more. Are you OK?' He studied her face with a penetrating look and she very nearly said, 'You wouldn't like Yves'.

Instead she nodded ducking her head, not wanting him to see her face.

His voiced softened and nearly finished her off. 'Why don't you go join the others, send Ben over and we'll bring the drinks back?'

Giving him a tremulous smile, she did as he suggested.

It wasn't until she'd almost finished the first glass of fizz, she started to felt more like herself again. Everyone else had loosened up too. The volume in the bar had increased five-fold since they'd arrived and it took considerable effort to wriggle through the crowd to get to the very plush toilets.

'So Siena,' Ben came and stood next to her, 'Jason says you live in France. How come your English is so good?'

'Because she's English, you pillock,' Jason ribbed him.

'Are you?'

Siena nodded her head, amused by the relationship between them. 'But I've lived in France since I was seven.'

'What?' Jason sounded startled. 'But you're Laurie's sister. She grew up here. Went to school here. How does that work? '

Siena shrugged. She'd rather not air the family laundry in front of an audience.

'So say something in Frog,' said Ben, completely oblivious to the nuances of the conversation. 'It's a real turn on when women talk foreign.'

Across the other side of the table, Claire rolled her eyes. 'Only to a cretin.'

Ben ignored her. 'Go on.' He bounced in his seat, his enthusiasm infectious.

'What do you want me to say?' For some reason she felt self-conscious and Claire's hostile stare wasn't helping.

'Anything. I dunno. Something like *voulez-vous couchez maverick moi*?'

'That is French, you numpty.' Claire's scathing words spilled out.

'I think you'll find it's *avec moi*,' interjected Jason with a reluctant smile.

Siena sneaked a peak at him, it wasn't the first time he'd taken the sting out of the other girl's sharp observations.

'Whatevs.' With a good natured grin, Ben added, 'Come on, speak some Froglish. Geddit? Because you're half and half.'

'Ben, grow up,' snapped Claire. 'You're so stupid.'

'*Bonjour Ben. C'est un plaisir de vous rencontrer*,' Siena blurted out, wanting to defuse the toxic atmosphere Claire seemed determined to create. Temptation shimmered like a naughty fairy for a second. It would be quite cool if she said in French, 'stop being a bitch,' but Siena had a feeling that with his probing looks, which seemed to see right through her, Jason would probably get the gist.

44

'Phwoar. Say some more.' Ben moaned in pretend delight completely oblivious to the other girl's displeasure. 'What's it mean?'

Siena punched him on the shoulder laughing, as Jason shook his head and the others all burst into gales of laughter. Lisa giggled like a loon. Only Claire remained unamused. She tutted.

'*Ça ne veut rien dire en particulier,*' she obliged.

'So, what are you saying? Something really sexy I bet. It had to be. Maybe I should learn French, pull the birds. I could get one of those lesson things on my iPod. Learn while I'm at work.'

'Oh God, please don't,' said Jason with a heartfelt groan. 'It's bad enough when you're murdering Coldplay with your headphones on.'

'I could teach you,' offered Siena.

'Seriously?' Ben bounced in his seat like an overenthusiastic puppy. 'Couple of chat up lines? That would be so cool.'

'She's not going to be here long enough,' said Jason.

'No,' said Claire with a derisory snort. 'Besides she'd be in her eighties before you picked it up.'

Ben's face crumpled for one swift second before a cheerful mask slid into place as he said to Jason, 'So boss, what's the plan for Monday?'

Embarrassed for him, Siena pulled out her phone on the pretext of checking it for messages. Scanning it quickly she stuffed it back into her handbag as a fresh conversation started up. More missed calls, all from the same two numbers. She couldn't bring herself to even text them, knowing it would unleash a flurry of communication. Normally her iPhone never left her side but lately she wanted to bury it at the bottom of her bag. She couldn't visit Facebook, go on Twitter, post on Snapchat or Periscope. Everyone was asking where she was, with some impertinent acquaintances drawing their own conclusions. No she wasn't in Switzerland having a secret abortion nor on an exotic island in the Pacific with a well-known tennis pro and most definitely not in hiding after a botched eyelift.

Lisa let out a squeal. 'And you've got a Prada handbag and purse. They must have been a gazillion euros.' She reached out and touched them with reverence. 'I bid on a Prada purse on eBay. Nearly got it for forty quid and then some bitch pipped me at the last second.'

'Don't you hate it when that happens?' said Katie.

The conversation focused on eBay. Siena kept quiet, not wanting to volunteer that she'd never been on eBay in her life.

Chapter 4

'You're sure?' she asked for the second time.

'*Oui, Mademoiselle.* We received the instruction from the account holder. I suggest you speak to them.'

'And I can't use the card?'

'No, it has been cancelled. A new one will be issued to the account holder's address.'

Siena shook her head. Not careless then. Both her cards had been cancelled. She'd known Maman would be angry at her leaving, especially when they were due out to dinner that evening, but not this angry. What had Yves been saying to her? He could be so convincing.

With resolute determination, she switched off her phone. She wasn't going home. Not before Harry's birthday. She had a plan and exactly a month to get everything lined up. In the meantime, she could easily survive on this month's allowance. Admittedly she couldn't buy a complete new wardrobe for spring, but she could make a start.

For a minute she stared out of the window. An idea popped into her head and grabbing the pad she always kept to hand, she quickly sketched a tall willowy figure and outlined the dress. Cowl neck. Mid length pencil skirt, with hem dropped at one side. Three-quarter-length sleeves. After ten minutes, she put the pad down.

She groaned out loud. It wasn't right. What she saw in her head didn't translate onto paper.

Which is why she needed so desperately to go to college. This week she'd arrange an appointment at the London School of Fashion. With her fashion knowledge and contacts in Paris it shouldn't be too difficult to get accepted on one of their courses starting next year. Then she could go back and present Maman with a fait accompli. She was too young to get married yet.

In the meantime, she needed to find a bank and withdraw some sterling.

She grabbed the last clean towel from the guest stack – she'd have to ask Jason for some more – headed into the bathroom and ran smack into him.

Her mouth dried. *Ça alors!* With a white towel wrapped very, very low around his waist, dark hair dusting a mighty fine, firm chest and then tapering down there, he brought her to a dead stop. Her heart jumped in her chest, the irregular rhythm vibrating like a Mexican jumping bean. Last time he'd been half naked, she'd been too worried about her own nudity to take much in.

She took in a breath to steady herself. How ridiculous. She'd seen, almost seen, naked men before. She'd even slept with one or two. It wasn't like she was some blushing virgin, although her experience was pretty limited. Before Yves, they had been lights off, fleeting encounters. Certainly never up, close and personal with a tank load of raw virility chucked in.

'Seen enough?' The initial irritation on his face, half covered in white shaving foam which accentuated his tanned skin, had given way to suppressed amusement.

'Sorry. I didn't realise you were in here.'

Almost mesmerised by his chest, she realised she'd clenched her hands tight to her sides, to stop her reaching up to touch the smooth skin. The cramped room meant there was very little room to manoeuvre with him standing in front of the sink.

'I think we might need to establish some ground rules. Starting with not barging into the bathroom without knocking.'

'You did it to me the other day.'

Jason did that double take thing, which wasn't funny or clever, eyes bugging out in exaggerated disbelief. 'You weren't supposed to … Oh forget it. Ground rules. Don't …' his voice trailed away.

'Seriously, you want to do this now?' She put her hand on her hips. His eyes seemed to have gone a bit glassy. 'Can't it wait until I've had a shower and a coffee? I've spent the last twenty minutes on the phone to credit card companies.'

'Good idea,' his voice sounded suspiciously strangled and he turned his back on her, rather abruptly as if he'd definitely finished talking to her. How rude. What was wrong with him now?

With a sniff, she backed out of the bathroom, shutting the door with a bang, narrowly missing catching the hem of her nightie in … *nom d'un chien*! She looked down. She really needed to invest in some new nightwear.

Jason took a slug of milky coffee and leaned back against the draining board. Maybe he needed to go out and get laid; it had been a while since he'd had sex but Siena wandering around in that see-through thing wasn't helping. At this rate, living with her, he was going to burst a blood vessel or set his stomach off again. Correct that. He wasn't living with her. Her stay was strictly temporary and he needed to find out when she was going home. She couldn't stay here; she'd drive him insane. Only one day and two nights and already she seemed to have spread a detritus of belongings about the house. Ankle boots, sexy high-heeled fuck-me numbers, now littered the hall. OK, so two pairs, but that was still two pairs too many. A scarf draped over the banister might not be much, but it was the start of things. Like the leather jacket slung over the back of the chair opposite him. As for the bathroom, he was surprised he could still get in there. A lorry load of Clarins products had staked their claim along every available surface. He liked things tidy. In their place. He liked … the image of her exquisitely perfect body popped into his head. Only two days and he'd already seen far too much of that too. He didn't seem to be able to dislodge the image from the loop in his head.

'Morning.'

And there she was, as if he'd conjured her up; her complexion glowing. He wasn't prone to fancy imaginings but her skin did appear to have its own luminosity. Then again, hardly surprising given all those expensive lotions and potions upstairs.

Deciding to be on his best behaviour and follow her civilised lead, he said 'Morning. Would you like a coffee?'

A smile lit up her face. Damn, it really did light it up. 'I'd love one.' She sank gracefully into the chair.

She certainly was easy on the eye. Last night's gorgeous vamp had been replaced with this daisy-fresh dewy-skinned natural beauty. No doubt the simple lavender blue T-shirt which highlighted the clear tones of her blue eyes cost a fortune but with pristine white jeans hugging long legs and skimming very neat ankles, she looked like some supermodel in from a long country walk.

Dropping into the chair opposite he watched her take a cautious sip of coffee and wrinkle her nose. 'Is this instant?'

'Yes.'

'Oh no, really?'

'Seriously? You're complaining about *my* coffee?'

'I wasn't exactly complaining.' She shrugged her shoulders.

'Sounded like it to me.'

'I wasn't. Surprised, perhaps. I didn't think people really drank instant.'

'They do, but feel free to buy your own fresh coffee.'

'Sorry,' her smile faltered and he felt as if he'd drop kicked a kitten. 'I didn't mean to sound ungrateful. It's a cultural thing. In France most people drink filter coffee or from a cafetière. I wasn't complaining.'

50

Jason sighed. 'Look. I'm sorry. We got off to a bad start. I haven't had much sleep recently and I wasn't expecting a houseguest. When Laurie asked me to pick you up, I'd driven back from Scotland. It's further north than Yorkshire and takes at least six hours drive.' Siena nodded and he was glad he'd explained. Her knowledge of British geography seemed to be rather sketchy. 'I'm happy to agree a few house rules for the next couple of days. And then if I'm around I can take you back to the airport. But I'm not here to babysit you, you get that? I picked you up as a favour to Laurie. I'm not responsible for you. You're on your own. Not my guest. Not my lodger. A temporary visitor.'

He needed to stress that. Temporary. Not like bloody Stacey who'd imperceptibly drifted into his flat like the whisper of a ghost, imprinting herself bit by bit, until one day she'd moved in. If he'd been more observant at the outset, he wouldn't have had to be such a bastard at the end.

Siena leaned one forearm on the table and took another sip of coffee. He felt his nerve endings go on alert at her studied casualness.

'House rules.' She nodded at him, her smile dazzling. It did dazzle him too. He found it difficult to concentrate when she smiled like that, all attention on you. Distracting. Even so, why did he get the impression she was hiding something? That sunny smile certainly made it hard to remember that she was a royal princess pain in the butt. He'd already lost his dinner to her, parted with seventy quid on her behalf and driven several hundred miles on five hours sleep.

'Do you know I've never shared a house with anyone before? Well, that's not strictly true, obviously I live with my parents and the staff.'

'We're not sharing a house,' he bit out. 'You are a temporary guest. Temporary. Got it—' He stopped. 'You have staff?' No wonder she was so clueless.

She stiffened. He held up his hand in apology, it had come

out sounding rather judgemental. 'Sorry, even Will's family never had real staff. All sounds a bit *Downton Abbey*.'

'Hardly, times have changed.' The innocent smile belied her tart words. 'We even give the staff holidays these days.'

'Right. Back to the rules. I'm out of the house by eight most mornings. You can use the bathroom after then.'

'*Trop d'honneur, merci!*'

'I suggest you learn to knock on the bathroom door if you don't want any more surprises. You've probably realised there's no lock on the door. I don't mind sharing my instant coffee for the next couple of days but you'll need to pitch in and buy milk and your own food. I'm going to be away for a couple of days, so if you're booking your flight home, I can take you to the airport before or after then. Anything you need to know?'

'I was wondering when I might get some clean towels.'

'About the same time you put the dirty ones in the washing machine, I guess.'

Siena coloured and he felt like the kitten-kicker again, so he swallowed down his next comment. 'If you bring them down, I'll show you how the washing machine works. And the dishwasher. If you fill it up, put it on. If it's full, empty it. All the usual.' Was that a dumb thing to say? What was usual for her?

She was nodding like one of those crazy dogs in cars, so he assumed she was following.

'So,' he stood up and rinsed out his coffee mug. 'When do you think you'll be leaving?'

There it was again, the evasive study of her fingernails and the slight tension in her jaw.

'I'm not sure.'

'Are we talking not sure, tomorrow, or the end of the week?'

Siena opened her mouth and closed it again. 'I need to speak to Laurie.'

It was doubtful Laurie would want her up in Yorkshire. She and Cam had the builders in big time at the moment. There was no way they'd want Siena under their feet. Jason smiled. He'd be shot of her by the end of the week.

Siena let herself out of the front door, pocketing the front door key that Jason had handed over, after carefully sliding it onto a little Lego man key ring, so she wouldn't lose it. When he wasn't being grumpy, he could be quite kind. Although, that would go up in smoke if he found out what she was really planning.

Guiltily she looked back down the street. Satisfied she was out of earshot, she pulled out her phone, dialled and then carried on walking briskly, trying to warm up. A layer of frost coated the windscreens of the parked cars lining the street. It felt cold enough for snow and the tip of her nose tingled in the freezing air.

'Siena.' Laurie's voice rang with pleasure.

'Hi Laurie.'

'How are you? I am so sorry I'm not there. If you'd given me a bit more notice I could have made arrangements. It's chaos up here, otherwise I would invite you. We only got the water back on yesterday. And I can't leave Norah.' Laurie paused before adding. 'Do you remember Uncle Miles' housekeeper? She should have retired but she insists on coming to,' there was another awkward pause, 'to Merryview to help out.'

Siena winced at Laurie's careful mention of her inheritance, the house which had left their mother incandescent with affronted rage. A weaker woman might have taken to her bed. Not Maman. No, she'd called in a team of Paris's finest legal advocates to query the veracity of her brother's last will and testament.

Siena swallowed. 'It was sort of a spur of the moment thing.' That sounded much better than a nowhere-else-to-go flight.

'Next time, you idiot,' the warmth of Laurie's voice made the insult affectionate, 'phone me first. I'm gutted I can't see you. When are you heading back?'

Siena stopped and leaned against the nearest garden wall. 'Here's the thing.' She kept her tone shiny bright and upbeat.

'You know how you said I'd always have my own room,' she left the pause, hoping that Laurie would fill it with effusive acceptance.

Unfortunately Laurie didn't oblige.

'Remember, you said it was mine, 'whenever I want it'?'

'Yes,' Laurie sounded hesitant.

'And you decorated it and everything. Your house is gorgeous inside by the way. I love the way you've done it. I can't believe you did the bedroom for me. I've been dying to see it and,' she took a breath, 'I want to stay for a while.'

'Wow. I didn't see that coming. How long's a while?' Trust Laurie, Miss Practical Pants to get straight to the point.

'Quite a while, like a year or two or three.'

There was silence.

Siena rushed on. 'I've decided to do a fashion degree. In London. I need to apply. Maman won't be too keen but I figure if I go back, all signed up, with somewhere to stay and a place, she can't really stop me.' She didn't add that she hadn't realised that Leighton Buzzard was so far from London but she'd worry about that later.

'Siena, that's great. You said that's what you wanted to do. Good for you. I'm sure your, I mean, our mother will be fine.'

Siena pulled a face. She wasn't so sure.

'Of course you can stay. Although what about Jason? I can't kick him out. It's been quite handy having him there, looking after the place.'

'Oh Jason's fine. He doesn't mind.' Siena looked back over her shoulder.

'Really? I guess it makes sense. There's plenty of room and the two of you can share the bills. The council tax is a killer and I'm sure he'll be grateful to share that as well as the electricity, gas and water.' Laurie lowered her voice. 'Nice for him to have company too. I don't know him that well, he's a uni friend of Cam's so he must be alright.'

'And how is the lovely Cam?' asked Siena grateful to change the subject.

'Fine,' said Laurie matter of factly. 'In fact when we're a bit straighter you must come and see us.'

'Just fine?' teased Siena. 'Mighty fine, I seem to recall.' She might have met him only once but as men went, he was more than fine.

Laurie laughed. 'He's gorgeous, stubborn, opinionated, absolutely lovely and a pain in the arse in equal measure.'

Once they'd wound up their conversation. Siena started walking again, a grin on her face. Looked like everything was working out perfectly.

Electrical Assembler. What the heck was that? *Experienced assembler required.*

That counted her out. Her finger scanned down the rest of the column as she leaned on the dresser, studying the back pages of the local paper.

UK driving licence required. Perhaps they might consider a French one.

A possible.

Must be fully conversant with Word/Excel and have some knowledge of accountancy packages.

No, not suitable.

Car owner.

'You're back.' She jumped at the sound of Jason's voice and folded the newspaper quickly.

'Yes, I popped into town,' she said brightly as if sounding upbeat might dispel the leaden lump in her chest. 'I've got your money for you.' She handed it to him.

'Thanks.' He put the money on the side, leaving it there as he began to pull clothes from the yawning mouth of the washing machine.

It hurt that he left the crisp bank notes so casually on the side. They represented a third of all she had access to at that moment.

Her bank account wasn't as flush as she'd thought. Of course there'd been the first class flight to London, the new dress and boots from Printemps and this winter's collection new Prada handbag and the matching purse this month. Asking Maman for an advance on next month's allowance appeared to be out of the question.

'I really appreciated you lending me the money.' She fingered the ribbing on the sleeve of her fine knit jumper not looking him in the eye.

'No problem.' He shook out a pair of jeans.

'So the bills here. Are they quite expensive?'

'They're alright.' Jason picked up the basket and hummed to himself.

Hesitantly she watched as he started pegging out his washing on a rack besides the rather feeble radiator.

'So,' she said brightly, 'how much do you pay?'

He looked up from the task and glared at her. 'If you want to know how much rent I pay your sister, spit it out and ask.'

'No. I wanted to know what kind of expenses are involved in owning your own home. I'm thinking about buying an apartment in Paris.'

'It's probably different there but here, there's council tax which is a hundred and thirty-three pounds a month,' as he spoke, he flipped the clothes over the rack with efficient quick movements, 'electricity is thirty-five pounds a month, gas varies but again about thirty-five pounds and water is about three hundred pounds a year, plus the telly licence which obviously you wouldn't pay in France.'

'Right.' Her stomached flipped. 'That's really helpful.'

He raised a sceptical eyebrow and she gave him a half-hearted smile. Over two hundred pounds a month, so half of that was a hundred pounds, plus food and other expenses.

When his back was turned, she tucked the paper behind her back and slid out of the kitchen to head upstairs.

Settling on her bed she opened the paper again and sighed. The jobs either looked terribly dull or you needed previous experience.

'*Wanted: door-to-door canvassers who are highly-motivated, enthusiastic and professional. With a passion to meet and exceed targets. Quality individuals needed to represent our company.*

Hello, this sounded promising.

Whether you have previous experience or not, as long as you have a passion to succeed, we'd love to talk to you.

This position requires excellent face-to-face communication skills with a positive and outgoing personality.

Basic pay negotiable with fantastic commission structure in place.

Siena sat up straighter. Oh, yes. She could feel it in her bones. This sounded like a great job. Maman thought she'd go running home, but Siena would show her.

Chapter 5

Monday morning and brewing day. With a yawn and a stretch, he rubbed his bristled chin. Shaving was a chore and it wasn't like he worked in an office any more but after a few days, the stubble drove him crazy.

He staggered through to the bathroom and then stopped dead. The shower was running.

He knocked on the door. 'Siena? Is that you?'

'Yes, won't be long.'

Bloody hell. He wanted a pee, a shave and a shower. No, he needed a pee. Right now. He wanted his usual morning routine. For a minute he waited but there was no fricking sign of the water abating. Did the fact she was up so early mean she had a flight to catch?

He'd avoided her on Saturday night by inviting himself along to the pub with Ben. That had backfired a bit because Claire had been there and had somehow ended up hip to hip with him all evening and he might have had a drink too many and might have kissed her. But suggesting lunch on Sunday had probably been his stupidest move. He didn't want to lead her on and he had horrible idea that he might have given her the wrong signals.

Two full minutes later and his bladder was telling him he wasn't a freaking camel. He could have burst in but catching Siena naked again felt wrong. Stomping downstairs, he barged into the kitchen, knocking a toe painfully against one of the wooden chairs.

'For crying out loud,' he spat through gritted teeth. Grasping the hot tap, he turned it on full and looked up at the ceiling. 'Take that, madam.' A second later, he heard a squeal of shock. He let the tap run for a good minute until he heard the shower door slam.

With a satisfied wrench he switched the tap off.

Knocking on the bathroom for a second time made no difference.

'Siena, I need to get in there.'

'I won't be long.'

'You already have been.'

'I'll be out in five.'

'You've got five seconds before I go and pee in the wastepaper basket in your bedroom.'

There was no response.

'One.'

He heard Siena sniff.

'Two.'

'Three.'

He opened her bedroom door, listening with satisfaction to its loud, familiar squeak.

'Don't you dare!' She shot out of the bathroom, her hair bundled in a towel with another wrapped around her. 'I'm out.' She stuck her nose in the air. 'Honestly, some people have no patience.'

'Some people are trying to get ready to go to work. Alien concept I'm sure.'

She stopped, drew herself up and with a haughty stare looked right down her nose at him. If he hadn't been so damn desperate for the loo, he might have found it cute. Her attempt at snotty would have worked better if she were a few inches taller but he topped her by three inches.

'I've got a job interview, actually.' With that she sauntered off to her bedroom.

He dived into the bathroom, so full of steam he could barely see a thing. Blessed relief. Now he could think straight. What the hell was she talking about? He shook his head and climbed into the shower, promptly slipping on the fragrant suds all over the shower tray and banging his knee hard on the tiled wall. Christ alive, she was a liability. A job? Doing what? Smelling people?

Stepping out of the shower he went to pluck the towel from the hook. Pushing wet hair out of his face he tried again, his hand scrabbling against the back of the door.

What? No bloody towel. No doubt the one wrapped turban style around her head. He'd kill her. Swear to God, he would.

Still dripping, he grabbed the hand towel, which was about as much use as a hanky. Sourly he rubbed a section of the mirror clear of condensation which promptly fogged over again. She couldn't even open the damn window to get rid of the steam. His knee throbbed and he managed to nick himself shaving. Not even eight o'clock and this day was turning out shite.

'Would you like some coffee? The real deal?' Siena beamed at him and sipped at her mug with a beatific expression on her face as he stomped into the kitchen.

Unfortunately the rich smell of real coffee addled his brain and when he would have asked her what the hell was going on, all he could do was nod.

And bloody hell it was good coffee. Seriously good.

'Not a morning person, are you?'

Clutching the coffee to his chest in case she turned nasty and took it away again, he glared at her.

'You'll find most men aren't when the morning routine they've enjoyed uninterrupted for the last six months is hijacked by someone who doesn't understand the concept that there are only sixty seconds in a minute and not three hours, and they've been left without a towel.'

'I wasn't that long. You're exaggerating.'

'I needed a pee.' How did she manage to make him feel slightly inadequate?

'Seriously?' She looked incredulous.

'Siena, may I remind you, there's only one loo in this house. I'm sure you're used to an en-suite for every day of the week but if you could remember that we need to share facilities and what's this about a job interview?'

'For a job.'

'I get the concept of a job interview. What I don't get is why you would want one.'

'Gosh, is that the time?' Siena darted around the table.

He blocked her exit, feeling a faint sense of unease when she tensed and a flash of something flitted across her face. 'Not so fast. Job?'

'Yes, I rang them on Saturday. In fact today's more of a training day than an interview.'

Jason closed his eyes. Proper jobs did not fall out of the trees. What the hell had she signed up for?

'A training day?' He tried to sound interested. 'Training to do what?'

'I'll be representing the company. Telling people about their home improvement products.' She trotted out the phrases parrot fashion. 'How they can make their houses look better. Offering them discounts. Today I'll be learning about drawing up quotes. You never know, I might suggest they do this place.'

Jason pinched his lips together and stared hard at the wood grain of the kitchen table, fighting the snigger. It wasn't for him to burst her bubble.

'So you get paid for this job?' he asked, the strain of not laughing showing in his voice.

'Of course I do, silly. I wouldn't be doing it otherwise. It's commission based, twelve per cent on your first fifty thousand then fifteen per cent on your second. There's the potential to earn up to one hundred thousand in your first year.'

'What happened to the trust fund? Hang on.' He shook his head as if trying to clear it. Once again she'd managed to distract him from his initial chain of thought. 'More importantly. Why? Why have you got a job? Here?'

Siena's perpetual smile slipped momentarily.

'I've decided to stay for a while. I've cleared it with Laurie. It's my room. This was my dad's house. I've got every right to stay here. Besides we can share bills.' She spat the words out so quickly, it took a minute to catch up. Good coffee or not, his brain was still in wake up mode.

'Run that by me again.'

He watched as she rearranged her face into a smiling utterly-reasonable-won't-this-be-fun expression.

'I spoke to Laurie. It is my house too, sort of, and the room is mine. So I'm going to stay a while. I'll keep out of your way. You won't even know I'm here.'

At that he raised a deliberately sceptical eyebrow.

'And just think, we can share the bills. That will help won't it?'

'Share bills?' He had a horrible feeling her hot water consumption alone would double the bills.

'Yes. You told me how expensive they all were. I'll be able to help. Great isn't it?' she said with the confident sunny smile he was rapidly realising was her default. The real world was a concept she had yet to grasp. Her world seemed to roll along on sunshine and roses. 'I'm sure it'll be nice for you to have a woman's touch about the place.'

The coffee sliding down his throat at that moment almost went west and he choked back a cough.

'Pardon?'

'You know, a woman's touch.'

He closed his eyes, counted to five. Surely no judge in the land would send him down for strangling her.

'What, the woman's touch that means I can't even find my own shaving gel in the bathroom anymore?'

'My, you are a grumpy Gus in the mornings aren't you?' She stuck her tongue out at him, with a cheeky grin. 'See you later.'

As she walked off, leaving his scrambled brain still trying to work out how he now had a lodger, he realised his eyes were glued to her backside, perfectly outlined in some smooth fabric and not a panty line in sight.

'You lucky sod.' Ben stopped for a second, lowering the sack of barley to rest on his knee. 'She's staying.' Then he pulled a face of horror. 'Claire's not going to like that.'

'It's nothing to do with Claire.' He regretted that drunken kiss on Saturday. She seemed to be very good at seeking him out at the wrong or right time depending on which way you looked at it. He shouldn't have but it had been a while and when an eager, pliant body was offering, it seemed easy to take what was on offer.

'You're doing that protesting thing again.'

'So would you if you'd had a morning like I've had.'

'Doesn't sound so bad. She made you coffee.'

'She also decimated my bathroom.' He shuddered.

Ben shrugged. 'So, no one died.' There were occasions when Jason admired the younger man's horizontal approach to life; this was not one of them. When Jason got stressed about fulfilling an order, that bacteria might have tainted a brew, or the gravity wasn't right, Ben's calm 'there's always tomorrow' attitude was an asset.

'But the mess ...'

Ben shrugged his wide shoulders, lifting the sack of grain.

Will wasn't much better. He laughed. 'She's what?'

'Selling double glazing.' Jason stared morosely down into his pint, when he took a break at lunchtime.

Will pushed a ciabatta BLT over the bar towards him.

'What's the problem? You said yourself she won't last five minutes.'

Jason brightened. 'Yeah that's true. But why? A job suggests she's staying long term.'

Will sobered for a minute. 'Seriously mate, a) is she that bad? and b) like you said she's so flighty, she could get back to Paris under her own steam. She's not going to stick around here. Paris. Cannes. New York. Leighton Buzzard? She came to see her sister. Her sister's not here. She's not going stay. Doesn't know anyone … apart from you … and I think you've made your feelings clear. Transparent actually. Girl like that is hardly going to want to live with a baboon like you.'

Jason chucked a slice of tomato at Will, who promptly caught it and stuffed it in his mouth.

'And how was the date with Claire?'

'How the hell do you know about that? It was lunch.'

'Jungle drums. You're fresh meat round here. A lunch date is a considerable coup in someone's campaign. She's on a mission, that one. You want to watch yourself.'

Jason clapped him on the arm. 'If you want the truth, I did it more to get out of the house on Sunday and away from her royal highness. I'm not about to get myself ensnared. Claire's a nice enough girl but one lunch doesn't make an engagement. I like her. I'm happy enough to take it slowly and if it goes anywhere, fine. I'm not in and out of girls' knickers like some I could mention. '

Will gave him a good natured punch on the arm. 'Mate, I can't help it if I'm a babe-magnet. They can't get enough of me.'

After lunch Will walked back across the cobbled courtyard with him.

'I love this smell.'

Jason agreed. One of the best smells in the world. Finest Kentish hops boiling in the large copper kettle. 'I know what you mean.'

They laughed together. As far as most people were concerned, the smell of hops boiling up was pretty disgusting but Jason knew that to them both it signified a whole world of dreams and ambition.

'Want a hand this afternoon?' Will had the face of an eager schoolboy; it would have been cruel to turn him down.

'You can't keep away. Like having your own train set.'

'Man this is way better than a train set. Who'd have thought eh? One minute I'm mashing your face in the scrum, the next we're building a brewing empire.'

'Empire's pushing it a bit. Although the Chamber of Commerce have said there's been some interest from a distributor in France.'

Will laughed. 'Cool if you got one in Germany. Coals to Cologne.'

'Apparently the French are going ape for boutique beers. We did win that award.'

'Yeah we could do with winning another award.' For all his effete, floppy haired, public schoolboy looks, Will had an extremely astute business brain.

'I'm doing my best.'

'You're doing fine mate. Our second year, five awards. An international gong. Distribution is on the up and we're almost solvent.'

Jason raised his eyebrows.

'Almost, I said.'

'As long as we don't want to eat as well.'

'Mate, you know I'll loan you anything you need.'

'I'm fine. Just need to be careful. Hopefully this week when I go up to the Lakes I can secure another deal. Keep going like that and in another year those tanks will be paid off. That'll lighten the load.' He paused and pulled a face. 'Providing Stacey doesn't start up again.'

'I can't believe that bitch. She sponges off you for three years. Then expects to get a cut of your flat sale. *Your* flat, man!'

'I think she's given up now.'

'I should bloody hope so. Cheeky bitch. So when do you head off and when are you back?'

'I'll leave tomorrow, back Thursday, so I wouldn't mind some help today. It's going to be a late one. There was a leak in one of the bags. I've had to send Ben in the Land Rover to get some more barley. If you can pitch in for a couple of hours that would be great.'

'I can help out until opening time and then it depends whether Michelle deigns to turn up or not.'

'Still having problems with her?'

It was unlike Will to put up with that sort of thing from one of his waitresses. The blond ponytail might lull people into the false assumption that his real job was organising a summer music festival, but his was a tight ship. People came from miles around to eat at The Salisbury Arms. The pub itself had won several big food awards and Will had worked in some serious kitchens, with the celebrity chef burns on his arms to prove it.

'Yeah, if she drops a shift again. I'm going have to sack her. I was hoping to hang on for a couple of weeks to get through Christmas. We've got a lot of big dos on. I might have to get you and Ben to pitch in.'

Jason snorted. 'In your dreams. What went wrong? I thought she was the best waitress you'd ever had.'

'I might have, er,' despite being nearly thirty, Will pulled his aw-shucks I'm-so-innocent-face.

'You didn't.' Will had a dreadful habit of being led by his libido. 'I thought we talked about this.'

'Come on Jay, she's hot.'

'She works for you.'

'It was late in the evening.' He launched into the Ed Sheeran song, doing a more than a passable falsetto impersonation.

'You're a dick sometimes.'

'She was all over me, man. And no, I didn't make any promises.'

'You're still a dick.'

'I know, part of my charm.'

'Being a dickhead is not a charm in anyone's book.'

'Must be my suave good looks then.'

Jason gave up at that point.

'This week is all under control. Ben knows what he's got to do. Once the mash is on it's a question of maintaining the temperature. Ask him every day how it's going. He'll soon tell you if there's a problem.'

'Easy peasy, lemon squeezy. I don't know why I keep you around.'

Jason thumped his arm. 'Because, apart from giving you advice on your love life, which you clearly ignore, me and the bank own fifty per cent of those gorgeous silver tanks. You and the bank own the other fifty per cent, but you don't know what the fuck to do with them.'

'OK.' Will conceded. 'You stick to the brewery side and I'll run the pub.'

Go me, thought Siena giving herself a little fist pump as she stood outside the entrance of the Hotel Enigma. She'd successfully negotiated not one but two buses, although how was she to know that five pound notes weren't acceptable currency on a bus?

'Hi. Good morning. You here for the training for the canvassing job?'

Siena nodded.

'Welcome to Johnson Home Improvements. Name please?'

'Siena.'

He ran a finger down a typed list.

'Ah yes, Siena. I've seen your name on here somewhere. Like the film star Sienna Miller. No relative then?'

'No,' she shook her head a little bemused by the question, 'I don't think so.'

'Ah, found you. Siena Browne-Martin.'

'It's Browne-Martin,' she pronounced the *tin* as *tan*, 'it's French.'

'Right, whatever. We're all equals here.' He peeled off a label and held it out to her.

'It's Siena with one 'n'.'

He shrugged. 'It'll do for today.' He continued to hold out the label.

Siena took it and held it between two fingers, looking down while she tried to decide where to put it.

'If you could wear the badge, then the trainer knows your name.'

'Right, it's ... this top is ... Gucci. Dry clean only. Do you know what adhesive they use on the labels? Is it water-soluble?'

'Ad-what?'

'The glue.'

'Glue?'

'Tell you what, why don't I introduce myself to the trainer?'

'That won't be necessary.' He sounded a bit more certain of himself now.

'Oh?'

'I'm the trainer.'

'Right. But you know my name.'

He nodded.

'So I don't need to wear the badge.'

His brow crumpled. 'I suppose not.' A look of relief crossed his face and he shifted his attention to the person behind her. 'Ah, good morning, welcome to Johnson Home Improvements. Can I take your name?' He turned back to her. 'Do go in. Help yourself to tea and coffee and take a seat.'

'Thank you.'

Taking a seat, she took a sip and almost choked. The brown liquid bore limited relation to coffee, in fact the only relation she could successfully conclude was that it was wet.

She'd spent considerable time worrying about what to wear and had aimed for smart and professional. You couldn't go far wrong with a pair of Joseph trousers, Gucci shirt and a cashmere cardie, especially when you only had a capsule wardrobe to choose from. The Missoni scarf added that jaunty look that stopped her looking really serious like a banker or a doctor.

The poor woman next to her seemed terribly nervous. She kept picking at a loose thread on her black dress, the fingers with nails bitten down to the quick, worrying at the seam with repeated staccato attacks.

'Hi, I'm Siena. Are you here for the training too?' asked Siena when the woman looked up.

'I'm not here for a bleedin' massage lovie. The Jobcentre sent me. That's a laugh. I come to these things once every six months, to get them off my back.'

'Oh.' Siena nodded as if she understood but the woman had lost interest already and had gone back to picking at the seam of her dress.

'Hello, earth to airhead.' Siena looked up at the newcomer. 'Can you move your bag so I can sit down?'

'I'm so sorry,' Siena swept her handbag onto her own knee.

''S'alright, darlin'.' He leaned forward in his chair, legs wide open so that one knee nudged her leg. She shifted and he promptly took up the fresh space.

Shifting again, she perched on the edge of her seat. He seemed completely oblivious. She turned her head away slightly to get away from the pungent smell of stale tobacco. A couple more people shuffled in, helping themselves to the tea and coffee and sat down. No one said a word to each other. It felt a bit like detention at school except without the nuns.

After a painful fifteen minutes of silent fidgeting, Alan Johnson finally strode in.

'Morning everyone. Just waiting for a few stragglers. There are always a few and quite a few no shows. It's difficult to get the staff, you know.' He grinned to show he'd made a joke, which elicited some weak laughter.

He stood at the table, looking down at a folder he'd brought in for another five blank minutes. Finally he looked up.

'I think we'll make a start. My name is Alan Johnson, Staff Training Director and I'll be introducing you to Johnson's Home Improvements today. I'll be telling you about our fantastic product range. Some USPs. Promotional tools you can use. Discounts and the like.'

'It's bloody door-to-door sales, mate. Just tell us what the fucking commission rate is,' muttered the guy next to Siena.

'Sorry sir, did you want to contribute?'

'Nah, carry on mate.'

Alan nodded. 'I want to emphasise we're a family run company, not one of these big conglom corpalates. Family run. We care.' He slammed his fist into the palm of his other hand. 'We want to give our customers the opportunity to make significant improvements to their homes. Improve energy efficiency. Saleability of their property. I can't begin to list the pros, they're endless. And that, ladies and gentlemen, makes these products really easy to sell. Seriously they walk off the shelf. Walk off the shelf, I say. No hard sell needed. Although today I'm going to run through some handy tips for clinching that sale. We don't want to hear those death of a salesman words, 'I'll think about it'. No, we want signatures on dotted lines. What do we want? Signatures on dotted lines. Deposits upfront. Commitment. So we'll be doing some role-playing exercises. And developing some handy tips for clinching that sale. Overcoming objections. And in exchange we can offer you a fantastic commission on every sale.'

A hand shot up further along the row. 'Excuse me. Is there a salary? I was led to believe this wasn't commission only.'

Alan gave a non-jocular laugh. 'It's not commission only. We're giving you training, free of charge, your own patch. Committed individuals, who stay with the company for six months, can achieve a monthly salary. Before lunch I'm going to teach you some of our trigger phrases. Keep you on-message.'

He stepped towards a flip chart and turned over the blank page to reveal a list of words.

Siena began to scribble in her notebook.

'First is 'Quality'. Customers love quality. And a good deal.'

Lunch came and went, and when he strode into the afternoon session, Alan seemed to think it was a virtue that half his audience had departed.

'See, this job is for the bold, the fearless. You guys are up for the challenge. You want to do well. So, you will do well. And if you do well, you can earn a lot of money.'

'Now, we're going to do some role-play. Team up into pairs.'

Siena's partner was an older black guy with the drooping jowls of a bloodhound and pudgy hands which gave her an enthusiastic, clammy handshake.

'Don't you worry darlin', He patted her thigh and she flinched. He withdrew it smartly. 'Sorry my love. Didn't mean to be over familiar. I do apologise.'

'It's OK,' she said, realising it had been an unconscious friendly gesture. She relaxed, letting the sudden tension dissipate. She realised it felt completely different to that stomach clenching sensation when someone kept deliberately touching when they knew you didn't want to be touched.

'I was trying to say, I'm an old hand at this. You look a bit green. Done much in the way of sales before?'

Siena shook her head. 'Nothing. In fact,' she lowered her voice to a whisper, 'I've never even had a job.'

'Good for you darlin'. No preconceptions then. That could be in your favour. The punters like a bit of honesty now and then. You need to be good cop and bad cop. Come on let's get started and Uncle Gareth will show you how it's done. I'm not sure Alan here could sell his own grandmother a box of biscuits.'

Siena turned the page and cleared her throat. This could be fun. She'd always rather liked drama at school.

'Good morning sir, can I interest you in—'

Gareth held up a hand, palm towards her.

'No, no, no, girly. Do you know the first thing I'm gonna do, if you turn up on my doorstep saying that?'

Siena shook her head.

'Slam the door in your face, missy. No matter how good-looking you are, and excuse me for saying, but you are one attractive young

71

lady. Now you can use those looks to your advantage. Me, I don't have that advantage.'

Siena tried to pull a non-committal kind of face.

'Don't worry, I use my looks.' He pulled a hangdog expression, his mouth turning down and his eyes sad. 'Everyone loves an underdog. My patter is very much apology. "Hey I'm really, really sorry to bother you. It's my job, it's a lousy job but …"'

Siena stared at him, uncomprehending.

He patted her leg again, this time on the knee. 'You gotta start by pulling them in, building empathy with them. Build rapport before you even go near the sales patter. Who wrote this crap?' He shook his head. 'Get your pen out. You need your own hook. You need to bat those baby blues. Flirt a little. Be supremely confident. A good-looking girl doing this job because she believes in the product. She don't have no other job, not because she can't get one, but because this is a good one. A good product. I tell you young lady, you have got a serious advantage here.'

Over the next hour, gorgeous Gareth as she renamed him in her head, shared every last scrap of wile and guile that he had with her and by the end of it, she felt she knew what she was doing.

Alan came to check up on their progress.

'So Siena, with one 'n'. Pretend you're knocking on my front door.'

Gareth winked at her. 'You go girl.'

'Hi, sorry to disturb you, can I say this is a lovely house. I love what you've done with the garden. Have you ever thought of selling?'

'No,' said Alan with a smug smile on his face.

'See, there's that close down the question, the one I told you about,' piped up Gareth. 'Now remember what you do.'

'And I don't blame you,' Siena was enjoying herself, blossoming under Gareth's paternal gaze, 'this is a lovely house. Although, if you don't mind me saying so, you could make it even more appealing. I see next door is looking a bit tired. Their front door could do with a lick of paint, don't you think?'

'No, Siena remember. Open questions. Don't ever give them the chance to say no.'

'Sorry.'

'And don't apologise. You're in charge here, if they don't choose to buy your product, it's their loss.'

Siena nodded, thinking fast.

'Their front door could do with a lick of paint. If you were going to paint yours, what colour would you go for?'

'Much better,' said Gareth nodding at Alan, encouraging him to join in.

'A door says such a lot about you. Creates first impressions. Says the people who live here care. Now if you paint your door, you've got to maintain it. Johnson's Doors are virtually maintenance free. Guaranteed for twenty-five years. Now I think you could probably do a lot more with this lovely house. Show people in the neighbourhood that you care, unlike the neighbours who don't or maybe they can't afford to invest in what's important. Now with a bit of TLC, you could really show your neighbours, friends, that you've got pride, dignity and money. People respect that.'

Alan straightened. 'Hell yeah. Where do I sign on the dotted line?'

Gareth held up a hand and Siena high-fived him.

'You go girl. You are ready to go out on the road.'

Alan nodded. 'Yeah, I think you are. Do you know what, I think I can see a very long and successful relationship with Johnson Home Improvements for you, Siena.'

Jason returned as Siena was grating cheese, dancing around the kitchen and melting butter in the frying pan.

'What the fu—' Jason stumbled to a halt in the kitchen doorway.

'Hi,' Siena turned, pushing unruly hair away from her face.

Jason looked pained.

'What's wrong?' She followed his eyes as he scanned the table, the kitchen counters and the sink which was piled high with saucepans.

'It looks like Armageddon in here. What are you cooking?'

'Omelette. I'm celebrating.' Now she had a job, she'd been food shopping and treated herself to a bottle of wine.

'Omelette? For five thousand? You must have used every utensil in the kitchen.'

Siena looked around. Surely he was exaggerating. She'd used a few plates, a couple of bowls, two chopping boards, several knives and one cast iron pan. 'It's not so bad.'

He came closer. 'Have you ever cooked an omelette before?'

'Yes.' Typical English man, no clue about cooking.

'Really? I've never seen it cooked like that before.'

Of course he hadn't. Judging from the contents of the kitchen, he didn't know one end of a frying pan from the other. He was used to eating meals from plastic trays in sleeves of cardboard. He was no judge.

'Wait until you taste it. Have you eaten?'

He hesitated.

'Go on, try it. What have you got to lose?'

He still looked reluctant, until she tossed the pancetta into a Le Creuset frying pan with a sizzle, the scent quickly filing the air. She saw his hesitancy fade as the red peppers and slices of new potatoes went in. She let them cook for a minute. Much as she loved to cook, she didn't get the chance very much. A lot of what she did was trial and error but she certainly wasn't going to admit that to Mr Superior. It would have been nice to impress him but a basic dish like this was hardly going to hit the mark.

Even though she did think that perhaps he might be coming around, when she saw his nose lifting in appreciation of the warm cooking smells.

As the vegetables and bacon softened in the butter, she folded in frothy whipped egg whites into beaten egg yolks.

Jason frowned. 'Do you know you can beat the eggs and put them in? I've never heard of anyone separating them and then putting back together.'

Siena shrugged. 'Your loss then.' She winked at him. 'I suggest you withhold judgement until you've tried it. Would you like a glass of wine?'

She asked him to pour as she concentrated on pouring the omelette batter into the pan. The trick was to cook the bottom and then slide it under the grill to cook the top.

When she whisked the fluffy omelettes onto warm plates with a side salad of leaves and popped one in front of Jason, she smiled at the look of pleasure on his face when he tasted them.

'Wow, this is amazing.'

She smiled and took a happy slug of red wine. 'Told you I knew what I was doing.'

'I take it all back.' There was a silence between them and then as if he'd suddenly remembered his manners, Jason asked, 'So how did you get on today?'

'It was great. I met some really nice people,' she pulled a face, 'and some not so nice people. But I'm all trained and ready to go out on the road.'

'Trained?'

'Yes.' Siena felt rather pleased with herself. 'Apparently I'm an active seller.'

'And what's one of those when they're at home?'

She ignored his scepticism. What did he know? He hadn't been there today. She was looking forward to going out, helping people improve their homes. Help them reduce and eradicate unnecessary maintenance.

'An active seller is proactive. Forward thinking. Takes charge. We make the best sellers.'

'You mean you're pushy and don't take no for an answer.'

'No,' Siena drew herself up. 'We develop empathy with the customer and build a relationship.'

'Good luck with that, you're going to need it.'

Siena rolled her eyes. What did he know?

'How's the red wine?'

'Good. No, great. I guess if you're French you know a bit about wines.'

Siena shrugged. She knew what she knew. She'd never really thought about it before. 'I'm not really French. I'm English. I just grew up there.' Neither one thing nor the other.

'I really like this one. What is it?'

'It's a Bordeaux Supérieur.' The best the supermarket had to offer.

'What's that when it's at home?'

'A wine from the Bordeaux region obviously; but the grapes, mainly Cabernet Sauvignon and Merlot, come from the older plots.'

'It's very nice.' He toasted her and took a long sip and then spoilt it by adding with a naughty grin, 'Would you usually serve this with omelettes?'

'But of course,' she toasted him back with a wry smile. 'Eggs and red wine, always. Haven't you heard of nouvelle vin? Forget all those stuffy principles of white wine with fish and red wine with beef. That's all terribly vintage chapeau.'

'Really?' Jason looked half convinced until she gave a gurgle of laughter.

'No,' she raised her glass and took an appreciative slurp. 'I thought I deserved a treat after today.'

'So it went well, did it?'

Half an hour later they were still chatting as Siena emptied the last of the bottle into the two glasses. She was rather grateful that he got up to do the washing up. There did seem to be an awful lot of it.

'Only because you cooked, mind,' he warned.

She'd remember that cooking was much easier than the boring tidying up, besides she wasn't sure how much longer her manicure would hold up. She'd never gone this long between salon visits before.

Chapter 6

After two days sleeping in hotel rooms where the beds were great but the heating systems seemed to be programmed to suck every last bit of moisture out of your system, Jason pulled up outside the house desperate for a long, cold drink. The trip north had been mainly successful. He'd signed a bottling contract and got a deal with a distributor for the Cheshire area. All in all, a fruitful trip. It also sounded as if things in the brewery had also gone well. He'd maintained regular, if slightly obsessive, contact with Ben and he felt confident that there was nothing to worry about.

He'd deliberately not contacted Siena. The omelette and wine had been convivial the other night but it wasn't something he wanted to encourage. Not that it mattered. In fact he was guessing she'd probably packed her bags by now. With a soft chuckle shook his head. Door-to-door sales. He'd bet she hadn't stuck it for more than an hour.

The house was in darkness when he slipped his key in the door. Sliding off his boots in the hall and letting the wooden bannister take his weight, he mentally pictured taking the first long pull of cold lager.

He padded down the hall to the kitchen without bothering to put the lights on and as he crossed to the fridge he felt a prickling sensation run down his back. Dismissing it as a symptom of bone-deep weariness, he opened the door and letting the light from inside the appliance spill out, he went to grab a bottle of Bud but stopped when he thought he heard a muffled sob. He paused, but all he could hear was the hum of the fridge, the slight clink of bottles rubbing together on the glass shelf inside. He grabbed a Budweiser, already anticipating the cold slide down his throat and turned.

Like a spotlight, the beam from the fridge haloed Siena, hunched over the table, head buried in crossed arms. Jason could see her ribs lift and shudder through the thin cotton of a white silk shirt which lit up like a lighthouse.

'Siena?'

Like a turtle she tucked in tighter, another muffled sob escaping.

'Siena. Are you OK?'

The light picked out and highlighted her narrow frame. Not wanting to blind her by putting the main light on, he closed the fridge door and switched on the less invasive light on the extractor fan.

He heard her let out a shaky shuddery sigh, as if each breath she parted with was hard fought.

'Siena?'

As he got closer he could see her ribcage heave as if she were fighting to keep the sobs inside and something about the way she'd tucked into herself spooked him. He'd seen histrionics, tantrums and drama queens. He had two sisters. But this quiet, contained desperate crying tore at his heart.

She took in a juddering breath and he crouched down next to her. 'Hey, what's the matter?'

She lifted her head.

'Bloody hell,' he hissed, regretting making her start, but Christ alive, her face was a mess. He reached out to touch the swollen, grazed cheekbone taking in the red-rimmed eyes and the tear-stained face. Something inside him clenched at the utter defeat in her eyes. Siena's eternal sunshine was missing. 'What happened, sweetheart?'

Her throat worked, swallowing and her eyes filled with tears as she simply shook her head, as if the effort of getting the words out was too much. Her eyes went glassy and unfocused and she seemed to blank out for a couple of seconds. He had a horrible feeling, she wasn't quite there, making him worry she might faint.

Without thinking he scooped her up and swapped places on the chair, with her on his knee, enfolding her into his arms.

'Ow,' she moaned quietly as he pulled her tight to his chest.

'Sorry.' He loosened his hold but kept her head tucked under his chin and rubbed her shoulder. She shifted, wincing, and he inhaled the scent of her shampoo, light and fresh. Very Siena. Confident, unafraid of the world, self-assured, self-possessed but with that upbeat positive attitude which he couldn't help but admire. Yes, she irritated the hell out of him, but that probably said as much about him as her.

Her breath hitched and then she began to cry softly, the tears falling onto his neck and soaking into the cotton of his shirt.

'Hey, there come on.' He felt totally inadequate but let her cry for a minute, figuring she needed to let it out. Gradually her sniffs subsided and he leaned behind him and grabbed the kitchen roll, ripping off a square. 'Here.'

'S-sorry.' She blew her nose and wiped her eyes with the back of one hand. 'Ouch,' she twisted slightly as if to relieve the pain.

'What's happened, Siena?' he took her other hand. 'Did you have an accident?'

'No.' She gripped his hand and sucked in a breath.

'What? You fell over.' She did like her skyscraper heels.

'No, it happened at work.'

He stiffened. 'What, while you were out knocking on doors?' She nodded.

'Someone slammed a door on you?'

'No. It was a man.' He had to strain to hear her voice.

'Someone do this to you?' Outrage tinged his voice.

'Yes, but it was sort of my fault.' The death grip on his hand tightened.

He studied her face, the red swelling like a small plum above the cheekbone, congealed dried blood below. Looking down he realised her jeans were muddy all down one side and one shoe was missing, leaving a saturated, torn sock.

Tension rode his muscles, he tried to keep the anger out of his voice, she was already clearly badly shaken and he didn't want to upset her any more. 'Tell me exactly what happened. Take your time.'

'I was doing my job. Did you know? People are so mean.'

He almost smiled at the disbelief in her voice.

'They shut the door in your face. A man spat at me. They swear. I don't understand. How am I doing them any harm? That's just—' She lifted her shoulders.

'Unfortunately a lot of people who sell door-to-door use quite strong tactics. They have quite a bad reputation.'

She sighed. 'But I'm trying to help them. Improve their houses.'

He did smile this time, picturing Siena in sales mode. He liked that she started to sound a little bit indignant.

'Some people really don't look after their houses. The windows are all peeling, the doors need painting. You'd have thought those people would want to make their houses look nice. And then not have to bother with all the boring refurbishment and upkeep.'

Bless her, you'd think she'd swallowed the sales manual whole.

'I guess, it's not that important to some people.' He rubbed her hand, not wanting to point out that some people might find it offensive to be told their houses need improving.

'They don't have to be so rude …' she paused and he felt her sway forward, 'about it.'

'You OK?'

'Feel a bit sick every now and then.'

'Do you want me to get a bowl or something?'

'No, I think I'm alright now.'

She did look very peaky, but he felt that keeping her talking was the right thing to do. 'Whereabouts were you, er, selling?'

She named the least salubrious area of town and he very nearly dropped her.

'What?' He shook his head. 'Bloody hell, that's about as rough as it gets. I'm surprised you weren't—' He stopped, his eyes returning to the swelling on her face. 'Fuck. Did someone do this to you?' He lifted a finger, outlining the gash on her cheek. She flinched. 'Oh Siena.'

With his thumbs he wiped away the tears and pulled her towards him, feeling his heart pounding. Without thinking or questioning it, he placed a gentle kiss on her forehead. It felt soft under his lips. His pulse tripped. He wanted to pull her close, nuzzle the velvet skin, keep her there. Make her feel safe again.

Forcing himself to pull away and surprised at the sudden sense of loss, he asked again, 'What happened?'

'I knocked at the door. There were steps up to it. The man opened it. He was already cross. I should have realised. I said sorry for disturbing him, but I was polite.' Her lips crumpled and she let out a sob. 'I tried to tell him but he didn't let me finish. He said you will be. Then he started to say all sorts of horrible things, calling me—' She stopped. 'It was awful and I froze. I know I shouldn't have made him even crosser.'

Jason straightened puzzled by her choice of words.

'I didn't mean to … but then I didn't know what to do and then he,' her eyes widened, 'h-h-he punched me. I fell down the stairs, I forget what happened then. I might have fainted and then I was on the ground and I c-couldn't g-get up for a minute, everything was fuzzy. And he kicked me. And then kept trying to kick me again. Then I got up and ran away. Then I got lost and didn't know where I was. My phone's smashed and I walked and walked, then I knew where I was and I came home.'

His hands clenched involuntarily, so hard they hurt his knuckles. It took all his control to grit his teeth and not give in to the burning temptation to go out and ram the fucker's own teeth down his throat. What an arse. What kind of animal hit someone like Siena? Anyone could see she was an innocent abroad.

Every muscle felt taut but when he felt answering tension in Siena's body, he forced himself to relax. Let his jaw go. Breathe evenly. She needed gentleness now, not his rage.

He lifted her from his knee, turned and placed her on the kitchen chair before crossing to put on the kitchen light.

In the sudden light, she looked dreadful. Paper white, her eyes huge in her face, still with that slight glassy sheen to them and her beautiful hair tangled and matted. Her clothes were streaked with dirt.

'Did you hit your head when you fell?'

She nodded.

'Show me where?'

'*Ici*.' She pointed to a spot and his fingers delved into her thick hair to find a definite lump.

'Have you got a headache?' Stupid question really, after all she'd been through, it was more than likely. 'Do you feel sick or dizzy?'

'Sick? *Oui, j'ai mal au cœur*.'

'Do you think you're going to be?'

'*Je n'en suis pas sûr*, it comes in waves.'

'OK, what about where he kicked you? Can you show me?'

'It was my back, *en deçà*.' She pointed to her side.

'Does it hurt?' He moved his fingers down her ribcage at the back.

'Ow, *oui*. There.' She flinched as he probed one particular spot. 'It's OK until I move or you touch it. It's fine when I stay ...' she went even whiter. 'Sorry I think ...' she closed her eyes, her forehead crumpling in distress. 'No it's gone again. Thought I might be sick.'

'Anywhere else hurt?'

'*Partout*. Everywhere hurts.' He almost felt relief at her put out little girl tone and the pout that pursed her lips. Signs of the real Siena for a second.

'Apart from everywhere, is there anywhere else specific?'

'My legs, my ribs, my foot.'

Crouching down in front of her he lifted it and peeled what was left of the tattered sock away from her heel. Hell's teeth, no wonder it hurt. A large bulging blister had formed on the heel of her foot, while the rest of the sole was filthy with ingrained dirt and covered in lots of tiny bloody scratches.

'What happened to your boot?'

'*Perdu*. It came off when I fell down the stairs. *Merde*, my foot really hurts.'

'I'm not surprised. This needs some attention.' Maybe he ought to take her to hospital. She seemed in shock, but a four hour wait in casualty probably wouldn't be as good as a night's sleep.

'Your foot needs a good clean. We need to soak it, to get some of the grit out. Let's go up to the bathroom.'

Pulling her to her feet, she swayed for a moment. 'I feel sick again.'

'No worries.' Leaving her side he went to the sink and grabbed the washing up bowl. As soon as he'd got her sorted, he'd give Ben's sister a call, she was a nurse.

Supporting her as she limped slowly step by step, he led her upstairs. She needed to get out of her clothes and he didn't think she was really in any fit state to do it herself. Leading her to the bathroom, he settled her on the loo seat. 'Do you have a dressing gown?' he gave her a gentle smile, 'that's a bit less flimsy that the little number you had on the other morning?'

She managed a weak nod of her head, her lips curving.

'Wait there a minute.' He darted off to his bedroom to grab his, not wanting to leave her a second longer than he had to.

'I need to undress you, OK?'

Something tugged at his heart as she looked at him, complete trust in her eyes. Trying to be as quick and impersonal as possible, he undid the buttons of her blouse. He couldn't help but notice the lacy white bra and the creamy flesh spilling over the top but, rather proud of himself, he kept his mind on the task before looking at her back. He traced the curve of her ribs; she seemed so soft and fragile. Although tall, her build was slender. No sign of bruising yet, but the large red mark below her shoulder blade made his blood boil. He had to clench his fist to stop the hiss of disgust. As a veteran of the rugby pitch, he knew it was unlikely the hospital would do an x-ray for a possible broken rib, so not much point going to A&E for that, although her head concerned him. The glassy eyed stare that she kept lapsing into could be either shock or concussion.

The silk blouse slipped to the floor in a puddle and he tried hard not to look at her breasts, instead his eyes drifted down. He frowned. A fist-sized bluish tinge on her stomach caught his eye. A bruise but not a fresh one. Before he could ask her about it, she went rigid.

'I'm going to be ssss ...'

With seconds to spare he whipped the bowl onto her lap and held her hair away as she heaved and choked into the bowl.

'*Dieu*, that hurts,' she gasped and moaned as another spasm gripped her and she dropped her head again.'

With her long curls wrapped around his hand, he stood there, unable to do anything to help, hating feeling so damn helpless.

At last she pushed the bowl away.

'I–I think that's it now.'

Just as well he thought, those final dry heaves must have hurt her ribs. She really was in a pitiful state, reminiscent of a small bedraggled kitten that had been rescued from a canal.

'Do you want a shower?'

She nodded.

'I'll put it on for you, take your jeans off and I'll leave you for five minutes. Then I'll be back. Do you think you can manage?'

Another nod.

'I'll leave this for you, then you don't have to worry about drying yourself.' He indicated his navy blue towelling dressing gown and stood up, taking the washing up bowl downstairs with him.

Outside the bathroom door he prowled, pacing backwards and forwards. What kind of fucker could do that to a woman? To Siena. Calming his breathing he listened. The shower had stopped. He gave her a minute.

'Are you decent?'

No answer.

He knocked on the door. 'I'm coming in.'

She stood, trying to belt the dressing gown, intense concentration on her face, the sleeves hanging below her hands. With her damp curls, she looked like Little Orphan Annie and he bit back a smile.

'Don't laugh. I look ridiculous.' The shower had obviously revived her and to his relief he could see a bit of colour in her cheeks.

'I was thinking kind of cute.'

She let out a huge sigh. 'I feel so *stupide*.'

'Stupid? That's silly. Come on let's get you into bed. I think that's the best place for you.'

He led her into her bedroom, propped up the pillows pulled back the covers and ushered her in.

'Thank you,' she whispered as she settled in.

'Right, I'm going to get you a cup of hot sweet tea because I think you're in shock, and a couple of painkillers.'

She gave him a weak smile. 'I'm so sorry to be so much trouble. You don't have to look after me. I'll be OK.' He gave her a pointed look and turned to leave the room. 'It's not like you're responsible for me or anything.'

He stopped and looked back at her. The words were spoken softly, no hint of sarcasm, a bald statement of truth. They hit hard.

'Shut up, Siena.' Inside, his stomach clenched.

He took the stairs slowly, shaking his head. What an arse. A real gent to have given her the impression that he wasn't willing to help her when she needed it. That wasn't him, or at least it never used to be. When had he become so focused on protecting himself that he shut other people out? Had Stacey really skewed his view of other people and their motives that much?

At the bottom of the stairs, he stopped in front of the mirror in the hallway. He stared at himself. These days his mouth had a slight down turn. Even as he examined his lower lip, always too bloody girly, he could see his face settle into its default expression. It, he, looked grumpy. He swallowed. Was that how other people saw him these days? He closed his eyes but forced himself to look again. Practiced a smile, lifting the corners of his mouth. It looked forced.

With an impatient huff, he wheeled away and into the kitchen.

Ransacking the cupboards for painkillers, he found a dusty pack of paracetamol and some ibuprofen and then he hesitated. What if she had concussion?

A quick phone call reassured him, but he was in for a long night. Ben's sister had said paracetamol only and since Siena was reasonably lucid, she recommended Jason monitored her throughout the night, waking her every couple of hours to make sure she woke up and that her headache wasn't worse.

'Here, take two of these.' He passed her the tablets and the tea.

'Thank you.'

'How are you feeling?'

'Stupid.'

'You said that before.'

'I feel even more stupid now. And I threw up in front of you. That's so not cool.'

'What and stripping down to your bra and knickers is?' He smiled at her cross-patch face.

'A gentleman wouldn't mention that.'

He winced at the word *gentleman*. 'True and a gentleman wouldn't hit anyone. We'll call the police in the morning.'

'The police?' Siena looked fearful.

'Yes. That man assaulted you.'

'He. I made him cross. I-I do that t-to some people. You. I made you cross. Remember. I don't want to get the police involved. It was—'

'Siena, you didn't make him cross. He chose to be cross. And even if you are cross, you don't hit people. He chose to hit you and then when you were on the ground, kick you. Are you going to tell me that didn't happen? Because I suspect you may have a cracked rib and if the swelling on your face doesn't go down, possibly a fractured cheekbone. We're talking serious assault here, not just cross.'

Siena studied her tea. 'I don't want to go the police. I'm sorry.'

It wasn't worth pushing the issue tonight. She'd been through enough for one day but something she said nagged at him. 'Why do think it's your fault he was cross?'

'Sometimes I do things. It makes people cross.'

'People who?'

She looked sideways.

'Is that what they told you?'

She nodded but wouldn't lift her face.

'Siena, no one should hit you ever. No matter how angry, cross or upset they get. That's a non-negotiable.'

He sighed, now ultra-conscious of his previous motivations, wary of what he said and how he phrased it. It wasn't that he was trying to get rid of her, not for himself, but she had to see that this incident highlighted how ill-equipped she was to function in the real world.

'Don't you think it's time to go home?'

Her eyes fluttered closed, leaving Jason looking at her suspiciously. Yeah, she could hide but she couldn't run. This wasn't the end of this conversation. He looked at his watch. She could sleep for two hours and then he'd wake her, and every two hours after that throughout the night.

87

It was going to be a long one. He had half a mind to phone Laurie and get her to phone their mother but then they'd both worry. For tonight he could do the worrying for both of them.

Chapter 7

As soon as she surfaced, anxiety started to gnaw. It took a while for her brain to catch up and then as she moved, all the aches and pains exploded into her conscious. Ah *bordel*, every single part of her hurt. Especially her pride. Thinking about walking back yesterday made her wince. What must people have thought? In one boot, looking like she'd been in a fight. Thank goodness she didn't know anyone. If that had got onto Facebook or Snapchat …

Moving with the speed of an old lady, she swung her legs carefully off the bed and took a shallow breath as the pain in her rib lanced through like a lightning strike. Right, maybe it was going to take a while to get going today. As she pulled herself to her feet, she caught sight of herself in the mirror.

'Ah *putain*!' She lifted her hand to the cheek which had swollen to Quasimodo-like proportions. Ow, that hurt. Worst still, she had a black eye! Her hair looked like as if it had been whipped up with an egg whisk and then sprayed in place. Even when she'd dressed up for the Hallowe'en Ball at Versailles as a zombie, after three hours of make-up, she hadn't looked this horrific.

The gentle tap at the door made her want to go running back to bed and hide under the pillows, except there was no way she could move that fast.

'Siena, can I come in? You decent?'

Interesting question, given she wore his robe. It smelt of him, an undefinable scent evoking his kindness last night as he'd woken her gently every couple of hours, bringing her tablets for her headache and before that, she bit her lip, she didn't want to think how it had felt to burrow into his lap in the half-lit kitchen, tucked into the crook between his neck and shoulder or the haven of his arms. How could she feel so safe with a man she'd known a few days, when a man she'd known all her life could make her feel so powerless?

'Siena?' His voice sharpened.

'Yes.' She swallowed hard, facing him this morning also meant having to face up to a lot of things she'd rather leave buried. Time to come clean. 'You can come in.'

The tray of tea and toast he carried reminded her how long it was since she'd last eaten and her stomach rumbled in a most unladylike manner but then Jason had held her head while she threw up last night, so it was the least of her worries.

'Morning. How are you feeling?' He winced as he looked at her face, put the tray down and came closer to study it. He'd showered already and smelt of some manly soap she couldn't identify but he hadn't shaved and the dark bristles outlined his strong jawline. Looking at them, she remembered them softly prickling her nose when he kissed her forehead last night. She swallowed and looked down at her feet, worried by the sudden flush she felt at the memory of the brief touch of his lips. Comfort, that was all it had been and yet it touched her. Even in her battered state, the warmth of it felt like sunlight on a spring flower after a long winter. And wasn't that ridiculously fanciful? He didn't even like her very much.

He'd probably like her even less when she 'fessed up, which she felt was imminent.

'You shouldn't be out of bed. I've spoken to Ben's sister again and she suggests we pop to A&E to get you checked over this morning while it's quieter. And we also need to call the police.'

The rigidity of his jaw and the sternness of his face suggested she was going to have a battle on her hands on this one.

'Jason, I can't go to the police.' She didn't want to plead because that would make her look silly and hysterical, she needed him to see that she was serious and rational. 'I can't.'

'Why not?' Damn, equally rational and reasonable back. It would be easier if he tried to take control and insist. She was used to battling against that.

'You're a bank robber on the run?'

Her eyes widened. On the run. Yeah that was about right.

'France's most wanted? Stolen the Mona Lisa?'

She winkled her nose even though she was trying to be serious and with a reluctant smile shook her head. It would almost have been worth doing one of those things to deserve the notoriety her reputation was no doubt currently enjoying back in France.

'Hang on. You pulled a face. Not a robber.' He stopped and it would have been amusing if she hadn't felt trepidation at having to confess, watching him add things up. 'On the run. You're on the run?' He screwed up his face in disbelief. 'Seriously? What the hell from?'

She feigned interest in the coving around the ceiling, picked out in pure white, to match the pretty grey and white wallpaper.

'Siena?' He had that 'I'm waiting' tone in his voice, a bit like a teacher knowing a pupil is in the wrong.

With a sigh, she pulled the robe tighter around her and shuffled back to sit on the edge of the bed. He came to sit next to her, not crowding her but at a comfortable distance for which she was grateful. He handed her the cup of tea.

'Here, take a sip. It'll make you brave.'

The hot tea scalded her throat but she welcomed the warmth travelling down, it gave her a focus as she gathered her thoughts. What had happened to that gruff, grumbly man that had picked her up at the airport, channelling hostility and resentment like a medium on a direct line to the devil?

'I ran away,' she said in a small voice.

'You ran away?' His voice rang with disbelief.

A rueful half-laughed escaped as she said, 'Ridiculous, *non*? At my age.'

To her surprise Jason didn't say anything, he just nodded gravely.

'I left a note.'

He nodded again.

'I needed to escape. Sounds crazy, eh? I have everything. A nice home, everything I want. Maman wants me to get married. To Yves.'

She looked at him waiting for him to tell her that there were far bigger problems in the world and she was being ridiculous and foolish.

'And you don't want to,' he said, with gentle simplicity as if that were perfectly acceptable and reasonable.

The calm response, contrasting so sharply with the histrionics and rows she'd endured these last few months, made her heart turn over in her chest.

'No,' she whispered blinking back tears.

'So why can't you say that?' His steady gaze held hers waiting, patient but without judgement.

It sounded so easy when he put it like that.

Without thinking she rubbed at her stomach, at the remnants of the bruise there. 'I did try to talk to Maman and Yves. It made him cross. Maman says I'm being childish and ungrateful. I needed some time to think without them, without all the noise.'

'I get that. We all need a bit of thinking time.' He shifted his position on the edge of the bed, crossing one knee over the other. 'So now what?'

Siena sighed, took a big breath and looked him right in the eye.

'I told Maman,' she grimaced, 'in my note, of course, that I needed time to think and that I would be back for Christmas.'

'That sounds reasonable.'

'Only because my stepfather, who is lovely but always busy with business, is having his sixtieth birthday party on the twenty-third. It's for him really.' With a frown, she added, 'That's when Yves wants to announce the engagement.'

'Ah.'

'I lied.' She waited for Jason's response, he continued to look at her, his expression impassive. 'I did plan to go back but only to tell them that I'm staying in England to do a fashion degree. To be a fashion designer. I thought if I had somewhere to live and had enrolled on the course, Maman would see I was serious about it. Show them that I'm not ready to get married yet. Maybe persuade Yves to wait.'

'Hence the staying 'a while.'"

'You don't need to worry about that anymore.' Defeat gnawed in the pit of her stomach. Hastily she pulled her finger away from her mouth realising she was worrying at the nail with her teeth. She'd run out of options. Three days of knocking on doors. Getting appointments had been a lot harder than Johnsons' Home Improvements had led her to believe. She hadn't managed to earn a sous.

'I have to go home now. Back to Bresançon.'

'Bresançon? Where's that?'

'Eastern France, not far from the Swiss border.' She closed her eyes hating the tears prickling there. It didn't matter anymore. 'My mother cancelled all my cards and my allowance. I've got nothing.'

He stared at her, a startled look on his face and ran his hand through his hair. 'Seriously. She cancelled them?'

Siena nodded.

'What about the degree? Don't you still want to do that?'

'Yes, but I haven't been able to speak to anyone at the college. I don't have all the qualifications they want, but I'm sure if I can get an appointment I can show them how much I know about fashion.'

There was no doubting her enthusiasm.

'I'm going to regret this.' He paused and gave her an assessing look. 'Will needs a waitress at the pub to tide him over for the

93

Christmas period. Let me give him a call and see if he'll consider you. That way you can earn enough to stay until the twenty-third and see the woman at the college.'

'Really?'

'Really. On the condition that you go the police.'

Chapter 8

'You'll need a white shirt and a black skirt.' Will gave a ridiculously exaggerated wink. 'Short, if you want to make lots in tips.' He poured them both a glass of wine and pushed one towards her.

Siena laughed and thanked small mercies for painkillers. Her rib still hurt but not as badly. 'Is that all it takes?'

The Salisbury Arms had to be the prettiest pub Siena had ever seen, not that she'd had a lot of experience of English pubs. Since Jason had pulled up outside, her poor sad, sorry spirits had lifted the minute she saw the thatched roof curving low over diamond lead lined windows.

The pub sat at the centre of the village in a V between two roads, the sprawling timber framed and brick building, festooned even in winter with a profusion of hanging baskets overflowing with tiny purple and white pansies. Tubs with matching flowers flanked both sides of the front door, which was accessed by a huge porch filled on either side with logs and racks with several pairs of upside down wellington boots.

Impatient to get to the brewery, apparently in the building behind the pub, Jason had literally dropped her at the door, telling her she'd find Will inside somewhere. To be fair she'd made him late. Disguising her black eye had taken more time, skill and ingenuity than she'd realised. Not having her usual make-up box had limited her options.

Luckily Will didn't seem distracted by her dodgy make-up job.

'So it won't matter if I spill their soup all over them? Drop an eyelash in the wine?' Should she be drinking during an interview? Will had said he was having one and she fancied a glass, so why the heck not? He was funny and charming. She could have introduced him to any of her friends back home.

'I'd rather you didn't do any of those things. The customers tend to object. Although,' Will's blue eyes twinkled with devilment, 'with those legs I think you'll probably get away with murder.'

The blatant appreciation made her feel much more like herself. Will was all talk. No he wasn't actually, he probably would act if you gave him the right signals but he was definitely manageable. The sort that *would* take no for an answer and not be the least bit offended.

'Right so micro mini, then.' Siena tossed her hair back over her shoulder, hooked her legs around the bar stool and leaned in towards Will, pretending to tick off a list on her fingers.

'I do need the chef still breathing.'

'I'll be gentle with him.'

'You'd better be, I need him. More than you I'm afraid, unless you can cook.' He laughed. 'Scrub that, of course you can't. Jason mentioned you had staff back home, so we'll take that as no.'

He made it sound completely normal and Siena loved him for it, although she might take Jason to task for raising it. Then again he had fixed up this meeting with Will for her.

'Have you ever worked as a waitress before?' Leaning his hip against the bar, his arms folded behind his head, stretching his T-shirt over a lean, long torso, it was hard to imagine that this laughing, laid-back handsome man owned and ran this place. Jason had told her it had a stellar reputation for food in the area, winning countless awards. She could see that he had shifted back into interview mode.

She gave him a direct look and lifted her eyebrows, an

96

irrepressible smile on her lips. 'Will, you know that apart from my short-lived disastrous spell as a door-to-door double glazing saleswoman without a single sale to my name, I have never done a day's work in my life.' She tipped her head to one side, awaiting his response.

With a nonchalant shrug he moved forward and leant on the bar. 'I thought as much but I wanted to know what you'd say.'

There it was, the test question. For all his casual air, you didn't get to be that successful without being an astute business man too. Siena had seen Harry in action enough times to recognise the seamless segue.

'I say I'll work as hard as I can, try as hard as I can, be honest and truthful.' That was all she had to offer.

'Oh God, don't be too truthful with the customers, that could end in tears.' He straightened and held out an imaginary plate and said in a dodgy falsetto. 'Yes sir, of course sir, you're absolutely right the beef is undercooked, totally and utterly. And yes I agree, where do we get off calling it rare?'

Siena smiled as he minced down the bar.

He came back. 'I do expect you to work hard. No favours because you're Jason's friend. I'll give you a trial. I expect you to be punctual, turn up for every shift and do your best.'

She took a sip of wine, a cool refreshing Chardonnay.

'Now, what do you think of that?'

'What the wine?'

'No, the pattern on the plates. Of course, I meant the wine.'

She swirled it thoughtfully lifting the glass up to the light, looking at the light straw colour and watching the legs slide down the inside of the glass.

'French, I think, but more of a new world style,' she took a large slurp and savoured the cold liquid rolling it around her mouth, 'oaked but not overpowering, buttery, medium body with good mouth-feel and long cool finish.' As she put her glass cleanly down on the bar as if to punctuate her tasting assessment with an authoritative full stop, Siena took the chance to take a better look around. Under her fingers, the smooth and highly polished wood of the bar was pocked with scattered knots and whorls. She liked the rustic feel of it. Ceramic brass pulls punctuated the bar in groups of threes, with little plates naming what she assumed were English beers. You certainly didn't see anything like this in France. Chiltern Glory. William's Finest. Red Kite.

Will inclined his head. 'I'm impressed. You know your wine.'

'I know a little.'

'You sound like you know plenty, which is great with the customers. Actually, hang on a minute.' He darted off to the back of the bar through a door and then reappeared her side of the bar and then scurried through to the next room.

Swivelling around on the stool, she examined the room, which opened to a roof supported by 'A' frame wooden beams in pale wood. It gave the room an open, airy barn-like feel. She liked the mix of contemporary and period; despite this obviously being an old building, its whitewashed walls and pale sage green painted doors and trims had a modern feel about it. Little details like the trendy wood burner and the colourful paintings on the wall, water-colours of flowers in vibrant purples, limes and blues, not your usual Victorian botanical watercolours, gave the pub a distinctive style. Even the knick-knacks on the window were stylishly designed ceramic vases and jugs in muted shades of grey earthenware.

Someone had worked very hard to achieve this understated chic atmosphere and she wondered if it carried on through the double doors at the end through which Will now appeared.

'New menus.' He waved them at her as he crossed the room and plonked himself down on the stool next to her. 'Main meals on pages two and three. Wines, cocktails and gins on the pages five and six. Booze is the biggest mark up for us, i.e. we make the most money on it.' Siena narrowed her eyes. Did he think she was completely stupid? 'So any extra drinks, bottles of wine you can offer the customer is a win win for everyone. We make a profit. The pub stays in business. You get to keep your job.'

'Really?' Siena opened her eyes in exaggerated wonderment. 'And here's me thinking you did it out of the goodness of your little heart.' She paused and gave him a direct look. 'Will, I might be a bit, actually a lot green when it comes to some things but we did a lot of entertaining at home. My step-dad is a multimillionaire. He's not a cuddly puppy, he's a shark. I've seen him in action plenty of times. Don't get me wrong, he can also be very charming and he's always treated me like his own daughter.' She smiled, actually sometimes he was a real softy, but she was probably the only person that had ever seen that side of him.

'Sorry.' Will held up his hands in surrender. 'I didn't mean to patronise.'

She laughed. 'You weren't. I know you and Jason think I'm hatched from some exotic other-worldly egg. I have led a privileged life but I'm not an alien. I do have some understanding of life on earth.'

'You don't look like any alien I've ever seen,' drawled Will. 'Tell you what, I'll assume you know what I'm on about at all times, unless you tell me otherwise. Anything you don't understand, you ask. Agreed?'

She held out her hand and said, 'Agreed,' as he shook it.

'I don't want another cheese and biscuits fiasco.'

At her questioning glance, he rolled his eyes. 'I had a very young waitress start a few years ago. Someone ordered cheese and biscuits and we were very busy. The kitchen gave her the plate of cheese and told her to add some biscuits.' Will drew in a long breath. 'Dumb ninny only opened a box of biscuits we keep for the kids' pudding menu,' he shook his head as though even now he still couldn't believe it, 'and next to our beautifully sourced fine selection of English cheeses, she put two bourbon biscuits, a jammy dodger and three custard creams.' Will roared with laughed. 'The customer was so gobsmacked he didn't say a word to her. Classic. Absolute classic.' He stopped. 'You've probably no idea what I'm on about.'

'No, I do. I remember them.' And she did. Custard creams on a plate in the kitchen. With Laurie. And her Dad. The foggy image of the man from the picture on the mantelpiece suddenly materialised as a proper person in her head.

'You OK?' Will interrupted her thoughts.

'Yes, fine.'

'So the menu. Have a look at the wines, and the other drinks. I'm going to give you my food order, so what would you recommend to drink?'

'Oh God.' Siena groaned. 'Not role-play again. I did that on the double glazing training. Marvellous in theory, bloody crap in practice.'

'You like food?'

She nodded.

'You like drink?'

Again she nodded.

'You're selling something real that people have come to buy. No sweat. Right, so I'm going to have the salt beef with gherkins and miniature pickled onions, followed by pulled pork with barbecue seasoning and beans. What would you recommend?'

She burst out laughing. 'That's mean. Pickled onions?'

He gave her a reproving stare. 'I'm the customer here.'

She scanned the drinks menu. 'Definitely not wine.' She pulled a face at the thought of the clash of the two acidic flavours. 'Ugh.' She scrunched her face in thought, a slow smile blossoming. 'Do you know what sir, can I suggest a Gibson? A gin cocktail, six parts gin with one part vermouth poured over crushed ice with a cocktail onion. We have an excellent selection of gins on the menu. Personally I would go for the Burleigh, although the Tanqueray or Beefeater would be perfectly acceptable. The Burleigh has the right balance of flavours,' she held up her hand to her face and said a stage whisper, 'and it's the most expensive gin on the menu. OK boss?' She raised her voice again, 'I think that would complement the flavours of the beef and the pickles.'

Will raised his hand and she high-fived him. 'Whoa, I am impressed. What about the pulled pork?'

'I might wait until I saw what the rest of the table were having but for that,' she looked back at the menu. 'Strong flavour again. Mr Imaginary Customer has quite a palate, doesn't he?'

'Very discerning,' said Will, nodding trying to look serious but the tell-tale naughty dimple in his cheek told her that he was enjoying himself enormously. He and Jason seemed so different; she wondered how they knew each other.

'With pork, I would have thought a white wine but pulled pork, especially barbecued, needs something a bit more robust. A mid-weight fruity red, a Shiraz or a Zinfandel. That one,' she pointed to the list.

'Excellent choice. I like your thinking. We might make a waitress of you yet. Even if it's only for a couple of weeks.' He nudged her arm playfully.

'You haven't seen me with the customers yet.'

'I don't need to. They're always right. Now, other things. You'll need comfortable shoes. Much as I like those sexy mothers, you will die in the first shift.' Siena extended her foot to admire her high-heeled ankle boots.

'Thank you very much, I'm rather fond of them.'

'I'm not surprised. They are serious fuck-me shoes, honey.'

'Interview going well then.' Jason's dry voice interrupted.

'Yup, I think we're all concluded. Siena's going to do a trial and we'll take it from there.'

'Thanks so much Will. I'm really grateful you're giving me a chance.'

'Don't be too grateful. If you're shit I'll fire the socks off you. I need a waitress, you're available and this side of acceptable on the eye, so you won't frighten the customers away.'

She poked her tongue out at him with a grin. Reading between the lines, Will didn't have any trouble recruiting staff. For all his denial, he was doing her or rather Jason a favour and she was going to pay them both back in spades. It would be fun working here, for all Will's flirting and twinkling, she could tell he wouldn't stand for any nonsense. She was going to be the best waitress he'd ever hired. She couldn't afford to fail at this or let Jason down.

They discussed the finer details, starting date, pay rate and shift patterns. She could do this. She'd eaten in enough fine restaurants and been on the receiving end of some top end customer service, if there was one thing she did know, it was how to treat a customer. In fact the more she thought about it she thought this might suit her perfectly for the next few weeks.

'You and Will seemed to get on,' said Jason as they pulled away from the pub.

'Yes, he's lovely.'

'A word of warning,' Jason turned her way, 'he's a dreadful flirt and has no staying power when it comes to women. That's partly why he needs a new waitress, the last one thought that because she was sleeping with him, she could take liberties.'

With a laugh she shook her head. 'I don't fancy Will in the least. He's far too obvious. Give me some credit.'

Jason looked surprised. 'Really?'

'He's got player written all over him. I might not be very experienced and have rubbish taste in men, but I've seen enough of them in action to know.'

'As long as you realise that.' He lapsed into silence. As the Land Rover picked up speed, the roar of the engine precluded conversation. Siena did wonder if that was why he drove it. It was still as messy as the day he'd picked her up.

'Do you ever clean this car?' she raised her voice.

'Every now and then. When it gets really bad.'

'But you're so tidy in the house.'

'I don't have to live in this, it's a work horse. Besides I'm always transporting stuff. It gets trashed every time I do have a clean out.'

She shifted her feet trying to find a clear space. Shoes. And her phone!

'I don't suppose you know where I can get my phone fixed?'

'Sure, we can sort it today.'

'And I need to get some shoes for the job and some clothes. Affordable ones. I don't suppose you know where I could go?'

Jason glanced at her, amusement in his eyes. 'That's not my department at all. But I know someone who can help.'

Chapter 9

'This is really nice of you,' said Siena as they walked from Lisa's battered little Mini towards the shopping centre.

'Don't be silly. Who doesn't like shopping? Besides I need some stuff too.'

'I thought you might mind, since Claire's a friend of yours.'

'Oh I heard. She caught you and Jason shopping for a phone the other night.'

'There was nothing to catch,' said Siena indignantly.

'We all know that. Don't worry. I don't know why she thinks she has a chance with him. He's always made it perfectly clear he is wedded to the brewery. That comes first.'

Siena was relieved. The encounter with Claire had been unpleasant, especially as the only reason Jason had had his arm around her was to help her walk on her sore feet.

Thankfully it hadn't affected things with Lisa. Since the other girl had picked her up that morning, they'd hadn't stopped talking. When Jason had texted her and explained Siena needed to go shopping, Lisa had immediately volunteered to pick her up.

Christmas had well and truly arrived in the shopping centre.

The walkways were bedecked in huge golden wreaths lit up with thousands of fairy lights and there was an indefinable buzz in the air. Siena felt a frisson of excitement. The department stores sparkled with glitter and colour and all the concessions were dressed up in their finery to celebrate the season.

'I love Christmas shopping,' said Lisa with a quick twirl, gracefully managing not to bump into any of the shoppers bustling past. Both their hands were filled with bags and balanced like panniers.

Siena felt a little flutter of regret.

'Don't you?' asked Lisa when she didn't respond.

'Maman tends to do it for everyone.' Siena let out a half laugh. 'Even her own present.' Every year without any apparent effort, Siena bought her mother a bottle of Miss Dior perfume.

'All the presents are delivered, gift-wrapped. Maman has accounts at shops in Paris, so she places an order and has everything delivered.'

'Wow that sounds … organised.'

'She's got it down to a fine art. A big bottle of Guerlain perfume for Agnes, the housekeeper. Smaller bottles of Nina Ricci for the two maids. Aged brandy for Jackson, the butler. A hamper for the chef. Table gifts for all the ladies,' Siena paused not wanting to sound ungrateful, 'and I usually get something from Tiffany.'

'Lucky you. We do Secret Santa, that's my favourite bit. My aunt pulls names out of a hat, or at least she says she does, and we have to buy our name a gift for under a fiver. It's great fun as we all try to outdo each other in who can get the silliest, cleverest or most tasteless thing.'

'Sounds fun,' said Siena doubtfully; it was difficult to imagine that idea working among the multitude of guests that descended on the Chateau each year, business colleagues of Harry's, Maman's coterie of lunching ladies from the length and breadth of Europe and a few distant aged cousins.

'It is. Everyone comes up with great ideas. I've got my cousin this year. I need some inspiration. We'll pop in here.'

Lisa dragged her into John Lewis.

They wandered through the shelves, teeming with brightly coloured china, decorations, gift ideas punctuating their journey through the shop with, 'Isn't this gorgeous?' 'What about this?' 'I love that.' 'Isn't this cute?'

Siena enjoyed herself even though she really didn't have anyone to buy for except maybe Agnes, who didn't like perfume. If Siena was going to buy something for Agnes, it would be a jigsaw puzzle of London. The housekeeper loved her puzzles.

'So where do you want to go now?' asked Lisa after they reached sensory overload.

She gave Lisa a rueful smile. 'I need to go the cheapest place to buy a skirt, black tights and shoes, but really cheap.' The hundred and seventy pounds in her bank account had to cover everything from now until she went home and she was determined to give Jason some money towards bills.

Lisa glanced pointedly at her Prada handbag and her Miu Miu boots. 'You do?'

'I do.' She laughed at Lisa's horrified face. 'It's a long story. My mother cancelled all my credit cards.'

'Cancelled?' Lisa's finely plucked and pencilled eyebrows drew together in a frown, which barely wrinkled the perfect skin of her brow. 'Can she do that? And why would she? Have you run up a really big bill?'

'Yes she can and she has. She's not very pleased with me.'

'But, I don't understand. Aren't they your cards?'

Siena flushed, feeling like a fish floundering on the beach, uncertain. 'The accounts go to Maman.'

'What and she pays them? Each month?'

Siena shrugged. 'The accountant takes care of all that sort of thing.'

'You have a credit card that … what? Gets paid for you? You're kidding me. Seriously? You lucky cow.' Lisa grinned. 'Does your mum want to adopt me?' Then she looked at Siena's face. 'So what did you do to make her cancel them? Something really bad? My mum used to ground me. And make me do all the ironing and washing for a week.'

106

'Ugh. That would be bad.' Siena pulled a face.

Lisa laughed and nudged her. 'You've never touched the washing in your life, have you?'

Siena shook her head.

'Shit, are you properly rich or something?' Lisa's round-eyed curiosity was innocent of malice or jealousy.

'Or something, at the moment. I think I'm what you call broke currently but it's only temporary.'

'Yeah, your mum is bound to forgive you. Eventually.' Lisa gave her a wicked wink.

'Mmm,' she replied. She didn't have quite the same faith in her mother as Lisa. 'So until I get paid my allowance,' she laughed, 'even then, I need to be careful with money.'

'Don't you worry. I'm an expert on cheap and cheerful.' Lisa linked her arm through Siena's. 'What do we need? Black skirt? White shirt?'

'Yes,' she sighed, 'and tights and shoes. I probably don't have enough money.'

'Don't you worry, Auntie Lisa will sort you out. How much have you got?'

'A hundred and seventy pounds.'

Lisa's eyes widened. Her heart sank.

'Isn't that going to enough?'

'Enough! Babe, you haven't been to Primarni, have you?' With a kind smile Lisa added, 'Thought not. Come on.'

Thank God for Lisa. Without her, Siena wouldn't have had a clue where to start. She didn't recognise any of the brand names or clothing stores.

'How about this one? It's only nine ninety-nine,' said Lisa holding up a black mini skirt. They were in a store called New Look. Siena couldn't believe the prices. 'What size are you? OMG you're going to be an eight or something ridiculous. Look at you, you're so skinny. You could be a model.'

'You're kidding.' Siena laughed at Lisa's enthusiastic admiration. 'Have you been to the Paris shows? They are all size zero. I'm at least a size eight. None of the fashion houses even know what an eight is, let alone make samples that size.'

'Siena,' Lisa threw a hand on her hip and posed. 'Do I look like I've ever been to Paris in my life, let alone a blinking fashion show? Do you really see people like Gwyneth Paltrow and Victoria Beckham in the front row?'

'Yeah, they're usually there.' Siena shrugged. 'I saw Kim Kardashian and Kanye at the shows in March.'

'Seriously?' Lisa looked impressed. 'I don't get it though.' She scrunched up her pretty face. 'I've seen some pictures on Pinterest. Those catwalk collections. Seriously? Who the hell would be seen dead in some of that stuff? And paying gazillions. Most of it looks completely ridiculous.'

Siena burst out laughing. 'And you only see half of it. Some of it is crazy but that's the whole thing. I want to train to be a fashion designer.'

'Seriously? That's so cool.' Lisa looked wide-eyed. 'Katie – remember her at the wine bar? – her mum's sister works at the fashion school in London teaching students.'

Siena stopped dead and laid a hand on Lisa's arm to stop her. 'Do you know which one?'

'I think it's the London School of Fashion.'

'That's the one I really want to go to. I've been trying to speak someone there for the last week.'

'You should speak to Katie. We always have Prosecco and film night when Tom's playing away; you'll have to come. In fact I'll call her later. Although,' she pulled a face, 'I think a lot of it is bollocks if you ask me. I saw one picture, it looked like the model was wearing a lampshade with a huge great eyeball on her head. How's that fashion?'

'That's the concept stuff, rather than ready-to-wear.'

'Pardon? Can you say that in English?' Lisa had already skittered off, and was rifling through a rail of clothes a few aisles along. 'Isn't everything ready to wear?'

'They're showing off their ideas and the styles.' She followed Lisa. 'Illustrating a type of neckline, the dress shape, the hemline, the fabrics, the colours, an idea. It's more of a shop window than real clothes you can buy.'

'Still all looks a bit pants to me.'

Siena pulled a shirt off the rack next to her. 'Look.' She pointed to the military style pockets on the front. 'These pockets. Paris catwalk, the Josetti show, eight weeks ago. The whole show was off the scale. Pockets on everything and nothing. But the pockets themselves have taken off.'

'Oooh I really like that. I'm going to try it on.'

'Are you sure?' Siena didn't know how to tell her that both the colour and style were all wrong for her.

'What's wrong with it?'

'It will look awful.'

Lisa giggled. 'Tell me straight, why don't you?'

Siena stood in front of her and assessed her.

'You've got quite a petite frame.' She picked up the shirt and held it up against her. 'Look.' She pulled the fabric along the shoulder line. 'It's far too wide here, it will make your arms look short as it will be too long in the sleeve. And see here?' She pointed to the hem of the shirt. 'See where it finishes, right at the top of your legs? Your widest part, so it emphasises that.' Siena pursed her mouth and shook her head before proclaiming with great solemnity, 'You will look,' she paused, 'like a pudding.'

Lisa burst out laughing. 'A pudding? Charming.'

Siena grinned. 'You don't want to look like that, do you?'

'No I ruddy well do not.'

Siena darted to a rail nearby and pulled out a hanger with more fitted style top. 'This looks like Moschino, or a very near copy. You team that up with a pair of skinny jeans or those black harem pants over there, it will show off your waist and look fabulous.'

Lisa looked uncertain. 'Not really me. I don't like things with waists.'

'You should. You have a fabulous waist. Wearing those long loose tops makes you look shapeless. A bit squat and square, when you're not. I'd kill for a real waist. Look – ribs to hips, dead straight. I look like a boy.'

'Squat and square, thanks.' Lisa giggled. 'And you do not look like a boy. What, a boy with boobs? You've got a great figure.'

'So have you, you just aren't showing it off to its best advantage. Let me show you.'

Siena took her time, gathering a selection of clothes so that she could demonstrate exactly what she meant, passing them over to Lisa, until the pile in the other girl's arms was so big she could barely see where she was going.

'Siena,' she croaked in a muffled voice from behind the stack of outfits. 'Do you think this is enough? They won't let us take it all in.'

With a bit of smart talking, Siena persuaded the sales girl to bring in a rail and separated the clothes into batches of ten items which could be tried on one after the other.

'Right, try the pocket shirt on with these black jeans and come out and show me.'

'I thought you said—' Lisa clutched the shirt, which she clearly had formed an attachment to.

'I want to show you how bad it will look.'

When Lisa came out, Siena stood next to her in front of the mirror. 'See,' she pointed to the line where the shirt stopped, 'thunder thighs.'

Lisa gasped.

'They're not at all, but that length accentuates them. And now look.' She lifted the hem of the shirt a couple of inches and looked at Lisa in the reflection.

'You're forgiven the mean comment.' Lisa studied herself in the mirror. 'Wow, yes. That's amazing. I had no idea. What a difference. But you still didn't have to say I had thunder thighs.'

Siena gave her a ruthless grin. 'Yes I did. I said you had a waist, you can't have everything. Tough love. Now try this top.' Siena bundled Lisa back into a cubicle with the white Moschino copy. 'Right. White top. Black jeans. I want to see you in them now.'

'I had no idea you were going to be this bossy. It's like fashion boot camp.'

'You ain't see nothin' yet. And don't moan so much. You've got your own personal Paris trained fashion guru and stylist.'

'OMG. That looks fab. I never would have tried this on, and not with the jeans.' Lisa twisted and turned in the mirror to catch every angle. She gave Siena the thumbs up. 'I love it ... what next?'

For the next half hour, she had Lisa in and out of a variety of outfits, and kept running back out into the shop to get additional garments. They started to attract quite an audience and then other girls in the changing room started asking for advice and the more delighted they seemed with Siena's feedback, the bolder she became.

A very tall, skinny girl asked Siena's view on a mini skirt.

'God no, you really need a skirt which stops at the knee. You have lovely calves. That shorter length emphasises your spaghetti legs and your knees sort of bulge in the middle. Go find a longer skirt.'

The ruder she was, the more they asked her opinion.

'That top is too low-cut. You look like a hooker.'

'Too tight, you can see three bulges in your back. And your bra doesn't fit properly.'

'VPL, get the next size up and get some better knickers.'

No matter how brutal she was they all seemed to love it. At one point the manager of the store came into the changing room to see what the gathering crowd was up to.

'Have you got a card or anything? I'd really like to speak to my boss about perhaps you coming in to do makeovers and be an in-store stylist.'

'No, I—'

'She's having them printed, aren't you?' interrupted Lisa with a naughty wink behind the manager's back.

'This was so much fun,' said Lisa as they came out of the shop. 'Now all we need are some shoes.'

'Could we have got them in there?' asked Siena looking back.

'Yeah, but if you're going to be waitressing, you're going to need something comfortable, and I mean cushioning soles. You're going to be on your feet all day and if Will has his way, on your back too. Just watch out for him.'

'Will's fine.'

'Hmmph,' grunted Lisa tossing her hair disdainfully.

'He can't be all bad, he's giving me a job ... and I don't even have any experience.'

'He's a complete tart. I can't stand him. Make sure he doesn't try to get into your knickers. Whatever you do, don't sleep with him, he's a—' She made a rude gesture with her hand.

Siena laughed. 'He's harmless, a player. You're don't need to warn me, it's written all over him.'

Lisa let out a small sigh. 'Glad you're so smart.'

Siena realised she'd strayed into difficult territory. 'You and him?'

'Once.' Lisa shuddered. 'Big mistake. Huge. Have you ever seen Pretty Woman?' the lightning change of subject told Siena the subject was definitely closed.

Chapter 10

'Have you made coffee again?' Jason stomped into the kitchen clutching a bloody tissue to his chin.

''Fraid so,' she said, amused that making coffee now appeared to be a crime. 'Want some?'

He narrowed his eyes and nodded.

'It's not that hard to make.'

'Instant's easier.'

'And doesn't taste as good.'

Jason shrugged. 'Too much hassle.'

'Hassle. Come on. You put the coffee in the cafetière and pour water over it. Leave to stand, plunge and hey presto.' She picked it up and poured him a mug. 'How hard is that?' She wafted the mug under his nose. 'And smell the difference.'

'You're like a drug dealer enticing me over to the caffeine side.' He took the coffee, sniffing deeply.

'What happened to your face?'

'Cut myself shaving. My razor's not very sharp.'

'No, I noticed that too.'

'What?'

'When I shaved my legs.'

'Pardon?' Jason's eyes were glacial.

'Yes, I had to go over them a couple of times.'

'You used my razor to shave your legs?' His words dropped one by one like pebbles down a well.

'Yes.' She pulled the toaster towards her and removed the toast. English bread wasn't the same as at home.

'You used my razor to shave your legs.'

His eyes had narrowed even further. 'Is that a problem?'

'Funny you should mention that. I'd say it's a problem for my chin which is bleeding copiously. Apparently the result of shaving with a blunt razor. Blunt because someone, who doesn't own said razor, has been using it to shave acres of leg instead of a small area of chin.'

Obviously the boyfriend, Yves whatever, was a lot more tolerant of this sort of thing. The man had to be a saint to cope with someone like Siena. And now the poor bugger had to wait for her to make up her mind about if she wanted to marry him.

'Oh.' Then she brightened. 'Don't worry. I've got some really nice L'Occitane shaving balm, I'll go and get it for you.' He grabbed her arm as she darted past.

'Don't bother. It's almost stopped bleeding.'

Siena chewed at her lip. 'I'm sorry.'

'So am I. Buy your own razors in future.'

'I …' She didn't want to admit she couldn't afford to buy her own.

'There's a pack of disposables under the sink. Help yourself.'

'Thank you. To be honest, I usually use an epilator if I can't get to the salon for a wax.'

'A what?'

'An epilator. It pulls the hairs out.'

'Pulls them out.' Jason shuddered. 'That brings tears to the eyes.'

'It's not so bad when you get used to it.'

'And you use that on your legs.'

'And everywhere else.'

Jason paled, his eyes travelled to her crotch and then he blushed.

114

'Right Siena, you'll be looking after tables ten through twenty-one,' said Marcus, leading her to the section of the restaurant in the far right corner.

Will had handed her straight to the tall, well-built Scot as soon as she arrived. Unlike the day he'd interviewed her, today he'd been all business.

'It's all very straightforward, hen. Al, the chef, wee fella in the kitchen will talk us through the menu for today at around eleven thirty. Officially, we have a seasonal menu which changes every four to six weeks but if Chef can't get the right produce he'll tweak the menu for that day. He and Will are dead keen on using seasonal produce, so they can change it at the very last minute … can you type fast?'

'Not particularly.'

'You'll learn, especially if Will is standing over your shoulder. There are also new specials every day and Chef likes you to memorise these and we're talking precise details.' Putting on a posh accent Marcus launched into a singsong falsetto. 'Today we have,' he mimed uncovering a platter, 'confit of beetroot on a hazelnut blini with organic artichoke cream.' He pretended to pluck an item from the imaginary plate. 'The beetroot was grown locally at optimum temperature, avoiding ground frost with outdoor heaters programmed to exactly 16.4 degrees which has been scientifically proven to be the prime temperature for beetroot. The hazelnuts were hand ground by wood sylphs from Sherwood Forest and the artichokes kept in manure from my own bottom.'

With a laugh, Siena looked at the menu. Marcus' warm humour was irresistible and all her good intentions to be ultra-professional went out the window. 'I think you've got that wrong. Beetroot should always, always be grown at 16.3 degrees, no more, no less and why do you think those sylphs from Sherwood can be trusted when everyone knows that the fairies at the bottom of the garden produce a far superior grind?'

Marcus started to laugh, 'Superior grind. That's classic,' his mirth which rapidly turned into a hysterical wheeze.

'Who's grinding?' A camp voice piped up and the chef, complete in his whites and rather lurid trousers covered in a pattern featuring manically smiling purple cats, started twerking (at least Siena thought that was the official terminology having seen mini pop stars doing it on YouTube), grinding his hips up against Marcus. 'You're not taking my magnificent creations in vain are you, darling?'

Eventually Marcus brought his breathing into line. 'Would I, sweet cheeks? Al, meet our new waitress, Siena.'

'Hi doll. Welcome. Don't pay any attention to him. If you want to know anything about food, come to me. This man was brought up on haggis and swede, he wouldn't know fine food if it came up and bit him on his hairy great arse.'

Marcus playfully cuffed him round the neck. 'And this one thinks he's God's gift to the kitchen, but he wouldn't be anywhere without the service.' He nodded his head at Siena. 'That's you and me, this lunchtime. We've got one more, Hayley, coming in between twelve and two but she looks after the bar with Will. We're light on bookings as it's mid-week, so as long as there's not a sudden influx, it's a good day to show you the ropes.'

'I'd best get on and start knocking up me beetroot confit,' said Al, blowing kisses as he retreated back to his kitchen.

They spent the next hour setting up the tables and Siena rather enjoyed the methodical, mechanical task, it didn't require any thought at all and Marcus kept up a stream of cheerful observations about this and that. Before she knew it, it was eleven o'clock which was the official coffee break and a briefing with Al in the kitchen.

'Hello, have I missed elevenses?'

Siena turned to see Ben entering the kitchen from an outside door on the right, carrying a handful of dirty mugs, dangling by the handles from his big hands.

'By heck it's cold out there. Enough to freeze a gnat's gonads off.' He stopped short when he saw her.

'Hello Ben,' she said feeling boosted by seeing a familiar face.

He beamed. 'Hey up chuck. How are you?' He acknowledged everyone else in the kitchen with a cheerful wave. 'There's snow in the air, mark my words.' He lifted one foot and waggled it from side to side. 'I can tell. My ankle always plays up when it's going to snow.'

'I can tell too,' sniffed Al. He held up his phone. 'It's called a weather app.'

Ben wiggled his foot again and screwed up his face. 'Definitely snow in the air.' He looked over at Siena again. 'Jason said you were starting here. How's your first day going?'

Siena looked at the other three men. 'Interesting,' she said with a rueful smile.

'She's fitting in a treat,' said Marcus, putting a beefy arm around her.

'Got any biscuits?' asked Ben.

Al nodded towards the pantry at the back of the kitchen. 'Chocolate hobnobs, help yourself. And put the mugs in the dishwasher.'

'Any coffee?' asked Ben over his shoulder as he crossed to the cupboard.

'You've got your own kettle over there,' answered Will. 'Tell Jason to invest in his own bloody coffee. I'm not running a canteen here, it's a restaurant for paying customers.'

'I heard that.'

Siena whipped her head round at Jason's dry voice. Her nerve endings all stood to attention and it appeared she no longer knew what to do with her feet or her hands. She shifted to one foot and then the next, hoping that she could blend into the background. He'd been silent on the journey to work earlier and she'd been lost in her own nervous thoughts.

'Workers need proper fuel.'

'Workers can have fuel as long as it doesn't eat into my profits. And your sudden addiction to real coffee is going to impact on my bottom line.'

'Man, what the hell happened to your face?' asked Will pushing himself upright from the bench. Siena had noticed his habitual position was to lean against things. 'They take the learner plates off your razor?'

Jason shrugged. Siena closed her eyes wishing she could fade into the background. He didn't look her way at all. 'Still half asleep. Wasn't concentrating.'

'Bummer,' said Ben. 'I hate shaving.'

The other men began to rib him about his age and while they were all talking and teasing each other, Siena stole a look at Jason's face. He looked up.

She mouthed, 'Thank you.'

He rolled his eyes in pretend exasperation and shook his head and as he strolled out of the kitchen back towards the direction of the brewery, he shot her a thousand watt beam and a wink. The transformation on his face from his usual sombre expression hit her hard in the chest.

'What do you think Marcus?'

The shift was over and she felt rather grateful that Marcus had sunk onto one of the bar stools. She followed his lead and slumped for a minute.

Will arrived with a tray of coffee and plonked himself down between them, looking rather serious. Siena felt her palms go clammy.

Marcus sniggered and looked Siena up and down. 'The guy on table nineteen definitely had the hots for you.'

'What?' That had Siena perplexed. 'He kept asking for more stuff all the time. Impossible to please.'

'No, no, no.' Marcus shook his shaggy head and waggled his eyebrows suggestively. 'He wanted your attention.' At the back of the bar the phone began to ring. As he went to answer it he added over his shoulder, 'But as you were playing cool, he had to

118

keep trying.'

'For a first day, not bad.' Will nodded slowly with half an eye on Marcus. 'Not bad at all.'

Despite his serious face, she grinned. She felt like she'd won a medal.

A brief frown crossed Will's face and her happiness dimmed until she realised he was listening in on the phone conversation.

'Yes. Yes. I'll be sure to tell him. Right. No I'll make sure he gets that message. Yes. I'll remember. Word for word.' Marcus had begun smirking at Will and making throat slitting gestures with his free hand. 'No, I won't forget that. Or that.'

Will had folded his arms and was once again leaning against the bar, an amused twist to his mouth.

Marcus put down the phone. 'The tree's arriving tomorrow. But you're on your own with the decorations. Cordelia's not coming to do them. She's otherwise engaged.'

Will raised an eyebrow. 'What did she really say?'

'Verbatim or précised?'

'Give it your best shot.'

'You're a two timing rat-fink bastard with, excuse me Siena, a dick the size of a chipolata and she'd rather shove a ten foot Christmas tree up your arse than decorate it for you. That's about the gist of it.'

'Aw, fuck.'

'Perhaps she'll calm down,' said Siena hopefully. 'Maybe you could talk to her.'

Will laughed. 'Siena babe, you are priceless. I couldn't give a toss about Cordelia. I'm pissed off that she's talked me into spending a hundred fifty quid on said ten foot tree which I now have no one to decorate.' He knocked back the rest of his coffee. Marcus sniggered. 'At least I've saved myself three hundred pounds on paying for decorations and her to decorate the bloody thing.' At that point Marcus burst out into uproarious laughter with Will following suit.

119

Siena stared at the two of them. They were like a pair of children.

After a minute of enduring their full blown hilarity, she tapped Will on the arm. 'Three hundred pounds? You were going to pay her three hundred pounds?'

He nodded and slung an arm around Marcus, the two of them still laughing like loons. She grabbed his sleeve and shook it. 'I'll do it for half.'

Will sobered for a minute, held up a hand and tried to catch his breath.

Finally he got hold of himself. 'It's a big tree.'

'Not a problem. We usually have a twenty foot one in the hall at home. I've been decorating it since I was fifteen.' Behind her back she crossed her fingers. So she'd been watching Sandrine decorate it for most of that time. But she'd watched carefully.

'The job's yours. As you heard the tree arrives tomorrow. Oh and a bit of ivy and,' he mimicked speech marks, 'foliage.'

Chapter 11

'Gosh it's cold out there. But I thought I'd better walk.' Lisa handed over a bottle of wine.

'Thanks, you didn't have to do that, especially when you're coming round to help me. Again,' said Siena, ushering her in quickly to keep the freezing air out. 'In the end there was too much stuff to carry round to yours.'

'It's fine hon, you are doing me a favour,' said Lisa emphasising the words with feeling. 'Nanna turned up so it would have been wall-to-wall soaps for the evening.'

A sudden vision of a mosaic of lavender, verbena and rose L'Occitane soaps decorating a wall filled Siena's head. Luckily Lisa must have seen her blank expression.

'Soap operas,' she explained, pulling a face as she unwound a huge woolly scarf from her neck and tugged at her gloves. '*EastEnders, Coronation Street, Emmerdale, Hollyoaks.* My gran loves them. Has to watch all of them every night. Don't you have them in France?'

'We do actually. *Paris 16ème* and *Plus Belle La Vie*.' Agnes was addicted to the former and Siena had often sneaked down to the kitchen to watch it with her during the school holidays.

'They sound a lot more glamorous than *EastEnders* or *Corrie*. So what's the crack?'

Siena led the way into the kitchen where she'd lined everything up in readiness.

'Jeepers creepers! What the …?' Lisa stared at the mound of pine cones, rolls of red ribbon and can of white emulsion paint on the newspaper lined table and then her eyes flitted to the pile of ivy and poster tubes piled on the kitchen chairs.

Her mouth opened and she squealed. 'Oooh! Christmas!' She shimmied out of her coat and tossed it on the only spare chair, reaching for one of a series of large plastic pots on the dresser. 'You got glitter. Red glitter.' She whirled towards Siena, the pot held up to the light. 'I love sparkle.' Her eyes lit up. 'So what are we doing?'

Siena laughed. 'Will's decorator let him down at the last minute. So I'm doing the Christmas decorations at the pub.'

Lisa's face dimmed fractionally.

'He's paying me,' said Siena. 'And I can pay you.'

'In that case, I'll let you off. I'm happy to help *you*. And forget about the money.' She bounced on the balls of her toes, opening her arms out wide. 'I love Christmas. You can pay me in Prosecco when you come to mine. Providing Nanna's gone by then.'

Siena sucked a quick breath in.

'Moved out, not died.' Lisa giggled. 'Your face. She's staying with me at the moment. So,' Lisa picked up a pine cone, 'what's the plan, Stan?'

'We're going Scandinavian. Lots of red and white. Simple but stylish.'

She explained. They'd create the tree decorations by dipping the cones cone into watered down white paint, drizzle each with a pinch of red glitter, add a loop of gold wire and tie a red bow around the loop at the top. For the wall decorations, she had something else in mind.

'Get you. Sounds fancy. Ours isn't.' Lisa rolled up her sleeves. 'Gosh this is organised.'

Siena had pre-cut the wire and the ribbon and lined everything up.

'Nanna insists we put every ornament on the tree that she's ever owned since the world began. We always do it together. It's like a family tradition since I was tiny and my mum was still around.' Lisa smiled wistfully. 'Mum used to buy a new decoration every year.'

Siena sat down opposite her and the two of them began dipping their cones in unison.

'Is this right?' Lisa asked holding up a completed decoration.

Siena nodded, wrestling with tying a tiny perfect red bow. Lisa's was a bit more haphazard but if it was near the top, no one would notice.

'We always get our tree on the Saturday before Christmas,' said Lisa, starting on the next one. 'We get it up and put the lights on during the day and then, after tea, the box of decorations comes down from the loft. That's my favourite bit, unwrapping each one, from the tissue paper. Rudolf with the missing antler. Glass angels. A star I made in junior school. A pair of wooden ice skates Mum got in the church craft fair and of course the fairy for the top. She's seen better days but we can't throw her out.'

She beamed at Siena, her eyes dancing with pleasure. 'Brings back memories of all the different Christmases. The year of the mouldy pudding, the one Mum forgot the crackers and our favourite, the Christmas of the farting dog, when my uncle brought his ancient spaniel with him. God the smell was awful.' Lisa burst into peals of laughter. 'Me and Nanna almost refused to go to my aunt's this year but she's promised the dog's on medication.'

Siena swallowed and concentrated on her decoration which was a bit difficult with her suddenly blurry vision.

It sounded very different from Christmas at the Chateau, where Sandrine would arrive each year in September with a series of mood boards depicting different themes for the household decorations and trees. Her mother would study them for several days before making a final decision. Then, on the first of December, Sandrine and her team would rock up with a van and transform the house in readiness for the first party. Nothing was ever done by the family. Unlike Lisa, she had no warming memories of decorating the tree together. It had never bothered her before, but now she felt like she had missed out on something … and it wasn't something money could buy.

Two hours and several glasses of wine later, the pine cones were complete and they still hadn't stop talking. Siena showed Lisa how they were going to make wreaths for the walls of the pub.

'If we cut each of these tubes into six centimetre sections, we paint the edges white, glue the sections together to create a circle and then, in a couple of random sections we pop different sized gold baubles.' She held up her prototype. 'What do you think?'

'Here's one I made earlier,' giggled Lisa and then rolled her eyes. 'You never saw *Blue Peter* did you? I'm impressed. How did you get them all to stick together?'

'With my secret weapon.' Siena produced a glue gun, holding it up with a *James Bond* pose. 'Don't mess with a girl with gun,' she said with a grin.

'Cool.'

'Unfortunately, I haven't found anything to make cutting the tubes up very easy. At the moment I'm using a bread knife and this one took forever so we could be here some time.'

'No worries, I haven't got work tomorrow. Baggsie the glue gun first though.'

As Siena manfully sawed through the heavy tubing she heard the front door open and voices in the hall.

Jason walked into the kitchen followed by Claire.

'Oh my God, what the hell happened in here?' His horrified glance took in the mess. 'I thought you were going to Lisa's tonight?'

'It's Chriiiiistmas,' trilled Lisa happily. 'Hi Claire.'

'Lisa.' Claire nodded, her face stern. She didn't look very impressed.

'Don't worry, I promise I'll tidy it up,' said Siena with a cheeky grin at Jason's long suffering expression. 'Every last smidge of glitter.'

His mouth twisted but she caught a brief glimpse of amusement in his eyes. With a sigh he said, 'I'll believe it when I see it.' He turned to Claire. 'You remember Siena, my landlady's sister.'

'Yes. From Paris. I thought you were only here for the weekend.' Claire shot Jason a questioning look. 'I didn't realise you were still here.'

Siena smiled encouragingly. 'Yes, I'm afraid I was a bit naughty. I wasn't completely honest then but I'll be gone before Christmas.' She giggled, trying to show the other girl she wasn't a threat. 'Jason will be glad to see the back of me by then.' She picked up the bread knife and began sawing at the cardboard tube again.

'So what's this in aid of?' he asked.

'I'm the official Christmas interior decorator for the pub. Will's paying me to decorate the tree.'

'Paying you?'

'Proper decorators can charge a fortune.'

'So you've done this sort of thing before in France?'

'Not exactly. I've helped.' She winked at him. 'But Will doesn't need to know that. If he hates what I do, he doesn't have to pay me.' The breadknife in her hand slipped and nicked the wooden table. 'Oops. I keep doing that.'

'What the hell are you doing?' He leaned over and took her hand, carefully removing the knife from her already cramped fingers. It wasn't the best tool for the job. 'Apart from wrecking my best bread knife and potentially about to sever one of your main arteries?'

'This is your best bread knife? I'm sorry.' Siena couldn't resist teasing him. 'Where's the second best one?'

With a shake of his head, he said, 'Hang on a minute,' and disappeared out of the kitchen.

Claire stood rather awkwardly looking at the mess on the table, her lips pinched together.

'Would you like a glass of wine?' asked Siena suddenly. 'And can

I take your coat for you? Sorry it's such a mess in here. We've been making decorations for hours. We'll be done soon. The lounge is quite tidy.' Her face fell. 'Although I haven't cleaned out the fireplace. I'm going to be in trouble with Jason again. He likes it to be ready so he can light a new one.'

'It's fine,' said Claire, her voice level and cold. Siena caught the slight flare of her nostrils and felt guilty.

'So, have you been somewhere nice? Did Jason take you out for dinner?'

The other girl's eyes darkened and Siena felt she'd put her foot in it again but had no idea why.

'We went to the pub for a drink, with Ben and Tom and Katie.'

Out of the corner of her eye, Siena saw Lisa hide a smile.

'That's nice. Ben's a sweetie, isn't he?'

Any answer Claire might have made was interrupted by the return of Jason brandishing a hacksaw. 'I knew I'd got one somewhere. Sorry Claire, do you want a cup of tea?'

'Oh brilliant. Thanks.' Siena reached for the saw.

'I'd love one.' Claire began to unbutton her coat.

'Uh uh nuh.' Jason lifted the hacksaw high above his head. 'Don't even think about it. Give those tubes here. I'll cut them up for you. I've got visions of you sawing off the table leg.'

'I'm not totally incompetent,' pouted Siena with a laugh.

'Not totally, no,' agreed Jason, 'but your track record with other people's blades ain't so great.'

She bit her lip and looked at his chin. Without thinking she reached up and cupped his chin. 'It's looking better than it did this morning.'

As she smiled up into his eyes, a flash of something made her heart flip in her chest, a funny butterfly sensation that stalled her next breath.

'I'll make tea, shall I?' Lisa's over-bright words broke into the frozen tableau. Siena could have kicked herself at the angry and hurt expression in Claire's eyes. Jason's mouth flattened.

126

Her hand dropped away and she busied herself brushing glitter from her jeans. 'My boyfriend is always cutting himself shaving. I keep a special balm for him.'

'What's the name of it?' asked Lisa, her voice loud. 'I'm always cutting my legs shaving. It's a right pain. And don't razor nicks bleed? They make a right old mess. I end up with little bits of tissues stuck all over my legs.'

'I'll look it up for you.' Siena and Lisa exchanged looks.

'I don't want any tea thanks,' snapped Claire. 'It's time I went home.'

'I'll walk you round,' said Jason and tucked his hand under Claire's elbow, escorting her from the kitchen without looking back at Siena or Lisa.

Siena was about to tell him that his chin was covered in glitter but catching Claire's stern expression thought better of it.

Claire maintained a stony silence during the ten minute walk back to her house. With every footstep his heart sank. She was going to make a scene, he knew it. He hated that. What was he supposed to have done? She had absolutely no reason to be jealous of Siena. He should have stuck to his guns, kept his distance. Taking her out last Sunday had been foolish. Given her the wrong idea.

'There's not much point inviting you in, is there?' she sneered as she put her key in the lock. 'It's pretty obvious what's going on.'

He ran his hand through his hair. Should have put on a hat, his ears were red tipped and starting to hurt.

'Claire, there's nothing between me and Siena.' The injustice of it stung. Most of the time Siena drove him mad. Some of the time. And some of the time she was funny and kind. She made him coffee. And her relentlessly cheerful outlook often made him smile against his will.

'Who are you trying to convince? She seems to think there is. Pretty proprietary, if you ask me.' Claire put a high silly voice. 'Jason likes the fire cleaned out. Oh your poor chin.' She snorted.

'Siena's friendly. There's no side to her. She's my landlady's sister. It was her dad's house. I can hardly throw her out.' And now he'd got used to her being around, it wasn't that bad. At least she tried to stick to his rules.

'You think I'm pretty stupid, don't you? All looks pretty cosy to me. The two of you living together.'

'We're not living together,' he said impatiently.

Claire raised her eyebrows. 'She's biding her time. No wonder you never wanted me to come round.' Her voice broke.

Jason's bit his lip, feeling like seven kinds of shit. The only reason he hadn't wanted her to come round was because he didn't want to encourage her.

'I'm sorry. Night, Claire,' he said and turned away, wincing as she slammed the door. The first flakes of snow were starting to drift out of the dark sky. He lifted his face welcoming the cold bite of their touch on his face. It felt a fitting penance. He'd probably made Claire cry.

Chapter 12

'It's snowed!' Siena squealed, running over the kitchen window, skirting around Jason who was taking his first sip of coffee.

'Yup, it snowed.' He turned his back on the scene and cupped his hands around the coffee cup.

'Isn't it gorgeous? I love snow.' He glanced over his shoulder.

She leaned on the draining board, the blonde hair streaming down her back, staring out at the layer of snow. 'Do you know what I really love?'

'Nope.' He took another slug of coffee, watching her more closely. Her heel jumped up and down, the ball of her foot anchoring her to the floor. He'd noticed she did that a lot, especially when she was enthusiastic, as if without that anchor she might bounce up and down. She was never really still. It was as if a zest for life rippled through her and there was always some part of her body that had to give it release.

'When it's perfect like that, untouched except for the animals. Look you can see the bird footprints across the top of the wall. Something, a cat or maybe a fox, across the grass. It reminds me that while we're sleeping, there's a whole world going on that has nothing to do with us.'

Unable to help himself, he stood up and joined her at the window. A robin hopped onto the half hidden birdbath, its head cocked to one side as if to say, 'Listen to her, she's right.'

'And you cut all the tubes up for me.'

Jason shrugged. 'Said I would.' It had been something to do when he got back last night to stop his brain buzzing.

'I know but you didn't have to do them all last night. That's brilliant, I can take them to the pub with me and assemble them there before I start work.'

He gave a non-committal grunt.

'And you made coffee all by yourself.' She gave him another one of her brilliant sunny smiles and poured herself a mug. 'Cheers.' She lifted the mug in toast. 'Hmm, not half bad. Well done. Is it OK if I go in the bathroom?'

'Yeah, I've finished.'

'Great.' She headed for the door before turning back to him with a worried frown. 'How deep do you think it is?'

'A good foot I reckon.'

'Will we get to the pub OK?'

Jason laughed. 'You know you complain about my car?'

'It's not the car I complain about.'

'Land Rovers are built for extreme terrains. We'll be fine.'

'Right.' She frowned again. 'I don't have any snow boots.'

'It's really not that deep, only an inch or two. It'll be gone by the morning.'

'That's fucking amazing!' Will circled the tree, his ponytail bobbing as he shook his head. 'You did all this?'

'Brilliant, Siena babes,' added Marcus.

Siena blushed, a smile stretching from ear to ear as the men stood at the base of the tree, paying homage to her work. It had taken all morning and she had a severe crick in her neck but the resulting tree did look pretty special. Her toes tapped on the spot; she wanted to dance. The tree had turned out even better than she'd hoped. With lots of white lights and the white cones with their splashes of red and twinkles of glitter, the tall bushy fir tree evoked Norwegian snow and style.

Only Jason didn't say much. He'd been very quiet on their journey to work this morning.

She hoped he hadn't hurt his back carrying her out to the Land Rover. It had been the only solution to her lack of sensible footwear. Thankfully Will had a spare pair of wellington boots, ugly black things, she could borrow. She didn't think her system could take being swung up into Jason's arms all Rhett Butler style again. It hadn't meant anything, that sudden flutter in the pit of her stomach or the urge to bury her face in his neck. A purely physical response to a big strong man making her feel fragile and feminine, which when you were one metre seventy-eight, didn't happen that often.

'I'll finish the wall decorations tonight and bring them in tomorrow.'

'There's more?' Will put his arm around her. 'You're a star.'

'Now team, enough of the tree gazing, we've got a pub to run and it's gonna get seriously busy around here for the next couple of weeks.'

Siena collapsed onto the high stool at the bar. Thank goodness it was the end of the shift.

Marcus picked up one of her feet and put it on his knee, massaged the narrow arch with his meaty hands. 'You've survived the week and look who it is. The tip fairy.'

Will came through from the office and handed them each a brown envelope.

'There you go, this week's haul.' Siena's envelope had £25 scrawled on the front.

'What's this?' Panic set her heart fluttering. The hundred and fifty pounds for the tree had been a bonus, but twenty-five pounds for a whole week's work? Why had she thought it would be more? Had she got her sums hopelessly wrong? She could have sworn he said so much an hour.

'Well done. Those are your tips for the week.'

'What? On top of my pay?'

'Yes. Are you OK for money? I can pay you weekly to start with if you'd like.'

Had Jason been talking to him? She didn't want anyone's charity. Now she'd decided to go it alone. Sharing food costs with Jason would help as he'd insisted he shared the grocery bill now that she was cooking for him.

Watching him eat those horrible plastic wrapped, compartments of food had driven her to insist that it would be cheaper for both of them if she cooked. They'd fallen into a routine as she cooked risotto, ratatouille and pasta. Conscious of her meagre budget she'd stuck to simple vegetarian dishes. He would drive her home from work. She cooked. The first couple of times he'd been suspicious. On the third night he'd said, 'I didn't have you down as a cook. I thought that omelette was a fluke.'

The memory of the night felt like a turning point, as if he'd stopped thinking of her as completely useless.

'Thanks.' Siena had replied sipping at her water.

'Did you learn at finishing school or something?' he'd asked flippantly taking another pull of beer.

'No, they didn't do anything that domestic.'

'What?' Jason had almost spat his beer out. 'You're kidding right?'

'No, the staff cook, you supervise and choose the menus.'

'No, I meant … you didn't really go to finishing school. Do they even exist?'

Siena remembered sighing at his horrified tones. 'Yes I went to one. In Switzerland. Lots of my friends went. It was useful.' Fun too. One of the few times when she'd been away from home with people her own age.

'So where did you learn to cook?'

'Agnes, our cook and housekeeper. When I was younger, Maman and Harry would travel a lot and I'd stay home, so I spent a lot

132

of time in the kitchen.' The memory made her smile. 'She got fed up with me being underfoot all the time. So I started peeling and chopping vegetables and gradually she let me do more. Of course it was a huge secret. Maman would have been furious if she'd known.'

'Why?'

'She just would.'

Jason had raised his beer bottle and toasted the air. 'Here's to Agnes. I for one, am very grateful, this is delicious.'

'Earth to Siena. Come in.'

Siena shook her head and realised she was still in the pub. 'Sorry, I was miles away.'

'I said, 'Are you OK for money?"

'I'm fine. It hadn't occurred to me that I'd actually get tips too. This is great, thank you!'

'They're good tips. Marcus is thrilled, aren't you?'

Sitting next to her at the bar, Marcus nodded as he lifted his pint in toast.

'Why?' She didn't understand.

'We share tips among the staff of each shift. If you get good tips but your shift partner doesn't, you lose out.'

'Yeah,' interrupted Marcus putting down his half empty glass. 'If you have a good shift partner, it's win-win.' He glared at Will. 'If you have one the boss has been sleeping with and she thinks the world owes her, you get crap tips.'

Will's mouth firmed. 'Thanks Marcus, for broadcasting that enlightening titbit, I'm sure Siena was enthralled.'

'Oh, it's OK. Lisa already mentioned it.' The minute the words were out of her mouth she regretted it. Will looked like thunder.

'Moving on,' said Marcus with a rictus grin stretching his lips. 'Siena you get good tips. I get good tips. So we're equal. I like working with you.'

'Thank you.' From someone as experienced and at home as a waiter as him, that compliment resonated.

133

'We make a good partnership.'

Will's face softened. 'Yes. I have to admit, you've done brilliantly this week. Like I said at the beginning of the week, I had a few reservations—'

'You never said anything,' said Siena horrified.

He flashed her a wicked grin. 'The customers like you. You've loosened up with them. You can stay on for as long as you like. I know you only wanted until Christmas but if you decide to stay on, I could use the help in the New Year.'

Siena's heart raced. 'Seriously?'

'Yes Siena. You're good. It's not everyone's idea of a good job but,' he lifted his shoulders, 'you're actually pretty good at it.'

'Am I?' A warmth blossomed in her chest as pride radiated from her heart. It might not be everyone's idea of a major achievement but she wanted to burst. She'd got a job. By herself. Jason had arranged the first part but she'd done the rest.

'I'm not sure what my plans are after Christmas,' she said suddenly shy, 'but I'd like to stay for the next few weeks at least. I love working here. Some odd people,' she shot Marcus a teasing grin. 'But most of the time it's great.'

'Excellent. I can post next week's shift pattern. There's a wedding on next week, I'm going to need an extra pair of hands.'

'Well done,' said Jason when she went skipping into the brewery, running up the stairs to tell him. 'I'll be another five minutes.'

'Thank you and don't worry. I wait for you every day.' She turned her back on him, hugging her news to herself. It might not mean anything to him but she couldn't help smiling. She had a job. A proper job. Inside her heart sang. A job. Earning her own money, that no one could take away or tell her how to spend. It might not be enough to buy the designer handbags and shoes she was used to but it was all hers. Bursting with energy she shifted happily on the spot, still wanting to jump up and down, and turned back to face him.

As if he'd only just noticed her, he looked over the top of his laptop at her and sat back in his chair, closing the lid of the laptop, watching her fidget.

'Sorry I wasn't paying attention. What did you say?' He got up from his chair and stretched.

She sighed and smiled as he pulled his denim jacket off the back of the chair and began to shrug into it. The double denim look had definitely grown on her. 'I've got a place on the next manned mission to Mars, it's unlikely I'll be back.'

'Right ... what?' He walked towards her heading to the door and stopped beside her.

Good, he looked confused. She waited a minute, enjoying having his sole attention. 'I've got a job. Will's taken me on.' And then she did a little excited jump. 'I can't believe it. It's brilliant.' She paused, unable to stop the huge grin stretching her mouth. 'A proper job, not a horrid skanky one.' If hadn't have been for him, she might still be knocking on doors. She threw her arms around him. 'Thank you. Thank you.'

The spontaneous hug had come from nowhere and she still didn't know what instinct had prompted it. She wasn't a hugger. No one in the family hugged. She froze. What the hell was she doing? Throwing herself at him. What would he think? To her absolute relief, Jason returned the embrace as if it were totally normally.

'Well done you.' He smelt musky with the slightly sweet smell of hops clinging to his jumper. He gave her a reciprocal squeeze which surprised her and pulled her off balance so that she moved, closing the gap between the lower halves of their bodies. 'Will wouldn't have taken you on if you weren't any ... er.' He swallowed and she felt him shift slightly against her. 'I, er, only got you the, erm, interview, you did the rest.'

'No, you helped a lot. I have to do something nice for you.' As she said it their thighs brushed and a tingle of sexual awareness shot through her, at the same moment the double entendre registered

135

along with the slight bulge in his jeans. Jason's eyes narrowed and locked on hers. She swallowed, mortified, but couldn't look away. Desire pooled between her legs and her breath caught in her throat.

'Meat,' croaked Jason, managing to shift his gaze. The ceiling seemed to have sprouted grass or something because he appeared to find it fascinating.

They disentangled awkwardly and she hitched her bag onto her shoulders. Was this some English thing she was unaware of?

'Meat?' she echoed in a silly squeaky voice.

She saw his Adam's apple bob in his throat. Her fingers trembled, wanting to touch the strong column of his throat. Really wanting to touch his skin. Puzzled she resisted the urge, stunned by the revelation that she'd always been passive with Yves. She'd never felt that want or need to touch him, even though he was probably ten times better looking than Jason. No, that wasn't true. If Jason took more care and smartened himself up, he'd give Yves a run for his money.

Jason managed to combine kindness with strength. She'd seen him heft the heavy metal tanks around the yard and although she was tall for a girl, he topped her by several inches. Yet even at his grumpiest, she'd never felt intimidated by him.

'Yeah, meat?'

She focused on him. The awkwardness fading as he took control again. 'Don't think I'm not grateful. I like your cooking,' he lifted his brow with feigned enthusiasm. 'I really do, but,' he adopted a hangdog expression, 'to be honest. I'm bloody sick of the veggie stuff.'

Siena burst out laughing, the tension between them diffused. 'You pay for the meat, I'll happily cook it.'

'Really? God, I thought you were on some healthy French type of diet.'

'Have you ever been to France?'

Comprehension dawned. 'Right, yeah.' He nodded with a self-deprecating snort. 'Not exactly the first or last bastion of vegetarianism.'

'What do you fa—?' She stopped herself just in time. 'What sort of meat would you like?'

'Steak,' he said with unequivocal firmness. 'Come on woman, we are going to the butchers.' He gave her a little nudge and pushed her towards the door.

Siena's heart gave a funny little twist, half with relief that they were OK again and half with regret.

Maybe the candles were a touch too much but she left them anyway. Jason had bought the steak at the butchers and while he was doing that she'd nipped to Marks & Spencer, of which her mother had always been a huge fan, to buy some new potatoes, salad leaves and a pot of cream.

Rummaging in the sideboard, she'd found a dusty bottle of brandy which was great, as she'd resigned herself to going without because she couldn't justify buying it. Now she had an idea for a pudding. There were two fresh oranges in the fruit bowl.

She hummed as she gathered everything together. Funny how quickly the tiny kitchen had come to feel like home. Jason still grumbled that she wasn't very good at tidying up but was always appreciative about the food she served up.

As the potatoes went in to boil, she seasoned the steaks, tossed the salad leaves in a little oil and vinegar and heated the heavy cast iron pan. Jason had gone up to take a shower, after she'd had her soak in the bath which she'd deliberately not overfilled so there'd be enough water for him.

As she turned the steaks, he appeared in the kitchen, his hair damp, freshly shaven and barefoot in ancient jeans that were worn thin at the thighs and a faded T-shirt that hugged the contours of his chest and abdomen.

He was a million light years from the well-groomed, designer clad men she was used to, and her mouth went dry.

'This looks nice,' he said strolling to the dresser. 'I think I should open some wine. There are a couple of reds in the wine rack in the lounge. I've never touched them but I'm sure Laurie wouldn't mind, especially when we're celebrating you getting your first proper job.'

As she poured the brandy into the pan over the peppercorns she heard the satisfying pop of the cork. Jason squeezed between the kitchen chair and her, his body brushing hers. She felt the soft hairs on his arm tease her skin on her forearm as he placed a glass on the side next to her. Her heart stuttered in response. She gripped the wooden spatula harder.

'Thank you. This will be ready in a minute.'

'It looks great.' He remained behind her. 'Can I do anything to help?' She felt his warm breath on her neck.

'You could put the salad on the table and drain the potatoes,' she said gritting her teeth, praying he'd move before she gave in to the urge to melt back against him. 'There's a hot dish in the oven to put them in.'

Thankfully her voice sounded normal and he didn't seem to think there was anything amiss. Most of the time, she didn't register how good-looking he was, but tonight he looked utterly edible. Masculinity seemed to ooze out of every pore. The dark hair on his arms fascinated her. The smooth chin with a hint of dimple. That full lower lip that begged to be nipped. She almost laughed at herself. Miss Frigid wanting to jump someone's bones. What would Yves say about that?

She reached out and took the glass. 'Thank you. And thanks for helping me get the job.'

'Pleasure, and thanks for dinner.' He picked up his glass and chinked it against hers. 'Cheers.'

'Salut.'

The rich mouthful hit her like an explosion of cherry and fruit flavour. Her eyes widened and as she swallowed she stared into the glass. '*Merde!* Are you sure Laurie won't mind us drinking this?'

Jason shrugged. 'There were a couple of different bottles in the wine rack. This one was one of two the same, so I thought it would be better to open this one so at least there's one left.'

Siena nodded gravely and crossed to the other side of the table to pick up the bottle.

'Well picked,' she said her eyes brimming with mirth.

'It is rather nice, isn't it?'

'Very nice,' she agreed. Should she tell him that he'd opened a bottle of Chateau Lafite 1985 which was worth over four hundred euros? Hopefully Laurie would forgive her but what the hell; it was open now and she planned to enjoy every last mouthful.

She served up the steaks, pouring peppercorn and brandy sauce over them. It smelt great. He couldn't remember the last time a woman had cooked for him like this. Not Stacey that was for sure. They'd lived on take-away meals and eating out. He shuddered to think how much money they'd wasted.

Looking at Siena now, her blonde hair rippling down her back, kinked from the plait she always wore for work, she could pass for a normal down-to-earth person. Sometime in the week the vibrant nail varnish had vanished and she barely seemed to wear any make-up. He had a hard time remembering what she'd been like the night he'd picked her up. Luckily the pale blue, soft as butter leather jacket she wore – which must have cost a fortune – and the handbag with its designer badge, which she slung over her shoulder each day served as a timely reminder that she came from a very different world and wouldn't be here forever.

Funnily enough, Will seemed absolutely delighted with her and he was nobody's fool. Silly bugger had even gone as far as to thank Jason for suggesting her. To be fair, he had to give her credit. She certainly worked hard, but in three weeks she'd be gone. Back home. This was temporary and it wasn't so easy to slum it when it was indefinite. Living on next to nothing soon palled unless you had a damn good incentive. And even then, it sucked some days.

He couldn't stop the greedy moan that escaped with his first mouthful.

'Wow, this is bloody fantastic. You're a great cook. '

Siena flashed him a delighted and surprisingly grateful smile. Sadness lanced him as he realised that she wasn't used to praise. What sort of life had she led? He'd felt quite sorry for her when she told him how she'd learned to cook, reading between the lines, she'd been a lonely little girl relying on the staff for company.

'So, have you got any further with your fashion degree plans?'

'Yes.' With usual Siena enthusiasm, she tossed her hair back over her shoulders and put her elbows on the table. He'd never met anyone so constantly animated and enthused.

'Lisa's friend Katie has an aunt who works at the London College of Fashion. So I'm going to talk to Katie and hopefully,' Siena's face lit up with its sunshine beam, 'go from there.'

As they sipped their way through the wine, Siena asked lots of questions about the brewery, how he knew Will, how he knew Laurie and Cam.

'You played rugby?' She looked impressed and her eyes swept down his body. He straightened and determinedly ignored the brief jump to attention in his boxers. It had been a while, that was all.

'At university and then for a while after but I gave it up when I started to feel like I'd been crushed by a millstone the next morning.'

'Your ears are OK.'

'Pardon?'

She giggled. 'Not all turned inside out and lumpy.'

He warmed to the sound, realising it was the first time he'd heard her giggle since he'd come home to find her huddled in that very chair. Her black eye had faded and the gash on her cheek was a lot less vivid.

'You mean cauliflower ears.'

'That's the one. Like Fabien Pelous.'

'You like rugby?' She really didn't seem like the type.

'Love it. Harry has a box at Stade de France. I always go when I'm in Paris.'

'Lucky you.' He felt a dart of envy.

'Not in the box.' She shook her head and waved her hands. 'That's boring. It's much more fun with everyone else.' She giggled again. 'Especially the English fans. They are so funny. So polite and so sweary and then apologetic.'

'You looked like you'd been in a rugby match the other day.'

'Don't remind me.' She touched her face.

It seemed natural when every last scrap of steak was demolished and both plates were empty, to pick up the wine bottle and move to the lounge. He lit the fire and the conversation moved on, nothing complicated or searching. Relaxed end of the week, undemanding chat. And she was easy on the eye. Not exactly a hardship.

Throughout the evening he noticed her pick up her phone and, every now and then, give it a troubled look but she didn't do any more than that. It intrigued him, most women, actually most people to be fair, would be tapping away in response to texts, tweets or Snapchats.

She perched it on the edge of the coffee table within easy reach and curled her feet up under her in the corner of the sofa. Feeling relaxed after two glasses of wine and a beer, he stretched his legs out with his hands behind his head. Inadvertently he kicked the phone and it fell on the floor. He picked it up to hand to her. The display flashed into life.

'Bloody hell, you've got twenty-three missed calls and a bunch of messages on here. That's going some. You're a popular girl.'

She looked down at her lap but not before the guilt darted across her face.

'Your mother? Yves? Have you not spoken to them?'

She kept her head bowed.

'Not at all?' He tried to bite back his impatience. Surely she realised that they were concerned. She'd led a sheltered, pampered life, completely protected from the grittier side of things. For all her family knew, anything could have happened to her. They were probably climbing the walls.

'Siena,' his voice rose, 'I get that you're having problems. But they're family. They're bound to be worried about you.' He knew what his mother had been like when he was a teen. Waiting up, no matter how late he'd been.

All he could see was the top of her head. From her curled up position, knees up to her chin, it looked as if she were trying to burrow back into the sofa like an ostrich burying its head in the sand, hands wrapped around her knees.

'They'll be worried sick. Yes, I know your mother cancelled your cards but it was probably a knee jerk thing. If she's not heard from you since, she'll be really worried as well as feeling guilty. At least listen to your messages.'

'I can't.' He could see the white mounds of her knuckles on each hand pressed tight to the surface of her skin. 'It's easier if I don't.'

'Easier for you? Hardly fair on them.'

Her chin lifted. 'You don't understand.'

'Try me,' he glared at her. She had to understand that everyone had responsibilities, parents to children and children to parents.

Mutiny sealed her mouth with an un-Siena-like tight-lipped slash.

'For God's sake, it's your mother. Of course she's going to worry. She probably was angry at first that you'd gone without saying anything,' he paused until she lifted her head to meet his burning gaze, 'but now …'

Siena's stubborn attitude burned low in his stomach. Spoilt and thoughtless and, more annoyingly, seemingly totally unrepentant, just when he was starting to think there might be a bit more to her than met the eye. 'Excuse me for saying it but I think you're being selfish and unkind.'

Two spots burned in her cheeks. He ignored them; he knew what it was like to be responsible for other people.

142

She sat bolt upright, swivelling from her comfortable pose to perch on the edge of the sofa. 'You listen then, if it's so ... so,' her mouth worked as if she couldn't quite bring herself to swear, 'important.'

She tossed the phone onto his lap with a violent throw, which hit his thigh with a painful thud, just missing his balls. He winced at the near miss. Spoilt brat.

'Alright, I will.' He snatched up the mobile.

The first message, understandably, came from her mother.

'Siena, where are you? It's 7pm. We're going out to dinner in half an hour. I expect you home immediately. Yves is already here.'

Jason wanted to smile, that was one cool Mama. Imperious and calm.

Message two sounded equally measured. He had to give it to her mother, she owned froideur. *'I'm in no mood for your childish tricks. We're waiting and Yves is not impressed.'*

A man's voice in heavily accented French but flawless English, followed with message three. *'Where the hell are you? We're leaving for the restaurant in ten minutes. You'd better be here.'*

Jason frowned at the hint of threat. Mr-not-so-cool.

This was followed by. *'We're leaving for the restaurant. Meet us there.'*

Message five. The same man with hissed fury. *'Where the fuck are you? You're going to be sorry. Embarrassing me like this. I have clients here. How dare you?'*

Jason stiffened and sat upright listening intently to the next message.

Siena's mother again. *'I have never been so humiliated in my life. Poor Yves. How could you do this to him? I am mortified. Is this how you show your gratitude after all we have done for you? Harry is very upset.'*

His skin prickled. This wasn't what he'd expected to hear.

It was a missed dinner for Christ's sake. So they were cross, but this went beyond that.

143

'What were you supposed to be doing? Having dinner with Sarkozy?'

Siena worried at her lip and said in a dull flat voice, 'A meal with my parents, Yves and some business contacts. Then going onto a nightclub.' She shrugged.

The messages were still rolling and before he could comment, he heard Yves' angry voice again, '*You selfish stupid bitch. You'd better be at the apartment when I get there. These disappearing acts every time you don't get your way are becoming very tiresome.*'

Then her mother again. '*Where are you? I can't believe you are shaming us so badly. What will people think? I expect you back today by 6pm.*'

The loud angry voices were carrying and it was clear that Siena could hear every word. Her face grew paler and Jason felt a dart of guilt, although, they were still in the angry rather than worried phase.

'*Have it your way young lady. I've cancelled your cards and stopped your allowance. See how long you can stay away now.*' Her mother's voice carried a hint of spite.

Jason felt quite sick. Where was the concern about Siena's whereabouts or safety? She could have been lying dead or in an unknown hospital as far as they knew. They'd cut her off without a penny when she could be anywhere. They clearly had no clue where she had gone.

The final message came from her mother two days ago.

'*Wherever you are I hope you are happy at the damage you've done. Yves is furious with you, but is prepared to put up with your atrocious behaviour. I want you to call me immediately. I—*'

He stabbed the touch screen to stop the message. He felt heartsick at the lack of affection displayed.

Siena's eyes had clouded, filled with haunting grief.

'Oh fuck, I'm sorry.' Of course she knew her own family better than he did. What a fucking idiot, supposing, no *insisting* he knew better. For assuming that the rest of the world played by the same rules.

She shrugged, her face bare of any emotion, a blank mask. 'It's not your fault.'

With mechanical stiffness she took the phone from his limp fingers and switched it off with resignation.

He hated that he'd done that to her. Doused the euphoria she'd shared at getting her first job. Her face crumpled slightly and he saw defeat in her eyes. Siena was never defeated. The slump of her shoulders made him clench his hands. It was so far from her usual sunshine attitude. For the first time he realised how isolated she was. Everyone needed family. Someone on their side. His sisters drove him mad but he never passed a few days without receiving a call, a text or an email from them

Wanting to wipe the desolation from her face, he looped an arm around her shoulders and pulled her towards him. She wasn't completely alone. This defeated, bowed Siena wasn't the Siena he'd come to know in the last few weeks. He thought of her and Lisa, laughing as they covered the kitchen in glitter, Ben's puppy love adoration for her which she treated with gentle respect, Will's admiration for her and Marcus' quick loyalty.

Guilt tugged. No wonder Laurie had asked him to keep an eye out for her. She knew all this. And in spite of everything, Siena had blossomed. She'd been far more resilient than he'd given her credit for.

Under his fingers, her shoulders remained rigid and he wondered if it were to keep a tight rein on her emotions. He couldn't imagine his own mother speaking to him or his sisters like that. He rubbed her back, like he would a child's. She seemed so vulnerable and lost. Eventually she turned to him, her body softening and he leaned back into the sofa taking her with him. Silence held, punctuated only by their breathing. He had nothing to say, all he could offer was the comfort of his hold and reassurance that she mattered. Mattered to someone. She mattered to him. Honesty. Courage. Dogged determination. Her sunny nature.

Her head lifted from his shoulder and he looked down. 'Thanks.' She looked up at him, her face so full of hurt. He wanted to ease the sadness away, soothe the confusion from her eyes. A woman of contrasts, fragile and strong, brave and uncertain, sophisticated and naïve. He leaned down and kissed her.

It was purely innocent, a kiss to offer succour. Gently he caressed her mouth with soft kisses, tracing her lips with the lightest touch. He felt her sigh of pleasure. It kicked into him with a punch of desire that he hadn't anticipated and when she shifted, pressing closer against him, instinct and sense warred in his head, but her stuttered breaths made him want more.

He deepened the kiss, unable to resist the sharp scythe of want, feeling a satisfying sense of possession as Siena met him, her lips questing and nuzzling at his without hesitation.

For once it didn't feel as if he were in a race to the end. With painstaking leisure he explored her mouth, taking his time, easing out the kisses, his lips gliding over hers, his tongue making gentle forays to touch hers and his hand slipping up to cradle the fine bones of her face. As kisses went it was a slow, long burn, as if they had all the time in the world. His arms were full of her soft pliant body. He wanted to hold her closer still and pull her into his arms to keep her safe.

When he finally pulled away to catch his breath and to smooth some of her hair away from their faces, she moaned in complaint, her hands tightening on his arms.

'Ssh, it's OK.' Shifting, he pulled her down lengthways on the sofa and they lay there face-to-face. He stroked her face as her eyes, limpid and large stared at him. Words seemed out of place and he didn't want to spoil the moment of complete accord and understanding between them. There was no expectation, no explanation, just the two of them, anchoring each other. He hadn't realised how empty and lonely he'd been feeling. Perhaps he needed Siena as much as she probably needed him. Just for this moment, this time.

Her lips curved in a sweet secretive smile and she lifted her hand, her index finger tracing his brow as if to wipe away a frown. She tracked her finger, down his face to outline his lips, touching the lower lip that bugged him so much. When she did it, reverently with that enigmatic look in her eyes, it made him feel that maybe the stupid girly lip had its attraction. Invitation shimmered as she considered him and he answered with a plundering kiss, delving his hands into that mane of hair and holding her head. Conscious of her fragility, he held her as if he were holding the tail string of a balloon, enough to keep hold but gentle enough to let go if need be.

He felt her confidence grow. A hand caressing his neck. Her breasts nudging against him. Her leg slipping between his. Their bodies gradually entwining. Low level heat began to build. Sliding his arms slowly down her back with lazy intent, making it clear she could stop him at any point, he brought his hand inexorably down to her bottom and urged her to him. Hands full, he cupped and shaped the pert cheeks, massaging her through her jeans and failed to bite back the groan. She felt so damn good.

Scant seconds later, she stiffened, her whole body suddenly rigid. Corpse-like, she lay beneath him before suddenly lurching into life, pushing against him, hands scrabbling, knees flailing and her breaths short, sharp and panicked.

Immediately he rolled away from her, falling off the sofa onto the floor, to give her space.

Sitting on the floor, he waited and watched as she calmed, conscious of his heartbeat pounding hell for leather in his chest. He concentrated on that, as it gradually slowed to normal, listening to the fire crackle in the silence of the room and keeping absolutely still as if he were waiting for a deer to break cover in the woods.

Eventually, her eyes tightly shut, she pulled herself upright, knees to her chest, her arms clamped around her shins.

They stayed like that, he didn't know how long for.

'It was Yves that punched me.'

Her soft voice startled him. The flames had almost lulled him to sleep and Siena had been silent for so long, he'd given up on her talking to him tonight.

'The bruise on your stomach?'

'Yes. I made him cross.'

'He hit you?' Jason needed to say the words out loud to process them.

She nodded, her gaze tracking across the room.

'Quite a bruise.' He kept his words level.

'He gets cross with me. I ... I don't like.' She swallowed. 'Sex.'

Jason didn't know what to say.

The flames in the fire danced in sinuous rhythm. If she looked at them rather than at Jason, it made talking about it easier.

'We'd been to the races. When we got back. I was a bit upset. I said I didn't want to go out with his clients again.' She swallowed, watching the curl of an orange flame rise and roll back on itself, focusing on it instead of the images forcing their way back into her head. 'They touched me a lot. He wanted to go to bed. I didn't.' Her hand drifted to her stomach as she tried to hold back that awful sensation of being completely powerless. 'Then he ...'

'Siena look at me.'

His gentle tone, damn him, made the tears well up.

'What happened?

She closed her eyes, feeling of the usual sense of shame at her inability to do anything about it. Lifting her head to look up at the ceiling, she swallowed hard, forcing the tears to stay put. She wasn't going to cry. 'He ... insisted ... when I didn't want to.' She'd avoided putting it into words for so long, that now she said them out loud she realised how pathetic and spineless she sounded.

'Insisted?' Jason raised an eyebrow. Like a terrier, he wasn't going to let go.

'He knows I don't really like,' she blushed, 'sex. I'm not very good at it.'

'It takes two.' Jason spoke softly.

'Yves says I need to relax a bit more but it's hard. I know he's going to want to and it makes me tense and then it …' Her mouth crumpled as she tried to hold back that awful sensation of being powerless and useless. Lying there. Him pumping into her.

'He says I'm frigid and need more practice.'

'You mean he forced you.' Jason's eyes were glacial. 'Didn't you tell anyone?'

'Tell them what?' Anger sparked. 'I'm lousy in bed? Yves is rich, handsome. One of the most eligible bachelors in France. He's always on those lists. When I tried to say no … that's when he hit me. I avoided him for a couple of weeks after that, but then on Thursday, Maman said she'd invited him to the Chateau for dinner and that we were going out with a few of Harry's business colleagues. She told me that she was expecting us to get engaged. Yves father is one of my stepfather's friends. He owns the neighbouring estate and has part shares in lots of Harry's business interests.'

'Establishing a family dynasty?' Jason's face hardened.

'Harry doesn't have any children of his own.'

'Very neat and tidy.'

'At first it was OK. I've known Yves forever.'

'Same social set.'

Siena sighed. It had been virtually impossible to avoid him. The races. Skiing. Antibes. St Moritz and St Tropez. She'd been blind to it originally. 'I didn't think he was that interested. Then we started going to things together. Before I knew it we were a couple. And Maman seemed so happy and kept promoting it.

'That afternoon, when she went out, that's when I decided to run away.' She laughed hollowly. 'I didn't think it through. Just packed a bag. Flew to England, assuming I could stay with Laurie and then make plans here.'

'So the fashion designer thing?'

'I am serious about that bit,' she shrugged, 'Lisa's going to help me see someone.'

'Are you sure your mother wouldn't be supportive if you talked to her? Actually, you do know you could report Yves for non-consensual sex? It's still a crime, even if you know him or have been sleeping with him.'

Siena smiled at him; for once he was being the naïve one.

'Yves' uncle works in the Ministre de Justice. Yves is a pin-up. No one is going to take that case on, believe me.'

And then the dam burst, the shame, the hate, the self-loathing. The tears forced their way through so fast and furious, her breaths turned into incoherent sobs and suddenly Jason was beside her, taking her into his arms, holding her as she sobbed into his chest, his strong hands anchoring her there.

It took a while for the outpouring to calm. She felt exhausted and could barely open her eyes. She'd look a sight; they felt puffy and swollen. So she kept them closed and took comfort in Jason's arms, feeling safe for the first time.

A numb arm woke him. They lay wrapped together, her breaths fast and even, with a slight wheezy squeak to them.

The room had chilled, the fire a pile of embers, a flame guttering every now and then. In the shadows, Siena's features had softened. She looked so damned innocent, it pricked at him.

She stirred next to him and her eyes fluttered opened with a sleepy frown of confusion that sent his heart into a Catherine wheel fizz.

He pulled her round with him, rising to his feet and taking her with him.

'Come on. You need to go to bed.'

Pausing to blow the candle out, he led her to the stairs. Willing and biddable, still half asleep, she did as he urged. Outside her bedroom door he stopped.

'Goodnight Siena.' Unable to stop himself, he traced her face with his hand. Not all men were shits. He planted a gentle kiss on her forehead, turned her round by placing his hands on her shoulders and pushed her through her door.

He was too tired to make any sense of any of it. Peeling off his clothes, he fell face forward into bed, slightly regretting there was no warm body in there with him, but knowing he'd done the right thing. In her vulnerable state tonight, anything more would have been taking advantage.

Chapter 13

Siena stretched and as she awoke, last night came flooding back making her heart bump. What a disaster, when it had started so well. She shivered. Those initial sweet kisses of comfort which had turned into something else. Her whole body alert and alive with excitement. She'd felt pleasure. She wanted to hold on to that feeling even though she knew it probably didn't mean anything to him. Gruff, grumpy Jason had a soft heart and he'd been offering her sympathy and comfort. She wanted to hug herself, and keep the memories inside so that they wouldn't fade in the bright light of a new day.

He'd been so kind and lovely and then she'd gone and spoiled it all.

What on earth would he be thinking this morning? That she was some neurotic nut-job? A spineless, useless idiot? But talking about it had changed things. She wasn't going to be that person any more.

She rolled over to check her phone. Seven thirty. Almost groaning she slumped back in her pillows, too wide awake to get back to sleep.

Irritated she scrolled through her phone, relieved that the red dot telling her she had umpteen million messages had gone, thanks to Jason. Those voicemails had been as bad as she'd feared except instead of depressing her and being cowed by them, she had something to celebrate. Surviving. Managing. Feeling more confident, she opened her Facebook app and bit back a smile. The world went on without her.

A party in Cannes. Dinner at a newly opened restaurant. A private showing of an up and coming abstract artist on the Left Bank. Contemporaries pictured in their favourite designer gowns holding flutes of champagne.

All things that Siena had done a thousand times. She peered at the pictures. Funny, she didn't miss it at all. Funnier still, people had stopped asking where she was. No one even mentioned not seeing her. Short memories indeed.

The phone buzzed in her hand. A text. Lisa inviting her out for the day.

Quickly she tapped the keys back in response and bounded out of bed. Before she left the bedroom, she listened warily. Was Jason up? If she went in the bathroom now would she disturb him? Had he already used the bathroom?

Dithering by the door, she listened hard. No sign of life in the house. She'd be quick. In and out of the shower in record time.

What was she going to say to him this morning? If she was really quick and quiet, she might make it out of the house without seeing him.

It wasn't cowardly, well maybe it was a bit. Last night had been … last night. A one off. A beautiful memory. Jason had felt sorry for her. She wasn't his type, she knew that. And he probably wasn't her type. She didn't know what her type was. What she did know was that Jason could be kind. His gentle sympathy and protective enveloping strength had touched her. And she was in danger of a severe case of hero worship.

Luck ran out before she could leave, or maybe she only had herself to blame. Making the strong Italian coffee was asking for temptation. Maybe she'd done it on purpose, knowing the siren effect the rich aroma had on Jason. He seemed to be able to scent coffee with an almost superhuman ability. As he wandered into the kitchen, looking rumpled and sleepy, Siena's heart skipped and she fought the urge to go to him, slide into his arms and press against his body.

'Morning,' he muttered, his eyes bleary. Not knowing how to respond, she turned and busied herself pouring him a coffee.

'Here you go.' She handed it to him.

'Thanks.' He gave her a dopey smile. 'You're up early. Going somewhere?' His face creased in puzzled confusion, which was really rather endearing. Not a morning person at all.

'Going shopping with Lisa.' She tried to inject enthusiasm balanced with matter of fact statement. 'Then I'm going back to hers for a girly film and takeaway pizza.'

'The pizza part sounds great, the rest of it ...' He made the sort of face a toddler would be at home with.

She smiled, the awkwardness vanishing. 'Good job you're not invited then.'

'Hmm,' he took a sip from the cup. 'Oh, that is good.'

Trying not to look at the V of chest revealed by his robe, Siena tidied away her plate and cup. Last night's kisses were suddenly imprinted on her brain. Like a magnet, his lower lip drew her gaze.

The toot of the horn outside heralded Lisa's arrival and merciful release.

'Enjoy yourself, I think,' he mumbled.

'What are you going to do today?' she asked suddenly shy.

'Going back to bed. I only got up because I could smell coffee. You wicked caffeine temptress.'

Their eyes met and he smiled. A kick to the heart, a spike in her pulse.

The car horn tooted again.

'Gotta go.' She felt hot and wobbly. Grabbing her leather jacket, she started towards the kitchen door knowing she had to walk right by him. '*Ciao*.' Like a woodpecker, she planted the barest, briefest kiss on his check and scuttled away. The front door slammed behind her and she let out a long pent up breath still unsure as to whether she'd done the right thing or not.

Lisa waited in the driver seat, her tiny Mini parked on the kerbside.

As Jason had predicted, the snow had all gone. She'd hoped the few inches would stay a bit longer. It was still very cold as the bite of morning air hit her. She could have done with a warmer coat. In Paris she rarely walked anywhere. They had a driver or she travelled by taxi.

Grasping the handle of the door, she hopped in quickly.

'Morning, how are you?' Lisa's beam lit up the inside of the car.

Siena wondered what she'd say if she told her what had happened last night.

'I'm so glad you could make it. We're going to have such a great day. I was worried you might be dead on your feet after a week with the slave driver.'

Siena laughed. 'Hi. I really enjoyed it. Although my feet are sore, so please don't make me walk too far today.'

'Not sure I can guarantee that.' Lisa tossed her long hair and narrowed a stern look at Siena as she swung the Mini around a corner. 'Shop till you drop. That's the mantra. I thought you were the woman for the job. I am relying on you to complete our mission.'

'Aha! A mission, you say. I can resist everything but a mission.'

'Wasn't that temptation?'

'That too.'

'Yes, a mission to the death.' Lisa whipped out into the middle of the road to overtake another car. 'We leave no shop unturned until I have found a dress for this ball. Today we scour the charity shops of Harpenden, tomorrow or next week or next year we take Manhattan. You up for it?'

Siena nodded and tried to snuggle into her leather jacket. The heating in the car seemed to be taking it's time to get into gear.

155

'There are at least six charity shops over there. Hopefully I can find something for this charity ball.' Lisa rammed on the brakes as they screeched to a halt at a set of traffic lights. Siena swore she could smell burning rubber. 'Otherwise it'll have to be Primark and then I run the risk of ten others having the same dress.'

Siena gave a wistful thought to the row upon row of designer dresses hanging in her dressing room at the apartment in Paris. The boxes of shoes and the matching handbags, neatly organised for optimum co-ordination. Not that she had any place to wear any of them at the moment but it would have been lovely to let Lisa choose one of the dresses and the footwear to go with it. The scarlet Givenchy from two seasons ago would look fabulous with Lisa's colouring.

'You can come back to mine afterwards. Meet Katie and,' Lisa pulled a face, 'my gran.'

'Your gran? Does she live there?'

'On and off, yes.' Lisa gave a sudden mischievous grin. 'False teeth and incontinence pads everywhere. I think I'd rather have Jason to look at in the mornings. He is rather yum, yum.'

Siena raised an eyebrow and ignored the odd sensation in her chest, as she had a sudden fleeting memory of the feeling of Jason's solid arms around her.

'Much as I love her, bumping into Nanna's prune-face in the kitchen, having her first fag of the day is not the best wake up call. That woman has smoked forty a day for the last fifty years and has the lines to prove it. She's like a tree, count the rings and you know how old, with her it's count the lines and you can work out how many a day.'

Siena couldn't tell if Lisa was joking or not. 'Can't you tell her not to? Do you have live with her?'

Lisa's cheerful face fell briefly. 'It's more a case of she lives with me ... part time. Her boiler's packed up, so she's got no hot water. She comes round to mine to warm up and have a bath, bless her. Oh you berk.' Lisa gave the hapless driver ahead a furious toot of her horn. 'Families eh?'

Siena wrinkled her nose at the slightly musty smell and wondered at the wisdom of Lisa's tactics. The shop had a strange and eclectic mix of clothes, some of which she wasn't sure a tramp would choose to wear if he'd been given them.

'You have to rummage,' whispered Lisa, catching sight of her wary face.

'Right.' Gingerly fingering garments, wishing she'd brought some hand sanitizer, Siena rifled through a rack of decidedly synthetic fabrics, holding her grimace at bay. Truly hideous. Even more hideous. Nasty. Hideous. No, no, no. What had someone been thinking of? Oh. Wait a minute.

Siena pulled the hanger out. A dress, almost pristine, nice cut, lovely fabric.

'What make is it?' whispered Lisa materialising beside her, like an undercover spy.

'*Desmoines.*'

'Never heard of it,' Lisa pulled a disappointed face.

'That doesn't matter. Look at the cut and this fabric, lovely and heavy and it's a gorgeous style apart from the frill, but that could go.' Siena could see lots of possibilities for the dress. Only seven pounds fifty – that was insane. Didn't the people working here have any idea? A dress like this would cost twenty times that in a Paris boutique.

Lisa still looked unconvinced.

'See here. The cut. Excellent design. It won't pull across the shoulders, the sleeves are set in. And the fabric is good quality, it won't go shiny, or bobble, or crease.'

'Not wanting to sound ungrateful, I get that it's all those things but it's not really what I had in mind and it's also a size sixteen.'

'So have you got an idea of what you'd like?' Siena asked as flicked through the rest of the rail. No, nothing. Shame.

'No, sorry, but I'll know when I see it.

After rifling through a rail of skirts and finding a few very nice pieces, which were absolute bargains, Lisa came over with two dresses.

'What do you think?'

She held them up one by one.

Siena pulled a face. 'They all look a bit cheap.'

'They are cheap,' said Lisa poking out her tongue cheekily. 'That's the whole point of coming to charity shops.'

'Yes, but I thought the whole point was that they were originally more expensive. If you wanted to buy cheap, couldn't you go to a cheap shop?'

'This is Primark,' said Lisa looking doleful at one of the dresses she held. 'What about this one?'

Siena looked at her and then back at the dress. 'No, you'd look like you'd died. And probably a bit dumpy.'

'Thanks.' Lisa poked her in the ribs in mock outrage.

Siena shot her a mischievous grin. 'Thought you wanted fashion advice.'

'Yes, what I should be looking for. Not what would make me look hideous.' Lisa turned and half-heartedly pulled the hangers along rails.

They left the shop empty-handed but Siena's head buzzed with ideas. There'd been plenty she could have bought, if she'd needed anything. Conscious of what she had to live on until pay day, she was loath to waste a penny. The beige houndstooth Jaeger pencil skirt would have looked fabulous but when would she wear it? Same with the dark green Karl Lagerfield jacket which was definitely vintage, it had to date back to the eighties but would look great with jeans. Oooh, tempting. She could wear that. Only twenty-five pounds, which Lisa thought was still overpriced. Even so she kept going back to the jacket. No, you could buy a lot of groceries with that money.

Neither the first nor the second shop delivered Lisa's dream dress. The third offered definite promise, with a whole rail dedicated to evening wear. It was funny, thought Siena, obviously a certain charity or shop attracted a better clientele. How did the people making the donations decide?

'Lisa.' Siena called her over, excitement resonating in her voice. This was the perfect dress. She held up a pale pink shift dress, silk dotted with tiny sequins which twinkled refracting the light. The colour would complement Lisa's English rose complexion and her dark eyes and the style would suit her slender figure.

Lisa bounded over. 'Yes. Yes. Yes. That's gorgeous,' and then her face fell. 'It's also a size eighteen.'

'So?'

Lisa put her hands on her hips. 'Can you see me filling the boob department?' She cupped her chest and looked down with amusement. 'On a very good day I'm a 34B not a blinking 38DD.' She grasped the voluminous skirt and wrapped it around her waist. 'This will go round me at least twice.'

Siena tugged the fabric out of her hand and held the dress up against her and dragged her over to the mirror.

'Look. Focus on the colour and style.'

'I am, it's gorgeous but it won't fit.'

'Pish, that's not a problem. We can alter it.'

'That's going to cost more than the dress.'

'Have you got a sewing machine?'

'No.'

'Damn.' How funny that her sewing machine should be the one thing that she regretted not bringing with her.

Lisa brightened. 'My Nanna does.'

'Would she let us borrow it?'

'Yes, I'm her favourite grandchild.'

Siena nodded. 'That's good then, does that mean she won't mind?'

Lisa frowned. 'I was joking.'

'What, you're not her favourite?'

'I'm her *only* grandchild. That's the joke; grandparents aren't

159

supposed to have favourites.'

Bemused and feeling she'd blundered, Siena focused on the dress. She'd never met any of her grandparents. 'If we cut here and here, and reshaped the neckline proportionally. That would probably work. Taking in the seams wouldn't work. That would ruin the shape of the dress.' Yes, she had a pretty good idea what she'd need to do.

'What … you can do it?'

Siena shrugged. 'I think so. I've altered things before.' She crossed her fingers behind her back. Not quite, she'd been there and helped while things were being altered. At the Chateau, Agnes' daughter, Elena, was a seamstress and had spent many evenings altering clothes in the kitchen letting Siena thread her needles, help pin the seams and sew hems.

'How much is it?' asked Lisa examining the dress front and back.

'Six pounds fifty,' Siena lowered her voice, 'but it's a Ben de Lisi.'

'If you say so.' Lisa's smile lit up her face. 'But if you can make it the right size, it's gorgeous. And a screaming bargain. I'll take it. You can do it tonight. Katie's coming round so you can ask her about that fashion course.'

Despite making the purchase, Lisa was loath to leave until she'd checked out every charity shop in case she might have missed another more perfect dress. By this time, Siena was thoroughly enjoying herself and had picked up two lovely black skirts for work, which she felt she could more than justify when they came to the princely sum of nine pounds fifty and Lisa had found another dress she adored, a taffeta black number with fuchsia pink details which at size twelve would only need minor alterations to make it fit.

In the last shop, all of her good intentions and careful budget considerations were blown to the wind when she caught sight of a red wool coat. Max Mara. Size fourteen. Too big but criminal to walk away from, especially when she really did need a warm coat. Leaving Paris with a single leather jacket had been reckless and now she was in England she regretted not giving more thought

160

to her wardrobe choices. She tried it on. Gorgeous, but too big. Taking it off, she looked at the seams. The whole thing would need a remake, to cut down the size would be an ambitious project as it would be harder to work with this heavy fabric than the light-weight fabrics of Lisa's dresses but it was a beautiful coat. And seventeen pounds. She touched the fabric again. She'd already spent the money on the skirts. Three weeks ago she would have paid full price for Max Mara without a second thought. Now ...

'I'm desperate for a cup of tea,' said Lisa shoving her key into the lock of the terraced house. It looked even smaller than Laurie's house, if that were possible. They stumbled through the front door straight into a minuscule lounge. A tiny bird of a woman jumped up, unmistakably related to Lisa.

'Nanna, hello.' Lisa swooped down on her with a hug and a kiss. 'Got too cold for you again?'

'Hell yes. Freeze a witch's tit off. Who's this?'

'This is Siena, my friend. Siena this is my gran.'

'That's a funny sort of name. That where your parents conceived you? Seems to be the fashion these days. Brooklyn. India. Chardonnay.'

'Chardonnay's a wine, Nanna.'

'Is she? Takes all sorts I guess.'

'Hi,' said Siena feeling slightly shy.

Nanna gave her a thorough up and down inspection.

'Bit skinny aren't you?'

'Probably,' replied Siena, completely nonplussed.

'Nanna, that's rude.'

'How is that rude? I made an observation. Did I lie? The girl's as skinny as a pikestaff.' She shot a suspicious look at Siena. 'Do you eat properly? Not on one of these weird Hatkins diets.'

'It's Atkins, Nanna,' replied Lisa rolling her eyes at Siena behind her gran's back. 'Sorry,' she mouthed.

'Hmph. Far too many girls worrying about their weight.'

Siena smiled, her face stretched in a rictus which said I'm humouring you but I really don't know how to handle this.

'Nanna, do you still have your sewing machine?'

'You lied, you said she had one.' Siena shot Lisa a horrified look and the other girl smiled blithely back. 'I thought if Nanna doesn't have it any more, we'll get one somewhere. If not you could do it by hand.'

There was no answer to that. Siena had to laugh. It was exactly what she'd have done. Act first, plan and think later.

'Of course I still have my sewing machine.' Nanna drew all four foot nine inches of herself up with great hauteur. 'I'm not in the habit of getting rid of something or throwing it away because there's a newer, shinier model for sale.' With a wicked laugh she added, 'If that were the case, I'd have traded your grandfather in a long time earlier. Got myself one of those Chippendale fellas.' Nanna's attempt at a dirty wink, which was more of an owlish blink, had Siena desperately trying to hold back her giggles.

'You're not sewing blankets for babies in Africa are you? Because I've been crocheting squares for the WI and I'll be cross if they don't want my squares anymore.'

'Nanna, I think you're safe. You keep crocheting. Siena is a bit of a whizz at sewing. I got a couple of dresses in the charity shop, she's going to alter them for me.'

Nanna's eyes lit up. 'I've got some trousers that need altering, remember, love? Those ones I bought in BHS.'

'Nanna, that was nearly five years ago. She can make things smaller, not grow them.'

'I don't know what you're trying to say, young lady.' Nanna tried to look down her nose which made Siena laugh as she had to look up to Lisa do it.

Lisa winked. 'Can I pop round and get it?'

'Course you can love. Actually while you're there you wouldn't collect my slippers would you? I forgot to bring them with me.'

Lisa tried hard not to laugh but then gave up the fight. 'Nanna, you've got them on.'

Nanna looked down at her feet and pursed her wrinkled prune mouth. 'Bugger me, what must the neighbours have thought?' She shook her head. 'They'll think I've lost my fricking marbles.'

'No comment,' teased Lisa.

'You're not too old to put over my knee, cheeky miss, you.' Nanna's wrinkled face split into what seemed like a thousand smiles. With a stab of envy, Siena wondered about her own grandmothers. She didn't recall either of them and in an uncharacteristically self-pitying moment, she felt cheated.

'Another glass?' Lisa topped up Katie's glass but held out on Siena.

'Oi, where's mine?' mumbled Siena through a mouth full of pins.

Lisa giggled and held the bottle high up out of reach. 'You need to make sure those seams are straight. I don't want you drunk in charge of a sewing machine.'

Siena frowned and continued pinning the seam. The pink dress had been a bit more complicated than she'd anticipated. The slippery chiffon and silk was a tricky combination. Now after cutting and pinning, she was starting to feel a little more confident. Lisa had been in and out of the dress fifteen times, as Siena was terrified of making a wrong cut.

The sewing up bit was easy, especially with this Bernina machine; like a vintage Rolls Royce, it had a few years on the clock but ran beautifully. She used the pedal cautiously, the foot trundling along the pinned seams like a steady old cob put out to pasture. Nanna had obviously looked after it well and she'd hovered anxiously over Siena and the machine as the first few seams were run up, even checking that they were smooth and straight.

'Not bad. Not bad.' Her beady eyes assessed Siena. It was mildly terrifying, the older woman's piercing raisin-eyed stare made Siena want to confess all her secrets. 'You'll do.'

'Thank you.' Siena felt like she was five.

'You shouldn't care so much.' Nanna narrowed her eyes and

looked over her shoulder to where Katie and Lisa were engrossed in a conversation of their own. 'I can see.'

'See what?' asked Siena, nerves shimmering at the directness of her gaze.

'Inside you're like a mummy. Bound. Tight. Don't be. When you get to my age, you don't care what other people think.' She grinned, a missing tooth making her look like a mischievous pixie. 'Damn shame, I didn't know that when I was your age. I'd have had a lot more fun. Now I'm too shagging old.' She gave a wicked wink. 'Now, run up another seam and let me have a look.' She waited at Siena's shoulder, the scent of lavender strong. 'Put your foot down a bit. You're not going to kill it. Although bloody stupid fabric. Trust our Lisa to choose the most difficult stuff to sew with. That's why you need so many sodding pins.'

When Siena slipped the silk and chiffon out from under the foot and neatly snipped off the ends of pink cotton, Nanna snatched it from her and, holding it up scant inches from her eyes, peered at the stitches.

'It'll do, although this flibbertigibbet will probably spill wine all over it first time out the traps. Wontcha love?' she called over to Lisa.

'What's that Nanna?'

'Nothing. I'm ready for my bed.' Her face fell.

'Don't worry Nanna, we'll soon get you back home.'

'Hmph,' she grumbled. 'Don't go keeping me up with all your noise and high jinks.'

'No, Nanna,' said Lisa crossing over to give her gran a kiss on the cheek.

'When's her boiler going to be fixed?' asked Katie, once the older woman had left the room.

'Not for ages.' Lisa sighed. 'She can't afford it. Needs a new one and we're saving but we need another six hundred pounds. I don't mind having her here. I love her to bits. Not like she's any trouble. Most of the time.' She rolled her eyes and snorted in a very unladylike way. 'When she's not arguing with the milkman over the price of his milk. But she wants to be in her own home.' She broke off. 'I know she only lives two streets away but she really misses her neighbour, Laura. They've been mates for twenty years and have seen each other every day. I can't imagine that. She wants to be in her garden; she grows prizewinning dahlias. I know there's probably not much going on at the moment but she likes to potter out there every day. She never moans but she's a bit down at the moment.' For the first time, Siena saw the tiredness and sadness in the other girl's face.

'Once the weather warms up she can go back, she's got an open fire in the sitting room but she won't have any hot water. I reckon it'll be spring before I'll have saved up the rest and she'll have put a bit more by. She's only got her pension.'

'What about your family?' asked Siena. Not having hot water or heating for months seemed utterly ridiculous in this day and age. Was that what it was like when you had no safety net? Things became huge and difficult when with a bit of money they were so easily solved. It didn't seem right.

With a lift of her shoulders Lisa said matter of factly, 'This is it. Mum died six years ago. Dad lives in Italy and is about as much use in the father stakes as a chocolate teapot. We're fine, most of the time. Every now and then though a biggie hits you out of the blue.

'Right, back to work, slave. You need to earn your Prosecco. How's my dress coming along?'

'Nearly there,' Siena looked mournfully into her empty wine glass. 'Although the supplies have dried up. So I might have to withdraw my services.' She tipped the glass as far back as it would go, to suck up the very last drop. Funny, it wasn't the best wine she'd drunk, in fact was possibly some of the worst, but it tasted fine.

'Katie, crack open another one quick,' called Lisa jumping up and grabbing the empty wine glass. She paused to drool over the dress. 'It's looking good.'

Siena grimaced. 'God I hope so. '

'Seriously, don't fret. It if goes horribly wrong, it only cost a few quid.' She stopped and waggled her eyebrows in what was supposed to be a menacing fashion but had Siena dissolving into giggles. 'Although, I might want my Prosecco back.'

When she stopped laughing, Lisa patted her on the shoulder. 'We've got a backup plan.'

'I know, the black dress is lovely and I have to admit, it will be a hell of a lot easier to alter. Have you always been this difficult?'

Lisa nodded. 'Of course.'

'But this one is the one you really like and it suits you.' More importantly Siena wanted to prove she could do this. It wasn't real designing, it was modifying someone else's work but she still wanted it to be right. Besides if she could get it right, Lisa would look stunning.

'Right, try it on again.'

'Again!' Lisa pouted. 'Do I have to? I'm sure it will be fine.'

'Strip. Strip. Strip,' chanted Katie, raising her glass. 'Get your kit off for the girls.'

Lisa gave her a withering stare. 'You've been spending far too much time with Tom.'

Siena waited, patiently holding up the dress. 'Come on, we're nearly there.'

'Can we eat pizza and watch the film when this is done?'

'You can, I'll make a start on my coat.' Siena felt rather excited about it. She'd planned to make a couple of changes to the design, like a proper designer.

Lisa peeled off the casual loungewear she'd changed into when they got back and shimmied into the pink dress.

'Whoa!' Katie toasted her, slopping Prosecco down the side of her glass and then hastily licking up the drops. 'That is lush. Oh Siena, make me one.'

Siena laughed. 'I didn't make it, I fixed it.'

'It's ... It's ...' Lisa did a twirl and a little skip. 'I love it.'

'Don't cry, you big wuss.' Katie shook her head at Siena. 'She looks bloody lovely though. Good job that, girl.'

Siena looked longingly at the red coat. More of a challenge but if she could do as a good a job …

'Go on, you know you want to.'

'I thought you wanted to watch—'

'As if, we always say we're going to watch a film.'

'We never do. Katie always falls asleep after the second bottle of fizz.'

'Do not. Third maybe.'

Siena smiled and grabbed the coat. Fingers crossed this would work as well as the dress.

Chapter 14

He'd planned to be more casual about it, but the minute Jason heard the key in the lock, he shot down the stairs. Lack of sleep tended to make him edgy. He'd chomped his way through half a pack of Rennies, after virtually giving them up in the last week. Worrying and having your imagination run away with itself rubbed your temper and your stomach lining raw. If she hadn't swanned in wearing a new coat and carrying a couple of shopping bags, he might have waited until she got through the door.

'Where've you been?'

And she could stuff the round-eyed, innocent, pink-cheeked expression on her gorgeous face. He wanted to shake the living and dying daylights out of her cute little arse and clutch her to him at the same time.

'Lisa's?' she sounded puzzled.

At Lisa's, of course, not dead in a ditch, not lying in a hospital ward, not any of the things he'd pictured in the middle of the night as he lay listening to every last crack and creak of the house, straining to hear a car or the squeak of the front door.

'Of course you were at Lisa's,' he growled. 'And I was supposed to know that, how?' His blistering sarcasm could have stripped wallpaper.

She paled but stood her ground for a moment, looking like

Bambi about to spring away. He ignored the flicker of guilt.

'You could have phoned.' Anger had got the better of him. 'Wait, no. Or even texted. You know, use that thing welded to your side.'

In a gesture he was now familiar with she lifted her chin. Relief punched into him because he'd gone too far. Warrior Barbie had stepped up.

'Don't shout at me.' She stood with her hands on her hips, with a pugnacious tilt to her head. 'I told you this morning I'd be with Lisa all day.' His annoyance faltered; had she? He couldn't remember. He'd been half asleep after a night of no sleep because he couldn't get her out of his mind. 'If you were worried, say so. You don't have to shout.'

'Who said I was worried?' he snapped. 'I wasn't worried. Why should I be worried?' He really needed to shut up. Stop talking. Right now.

His anger evaporated. 'I was worried. After everything you told me last night, someone needs to worry about you. You could have been hurt, in hospital on your own. I don't know, but you could have called.' Oh shit now he sounded like his mother.

'Jason. Make up your mind.' Her voice softened as she said it, then in a firmer tone she added, 'You made it quite clear when I came here that you weren't responsible for me. More than clear. Remember?'

'That was then.'

'So what's different?' Puzzlement clouded her eyes.

He sighed and rubbed at his forehead realising he'd made an absolute dick of himself.

'That was before I knew what Yves had done. Before you got beaten up in broad daylight in the street. Before I heard how your mother spoke to you.'

She took a step closer, her eyes locked on him. 'You're not responsible for me. I can,' she gave a wistful smile, 'stand on one foot at least. It will be two soon but you don't need to ...' she shrugged, guileless, trust in her open gaze.

'I might not be responsible for you but,' he sighed wondering how it had happened, 'I care what happens. We're … we're sort of friends.'

Siena quirked an eyebrow. 'Sort of friends. I've not come across that before. What's a sort of friend?'

He stepped away. Did they have to get into this now? He glowered at her, hoping it would make her back off a bit. Duh! He was the one that moved in on her. Definitely losing it. A relief then that she was being a typical woman. Had to analyse every last thing. Find a definition. Put things in boxes. He shrugged. 'Friends, then.'

'Friends?' she looked amused.

At his expense. 'Friends,' he growled and squeezed past her and walked off down to the kitchen. Surely she'd leave at that now.

Thankfully, he heard her trot up the stairs, carrier bags rustling. Being friends was good. It wasn't as if she were going to be here forever. God knows what would happen with her mother, but surely she'd come round eventually and they'd make up. In the meantime, judging by the new coat and purchases, Siena was starting to miss her old lifestyle. It wasn't as if she'd want to slum it forever. He looked around at the small, homely kitchen. This wasn't what she was used to. Being here was easy. Rent free and belonging to her sister. Siena might think she was on the first steps on the ladder of independence, but she still had this as a safety net.

'Siena, what is the matter?'

'Nothing,' she answered distractedly, still frowning down at her phone.

'Will you quit with the sighing and the tutting then?'

'Sorry.'

Jason turned back to the newspaper. Sunday afternoons were best spent with the rugby on the TV, a pile of supplements and a nice bottle of beer, peace and quiet.

Three out of four wasn't bad.

Siena tutted again and pulled a long, disgusted face. Then looked up. 'Sorry.'

She turned up her nose, her features scrunched in concentration. Amused he watched the contortions of her face.

'What are you trying to do?' Exasperation finally won, he'd never watch the match at this rate.

She sighed heavily. 'I'm trying to do eBay.'

'You mean use eBay?'

'Yes. I want to sell something but I don't want it to go for too little. I need to guarantee I get a certain amount for it, otherwise I don't want to sell it.'

'That's easy, you need to put a reserve on it.'

'Oh. It really is confusing.'

'It's probably not that easy on a screen that size. Would you like to borrow my laptop?'

'I didn't know you had one.'

He felt the streak of colour flood up his face. 'I keep it in my room.'

'Ah,' she nodded knowledgeably, 'watching porn.'

'No, I was not.' He sounded about fifteen in his denial and immediately thought of sweaty episodes and magazines in his teens, best forgotten about, which made him blush even more.

'There's no need to be shy about it. I understand lots of men do.'

She was such a bizarre mix. European candidness about some aspects of sex and then so naïve about others.

'I was not watching porn.'

It seemed petty to admit now that he'd deliberately kept his laptop out of sight, working on it upstairs when he needed to, so that he could keep out of her way the first few weeks, in the deliberate hope she'd get so bored and lonely she'd go home.

'If you say so.'

He rose and went to get the laptop. 'Have you got an eBay account?'

'I have now. It's taken me ages to set it up on my phone.'

171

'Log in on this and show me what you're trying to do.'

'Here, see. I've got as far as this.'

'Right you need to say you want to set a reserve. How much do you want to set it as?

'Six hundred pounds.'

'Fuck, what are you selling? State secrets?'

She gave him a frosty look. 'My handbag.'

'And it's worth six hundred pounds? Fuck me.'

'It's worth more actually, but that's the minimum I'd like to get.'

'There'll be fees on top. You have to pay eBay a percentage of the sale.'

'OK, make it six hundred and fifty then.'

'Short of cash after your spending spree this weekend?' She looked at him puzzled. 'I saw the new coat. Must have set you back a bit. I suppose going a whole three weeks without shopping must have been tough.' Why was this stuff spilling out of his mouth? Why did he sound like the spoilt child? What she did with her money was her choice?

He got the ice princess look.

'Sorry. As long as you can pay your share of the bills at the end of the month, it's nothing to do with me.'

'No. It's not,' she said, her usual sunny smile surfacing. She also looked a tiny bit smug which rang alarm bells. He looked at the screen then back at her. Was she up to something? Or was he being paranoid. No, open book and Siena went hand in hand.

Chapter 15

'Right.' Instead of gathering in the kitchen or propped up at the bar, Will had convened the team meeting in the restaurant around a table and had a pen and notebook in his hand.

'Looks like important business,' muttered Marcus. 'That's a strategy notebook if ever I saw one.' He nodded seriously, making Siena smile.

'Stop taking the piss,' said Will chucking the pen at him. 'We've got a do.'

'What, a proper do?'

Will ignored Marcus silliness. 'An important do. Medical supplies company. The MD, Mike, has asked us to lay on lunch for a group of Japanese businessmen. Private dining, special menu. There's a big deal riding on the visit and Mike wants us to put on a really good show. We'll use the private dining room. I need ideas for the menu. Decorations.'

'Teriyaki and sushi.' Al rubbed his hands together. 'Great.'

Will looked pained. 'No.'

'Why not? It will make them feel right at home.'

'Because, you great noodle,' Marcus leaned against Al with a show of affection, 'how would you feel if you went to Japan and got served crap roast beef and soggy Yorkshires?'

'I wouldn't be serving crap teriyaki.' He tossed his head and nudged Marcus back before looking at Will. 'I could put an English twist on it.'

Will shook his head. 'No.'

'I know a bit about hostessing,' Siena piped up.

'Hostessing?' Will raised an eyebrow. 'I'm intrigued.'

'What? Is that like, you know, escorting?' Al's voice held a note of salacious horror.

'No.' Siena threw a napkin at him.

'Al, does our Siena look like a hooker?'

'How would you know what a hooker looks like?' Al retorted.

'Boys. Boys. Behave.' Will shot them both the sort of look a primary school teacher might use.

She'd started now, so she'd have to finish. She sniggered at her own pun. 'I went to—' She closed her eyes. If she it said really quickly she might get away with it. No, working with the three of them over the last few weeks, she knew they were going to rip the piss out of her – her English colloquialisms were coming along nicely.

'Earth to Siena,' sang Marcus and held up his hand opening his fingers to make the traditional Vulcan greeting which had become their private joke.

'Here's hoping Scotty will beam you up.' She poked her tongue out at him. 'I,' she took a deep breath, '*wenttofinishingschool.*'

'What? Run that by me again.'

Siena groaned. They were going to drag this out, she could tell by the universal mirth that now lit their eyes.

'You heard.'

'No, surely not. Did you say you *went to finishing school*?' Al emphasised every last consonant, the little weasel.

'Finishing school?' Will actually looked quite impressed now. 'What do they finish?'

'Would finish me off,' declared Marcus shaking his head. 'Sounds awful. Don't you walk around with books on your head and that sort of stuff?'

174

Siena let out a gurgle of laughter. 'You're caught in some 1960s time warp, sweetie. These days it's all about playing the perfect supporting role. Training to be wife of a multi-millionaire businessman.' It had been fun at the time, being away from home with girls of her own age but when she said it aloud, it sounded as if it were still the 1960s. She'd never questioned it before. All her friends had gone.

'What,' Al's eyes widened and he dropped his voice, 'they give you training in that?' His eyes dipped to her crotch.

Will burst out laughing. Marcus rolled his eyes.

Siena sniggered and then couldn't hold it in. 'I d-didn't sign up for that class.'

Will held up hand. 'We're getting off track here. I can't even remember what we were saying.' He ran his eyes down his notebook. 'Food.'

'That's what I was trying to say.' With a stern look at Marcus, she said, 'We were taught how to look after different guests.' She glared at Al. 'Stop right now. Enough of the double entendres.' She pointed a finger at him. 'Make them feel comfortable.' Marcus kept his mouth shut but his eyes danced. 'By observing their cultural manners.'

'That's how you attract a millionaire husband?' asked Al disappointment echoing in his voice.

'Go on,' said Will, the only one who seemed to be taking this seriously.

'I'd suggest putting in Japanese flower arrangements, which would be a nice welcoming touch. In a lot of Japanese restaurants you are given a warm towel to clean your hands before you start. We could decorate the tables with folded origami cranes, which represent good fortune and longevity.'

'That sounds nice. I like it. Any ideas on food?'

'Traditional roast beef and Yorkshire pudding but with a twist. If you go to another country you want to try their traditional food but it would be a nice touch if it had a nod towards Japanese food.

Perhaps beef carpaccio styled like sushi. Use horseradish in the same way you add wasabi to things.'

Al leant forward. 'That's a genius idea. I could make a lovely teriyaki style gravy. Loving it.'

Will also looked very happy as he wrapped up the meeting and Siena got on with laying up tables for lunch, keeping an eye out for Hayley. Hopefully the other waitress wouldn't mind swapping a shift later in the week. Katie had come good on her promise to talk to her aunt. This time in three days she'd be at *the* London College of Fashion. Please God, let them like her portfolio. Butterflies jumped in her stomach at the thought of actually showing it to someone. All those drawings she'd poured her heart and soul into.

'Excuse me?'

Siena looked up at a smartly dressed gentleman.

'Sorry, good morning. Would you like a table?'

'Yes, please. For four.'

She showed him and his wife and the couple with them to a table.

'Here you go. Can I take your coats?' With professional ease, she had them seated with menus in no time at all. Funny how, it all seemed second nature now. 'Now we have some lovely specials on the board today, which I can talk you through.'

'Can't we order drinks first?' The woman had a sulky look on her face as if the restaurant was the last place on earth she wanted to be. Her three companions all looked a little wary.

Siena, aware of the tension, favoured the woman with her best smile. 'Of course you can. What would you like? I could get you a nice aperitif. A sherry. A gin and tonic. We have a fabulous selection of gin if you're interested.'

The woman's face lifted slightly. 'Do you know what? I could murder a G&T.'

'Me too,' piped up the other woman looking relieved.

Siena offered the drinks menu to each of the women.

176

Sulky lady frowned. 'I've never heard of half of these.'

Siena leaned forward and in a conspiratorial whisper said, 'Neither had I until I worked here.' She pointed to the list. 'That one's very nice.'

'Is it?' The woman's expression lightened, 'What about this one?'

'Ah, that's good too,' enthused Siena. 'To be honest, I don't know much about it,' she confided, 'but it tastes good. Goes particularly well with the Fever Tree tonic.'

'You've sold me. I'll have that one.' With a reserved smile that made Siena feel like she'd overcome a huge hurdle, she handed back her menu.

'It's all too confusing for me,' the other lady chipped good-naturedly. 'What do you recommend?'

Siena ran her finger down the list. 'That gin and the Fentimans tonic are my particular favourites,' said Siena.

'I'll have that, thank you.'

The first lady smiled. 'I think after the morning I've had, I need it. Sorry guys, for being grumpy.'

As Siena left to get their order, she saw the older man place his hand over hers.

'Nice work.' Will nodded as she waited for him to pour the drinks. 'You've turned into a real pro.' He waited a beat. 'Mind you, you've had training. Hostess training.'

As she took the tray of drinks, she gave him her best we-are-not-amused look and walked off to his laughter.

As it turned out, once they'd got their drinks, they were quite a jolly group.

There was a tiny minority of people who you couldn't please ever. Like the Colonel Plum type yesterday, who'd been determined to find fault with everything, despite his wife's equal determination to be delighted with everything. It must be so exhausting to be married to someone like that, who you had to constantly apologise and make up for.

Like a cloud passing over, she had an image of her and Yves in a restaurant. Two months ago. The wine had been corked. The steak overdone. The table too draughty.

'You alright?' asked Jason catching her pulling faces as he arrived to take her home. He'd taken to coming over to get her and they'd often have a quick drink with Will, Marcus and whoever else was working the shift, before they headed off.

'Fine,' she lied. 'Just thinking.'

'Ah, that explains it. You probably don't want to do much of that. Scare away the customers.'

'The customers love me,' she said putting a hand on her hip and posing like a pouting starlet.

'They do,' quipped Marcus coming to join them. 'My tips have never been so good.'

'Ready to go home?' asked Jason. 'Can I whip Cinderella away, Will? She's got my tea to cook.'

Will groaned. 'Please tell me you're not cooking for this oaf?'

'I open a mean tin of beans,' answered Siena, 'and Jason has to do the washing up.'

'You should see the state of the kitchen when she's finished, it's like Gordon Ramsay on speed has whipped through the place.'

'That's so mean Jason, I'm much better now.' She pouted.

'You are,' he winked at the others so hard it was a wonder he didn't dislocate his eyeball. 'Although it's all relative.'

She joined in the laughter and grabbed her coat. 'If I'm Cinders, you certainly aren't the handsome prince.' Although he had rescued her. Several times over.

'Before you go, Jason. We've had an enquiry on the website from that Chamber of Commerce programme. And that French company are really interested in a distribution deal.'

'Cheers, I'll have a look at it when I get home. Great news!'

Cupping her elbow, Jason ushered Siena out of the pub and into the tatty Land Rover.

'That's a bit of a result, a French company wanting to stock our beer.'

'Is it?'

'Siena, I don't wish to be rude to your home-country—'

'I'm English, I keep telling you.'

'You should know that the French have a pretty dim view of our food and drink. This is quite a compliment. And,' he punched the dashboard, 'being able to send them an email response in fluent French, was a bit of a blinder. Thanks for that.'

Siena did smile at that. She'd helped him compose the email last week. It did seem to be a point of pride that French people refused to believe that any foreigner could possibly do justice to their language.

'One day I am going to clean this car out,' she said as they drove along. For all her complaints, she'd become rather fond of this car; she liked being this high up on the journey home.

She could see horses in the field, five of them thoroughbreds, who usually congregated by the gate at this time of the day and marked the halfway point home. No sign of the idiotic pheasants in the opposite field which lead up to a copse of trees.

'Feel free.' He grinned at her.

'I think you're deliberately making it worse at the moment, so I will.'

'Who me?'

'Don't you give me that innocent look. There isn't an innocent bone in your body, Mister.'

'Hello? I'm lovely. Will's the wicked one.'

'At least he's not Captain Grumpy Pants in the morning.'

'Usually because he's rolled out of bed with some hot totty. Whereas I have to put up with Petunia Sunshine. And don't think I haven't noticed your Pollyanna act these last few mornings.'

'Don't know what you mean.' She looked out of the window with a smile. 'So what's the story with Will and Lisa?'

Jason gave her a sharp look. 'What do you know about that? Has Lisa said something?'

'Nothing explicit,' Siena lied. It wasn't for her to repeat what

Lisa has said about them sleeping together. 'Their body language was very interesting when we went to the wine bar that time.'

'You know as much as I do, then. She and Ben have been friends since school, along with Katie and Tom. Tom and Will are cousins. Did you know that?'

'No, they don't look anything like each other.'

'They used to come out to the pub all the time. And then Lisa stopped coming. I thought it because money was tight but ...' he shrugged. 'No one seems to know anything but overnight they seemed to hate each other's guts.'

'I got the impression she really doesn't like him.'

Jason raised his eyebrows. 'I got the impression she'd happily rip his balls off and feed them to the crocodiles, followed by every last bit of him.'

Siena smiled ruefully. There was certainly something between the two, but there was a thin line between love and hate.

Chapter 16

Emerging into the weak sunshine onto a busy Oxford Street, Siena felt like a mole coming out of a hole. The street was filled with shoppers loaded with carrier bags and from the teeming shops, fragments of carols and Christmas songs blared in quick bursts as she walked by.

Although it was only two o'clock there was a party atmosphere, lights flashed, stalls with Santa hats abounded on every corner and it felt as if the festivities had started already despite it being early December.

One day she might be doing this journey regularly. Train from Leighton Buzzard, a few stops to Euston. She tried to adjust her pace as she joined the stream of people but it was impossible to keep the skip out of her step. She loosened the pashmina wrapped around her neck. It already felt slightly warmer in London than out in the country.

The directions were imprinted on her brain, saved on her iPhone and written on a bit of paper but her feet carried her along. Slow down, plenty of time. Getting there too early would only ramp up the nerves, which were already threatening to spiral out of control. She'd babble. Talk nonsense.

The London College of Fashion. There it was. Bold black letters. Her future. With a clammy palm she hauled the black portfolio case higher under her shoulder, pulled back her shoulders and took a deep breath, conscious that her heart had tripped into overdrive. Just think, the likes of Jimmy Choo, Patrick Cox, Philip Treacy had all passed through these doors. God, she wished she'd got something new to wear. Would they notice the Stella McCartney was last autumn or the Max Mara coat several seasons old?

'Take a seat, Ms Williamson will be out soon.'

Siena sank into the hard green plastic chair which had seen better days and surreptitiously took a quick peek around. The grey lino floor surprised her and she still couldn't believe that the walls were all painted in a uniform pale grey green that stretched away down the long corridor. It looked like a municipal school. Then she told herself off for being so stupid. This was the administration area. Of course it wasn't going to be impressive. The studios and galleries, the workshops, the areas where students got down to real work were obviously on a different floor.

She crossed her legs. Uncrossed them. Picked up her portfolio. Put it down again. A couple of students walked down the corridor. As soon as they'd passed, she took a good look at what they were wearing. Jeans. One of them wore a huge baggy cardigan, actually it wore her, dropping below her knees and then there were all those weird coloured feathers woven into the hem.

They were fashion students? Not a designer item on either of them. Although to be fair, Siena guessed, like her, they were on a budget.

The chair became increasingly uncomfortable and the passing students more and more disappointing. Her growing disquiet about their fashion sense was tempered by the reassuring thought that she did know her stuff.

'Miss Browne-Martin? Come in.' A tall brunette woman, wreathed in a russet rainbow of scarves and wide legged palazzo pants appeared at one of the doors lining the corridor and Siena knew those sharp brown eyes had taken in every last centimetre of her.

With a loping stride, she took her seat behind the desk and sat down in one fluid movement.

'Take a seat.'

'Thank you.' Nerves erupted with the woman's brusque manner. She hadn't even offered to take Siena's hand.

'Thank you for coming today.' She glanced at the paper on the desk. 'You have a baccalaureate. No further qualifications. You would have to do our foundation course. As an overseas student you'd be liable for the full fees.'

'Oh, but I'm English and a resident here.'

The woman pursed her mouth. 'That's not down to me, to be honest. That would be admissions. However, I can see from your representation that you are passionate. What was the last exhibition you went to see?'

'Exhibition?' She'd attended every Paris, Milan and London Fashion week in the last three years, been to private viewings at Givenchy, Dior and Yves Saint Laurent and this woman wanted to know about exhibitions? 'What sort of exhibition?'

'Any sort.' The woman heaved a sigh. 'Art. Dance. Fashion. Food.'

Phew, not a trick question then. 'I saw the Paris and New York collection shows ...' She reeled off several more, everything she'd seen this year.

Ms Williamson nodded and continued to study the sheet of paper. 'Got a portfolio to show me?'

Siena lifted the black case and unzipped it with shaky fingers. No one had ever seen these sketches before. If she had children, which clearly she didn't, but if she did she was pretty sure this would feel like they were being offered up for sacrifice.

With a toss of her scarves, Ms Williamson, cleared a space on her desk and took the portfolio. A clock in the corner of the room ticked. It was all Siena could hear, apart from the unsticking of the plastic pages as they were peeled apart.

The time it took to turn each page felt as if it were branded on her soul. Siena worried at her lip, her stomach hollow as the woman flicked past the dresses she'd imagined, cowl necks, raglan sleeves, smart trouser suits with clean, asymmetric lines and jackets with detailed piping in jewel colours. How often had she fantasised about her own show? The vision was absolutely clear. Models with pacey, fierce strides, eating up the catwalk, the designs silhouetted with clever lighting, faces highlighted with striking make-up. The pulsing beat of the music. Every step, turn and pose choreographed in her head.

'Hmm, very interesting.' Ms Williamson closed the portfolio. 'You could do with a few lessons in basic drawing. Form. Proportion. But on the whole. Nice outfits.' Siena felt she was missing something. The woman nodded. 'Very nice. But I have to tell you. Competition to get in here is very fierce. You have to be very hungry.'

What the hell did that mean? Hungry? Was that the same as passionate? Determined?

'I suggest you have a few drawing lessons.'

'Right. And if I did that?' It wasn't what she'd wanted to hear. 'Would I get in?'

The woman looked at the portfolio and shrugged. 'Possibly, but as I said competition to get in here is extremely tough. We only take the very best. You need to immerse yourself in fashion.' She looked at Siena's top. 'Real fashion. Up and coming. Urban. Edgy. But there's absolutely nothing to stop you applying. I'm not on the admissions panel. They look at your results first. So I'm afraid you do need the qualifications.'

Siena nodded. Urban. Edgy. Real fashion. What the hell did any of that mean? But she could apply. That was positive.

'But thank you for coming to see me. It was very nice to meet you. I wish you luck in finding the right course for you.' She rose and held out her hand, leaving Siena no choice but to shake it back and scoop up her portfolio. Feeling wrong-footed and rushed, she stumbled out of the room back into the corridor, disorientated for a second as she tried to remember the way back to the stairs.

She had absolutely no idea how that had gone. The woman had hardly been encouraging but then she hadn't been totally discouraging. She'd said Siena's ideas were nice. She hadn't said they were awful or laughed. That had to be good, didn't it? Siena wrinkled her nose. They seemed to be more interested in qualifications rather than her ideas. A small part of her had hoped Ms Williamson would take one look at her drawings and love them the way Siena loved them.

As she reached the bottom step of the flight of stairs, her hand went to her neck. Damn, she'd left her pashmina in Ms Williamson's office. Turning back, she quickly mounted the stairs and headed back along the gloomy corridor. The door was ajar and she was about to knock when she heard Ms Williamson's low tones. Pausing, not wanting to interrupt she waited a moment.

'God, I kid you not. They were dreadful. Not an ounce of originality or creativity. Stultified middle class crap.' She laughed down the phone. 'Yup, you got it. Typical spoilt, indulged brat.' She slapped the desk hard laughing along with the person on the other end of the phone. 'Never bought anything but designer.' She cackled again. 'No, every last one was a bit of this and a bit of that. Christ it was like a Paris designer jigsaw, not an original idea in there.'

Siena froze, the hand clutching her portfolio cramping like a claw, the tendons standing proud. Pain seared through her chest. Was it possible to feel your heart shattering?

'And you should have seen her. You got it. Victoria Beckham's blonde twin sister, all cheekbones and snooty look-down-her-nose attitude.' More raucous laughter. 'Seriously, she wouldn't know fashion if it bit her on the arse. I had a bloody hard time keeping a straight face. Absolutely clueless. I did it as a favour for my niece. Had to be done. Thank God admissions deliver the bad news and not me … oh … shit.'

Ms Williamson looked up and her eyes met Siena's as the portfolio dropped to the floor with a sickening thud.

'Gotta go.' The woman sighed. 'You weren't meant to hear that.'

At least she maintained eye contact, Siena thought. 'I'd rather hear the truth.' After the first hot flash had raced through her, she felt calm. In control. 'Saves a lot of time later, don't you think?'

The woman nodded to the chair Siena had vacated barely ten minutes before.

'Look. The truth is, there are thousands of girls out there who want to be fashion designers.' She gave Siena a kinder look. 'I was harsh, but do you live and breathe fashion? Or just think you do?'

'I thought I did.'

'Going to the shows is great, but you don't see the inspiration or the origin of the ideas.' She stood up and pointed to a couple of pictures on the wall. 'Look at the Sahara, the sinuous shapes of the sand.'

Siena stood up and went up to the picture; it had life and shape. She could almost feel the sun on her skin as she looked at the rippling sand.

'Now look at this.'

The second picture was a model wearing a bizarre all in one type of playsuit, the sleeves and legs blouson, gathered at the ankle and wrist but with a slit running the length of each of the long lines. Silk fabric billowed and rippled in shades of gold, auburn and sand.

You could almost imagine a lizard running across the fabric, thought Siena with a start. She looked more closely at the design. Never in a million years would you wear it out of the house but the billowing shapes and the amazing print was an absolute work of art.

'Do you see this when you're at a show?' asked Ms Williamson as Siena lifted a finger to trace the ripping effect of the silk.

Siena shook her head and turned to face the other woman, a sense of sadness blooming in her chest.

'You're too far removed from it. That's the end of the line; you need to be at the start. Unravel the thread to the very beginning. In this case, the sand. I don't think you've been exposed to real life very much.'

Siena stiffened.

'You need to get out there, experience different things.' The woman talked with her hands, a very different person to the earlier version. 'I'm really sorry.' She did look genuine this time as she nibbled at her lip, a gesture all too familiar to Siena. 'What you showed me? Perfectly acceptable. Nice and perhaps ninety percent of women would happily wear those clothes you've drawn. But that's what you've drawn, clothes. Not designs. Not ideas. I can see little bits in what you've done but not enough to say with any conviction that you've got real design talent.'

Siena nodded and closed her eyes thinking of the hours she'd spent on all those dumb drawings.

'That's not what I'm looking for. It all seemed a bit safe and pedestrian. Personally I don't know if you've got what it takes. And you could spend a long time finding that out.'

Siena met her eyes and saw a touch of sympathy.

'I've seen too many people chasing the dream, with all the talent in the world and never getting anywhere. But,' she held up her hand, 'that's not to say I'm right.'

'I see.' Siena felt stiff and stupid. All she wanted to do was get out of there.

The woman exhaled. 'Look, why don't I show you round? Let you see what we do here.'

As Siena warmed to Ms Williamson on the tour, her ambition waned. Embarrassment burned in her stomach that she'd even dared to think that her, quite frankly, schoolgirl drawings were good enough. The standard of work that she saw was staggering, beautiful, frightening, shocking, weird and often quite unintelligible but all of it evoked emotion.

'So what do you think?' asked Ms Williamson as they came full circle and back to reception.

'I'm blown away. The passion. Energy,' she gave a mocking laugh 'and embarrassed. I loved it all but I'll never be a designer. Not out there enough.'

'No,' the older woman gave her an assessing look, 'but I like you. I am guilty of perhaps judging on appearance first. I didn't give you a fair chance. I'm not sure you have what it takes to be a designer, but clearly you have a genuine love for fashion. Design is my specialism. We do lots of other courses here related to careers in fashion. Have you thought about a related area, like fashion journalism or blogging? Let me speak to a couple of people. Here's my card. I'm Ruth by the way. Give me a ring.' She placed the square of card into Siena's hand. 'Nice coat by the way. Who's the designer?'

Siena smiled ruefully.

Jason had promised Siena he'd pick her up and had to get a move on when he got her text. With a bit of wild driving and at least three penalty points if he'd been caught, he made it to the station by the skin of his teeth, but to his surprise she was already there, sitting outside the station on a bench, huddled into her coat, lost in thought.

'Hey, sunshine. Want a lift?' He called through the window over the noise of the diesel engine. This car was starting to sound more and more like a tractor. Looking slightly dazed, she lifted her head and he saw the faraway expression clear as she registered it was him.

She hopped in beside him, her feet sinking into the rubbish without her usual huff of disapproval. One day he'd surprise her and clean out all this junk.

'You OK?' He looked down at her feet, frowning.

'Yeah, fine. Thanks for picking me up.'

'Sure?' Her feet rustled as she pushed aside a McDonald's bag without a murmur.

She nodded, her hands clutching the Prada bag in front of her, all prim and upright. Guarded. Something tugged at his gut.

'How did you get on? Did they think your designs were *fabulous darling*?' He gave a grin which faltered when he saw stark pain fill her eyes and he regretted not listening to his instincts and treading warily.

'No, they didn't. They thought they were a bit crap, actually.' She smiled dolefully and shrugged her shoulders despondently.

'Ouch, did they really say that?' No one would come out and say that. Surely. Was she exaggerating? Maybe they weren't as fulsome with their praise as she'd hoped.

'Yup, she really did say that. "Stultified middle class crap" to be precise.'

'Whoa!' He leaned over and laid a hand on her thigh. Her leg jittered beneath his touch. 'That's harsh.' How did you come back from that? He squeezed her thigh. 'I'm really sorry. That sucks.' He squeezed again. 'Really sucks.'

She sighed, gazing out of the window. 'It's better to know, I guess.' She seemed numb and disconnected, as if the sunshine had been drained away.

'Yeah, I agree with that, but there are ways.'

She turned and gave him a level stare. 'Doesn't matter now. I can stop wasting my time chasing rainbows. Do you mind if I open the window? I've got a bit of headache.'

Jason looked at her pale face. 'Come on, I'll take you for a drink.'

Chapter 17

They managed to get seats near the open fire and when he returned with their drinks, he found Siena with her hands stretched out, warming them up.

'This is nice. Thank you.'

'You OK?'

'Not really. I feel stupid.'

'Stupid?' he asked, sitting down placing his pint on the table and a half in front of her.

'Being so clueless. But,' her face lifted, 'the woman, Ruth, did say to call her back. You know when you're so fixed on one thing, you don't see other things.'

'I know that feeling. Now try your beer.'

'Do I have to?' she asked. He had to hand it to her. She bounced back quickly.

'Yes, it's your beer education.'

'Really? Do I need one?'

'Yes. I've had an idea.'

'Are you allowed to do that?' Signs of the back to normal Siena filtering through. The twinkle was back in her eyes. 'I thought Will was the brains of the operation.'

'Only when he's thinking with his pants on.' He took a long swallow from his pint. He had no idea what Will would say, given he'd only thought of it fifteen minutes ago. Scraping together the cost of a second flight probably wasn't the best use of the business account but fuck it. What was the point of running your own business if you didn't get the occasional perk? 'That contact from France. He wants a meeting.'

'That's brilliant.'

'In Paris.' Jason pulled a face.

'Paris is wonderful at this time of year.' Siena nudged him. 'You philistine. I could tell you all the best places. You'd love it.'

'Hmm not sure about that, but I could do with a guide and translator.'

He watched as a range of emotions ran across Siena's face. Initial excitement quickly doused by uncertainty.

'Do you really need a translator?'

'Yes,' Jason rubbed at the stubble on his chin. 'You should have seen me trying to translate that bloody email this morning using Google. Yes, I mean it.' Her face fell and he could see her reluctance. 'Too dangerous?'

'No, everyone's gone skiing. It would feel a bit strange, that's all.'

'Don't worry, I'm sure I could get by fine.' Jason reassured her. 'I can't really afford it anyway, to be honest, but it would be a great foothold in France for you. There's real interest in British beer over there at the moment.'

She suddenly straightened and began digging in her handbag. 'Voila!' She pulled out a credit card sized piece of plastic and waved it excitedly. 'You shall go to the ball, Cinders and Buttons will translate. Sorry, I'm being silly. There's absolutely no reason why I can't come and help you. *Ça alors*, you've done loads for me. I can do the flights.' She beamed at him. 'Pay you back for letting me stay.'

'You don't need to do that. It's a business expense.' He laid a hand over hers. She had even less money than he did.

'No, you don't understand. Air miles. Air France.' She laughed. 'I've got enough on here to circumnavigate the globe several times over. We can go business class.'

'We don't have to do that. It would be great to have a native speaker though.'

'And, ta dah! Marriott Rewards points. Accommodation too.'

'Cool. I'll speak to Will and we'll get online when we get home. Now try the beer. If you're going to be our new Head of Sales and Marketing, you're going to need to know what you're talking about.'

She grimaced and took a hesitant sip.

'What do you think? That's our session ale. Nice, light.'

'Mmm,' she said putting the glass down with one of her trademark dazzling smiles. 'Interesting.'

A man walking past them suddenly stumbled. Jason bit back a smile. Too busy gawping at Siena.

He studied her as she wrinkled her nose, in a gesture he knew was her preface to asking a big question. 'So how did you get into making beer? It seems like the sort of the thing old men do.' She tilted her head towards him, waiting for his answer.

Funny, he'd become so used to her being around, he'd forgotten how beautiful she was. He swallowed as his gaze travelled down the smooth golden skin of her throat as she tilted her head back. Not his type. He'd end up in the same situation as before.

'Funny, that's what one of my sisters said.'

'You've got a sister?' Her head snapped down and she turned to face him, her hands resting loosely on the table.

'I've got two. Why would that be such a surprise?' He sounded ridiculously defensive.

'I don't know, I had you pegged as an only child. You seem quite happy on your own. Actually no, maybe that's why you're always so grumpy,' she caught his eye, a dimple in her cheek deepening. 'Less grumpy these days.'

'I can't be grumpy, you're always on my case about it. And living on my own was easier for a while.' It had been what he'd needed to get his balance back. 'I'm not living on my own now, am I?'

'No and less grumpy,' she teased. 'See, I'm good for you.' The words hung in the air as the teasing expression died. Her eyes met his and tension shimmered between them.

He snapped his eyes away. There was no way he wanted to get cosy with her. Time for a change of subject. He crossed his legs and folded his arms.

'Will and I were at university together. We liked beer.' That was the short and simple story. His eyes clouded at the memories.

'Most men do, it seems.' At that moment, the girl-woman seemed all woman. 'They don't all go off and start a brewery.' Her voice softened and her eyes watched him, open but keen as if she'd caught his lingering sadness.

'We shared a house and started home-brewing.' He shuddered, the taste of that first pint still horribly imprinted. 'Ugh, the first batch, it was disgusting. Even as students we couldn't drink it.'

'Must have been bad, I heard students drank anything.'

'It was shite. Unfortunately we'd bought all the kit and were broke. Will insisted we had another go. That lot wasn't quite so bad.' He shook his head. 'Not great but almost drinkable. So we did another batch. To cut a long story short, eventually we got quite good. Played around with recipes, tweaking it. Started to sell it.' He looked around and put his finger on his lips. 'Totally illegal of course. You're supposed to pay duty on alcohol. Do the proper environmental health stuff. Not boil it up in a couple of old pressure cookers and hope for the best.'

'You mean that's not what you do now?'

'I won't tell Ben you said that. He spends hours cleaning and sterilising our equipment. We built up quite a reputation. Made some money. Always nice. Helped me pay my way through uni. Unfortunately, to do it properly needs a huge amount of investment. We had talked about it but then in our third year, Will's dad died.' His mouth crumpled, remembering that day.

'Poor Will, that must have been a terrible shock.'

Jason closed his eyes, ten years ago and it still hurt. 'A month later my dad died, too.' He let out a breath with a long exhale and looked away over to the other side of the canal. 'Tough times.'

Siena laid a hand over his and gave it a gentle squeeze. She left it there.

Her fingers were still slightly cold, their touch distracting. He stared at her neat, oval nails, the long index finger laid across his knuckles, fighting the urge to lace his fingers through hers.

'Will and I drank a lot of beer, wept, wrapped up our little operation and went out and got proper jobs.'

'What type of proper job?' asked Siena, softly.

'Merchant banking. I was quite good at it.'

He felt Siena pull back in surprise and it was a relief that she'd removed her hand before he did something stupid. She broke the moment perfectly.

She ducked her head under the table to look at his legs and then popped back up again, a pronounced and rather put out frown wrinkling her forehead.

'So those jeans are not surgically attached. Are you telling me that you once,' she gave a theatrical gasp, 'wore a suit?'

'Believe it or not, I owned several. Hugo Boss, actually.'

Siena seemed speechless, her mouth worked but nothing came out.

'They're in a box somewhere at my mum's.' He grinned, pleased he'd managed to surprise her.

'Merchant banker. Brewer. Not a short hop.'

He sobered. 'No. I worked in the city. Luckily I earned huge bonuses, as Dad's pension bombed. I had to help Mum and my sisters.' Those really had been tough times, although ironically had helped in the longer term. 'It meant I could only afford to buy a flat in an old mansion block in a duff part of London. The area went up in desirability. The flat escalated in value. A property developer made me an offer.'

'Handy. So it was meant to be.'

'Not exactly.' He stopped, swallowing. Acid swirled in the pit of his stomach. That familiar burning sensation. And he didn't even have his indigestion tablets with him. Might as well spill all. Show her what he was really like. 'I had a girlfriend, Stacey. She lived with me. She didn't want me to sell. Didn't want to move out to the country.'

Siena frowned. 'That seems a bit unfair on you.'

That wasn't what she supposed to say.

'Not really. I had a responsibility to her. Stacey. She— We— We'd been living together for three years. She lost her job and,' he stared off at the view outside the window, 'never got another one.' Not that she'd tried too hard but he'd been so busy working and by that stage was earning enough. With hindsight he should have pushed harder on that one. 'She was financially dependent on me. What could I do? So I stayed put for another year, but I couldn't hack it.' He closed his eyes and then looked Siena in the eye. 'I did the selfish bastard thing. I sold the flat and kicked her out.' And had hated himself ever since. He waited for her to withdraw her hand, instead she maintained her gaze.

'What happened to Stacey?'

He bowed his head, the churn of his stomach ramping up a notch.

'She moved back in with her parents. Took to sticking pins in voodoo dolls of me. She's never worked since. She's ill.'

'Ill?'

'Severe depression.' Acid swirled again. 'Because of me.'

Her hand crept onto his again. 'But what if you hadn't done it, set up the brewery? Wouldn't you have been depressed? You said you couldn't hack it.'

He'd not thought of it like that. 'I guess.'

'I'm sorry that she's not well,' Siena leaned over to him, 'but do you know what, I've learned something since I've been here, you can't be dependent on other people for your own happiness. You have to be happy with yourself. You have to be responsible for yourself.'

She meant well, but sunshine Siena had no idea of the depth of his guilt, or the realities of the real world. She'd be going home soon, back to her world insulated from the everyday problems of real life. A visit to Paris would probably speed up the process, make her realise what she was missing.

'So you used the money to set up the brewery?'

'What?' Was that it? No more on Stacey.

'The brewery. How did you set it up?'

'Will's family have owned the pub forever but it hadn't been doing well. Between us we set up a company which owns both the pub and the brewery. He took over the pub, gave me the premises. We bought the kit together with a loan from the bank, secured on the pub. All a bit scary but,' he tapped the table, 'touch wood. So far, so good.'

Every last penny he possessed rode on the success of both.

Siena frowned; that seem to bother her more than his revelations about what a bastard he was. 'I didn't know you owned the pub too.'

'The two operations are completely separate. I had absolutely nothing to do with Will hiring you. If you weren't any good, he wouldn't have kept you on.'

The mulish tilt to her jaw dropped. 'Hmm,' she said taking another sip of beer. 'This is growing on me.'

'Want another?' He laughed as she tried to find a diplomatic response. 'Wine?'

'Yes please. Red,' she responded with alacrity. He laughed and headed to the bar.

'What are you going to do?' asked Lisa. She had texted as Siena left the pub with Jason asking if she could pop round for an update on Siena's visit to London.

'Hand me another pin.' Siena looked critically at the black dress which lay the length of the kitchen table. Yes, if she put a dart in under the bust on both sides, the black dress would fit Lisa perfectly.

Lisa was having a wobble about wearing the pink dress to her Christmas do and had brought the black dress round for Siena to make one final alteration.

'I'm going to go back to the drawing board. Ruth said to look at some of their other courses. They do merchandising, fashion journalism. All sorts of things I'd never even considered.'

'Not going to give up then?' Lisa teased.

Siena looked up. 'No, I am not.'

'Good for you.'

'It might not happen next year or the year after but one day. I can't bear the thought of not doing anything. It's weird. I've never worked before in my life and now I have no idea what I used to do with my time all day.'

Lisa put her hands on her hips and gave her a mock glare. 'I'd swap places.'

'No you wouldn't.'

'Are you sure?'

'Positive. It's hard work being the idle rich.'

'I'd be willing to give it a go.' Lisa refilled their glasses with the last of the bottle of Prosecco, she'd brought around along with Nanna's sewing machine. 'Cheers.'

'Cheers. This is almost finished. Are you sure you don't want to wear the pink?'

'I do, but this looks better with my black shoes. Unless I strike lucky in a charity shop between now and next Saturday and find some pink shoes.'

'I know exactly where I can get you some. Trust me and don't ask any more questions. You will go to the ball in the pink dress.'

Siena handed the dress to Lisa to try on. She jumped up and peered through the doorway to where Jason poured over the laptop. Her heart lurched. She'd seen a very different side to him this evening in the pub. Kind and strong. Looking out for everyone else, putting them before himself. She thought he'd been more than fair with Stacey although he was obviously still beating himself up about it.

'How are you doing?' she asked softly.

'Almost there, thanks to you. It's very generous. I'm not sure how I can repay you. Business class flights. Five star hotel.' He looked bleak at the thought.

Typical Jason, she realised. Worrying about money but never for himself. When was the last time anyone had looked after him? She wanted to cross the room and smooth away the lines around his downturned mouth. The thought of raising her fingers to touch his mouth, set off a strange fluttering low in her belly.

'I'll have to pay you back somehow.'

She wrenched her gaze from his lower lip, trying to focus on what he was saying.

'What?'

'Pay you back.'

'You can make coffee in the mornings.' She held up the cafetière with a wink. 'And clean it out every day.'

'What proper coffee?'

She nodded and raised her eyebrows. 'Reneging on the deal already.'

'Never.'

'When do we fly?'

'Fly? Where are you two off to?' Lisa looked intrigued.

Siena jumped up and gave her a big hug.

'What?' Lisa glanced between the two of them. 'You're not going home are you?'

'No.'

Jason folded his arms, reminding her of Will as he leaned against the dresser, and grinned broadly. 'We're going to Paris.'

'The City of Lights,' she said at exactly the same moment as Lisa said, 'City of Love.'

Chapter 18

Travelling with Siena was a lesson in luxury and efficiency. At Heathrow's Terminal 4 there was no queue at the Business Class check-in.

The last flight he'd taken, from Luton to Zante had been a nightmare of delays, cramped seats and drunken passengers. Being in the business class lounge was definitely more like it.

'Would you mind grabbing me a glass of champagne?' asked Siena, giving the wine list a quick glance. 'Number three, please. I'm going to see if there's any chance of a manicure at the spa while we're here.'

Before he could answer she'd gone, leaving her Louis Vuitton cabin bag with him. Luckily he still had the good leather bag from his city days and the one Hugo Boss suit he hadn't stored in his mum's, so he didn't completely feel like Siena's county bumpkin cousin. The minute business was over he'd be back in his jeans.

He took a seat. He felt as if he were in a New York loft rather than an airport. With a disbelieving shake of his head, he picked up *The Times*, complimentary of course, and drank his coffee glancing idly at the pages and looking round every now and then.

Things had changed since he'd last travelled business class. What the hell was an Oxygen bar?

'What do you think?' She held out shiny red nails. 'Holiday Holly Berry.'

'Very nice.' They did actually look rather stylish, although he'd chew on glass before he'd admit that out loud to anyone.

'You're so English.' She teased and her eyes lit on the empty champagne glass.

'Sorry, I'll get you another. I was worried it might go flat.'

'A likely tale. Don't worry I'll go and get one. Want another?'

What the hell, it wasn't as if he got to do this every day. 'Don't mind if I do.'

She returned with two sparkling flutes of straw coloured wine.

'So what time's our meeting?' she asked taking a sip, holding the flute at the stem. It was a rather nice champagne.

'Nervous?'

'How did you know?' she asked. So much for trying to appear cool, calm and collected.

'Because that's about the ninth time you've asked.'

'It's at ten thirty. I know that. We should have plenty of time. I know that. The plane lands at eight thirty. I know that. I can't help it. I've never ever been to a business meeting before.' Siena's face fell, worried lines creasing her face and she flung out one hand in front of her, slopping champagne over her glass with the other. 'Do you think the nails are a bit frivolous? Too party girl. Shall I go and get a more neutral colour?'

'Siena. Calm down. It's fine.'

'Why did Will have to book another appointment?'

Jason patted her knee. 'Because it made sense to make the most of our time. We couldn't get a flight back on the same day anyway. I'd make the most of it. Think of it as a holiday. Over the next few weeks the pub is going to get really busy. Think of me. Totally at your mercy in Paris. I'm a bit apprehensive. Promise me there'll be no shops involved.'

He didn't trust the wicked smile that curved her lips or the mischievous expression heightened by the two dimples that appeared on her face.

'These *are* Parisian shops, darling,' she purred. 'Surely you need to do some Christmas shopping? I'm going to do some.' She'd decided to buy presents for Lisa, Will, Al and Marcus. And wrap them herself.

He let out a huff. 'If we have to do shops, you have to help me choose something for my mum and my sisters. I never know what to get them. I was hoping to avoid it all together by not going home for Christmas.'

'What will you do instead? You can't be on your own.' Although even in a house full of people you could still be on your own.

'I'll go to the pub. Will opens for drinks only, most of the village come and then when he's kicked everyone out, whoever's working sits down to a proper turkey dinner with all the trimmings and then we play Trivial Pursuit all afternoon.'

'That sounds fun.' The timetable for Christmas at the Chateau was driven by protocol and endless formal meals in the dining room. Not so fun. She was realising there was a lot more to Christmas … and a lot more to life.

On the flight Jason reverted to small boy mode, wanting to press the buttons, see what all the controls did and most of all try out the mechanism that turned the luxurious business class seats into proper beds.

'Stop it.' Siena giggled at this wide-eyed un-Jason-like enthusiasm.

'Go on. You could pretend you need a little nap.'

'But I don't and neither do you. We've only been up a few hours.'

'A power nap then. All good business people have power naps. Richard Branson, Donald Trump. Now that you're going to be a business woman.'

'I'm not in their league. Now behave.' She groaned as the air hostess approached.

'Can I help?' she asked indicating the call button above Jason's head, which had lit up.

201

'No, I'm sorry.' Siena glanced at Jason. 'He's got an obsessive compulsive disorder about buttons and switches.'

With a deadpan expression the air hostess nodded. 'We get that a lot. Although not normally on this particular flight. This is a replacement aircraft, usually used for intercontinental flights. You struck lucky today.' With barely a wink, she switched off the light and moved down the cabin.

In the cab, Siena took charge. It was nice to be the one who knew what she was doing for a change. Over the last couple of weeks with so many firsts, she'd made a fool of herself a gazillion, as Lisa would say, times. Their meeting with the distributor was off the Boulevard de Magenta in the 10th *arrondissement* near the Gare de l'Est, and she made it clear to the driver that she knew her way around.

'What's an *arrondissement*?' asked Jason, grabbing the armrest as the taxi pulled off like a stunt man in a Bond film.

'Paris is divided into twenty *arrondissement*. They're administrative municipalities. Number one is right in the centre of Paris on the Seine. From there, the remaining areas spiral out like a snail shell to circle the city.'

'Sounds confusing.'

'Not as confusing as London. It's quite logical and the street signs usually have a roman numeral to tell you which arrondissement it is. You always know where you are.'

'Christ. Is it always like this?' Jason inclined his head towards the traffic chaos outside the cab window.

'It's rush hour, although the *Périphérique* is always hell.'

The Lefoute et Fils' offices were on a busy tree-lined boulevard, its nearest neighbours a couple of opticians, a pharmacy and a men's clothing store. Siena had been down here a few times before but there was nothing memorable about it apart from the rather pretty Eglise Saint-Laurent across the way.

'There it is. Those big wooden doors.'

Jason paid the taxi driver and she got out, buttoning up her coat. Hopefully her faithful Stella McCartney top and Joseph trousers would look stylish enough, even if they weren't standard office wear.

She looked around with interest once they arrived at the first floor reception. The offices were typical of the grand apartments in this part of Paris with their high ceilings and huge arched wooden doors. Everything felt very formal as the young man at the desk took their names and in stilted English invited them to sit down.

Jason fiddled with his phone while they waited and suddenly gave an exclamation of disgust.

'Damn! I forgot to get my phone set up for roaming abroad. It doesn't work.'

'Don't worry.' Siena reassured him. 'Mine does. You can use it if you need to.'

'Thanks Miss Jet-set.' He nudged her with his knee, a teasing note in his voice. 'I bet it was like that from birth.'

'Don't be silly Jason.' She poked her tongue out at him. 'I didn't get my first phone until I was at least eighteen months old.'

Their shared laughter was cut short when, with a grand flourish, the double wooden doors to Monsieur Lefoute's office were opened and he invited them in. Her fears evaporated and she swallowed a giggle, immediately looking down at his feet to see if he wore spats. Short and portly, he carried the waxed Poirot-style moustache off, with a dash of old-fashioned villain. At any moment she expected him to start twirling the pocket watch and chain he had tucked in his waistcoat.

Siena sneaked a look at Jason. His expression had never been so grave and controlled. Then she caught sight of the way he'd sucked in that full lower lip of his, as if trying not to laugh.

'*Bonjour*, Monsieur Landon and Mademoiselle Browne-Martin. Welcome to Paris.'

The meeting had been going for thirty minutes and seemed to be progressing nicely, as far as she knew. Everyone was still nodding and smiling. Jason had been doing a lot of talking. Siena kept quiet; he didn't really need her. It appeared that Monsieur Lefoute, when he wanted, had a perfect command of English. They were close to finishing, with a clear agreement seeming to be on the table when the phone on the leather topped desk near the window rang.

'Excuse me, I must take this call.' He answered the phone and began a conversation in French. 'Gustave, thank you. Yes they're here now. I'll be tying him into an exclusive deal.' There was a pause. 'No, on the least favourable terms we can offer. He's English. He won't know that every distributor in France is looking for a rustic English brewer after that film star idiot started a trend for English beer.'

Lefoute rattled on in French, his back to them.

Siena leaned towards Jason and whispered quickly. 'Don't agree to anything today. Tell him you have another meeting with another distributor.' She nodded towards Lefoute with a quick frown.

Jason nodded without demur or query.

When Lefoute returned to the table, he beamed. 'Sorry about the interruption. I'm happy we have an agreement. It is our standard contract, which we have with all of our suppliers. The paperwork can be provided today. It can be signed before you leave Paris and we save lots of trouble with lawyers and signatures here and there.'

Without any prompting, Jason put his hands together in a considered pose. 'I do have several other meetings in Paris in the next two days. However, my legal representative and French colleague, Miss Browne-Martin, will be happy to read any documentation you have to hand.' Jason emphasised the French pronunciation of Martin.

His absolute faith sparked a small glow of gratitude.

'You are French?' Lefoute paled as he turned to Siena.

'*Oui*, Monsieur.' She maintained her grave expression.

'Apologies, I did not realise. You live in Paris?'

'Not at the moment. My family lives in Bresançon.'

'I have relatives there. Whereabouts?'

'Just outside. Le Chateau Descourts.'

The Frenchman paled even further. 'You are related to Monsieur Harvieu?'

'*Oui, il est mon beau-père.*'

Siena didn't think it was possible for him to get any paler.

'I missed quite a bit in translation back there,' said Jason as they sat in the back of a cab headed for their hotel.

'Lefoute was trying to tie you into an exclusive deal at the lowest possible terms when apparently English beer is suddenly all the rage and there are distributors who would bite your hand off for an authentic boutique British beer.'

'And the last bit?'

Damn, Jason was too astute for his own good.

'Exchanging small talk.'

Jason narrowed his eyes.

'His family comes from a small village near the town where my mother lives. Look there's the Eiffel Tower.'

They pulled up outside the five star hotel, the Arc de Triomphe clearly visible down the busy boulevard and climbed the stairs into the hotel lobby.

'This is nice, I've not been here before.' She nudged Jason as they crossed the marble tiled floor into an astonishing atrium lobby which was at least six storeys tall. A vast circular dome of glass high above them lit the airy room which, with its stone façades, made you feel as if you were outdoors, except for that distinctive hotel lobby hush.

A Christmas tree decorated with tiny golden lights dominated the centre of the room amid stylish sofas and contemporary armchairs upholstered in textured fabric of golds and greys. Each of the occasional tables dotted about was adorned with a simple arrangement of poinsettia and white lilies, matching the more elaborate displays interwoven with more fairy lights, flanking either side of the wooden bar on the left hand side of the room and the registration desk opposite. Siena sighed; the Christmas display was gorgeous but the lobby was not so dissimilar from any other five star hotel.

A grey suited member of the concierge team with practised efficiency scooped up their bags as soon as they'd been registered and led them across to the lift.

Once outside their neighbouring doors they agreed to a quick freshen up. 'And then I'm going to take you on a tour.'

'Do I get lunch?' asked Jason in a dry voice. 'I've got a feeling from the way you said it, that I'm going to need my stamina.'

'We'll start on the Champs-Élysées. Go through the Christmas Market. It's not the best one but it's fun and we can grab something at one of the food and drink stalls. Then we can walk and eat. We're only here for two days; we've got a lot of ground to cover.'

'No rugby and beer then.'

'Not today.' She grinned at him, his words sparking an idea.

'Then I'm going to take you on a whistle stop tour through the Place de la Concorde, the Tuileries, past the Louvre. Up Avenue de l'Opéra to Galeries Lafayette, my favourite shop in the whole world, and then take the metro to Abbesses, the *funiculaire* up to Sacré-Coeur and dinner in Montmartre. It's a bit touristy up there but,' she wasn't going to tell him what she had planned, 'it's worth it. How does that sound?'

She'd done her best to think of a route that would show Jason a glimpse of the best of Paris that he would enjoy and perhaps let himself relax for a change.

'Dead sexy. I could almost forget you are dull English waitress, Siena Browne-Martin.' He quirked a cheeky eyebrow at her. 'You could be some hot French chick the way you say all those place names.'

She playfully batted him on the arm. 'Or we could spend the day on the Rue Saint-Honoré.'

'I don't know what that is but I've got a horrible feeling I wouldn't like it.'

No, designer shops were definitely not his thing. 'Give me ten minutes to freshen up'

Under a brilliantly clear winter's day sky, the Champs-Élysées thronged with people and languages from all over the world. They kept getting separated until Jason grabbed her scarf, pulled her to him and threaded his arm through hers.

'Otherwise I'll lose you and I need my translator. I'm hungry.'

'I can tell, the grumpy face is back.'

With a quick tug on her arm he bared his teeth before laughing. 'Then feed me.'

The stalls were brimming with sweets and wooden gifts. Nothing Siena would buy but it was fun to watch the children, wide-eyed and excited, picking up little wooden boxes shaped like birdhouses

She guided him over to a stall where steam pumped from a little chimney on the sloping roof. Huge round pans sizzled and a cheerful blonde woman pushed around potatoes

'You have to try some *tartiflette*.'

'Smells good. I'm sold. Although, what's in it?'

'Potatoes, cheese, bacon, onions, cream. It's delicious.'

Jason gave a greedy moan. 'Sign me up now.'

In quick French she ordered two and winced at the tourist price but it was a good-sized portion and hopefully would keep Jason happy.

'You want some *vin chaud* too?'

'Don't think we've got enough hands,' said Jason as he took the polystyrene rectangle, his fork already digging into the steaming potatoes and pulling out strings of melted cheese. 'Later, maybe.'

Her stomach rumbled and she dug into hers. The hot creamy potato almost burnt her mouth.

'Mmmm.'

'S'good,' muttered Jason through a mouthful of food, waving

his plastic fork in appreciation. 'Delish.' He winked at her. 'Proper man food. I was worried it was going to be wall-to-wall snails and frogs' legs.'

'Not in winter. They go into hibernation.'

Jason looked incredulous for a moment. 'Seriously?'

She looked down at the pavement, her lips twitching.

With a suspicious narrowing of his eyes, he nudged her. 'You made that up, didn't you?'

With a smirk, she bit her lip trying not to laugh. 'It's most likely true.'

Strolling down the Avenue des Champs-Élysées, they soon came to the Place de la Concorde.

'This is all very grand,' said Jason pointing to the imposing buildings around the edge of the square.

'Come on.' She took his arm and guided him across a couple of busy roads to the fountain in the centre of the square.

'Wow, that's one hell of a fountain, or rather I bet it is in summer.' Jason leant on the parapet looking at the water full of chunks of ice before studying the black, green and gold statues in the centre, the golden fish clutched in the hands of a goddess rising up out of the water.

The sun highlighted the chestnut tones of Jason's thick dark hair and she stared for a moment. When he was relaxed like this, close-shaven and slightly windswept, he exuded health and masculinity. Manly. So different from Yves who in comparison seemed effete. She rubbed her fingers together. They had a mind of their own, itching to touch that strong jawline. He'd kissed her. Held her. And the stupid memory of that solid strength and those slow, gentle, languorous kisses wouldn't go away. Why did they have to pop up at inappropriate moments? Did he think about it? They'd never mentioned that evening since.

'Yes, it is,' she said looking away quickly as her pulse started misbehaving. 'Water comes up in jets out of the fish mouths. It's quite spectacular. Lovely on a hot day. The spray's quite refreshing.'

She turned and parked her bottom on the low parapet wall. Focus on the tour of Paris. 'Know much about French history?'

'A bit. The revolution. The guillotine. Marie Antoinette. Let them eat cake.'

'For a brief time, this was the Place de la Revolution, where the revolutionary government erected the guillotine. It would be full of people waiting to see the public executions. A spectator sport. Louis XVI, Marie Antoinette, Robespierre – they were all executed here.' She shivered. The spectre of the horror seemed so at odds with the exotic lushness of the fountain. 'Can you imagine waiting to be brought out, hearing the crowds baying outside? It must have been awful. History, it was brutal *non*? But we learn.'

'I'm not sure we do,' said Jason scanning the square in front of them. 'People repeat the same mistakes all the time.'

'That's very pessimistic. I like to think they at least think about doing things differently.'

'That's because you're the eternal optimist.'

'Are you really that much of a pessimist?'

He didn't answer.

With a sunny smile, she got up and led him on through the Tuileries gardens, their feet scrunching on the gravel paths.

'In summer it's lovely here. Although very bright. You need to wear sunglasses because of the reflection from the white.' She pointed to the stones underfoot.

It was too cold to linger for long, with a choppy wind coming off the Seine and she huddled deeper into her coat. Once again, without saying anything, Jason pulled her closer and together they walked arm in arm, picking up their pace to keep warm as they headed along Avenue de l'Opéra.

'I sense a shop coming on,' said Jason. 'You've perked up.'

'I have not,' she denied a bit too smoothly. Was he a mind reader or something?

'You have. You're walking quicker and you've got your girl-on-a-mission look on your face.'

'OK. I admit it's a shop, but it is special I promise.'

He groaned. 'What, better than Harrods?'

'I think so,' she said raising her eyebrows with a supercilious tilt and pretending to look down at her nose at him.

'Typical Frog,' he teased back, squeezing her arm.

'Monster Christmas,' said Siena translating the huge sign on top of the Galeries Lafayette building, for Jason's benefit.

'I think I might have got that,' muttered Jason dryly in her ear.

Pressing through the crowds, they came to the first Christmas window.

'Oh, isn't that so cute?' She peered over lots of well-wrapped up children in bobble hats and mittens, pointing and giggling as three pink monster princesses in tiaras and tutus twirled in the window obviously getting ready to go to a party. Everyone in the crowd laughed and smiled at the animated figures.

The longer they stood there the more hidden little details she spotted. 'Look,' she pointed at one of the monsters pinching one of the other's lipsticks. 'Aren't they fab?'

'Brilliant. Princezillas.' Jason laughed with her.

At the next window, Day-Glo one-eyed rabbit monsters in varying sizes popped out of assorted top hats, making children and adults, alike, laugh and wriggle with excitement. Jostled by the crowd, Jason slung an arm across her shoulders pulling her up alongside his solid body.

'It's like being in the middle of a very good-natured scrum,' he muttered into her ear, his breath warm on her cheek.

'Isn't it gorgeous?' she couldn't stop smiling. The monster theme seemed so irreverent and un-Christmassy in one way and yet so joyous and fun, it was appropriate in entirely another. Inviting adults to share the childlike joy of the ridiculous, in the same unself-conscious way that children enjoyed Christmas.

She felt bleak for a second. When was the last time she'd really enjoyed Christmas?

It took them nearly an hour to examine every window thoroughly but Jason seemed perfectly happy to wriggle through the crowds with her.

'The one-eyed bunnies were definitely my favourite,' said Siena.

'Not the pink ballerina monsters?'

'No, the bunnies. Come on.' She took his hand. 'You've got to see this.' She tugged, smiling up at him as he rolled his eyes. 'Time to see the tree now.'

'I take it from your hushed, reverent tone, that this is a *big* deal.'

'It's a Parisian institution.' She put her finger on her lips. 'This is the best tree in Paris. Every year the big shops vie with each other as to who has the best Christmas tree but Galeries has a huge advantage. You'll see when we get inside.'

Jason spotted the tears Siena was surreptitiously trying to blink away. He had to admit the inverted Christmas tree suspended from the Art Nouveau dome, several stories up was quite a spectacle. She sniffed again, her lip quivering.

Jason gave her a hug. 'You big softy.' With his thumb he swiped away a wayward tear. 'Although,' his eyes met hers, twinkling and teasing, 'I admit it is pretty amazing.'

He pulled her to him, so they stood side by side gazing up at the tree made entirely of lights. 'I can honestly say I've never seen anything like it.' His head tilted back as he took in the full spectacle and the glory of the balconies on each layer overlooking the central shopping hall.

'It always reminds me of an elaborate inside out wedding cake, with all the tiers. Sometimes I visit each floor to look down. I love all the wrought iron tracery on the balconies.'

Definitely a Siena place. This was rich kid paradise. The labels. Well-heeled shoppers. It was her to a 'T'.

'Galeries Lafayette is my favourite store in Paris. In the whole world. I come every Christmas to see the tree and the windows.'

Why didn't that surprise him? But he owed her. She had done

211

a great job this morning, the least he could do was humour her and the decorations were rather cute.

'Come on, I'll buy you a drink and you can sit and feast your eyes on this rather wonderful upside tree.'

The champagne was ridiculously expensive but you were probably paying for the view and he couldn't imagine Siena drinking anything else while here. They managed to snag seats looking out over the store, although it was difficult to look anywhere but the violet, orange, blue and white bejewelled lights of the tree. Talk about blinged up on speed. Not his taste but Siena seemed mesmerised by it.

'Cheers and thank you.' Jason chinked his glass with hers.

'Salut,' she tapped hers back. 'This is wonderful. I could spend all afternoon in here. Dior have got a new perfume and the new Michael Kors collection for spring has arrived. Oh, down there. In the men's department. Did you see? Grégory Fitoussi.'

'Who?'

'He's an actor. Very good-looking. I've seen him in English programmes.'

To his surprise, Siena was happy to leave after they'd finished their drinks. He'd half anticipated that she'd want to spend the whole afternoon in there.

It was quite relaxing to be in the hands of a native, especially on the Métro. The London Underground he got, but the Métro seemed even older and dirtier.

She told him they were getting off at Abbesses and he was glad to put his feet up for a few stops. When they came out of the station, dusk had fallen.

'Where are you taking me now?'

'On the funicular up to Montmartre.' He might have heard of the area but he only had a vague notion of where they were. Somewhere north. 'The artists' quarter?'

'That's right. Place du Tertre. There's another market up here. It's busy but nice. More French people come here. It's still touristy but different. There are lots and lots of cafés. I thought we'd eat here.'

'Thank God for that.'

'Do you ever think of anything but food?'

Jason's face fell, but he ought to be grown up and tell her. It wasn't as if it was anything to be ashamed of. 'I had an ulcer a while back. I need to make sure I eat regularly.' He scrunched up his face. 'And sensibly. I miss a damn good curry takeaway.'

'Hence the tablets I've seen you take.'

'It's much better. Only indigestion tablets now. They're few and far between.' Thankfully, he was off the heavy duty stuff.

Artists' work lined the square, on the pavements, on easels and pinned up on walls. Everything from contemporary, clever symbolic scenes of Paris, well executed watercolours of famous landmarks through to cutesy hideous depictions of stereotypical geranium festooned balconies populated by enormous-eyed children wearing black berets on display. He couldn't believe anyone bought the latter, although he had a vague memory of something very similar on his grandmother's wall in the seventies.

There was a definite buzz here. Earnest artists, young and old, hoping to emulate the famous painters who'd inhabited these streets a quarter of a century before. Although, as he recalled, a lot of them hadn't been that successful until after their deaths. Montmartre seemed more like a separate village, with its cobbled narrow streets and the abundance of cafés which looked as if they hadn't changed since the thirties. Lovers and couples wandering together, leisurely and unhurried. Siena had slowed her pace too, now that she'd got the razzle dazzle bit of the day out of the way. At one point he'd thought he might have to stop her leaning over the balcony in that mind-blowing store to touch the magical Christmas tree.

She reminded him of his nieces on Christmas Day. Manic and excited, rushing through everything in the morning, thrilled with the bright lights and presents before calming down to enjoy the traditions and the family element of the day with the long, drawn out lunch and time spent talking to the relatives. She also reminded him of the glow of Christmas, something he'd missed in the last couple of years. Last year had been miserable, battling with his stomach problems and trying to sort Stacey out before he'd realised she was beyond his help. Before that somehow they'd never managed to compromise on whose family they should visit, so they'd usually spent Christmas Day on their own with a feeble turkey crown for two and bung in the oven pre-prepared veg before going to their separate ways to respective family on Boxing Day.

Christmas wasn't far away and, based on past experience, he couldn't raise much enthusiasm.

'Earth to Jason. Look, what do you think of these for Lisa?' Siena was dancing in front of him holding up a set of Russian dolls. They'd been wandering around the Place du Tertre for an hour, with Siena darting from stall to stall like a golden firefly.

Her excitement was contagious but she didn't badger him. She left him to wander and size things up on his own. She smiled and skipped, here and there, keeping her counsel as if she didn't want to impose her relentlessly upbeat cheer on him. It was weirdly restful and rather endearing.

'I want to get her a little something, although I'm going to give her a big something as well but that's second-hand, so it's a bit of cheapskate present.'

'Nice.' If you liked that sort of thing.

'Stop being a grump. They're lovely.'

She was right, he was being a misery. 'Actually, I think my nieces would love them.'

'Now you have nieces?' Siena looked quite put out.

'I had nieces before.' His shoulders shook with silent laughter. Was not mentioning his nieces some sort of crime?

'You didn't say anything about them when you talked about getting your sisters' presents. So you need more than presents for your mum and sisters. What about brothers-in-law? Do you have those? I hadn't allowed for them.'

He had no idea what she was on about.

'Pish.' She thumped his arm. 'Christmas presents. I said I'd help you. Mums and sisters I can do. I have those.'

'I'm sure we'll manage but, to fill you in, I have two sisters. One of whom has a long term boyfriend. They're both legal eagles. Barrister and solicitor. They live together in Birmingham. She works for Aston Villa, the football club. My other sister is five years older and she's married with two daughters. Karla, who's nine and Amelia, who's seven.'

'So Russian dolls all round for Lisa and your nieces.'

It turned out Siena was quite particular about present buying, refusing to commit to any particular colour until he could make reliable guesses at his nieces' favourite colours or the colours of their bedrooms.

'Pink it is for Lisa, blue for Karla and purple for Amelia. And I've seen a lovely print for Marcus and Al. It's so them. They'll love it. A hat for Lisa's nan which matches her slippers perfectly.'

Why that was of any relevance he had no idea. Maybe it was a French thing.

'Now I need to find something for Will.'

'He won't be expecting anything from you.'

She looked horrified. 'That's not the point. I want to get him something. But it's got to be the right thing. It's easy to order something. Have it delivered. I want my presents to show I've put some thought in.'

That was all well and good when you had all the time in the world and nothing to do but shop all day.

He had to admit her final choice, a wooden wine stand, was very tasteful.

A successful day. She'd managed to get something for everyone. Things she was sure they'd like. Nanna was going to love that hat. She squirmed in her seat at the thought of Lisa, Marcus and Al

215

opening her presents. She couldn't wait to wrap them with the gorgeous paper she'd seen with Lisa in John Lewis and she'd buy ribbon and matching tags, making all her presents look beautiful.

Jason had been quite patient as she'd browsed but he'd started to get bored towards the end. Now replete after a meal of steak-frites polished off with red wine, he looked much happier.

Jason asked for the bill as Siena fidgeted on her chair. She'd wanted to share the bill but he'd insisted on paying for dinner. 'For services rendered.' He winked. 'As well as flights and hotel rooms.'

'Have you finished your coffee yet?' She'd already pulled on her coat. He was taking forever. She wanted to show him something. She hadn't managed to get him a present today. A bit tricky with him underfoot. This would be a memory for him.

'Where's the fire, hot pants?'

She tapped her foot under the table. At last he drained his cup. 'Ready?'

She'd been ready for ages. It was truly dark outside now.

'Come on,' she grabbed his hand and dragged him outside. It had become much busier and they had to slow down to weave through the crowded lanes. She knew the way and kept up her pace. They skirted the cathedral, dramatically up lit, the milky walls looking more like a fairy castle than a religious centre. She barely gave Jason chance to look up or take a second look.

Then she stopped and pushed him to the side of the lane up against the wall.

'Close your eyes,' she said.

'What are you planning to do with me?' His voice held a trace of amusement. She didn't put it past him to cheat.

'Take off your scarf.'

'It's not going to get kinky is it?'

'No,' she laughed, 'I don't trust you not to peek.'

She tied the scarf around his eyes and took his arm, guiding him through. People smiling at her, moving out of their way, so that when they approached the balustrade on the terrace a gap magically appeared.

With a flourish, she whipped the scarf off.

'Paris!'

Spread out below them the city shimmered with light. Together they stood there without saying a word. Like a golden sentinel standing guard, the Eiffel Tower dominated the distant skyline. He reached for her hand and squeezed it.

'I can see where it gets its name,' said Jason looking down at her.

'I love this view. It never gets old.' She smiled up at him. His eyes locked with hers and for a moment her breath caught in her throat. Her eyes fluttered closed.

'Thanks for a great day,' his voice sounded brusque. When she opened her eyes, he'd turned to look back out over the city.

She swallowed hard, battling to hide leaden disappointment.

She darted forward. '*Excusez-moi*?' She held out her phone. '*Est-ce que vous-pouvez prendre une photo*?'

The man obliged and she went back to stand next to Jason, he slung his arm around her and she squeezed in close to him.

'That's lovely, *merci*,' she said as the man handed back her phone. 'A nice memory of the day.'

'I've enjoyed it.' Jason nudged her. Matey and jolly. 'More than I thought I would.' He gave a small laugh. 'I expected you'd take me on a tour of all the designer shops and art galleries.'

'No,' she shook her head. 'There wasn't time today.'

Mustering her spirits, she added. 'But tomorrow's a whole other day. Our appointment's at nine fifteen and our flight's at six. There are a few hours of shopping time in between.'

He groaned. 'I thought I'd got off lightly.'

Chapter 19

'I do love a good breakfast,' said Jason as he set down the plate he'd piled high with croissant, cheese, ham and little packs of Nutella.

'So I see. How come at home,' she paused, Laurie's house did feel like home now.

'How come at home ... what?'

'You don't eat in the mornings. You drink coffee.'

'Because, sounds awful, I know but, I can scrounge something at the pub later. There's always something left over, so I feel I can justify it.'

He didn't need to justify it to her either but it was rather sweet that he did.

'Sleep well?'

She nodded, although sleep hadn't come quickly. She couldn't get that near miss of a kiss out of her head last night. When had grumpy Jason turned into this teasing man with a hidden sensitive side?

'So where are you taking me after our meeting?' asked Jason, as she gave a small sigh.

'We're going to Saint-Denis. It has a very nice mediaeval church there and an excellent museum of art and history.' She didn't actually say that they were going to visit them.

'Sounds fun.'

She hid a smile, watching him manfully try to summon up some enthusiasm as he swallowed down his coffee.

'I need to take a quick detour this morning. Before the meeting.' Toying with her napkin, she folded it into a neat square before changing her mind and pleating the white linen. 'It won't take long.' She rearranged the salt, pepper and toothpick holder in the centre of the table. 'Straight in and out, really.' She took a toothpick and ran her fingers up and down it. 'We'll need to leave half an hour earlier or,' she lifted her shoulders, 'I could meet you there?'

Jason leaned over and removed the toothpick from her fingers. 'It's not a problem. I'm ready to go whenever you are.'

From the hotel they turned left down the busy street, took a right, another left and another right. Less than five minutes after leaving the hotel, she stopped outside an elegant mansion block, its tall windows bordered by beautiful wrought iron balconies. Thankfully the street was empty but she took a quick look around in case.

'Come on.' She nodded her head towards the tall entrance door and ran lightly up the stone stairs. Punching in the code as quickly as she could, she hauled Jason through the front door and tapped quickly across the black and white tiled hallway to the internal staircase.

'Are we meeting a Russian spy or something?' Jason asked.

She ignored him, taking the shallow stairs two at a time without bothering to check that Jason kept up, her hand running lightly along the brass hand rail spiralling up the centre of the stairs which gleamed from years of tender care by the concierge and his family. She wanted to be in and out as quickly as possible.

'Where are we?' asked Jason when they came to an abrupt stop outside a glossily painted door.

'Shhh,' whispered Siena. The Amiens who lived in the apartment across the way didn't spend much time here but they could be in town for some Christmas shopping.

Finding her key, she unlocked the door and glancing down the empty hall with a sigh of relief, she pulled him in, quietly shutting the door. The burglar alarm flashed, which was a good sign; it meant no one was home. Tapping in the code, she silenced the beep.

'Should we be here?' asked Jason with a worried frown.

'Technically. Yes.' But in reality being here was horribly uncomfortable. She wanted to grab what she'd come for and go as quickly as possible.

She opened the first door on the right and peeped in even though she knew the place was empty.

The kitchen with its grey hi-gloss cabinets, dark granite worktops and hidden appliances felt ominously quiet. A whisper of unease prickled along her skin.

Jason stepped into the centre of the room and looked around, hands planted on his hips. 'Design by Darth Vader? The Death Star range? Installed by a team of storm troopers?'

'It is a bit grim isn't it? But it was the feature spread in *Homes & Interiors* when it was done, so it set a trend.' One her mother was inordinately proud of.

Without stopping to gauge his reaction to the high ceilinged salon, she cut through, coming onto a second corridor but behind her she could hear him muttering. Walking straight through the bedroom, she opened the doors to her dressing room and threw open the first set of doors.

Dropping to the floor, she cast her eye along the rows of shoeboxes. On the front of each was a digital print of the shoes inside. The boxes were arranged by colour, which made it easier as all the pink and red tones were at the far end.

'Bloody hell. What is this?' Jason's semi-horrified tones startled her but she'd found what she was looking for – the pink satin Dolce & Gabbana sandals she'd worn at her birthday ball on a boat on the Seine last year and a pair of unworn Yves Saint Laurent rose coloured leather peep toes.

'Can I ask? Are we breaking and entering? Or is it allowed under French law to wander around some Russian oligarch or oil rich sheikh's place?' asked Jason watching her pop both pairs, along with matching clutch bags, into a wheelie case she'd grabbed from the cupboard opposite. 'Are you stealing shoes?'

Ignoring him, she crossed to the chest behind him and rifled through to find a pair of thermal long johns and vest, some ski gloves and a hat.

'And ugly underwear?'

'I had no idea it was going to be so cold in England.'

'Quite.'

From the last wardrobe on the run, she pulled out a pair of snow boots and a pair of UGG boots and tossed both into the case.

'You certainly seem to know your way around.'

'All done.' With brisk efficiency, she zipped up the case and pulled it past Jason, back out to the front entrance.

'Come on,' she said, waiting impatiently by the alarm panel.

He looked completely bemused but followed nonetheless.

'Jason you can stop worrying. It's my stuff. This is the family apartment. Where we stay when we're in Paris. But I didn't feel we could stay here. Maman's cancelled my cards. It's a point of principle.' She tossed her hair over her shoulders and gave the black gloss door a final backward glance. Staying here would have been an admission of defeat.

'You're fucking kidding me.' He looked back over his shoulder.

'I think that's a done deal,' said Jason as they boarded the Métro at Invalides. Will would be pleased with the outcome. Selling beer to the French. Who'd have thought it?

'Much nicer people to deal with,' agreed Siena, settling her bag on her knees.

'Nicer everything. Offices. Coffee. Cake. Old Lefoute was too busy peering at us like we were a pair of slugs to offer us a drink yesterday, let alone take us out to a cake shop.'

'*Pâtisserie*,' corrected Siena. 'You can't call it a cake shop!'

'I'm not sure I'll need to eat again before we get on the plane.' He didn't normally have that much of a sweet tooth but the amazing gateaux and desserts on display had been too mouth-wateringly enticing to refuse. 'Are you sure we've got time to go to this church and museum place?' An afternoon in a café drinking coffee and watching the world go by sounded peachy to him.

'Where's your sense of adventure?' teased Siena.

That's when he realised she was up to something. She was about as interested in old churches as he was. Every now and then he caught a secretive smirk on her face.

Yesterday had been a surprise. He'd resigned himself to a lot of high end window shopping and a visit to a gallery or two but she'd gauged his preference for being outdoors perfectly. There was no way she'd inflict a church on him. What was she up to?

Twenty minutes later they arrived at Saint-Denis Porte de Paris Métro station and Siena got out her iPhone and sent a quick text.

'Any clues yet?' asked Jason.

'*Non.*' She shook her head, an impish look upon her face, dancing out of reach when he grabbed her, pretending to shake her. 'Patience is a virtue.'

'So is not being irritating.' She walked backwards for a minute facing him and poked out her tongue.

They were walking along a busy road in a not particularly attractive area and he was clueless until they rounded a corner and a huge stadium rose above them.

'Is that …' Words eluded him. Speechless. Genuinely. He didn't know what to say.

Siena beamed at him, her face lit up with delight at his surprise and her eyes wide with anticipation. 'Surprise. Stade de France. The home of French rugby. It was the best I could do. Unfortunately there isn't a match until the twenty-first, although Harry will be using the box that day. It's his birthday. Maman was a bit cross that she had to rearrange his birthday party for the twenty-third.'

She was babbling and he could tell it was nerves.

'I thought you might like a tour. I called Georges. He's the event manager who looks after the boxes. I told you Harry has one.'

Jason began to laugh. 'We have the whole of Paris at our feet; the Louvre, the Musée d'Orsay, Notre-Dame, the Eiffel Tower and you bring me here?' He grabbed the ends of her scarf and pulled her towards him, until her laughing face was within kissing distance.

A punch of longing seared, fast and sharp through him. With both hands he let go of her scarf as if the fabric had burned him. Shit, he'd nearly kissed her last night as well. What the hell was wrong with him? Keep it light. Keep it friendly.

He dropped a quick kiss on her nose.

'Thanks Siena.' He straightened, patting her shoulder, putting distance between them. Shit, that shook him up. 'What a brilliant idea. Really thoughtful. Fantastic.' Now he was the one babbling.

Bugger, she looked disappointed. He had to be more careful about keeping his distance. Truth was, he'd have happily snogged the living daylights out of her, but luckily the common sense fairy paid a visit in the nick of time. Kissing her came under the heading marked an extremely bad idea. He'd travelled down that road before.

'My pleasure.'

He hated himself for dimming the happiness that had radiated from her eyes seconds before. Her mouth pursed. 'Come on, we can't be late. Georges will have pulled out all the stops.'

Chapter 20

'I don't fucking believe it.'

Jason shook his head, speaking out loud to no one in particular. 'Welcome back and yes the trip to France went well, thanks very much for asking. Despite the fact we didn't get in until three this morning.'

Heavy snow had started to fall as they'd left the stadium, a cold front advancing from Siberia which meant their plane had been delayed and when they landed, the snow had already begun to fall in London.

Will was jumping around, his blond hair loose for a change, looking like a very unhappy and demented elf – a far cry from his usual reserved, Legolas self. Siena often thought he looked like the character from Lord of the Rings. Today had her wondering if a pack of orcs had rampaged through the pub and murdered every last customer.

'What's wrong?' asked Jason, totally ignoring Will's dancing histrionics. He strode past him into the pub, shaking the snow from his boots. The Land Rover had made short work of the snowy roads on the way back from Heathrow late last night and into the village this morning.

Siena followed more slowly, eying Will doubtfully. His feet were bare, an unbuttoned white shirt flapped open over jeans which he had yet to zip up. Her eyes hastily slid upwards. Someone went commando.

'Fucking, pissing, fucking power cut, thanks to the dump of snow overnight. How the hell am I supposed to run a pub with no power? The electricity board says it won't be back on until tomorrow. The whole sodding village is out.'

Jason whirled round. 'You're kidding? Phew, thank God we bottled yesterday.'

'Bully for you. I've got a wedding party in the barn in three hours. Fifty people expecting food. Booked for frigging months. The Elmsleys! They'll go ape.'

'You'll have to cancel,' said Jason, being a man and saying the most obvious thing. Much as she admired his calm, no nonsense attitude in the face of possible calamity, Siena nearly choked and for a minute wondered if Will might punch him. She stepped between them as Will danced over on the balls of his feet, his face dark with anger.

'Why don't we calm down and consider all the options?' she suggested.

'Why don't we, Miss Polly-fucking-Anna?' Will snarled, 'You think a positive mental attitude is going to solve this, do you?' He loomed over her. Like Yves. Siena froze, her feet welded to the floor, her heart in her mouth.

With incredible grace, Jason slid in front of her, grabbed Will's arm and gently pushed him back up to the wall with the implacable force of a bulldozer at full throttle. It defused any sense of violence and a breath eased out of her lungs.

The simple action almost floored her. Warmth rushed through her with a flash of heat, her mouth went dry as she stared at Jason's broad back, shielding her from Will.

'Don't,' he said with deadly calm.

Will blanched and read something in Jason's eyes. Siena saw the fight go out of him, like a hot air balloon deflating.

'Shit, sorry Siena. I'm really sorry. That was uncalled for.' Will stepped forward.

Jason whirled round, slapped a hand on his shoulder and pulled him back. His eyes blazed. 'Just keep your distance.'

It would have been easy for Siena to say. 'Don't worry, it's fine.' Accept his apology. But she'd been down that road before. Not this time.

She caught Jason's eyes dip to her stomach. Reflexively she rubbed at the faded bruise under her shirt.

In a voice that sounded considerably cooler than she felt, she said, 'Make sure it doesn't happen again.' She held Will's gaze, eyes boring into his. Shame filled his.

'I really am sorry. I ...'

She inclined her head. 'Now sit down and tell us what the problem is and we can think *sensibly*,' she emphasised every syllable and gave him a sharp look, 'about what we can do.'

He nodded, chastened. Jason still looked furious and she touched his arm to reassure him she was OK. With a questioning look, he laid his flat palm on her stomach.

The gentle, unexpected touch heated her skin through the cotton of her shirt, the sensation spiralling through her to make her breathless. Something in his stance, a wary unhappiness, made her rise to her toes and plant a gentle kiss on his pugnacious jawline.

Warmth exploded in the pit of her stomach and she saw his gaze soften.

'Go make beer.'

He raised his eyebrows.

'Do paperwork then.' She gave him a shove.

It was a measure of Will's docility that he didn't make a single comment on the exchange; her repressive gaze might have helped.

Inside her heart was beating a furious tattoo. Trying to pretend everything was completely normal, she spoke, horrified to realise that her voice squeaked slightly. 'Right. Are Al and Marcus here?'

'Yes, they're in the kitchen.' Will started to get agitated again. 'We can't even use the effing gas rings because they won't work without the electric fans. Bloody health and safety.'

'Go and get them.' She barked out the order, pleased to see Will obeyed without question.

Will slunk off to the kitchen and Siena arranged the bar stools into a semi-circle and hopped on the one nearest the bar to wait, rubbing her stomach absently. She felt warm all the way through, especially from the way Jason's eyes had widened and his breath hissed out when she sneaked that kiss in. She'd had about enough of his backing off. He'd kissed her quite happily that night until she'd told him about Yves and then in Paris, he'd chickened out one time too many.

Was it too early for a nip of gin? Twisting her mouth, she looked up at the rows of optics. It might calm Will down. That or Valium.

He returned with the other two, Al wringing his hands and Marcus silent but constantly rubbing at the lines on his forehead, as if trying to figure out what to do. He didn't know it, but he'd been recruited as her second.

'Sit.' Siena pointed to the bar stools she'd grouped. All three of them obediently plonked their bottoms down.

'Right,' she said, making it up as she went along. The demoralised trio in front of her needed to believe that everything was going to be fine. She could do this. They'd hosted a million parties at the Chateau and come up against every type of eventuality with Maman making her impossible demands and leaving it to Siena and Agnes to sort out how to achieve them. It would have been handy to have the calm, unflappable housekeeper here now.

'Al, what food have you got that doesn't have to be cooked? Or that needs to be used. Presumably we'll lose everything in the fridges and freezers as soon as we open them.'

'That's right,' he said gloomily. 'Although the meat I can leave in the freezer that should be OK. In the fridges we've got—' He reeled off a list.

'OK.' Siena ticked things off on her fingers. 'Ploughmans are still on the menu. So we can offer that to lunchtime customers.'

She turned to Will who looked morose as he played with a beer mat. He needed to pull himself together. 'You need to put a notice on the door explaining to customers we've had a power cut and are running a limited menu today. If they've got this far through the snow, they'll probably stay if we can offer something.'

'Yes, but what about the Elmsley wedding?' Will put his head in his hands. 'That's my biggest worry. Sorry Siena, I can't see how we're going to get round that.' His face crumpled as if he might cry any moment. 'It's their wedding reception. We can't cancel that. Fifty people. Coming straight here from the church.' They all stared out of the window, where they could see the church on the other side of the green. His fingers crawled all over his face, rubbing and worrying. 'I can't bear to let them down.'

'We're not going to cancel.'

Will shook his head despairingly. 'Seriously Siena, I don't think we can do this. I haven't even got the right tablecloths for the tables because we can't iron them.'

'Marcus, you need to go to Ikea. Jason can take you in the Land Rover. Buy loads of tea lights. Holders. Strings of lights. Battery operated to make the room look beautiful. Coloured napkins. Not patterned. See if you can buy any jars or small cheap vases that we can wire up and hang from beams. If in doubt, FaceTime me from the store.'

'Isn't there a whole load of stuff like that upstairs in the old flat?' suggested Al.

'You're right. We dumped all those banqueting rolls up there,' said Marcus. 'I'll have a quick shufty before I go to Ikea. Come up with me Siena.'

'Great, that's all bloody marvellous. But what about the food? They're expecting a three course meal.' She was pleased to see the bite of Will's sarcasm. There was some fight in him somewhere.

'And they'll get one.' She turned to Al. 'What were you—'

Will's phone rang and he pulled it from his jeans pocket.

'—planning for the meal?'

'Shit, it's them,' Will groaned.

He stared down at the screen as if it were a bomb he'd been invited to defuse. Siena took it from his frozen fingers.

'Good morning, The Salisbury Arms.' Deliberately she turned her back on Will. She couldn't maintain this calm façade and deal with him panicking.

'Hello, yes Mr Elmsley ... No, we've got everything under control ... Absolutely nothing to worry about ... We will accommodate you. Yes, slight change to the menu. Still Thai. I promise you will have a wonderful wedding reception. All you have to do is go and get married. Leave everything to us.'

She handed the phone back to Will, still wide-eyed with panic.

'You could have told him then. Warned him that they might have to make do with Ploughmans.'

She patted him on the arm. 'What and spoil their wedding? Right.' She rubbed her hands together. 'To work. We need Ben and Jason to be our runners. I'll call them in a minute. You, Will, go lay up the tables in the barn, get the fire going and stockpile plenty of wood so that we can get it warmed up. Al and I are going to do a spot of cooking without gas.'

'It's cooking with gas,' Al pointed out.

'Not today it's not.' She rolled up her sleeves.

Ducking her head under a beam, she took the string of lights Marcus handed her. 'This place is like Aladdin's cave.'

'It's full of rubbish. Everything gets dumped up here.' He picked up a plastic gnome.

'What's that for?' Siena took a step back.

'Left over from last year's Allotment Society Christmas do.'

'So did someone live up here once?' There was a fully equipped kitchen. 'The appliances all look new.'

'Me and Al lived up here when we first came out of London. The flat went with the job which was great, but we wanted to put a bit of distance between home and work and it's a bit quiet.'

Siena peered out of the dormer window out over the fields. 'It's lovely. Shame it's full of all this junk.'

'Ah! Have you seen the time? You need to go.'

The two of them, clutching their haul of tea lights, vases and candle holders, clattered hastily down the tiny wooden staircase which led back into the bar.

By eleven, she had the troops well and truly marshalled. She felt a bit like the fairy godmother in Cinderella, flinging orders at people with the gay abandon of a bibbity bobbity boo.

Humming, she lined up the ingredients for the Thai beef salad on the stainless steel prep tables. Al performed a sterling service, knives flashing with professional speed.

Marcus and Jason had returned from their trip to Ikea, a huge relief because even though Will had calmed down a lot, he still wasn't firing on all cylinders yet. There was still a lot to do. Even Jason and Ben had now been given kitchen porter duties.

'Ben, you're on carrot duty.'

'I've always wanted to be on carrot duty,' said Ben with a very straight face.

'Me too, love, me too,' said Al grinning.

Siena hid her face, clamping her lips shut to stop a laugh escaping. 'Peel this lot and hand them over to Al to chop.'

Jason appeared in the doorway and from the mischievous glint in his eye had caught onto the rapidly lowering tone of the conversation. 'Al's getting his chopper out is he?'

'You,' she gave him a stern look, hard when her heart suddenly decided to do a quick canter at the sight of him rolling up his shirtsleeves to reveal strong, capable forearms. What was the matter with her? She'd seen arms before. 'Peel cucumbers.'

'Very masterful. And what would you have me do with my cucumbers?' He waggled his eyebrows and she couldn't stop the gurgle of laughter that flowed. Who'd have thought that being at work, even on day like this could be so much fun? She hadn't laughed like this in … ever.

'Pass 'em over here, love,' piped up Al with a dirty laugh.

'Chop them finely,' Siena mimed a very decided chop, to winces all round and smirked. 'After that I need this coriander and mint de-stalked and finely chopped.'

The four of them worked in perfect tandem, the little production line bolstered by silly jokes and ridiculous innuendo. Her diaphragm ached with the constant laughter despite the looming deadline of one o'clock and the pressure to make this work.

With Marcus' arrival, after he'd unloaded all his goodies in the barn, Siena swapped with him to take over in the kitchen.

'Jason, Ben.' She beckoned a finger. 'I need you in the barn now.'

'And that's not a phrase you hear every day,' murmured Jason in her ear, as he brushed past her in the doorway of the kitchen. The almost brush of his lips sent a skitter down her spine.

The barn had already started to warm up; Will had got quite a blaze going in the huge fireplace. Apparently it was rarely lit because it threw out so much heat.

Mercifully he seemed to have got his mojo back and had picked up his pace, whizzing around the tables with Hayley, laying place settings and, aside from the napkins, they were almost done.

Giving Ben and Jason their orders, Siena left them to it and turned to show Hayley how to turn the jewel-coloured selection of napkins Marcus had bought, into crane-shaped decorations for the tables. Another valuable lesson she'd learned at finishing school, which made each napkin worth a good hundred pounds in her book.

As she moved from table to table, she couldn't resist looking up at Jason who'd been charged with climbing ladders to tap nails into the beams to string up the battery operated lights. With each stretch upward he revealed a taut stomach with dark hair arrowing down into his jeans. Her mouth went dry. She couldn't bring herself to leave, so hung around supervising the arrangement of the lanterns hastily made out the jars Marcus had rounded up.

By twelve thirty, the barn was done. Tea light holders lined every available level surface. In a move which earned him a huge hug, Ben had borrowed the Land Rover to nip home and had come back with three packs of battery operated fairy lights.

A row of barbecues, which had been requisitioned from everyone Will knew in the village, made up a make-shift kitchen in the courtyard to the left of the barn. Steam rose in great plumes into the cold winter air. Several joints of beef had been gently roasting in two kettle barbecues.

Chicken kebabs were lined up on trays ready to be cooked on a second string of barbecues.

Will had also turned into a human being again. Standing beside the row of barbecues with the whole team, wrapped in coats, scarves and hats, assembled with another twenty minutes to go, he apologised. 'Sorry guys. But there's a lot riding on this. Elmsley was my Dad's best friend. He lost his wife not long after Dad passed.'

Jason and Will exchanged a telling look and Jason clapped him on the back.

'He met Bev on holiday in Thailand eighteen months ago and they've been inseparable ever since. Today, I wanted it to be perfect for them.' He looked at his watch. The now married Elmsleys would be there in fifteen minutes.

Hence his panic over having to abandon the original menu of a fragrant tom yum prawn soup, Thai green chicken curry and a beef massaman curry to be served with jasmine rice and fried noodles.

Siena was pretty pleased with the alternative she and Al had come up with, utilising most of the ingredients, which was just as well because the freezers were likely to defrost overnight.

'Siena, you're amazing,' said Al, as he stirred a pan of coconut milk on top of one of the barbecues.

'I wouldn't say that until we're sure this is going to combine.' It was a cheat's satay sauce recipe that she was hoping would work. The coconut milk only need to be warmed and added to crunchy peanut butter and ground chillies.

'Even if it doesn't, the Thai beef salad is going to be a triumph. The chicken kebabs will be fine on their own and that prawn dish with chilled cucumber is divine.' He put up both hands and they high-fived each other. 'We rock.'

Will wandered by holding a plastic bucket half full of ice. Behind him, Ben carried a crate of champagne. 'Looking good Siena.'

'They're here,' called Hayley who was manning the bar in the pub. At her signal, Ben and Jason moved back inside the barn to start lighting all the tea lights. Marcus and Will had obviously begun to pop corks and pour champagne into flutes.

'You OK?' she asked Al, whipping off the apron which had been protecting her white shirt all morning.

'Yup.'

'Best go do my other job.' She smoothed down her skirt and scooted to the double doors at the front of the barn.

Jason was coming out, carrying the ladder.

'All done,' he winked and paused. 'You've got—' he made a gesture with his finger.

'What?'

'Stuff on your,' he wiped her lower lip with his index finger. Was it her imagination or wishful thinking that his touch lingered? 'I'll be right back.' He hoisted the ladder under his arm and whisked away around the corner.

Will stopped her at the door. 'Wait a minute. Close your eyes.'

'We haven't got time for this, they'll be here any second.'

'Tough, they'll have wait.'

She sighed and glared at him and Jason who'd returned and stood watching, his arms folded with a smile on his face.

'Close your eyes,' said Will.

Siena immediately looked at Jason. Will's words evoked that almost kiss in Montmartre. Jason looked back steadily, a brief flicker of something in his expression. So he hadn't been totally

233

unmoved that night.

Flanking her, the two men escorted her into the barn.

'Open.'

'Oh,' she gasped, feeling tears well up. Like a magical starlit world, tiny lights flickered and twinkled throughout the room making her heart swell with the simple romance of the clear white lights. The stately old wooden beams looked golden and the jewel colours of the napkins she'd taught Hayley and Marcus to fold into pretty flowers, made elaborate table decorations which transformed the traditional white settings into something exotic.

'It's …'

She turned to examine the trestle tables lining the wall. The huge platters of salads even covered in cling-film, looked beautiful and no one would ever know this was a make-shift menu which had been cobbled together using what was to hand.

'It's fucking amazing, that's what it is. You're a bloody genius. I was all set to cancel this morning.'

'Yeah,' growled Jason making it quite clear he had yet to forgive Will, 'that makes you an idiot doesn't it?'

Will nodded. 'You're not wrong there. Siena, you are utterly, utterly brilliant.' He pulled her towards him and gave her a huge hug followed by a kiss right on the lips.

She stepped back slightly surprised and saw him wink and incline his head ever so slightly towards Jason, who looked mightily pissed off.

'They're here.' Marcus came through the doors, moving straight to the tray of champagne. Jason melted away but not without a proprietary look her way. Will looked smug.

'Oh my!' The new Mrs Elmsley, clad in a cream shift dress, beamed and turned to the man at her side, who had to be her husband. 'This is stunning. Just like the beach café in Phuket.' Tears sparkled in her eyes as the two of them shared a long, telling look.

Marcus winked at Siena and mouthed, 'Job done.'

One by one the guests expressed their astonishment, as they

took their glass of champagne.

'Honestly I thought it would be cancelled.'

'Gorgeous isn't it.'

'So clever!'

As she stood there, watching the guests sipping their champagne and pointing at the roof, Siena realised she'd never felt prouder.

Chapter 21

The downside to going ahead without electricity was that there was no dishwasher, no reviving coffee and no lighting in the kitchen. Rows of tea lights and candles didn't make washing a hundred and fifty glasses, plates and cutlery any more appealing or romantic.

Siena looked around at the kitchen. She'd tried to stack everything neatly so that it didn't look too bad in there, but it was still pretty overwhelming.

'Leave it,' announced Will carrying through the last tray of plates. 'We'll catch up tomorrow when the leccy's back on. If the environmental health people come in, stuff it. You've done enough today.'

'Yup,' Jason swung through the door behind him with a crate of glasses. 'Time to go home, Cinders.'

Siena rolled her shoulders. Her body felt knackered but inside she felt a bit hyper.

As she left the pub, following Jason out to the Land Rover, Will stuffed an envelope in her pocket. 'You saved the day today. Well done.'

Half way to the car, bouncing along on her very sore feet, feeling like she'd conquered the world, she had a thought. 'Hang on, I'll be right back.'

When she came back to the car, Jason had started the engine

and was looking at her curiously.

'I can't stand this anymore,' she declared and began scooping all the rubbish out of the footwell in to a bin bag. 'If I'm sharing this car with you, this is going.'

'Blimey, you are the General today.'

'Yes,' she retorted, 'and when we get home, you can put all of this in the recycling.'

'Yes, boss.'

Happy that she'd laid claim to her seat, she chucked the bulging black sack in the back of the car.

'That feels much better.'

'Thank you.' Jason had the grace to look a bit shame-faced, she was pleased to see.

'Gosh, I feel like going dancing.' Siena stretched her arms.

'Dancing? I thought your feet would be killing you.'

'They are, but I feel like doing something.' Today had been one of the happiest of her life. She buzzed with the sense of achievement and satisfaction. It had been fun and she'd fitted. She belonged. She had friends. Real friends.

'I've never worked so hard in my life. You are a slave driver, woman.'

'Yes.' She grinned happily. 'I am.'

'You were bloody amazing today.'

Siena remembered the envelope Will had given her. Five ten pound notes fell out onto her lap.

'Wow. Will's given me fifty quid.'

'Good,' grunted Jason, 'he owes you. I nearly decked him this morning.'

'I noticed,' her voice turned husky at the memory, not of him defending her but the way he'd done it with such gentle firmness. Without violence. It said so much about him. Her heart flip-flopped.

'He was out of order.' Jason sounded defensive.

'He was panicking and you're over-reacting,' she leaned over and patted his thigh, 'but I appreciated the gesture.'

He laid his hand on hers, gentle again, it would have been easy to pull away but she didn't want to. 'I don't care whether he was panicking or not, no man should ever use his size or strength to intimidate a woman.

'However it was nice of him to give you a bonus. You must be rolling in it. What with the seven hundred and fifty pounds you made on eBay, you're rich.'

Tiredness made her speak without thinking. 'Oh, that's gone already, I gave it to Lisa's Nanna.'

'Sorry?'

She closed her eyes, wishing she hadn't said anything. She had a feeling Lisa's Nanna might be embarrassed if all and sundry knew her business.

'Siena?'

'Yes?'

'Let me get this straight.' He turned to her and then had to swerve as the car wandered towards the middle of the road. 'You sold your Prada handbag and gave the money to Lisa's gran?'

'Yes.' She wished she'd kept her mouth shut. 'So what?'

'Why?'

'Because she's eighty-seven, misses her garden and her next-door neighbour and doesn't have any hot water or heating because she can't afford to get her boiler fixed.'

Jason shook his head as if he still didn't understand.

'You sold your handbag to pay for boiler repairs for Lisa's Nanna who you've met how many times?'

Siena glared at him, his patient repetition starting to grate. 'Once, actually.'

He started to laugh, gentle sniggers rumbling out of his mouth.

She folded her arms and stared out of the window at the passing hedgerows.

His laughter had turned to full blown snorts. Why he would find that funny, she didn't know.

'S-seriously.' The car had slowed down as he tried to gain control of his increasing merriment. 'B-boiler. P-priceless.' He clutched his stomach, doubling over the steering wheel.

'I don't see what's so funny,' she said tightly, unaccountably tearful as he continued to wheeze and splutter, banging the steering wheel. A lump lodged in her throat.

'Siena?' She ignored him and hunched into her seat. 'Siena, I'm sorry,' his voice was still full of mirth as he twisted round. Like a gushing tap silenced, his amusement dried instantly.

The car swerved slightly as Jason pulled hard on the steering wheel and pulled over in a gateway, with an emergency stop.

Pulling off his seatbelt, he unclipped hers and jumped out of the car. Startled, she watched him cross in front of the car and wrench open the passenger door.

'Shit, I'm an idiot.'

'That's never been in doubt,' she snapped as he lifted her out of the car, cradling her to him. A flush of heat roared through her as he put her down, her body sliding down against him.

Lightly he threaded his fingers into her hair, cupping her head, his blue eyes intent.

'I wasn't laughing at you. I was laughing at me. For getting it so wrong. For being a prize dick. For underestimating you, again.' His hand slid to her chin and with a crooked smile, his eyes blazed with something that made her heart want to burst. 'You are amazing.'

'Yes, I bloody am and it's about time you realised it. And I'm not made of china either.' She wound a hand around his neck and pulled his head down. She'd had enough. Time to grasp life by the scruff of the neck and kiss it senseless, starting with Jason's mouth.

Who wanted delicate arms-length kisses, when you could have a full on snog that took yours and his breath away?

Taking charge of his lips, ranging hers over the mobile full mouth, she plundered, showing him what she wanted. Being protected in the face of danger was one thing, but she wanted to live.

Without a second invitation, Jason moulded his body to hers bringing her hips to his, nudging between her legs. They almost buckled and he turned them, still kissing her, to lean her against the five bar gate. Greedy for him and high on the passion that exploded like a nuclear bomb radiating out through every pore, she ran her hands down his thighs. Soft denim moulded taut muscles. She shivered and traced upwards to cup the bottom she'd eyed up so many times that afternoon. Standing in the circle of his arms, she explored as she savoured the relentless kiss. His tongue met hers and her pulse spiked. Dear God, she felt so hot. Bothered. Shaky.

She wanted more; the touch of skin on skin. Burrowing under his jacket, she teased his T-shirt upwards with determined purpose. Driven by the power of what she was doing to him. Her hands brushed hair roughened abs. Liquid heat pooled between her legs and she stroked upwards, tracing his rib cage.

He shuddered beneath her touch and pulled away from her mouth to nuzzle along her neckline, nipping under her chin, the tender patch under her ear lobe. It made her squirm, lust coiling hot and dark in her belly.

His hands slid down her back to cup her bottom and urge her up against him, against the erection bulging at his flies. Huskily, he breathed her name as her hands stroked down his back, slipping beneath his jeans. Intoxicated by the touch of warm skin, the desire in his heated kisses, she let instinct take over. Want and need pushed her. When his hand slid into her shirt and pushed into her bra, she moaned. The spark of heat darted straight to her groin and she ground against him, urging him on.

Hot and hungry, she pulled at the button on his jeans, fumbled with the zip and plunged her hands into the jersey fabric to release him.

'Fuck, Siena,' groaned Jason, breathing heavily.

Nuzzling kisses into his neck, she explored the smooth, heavy length of him, heady with the power of his laboured breaths.

'Yes please.'

He jerked his head back in amazement and she gave him a wicked grin. 'Oh my, this feels good.'

'Fuck,' he groaned.

'You said that before,' she teased. His ragged breaths were turning her inside out. 'Jeez … Siena … oh …'

His lips crushed hers, his tongue delving in to duel with hers, inviting her to fight back. He led but he didn't take control, letting her find her way. The power was utterly intoxicating.

Thrusting her body towards him, wanton and inviting, she urged him on. The ache between her legs had heated to an unbearable level. Impatience gave way to the sharp sweet ache. She writhed against him. She heard herself squeak. 'Please. Oh please.'

The bastard laughed.

 Looking up into his face, she half smiled but it was hard when the only thing her mind could possibly focus on was the heat building inside her. In fact it was hard to think of anything. It was like being in a race she couldn't see the end of, but knew she needed to get to. Desperate to take control and speed him up, her hold on him firmed. Sweat broke out on his brow, his face screwed up with intense concentration. He leaned his forehead against hers.

'You're … killing me.'

Her mouth curved in satisfaction.

'Good,' she whispered as she gave another deliberate slide up and down, he bucked slightly in her hand, trying to resist the pace. He stifled a groan but pulled back to give her a wicked smile.

'Good?' Her heart jumped at the intent in his eyes.

His had slid up her thigh in slow teasing circles. 'Good?' he repeated.

She caught her breath, frozen with anticipation.

He spun out the moment.

'Siena, stop.' He tried to slow her down but she kept up the relentless pace. 'Christ, if you don't stop I'm going to come.'

As if by mirroring her actions he hoped to stop her, his fingers stilled.

'No, don't please.' Her breath ragged, she turned pleading eyes up to him. 'I want this.'

'We're in full view. There's bloody snow on the ground.'

'Have you got anything?'

His eyes widened. 'Condom?'

'Yes.' Impatience made her fierce.

'Are you sure?'

'Oh for fuck's sake, a woman could die here.' Her face sobered. If she didn't give in to this burning need right now, she might never feel this wild abandon again.

'Not this woman, not on my watch.' He pulled out his wallet and shook it, dislodging a packet onto the palm of his hand.

She pushed open the gate and kissed him, pushing him into the field, out of sight of the road to a tree. Snow trickled out of its branches as she pulled him with her to lean against the trunk. It caught in her eyelashes making her giggle.

'You're mad.' He stroked her face with his thumbs, unable to tear his gaze from her face. She radiated life and joy.

'Please Jason.' Wanton and fierce, her expression was so intent. Condom on, he hardly drew breath before she'd tugged him to the ground. They sank into the snow but it didn't seem to bother her. Her hands raced over him, exploring his balls, pushing into his jeans to stroke his thighs. Her excited sighs and the wicked smile on her face turned him on so much that despite this being utterly crazy, he had to have her.

Never had a woman beneath him been so decided, so sure, so hell bent on having her way. This earthiness was a hell of a surprise and if she'd been shy or unsure, he would have reined back, had some common sense. Caught in the moment, her eyes dancing with delight and desire by turn, he sank down onto her and guided himself into the hot tight wetness.

Sensation exploded as he slid home. Her eyes grew round and locked on his, widened with wonder and her mouth curved with sudden joy.

Tucking an arm around her, he pulled her to him, with a fierce ache of possession, watching every expression on her face, feeling the spiralling sensation of fullness and desperation peak.

Her breath came in shallow pants, her eyes desperate with unspoken entreaty. Unable to stop himself and so lost in her wonder, he drove the pace, feeling her hips rise up to meet him. He couldn't, couldn't …

With a breathy sigh, she clenched around him. Her hands fluttering at his back. With one last plunge, he let go, sinking into her, coming with a force that made him shudder.

Lying, spent, on top of her, he buried his head in her neck. She still smelt of perfume.

'Jason.'

He tensed. Her voice sounded worried. Damn, he should have slowed down, but he'd been so caught up in the moment.

He lifted his head. Her eyes danced with merriment. A kitten that had well and truly had its cream and eaten it.

'You OK?' he asked.

'I'm fine, but,' she giggled, 'I think we might have shocked the horses.'

Chapter 22

Still high and soaked through, they raced for the door and juggled their keys.

'I can't believe we did that,' giggled Siena. 'Although, I think there might be something horrid in my hair.'

'Ugh, you might be right,' said Jason taking a peek at her dishevelled plait. 'I'm not sure my extremities will ever be the same again.'

She pulled at the edges of his very wet denim jacket and drew him down for another searing kiss. She didn't seem to be able to keep her hands off him and her skin tingled everywhere. 'You weren't complaining half an hour ago,' she teased.

'Not complaining now,' he said, his lips sliding over hers, 'although there is a bit of a pong. I wonder if we shouldn't get you into the shower.'

The idea set light to nerve endings and without further ado, she pushed the jacket from his shoulders letting it drop the floor.

'I'm feeling quite dirty. No, very dirty.'

'Nothing for it then.' With sure, deft fingers he began to unbutton her shirt, not a difficult task as only about three of them were still done up and even then not in the correct buttonholes.

Backing up the stairs, she tugged at his T-shirt. Half way up the stairs he managed to pull off her shirt.

'You're better at this than me.'

'Easier access,' he said with a triumphant grin as he unhooked her bra strap.

They paused at the halfway mark for another fumbled kiss as she fought with his zip and tugged down her skirt which pooled and slithered away down the stairs.

She swallowed hard as he took another step up, her eyes level with his bare chest. Dark hair spread down his sternum. Talk about gorgeous. She turned and raced up the last few steps.

Jason had the foresight to switch on the shower. Stripping off quickly, she laughed at him as he pulled off his sodden jeans one-handed and hopped about barefoot.

Clothes flew, pants, tights and then somehow they were in the shower, naked body to body, chest to chest, kissing under the flow of water.

Jason undid her plait and, while she reached up to wash her hair, took advantage and from behind thoroughly soaped her breasts while rubbing his erection up against her bottom.

Tumbling out of the shower, grabbing towels as they went, Jason pulled her out onto the landing.

'Your room or mine?'

'Don't ask difficult questions,' grumbled Siena, missing the warmth of his mouth on hers. 'I'm done with decision making today.' And if he slowed down, it would let memories crawl through her defences. Bedrooms and beds. Dark, heartless fumbling. Dry, forceful couplings.

Hooking her arm around his neck, she stroked the nape, pressing kisses down his chest.

'I'm going to hold you to that.' Tugging her hand, he pulled her to his room, clumsily barging the door, sending it flying with a loud crash and rattle. Stumbling, gloriously uninhibited, they fell through the door as he propelled her towards his bed. She felt soft cotton behind her knees as he pushed her down onto the bed, to join her naked, full-length skin to skin.

Panting and laughing, she looked up at him.

'I'm all wet.'

'I should think so too, otherwise I'm not doing my job properly.'

'My hair, you idiot. The pillows …'

'Will dry. Besides, I know where there's another bed.'

He dipped his head and returned to the serious business of kissing her, which she had no intention of complaining about.

In the aftermath, tucked under the duvet, legs entwined, she idly stroked Jason's chest, wondering at how comfortable she felt touching him.

'I'd never have done this with Yves,' she said. 'I know I'm not supposed to talk about another man straight after sex.' Sated and warm, the earlier buzz and restlessness of the day had died down to a low level hum and she was horribly aware that normality had to impinge at some point.

'So why are you?' asked Jason. The hug accompanying his sleepy words robbed them of any dissension.

'Because you know what happened before, but you didn't make allowances. You let me be me.' She plonked a heartfelt kiss on his cheek. 'It's never been like that. Fun, happy. Orgasmic.'

With a rueful smile, he said, 'By accident rather than by design, not the latter of course, because I am a highly skilled …' his words petered out into sniggers. He hesitated and she saw the vacillation in his eyes.

'What?' she asked.

'To be honest,' he paused and shook his head, 'you didn't give me much choice.' He sighed. 'I mean, one minute I was innocently trying to be nice, the next you'd vacuumed yourself to my lips and had your hand down my pants.'

'You!' she punched his arm, giggling at his pitiful attempt to look put upon.

He rolled on top of her, his chest rumbling with mirth, his hands stroking her bottom. 'Siena, I've never been so bloody

turned on in my life. Couldn't think straight. That is the best
…' he stumbled over the word, 'it's ever been.'

'Sex, you mean.' Her hands roaming over his back in wonderment that she was here in bed with this gorgeous man.

'Yes, er ahem, sex.' He cleared his throat and squinted down at her.

She beamed at him. 'It was amazing. Wasn't it? It's never been like that before for me. Has it for you?' She didn't regret for a moment the last few glorious, sexually wild hours. Feeling enormously liberated, now she knew what it was all about, she felt slightly aggrieved that she'd been cheated for so long.

Jason sighed. His discomfiture amused her. She didn't think he was uncomfortable with her questions but there was certainly something.

His eyes turned serious. 'Siena, it was more than amazing. You've turned everything on its head. I spent all that time in Paris trying to keep my distance. It nearly bloody killed me. And the trip to the Stade.' He shook his head and stroked his hand down her cheekbone to cup her chin, a tender smile on his face. 'Every time I think I've got you sussed, you show another side. I thought I had you pegged,' he closed his mouth with diplomatic inference but she knew exactly what he thought of her.

'Spoilt, rich, lazy, clueless, naïve, dumb,' she finished for him.

'That's a bit harsh. I never thought you were dumb.'

She planted her elbow in his ribs.

'Oof,' he grabbed her arm and began to tickle her.

'No, no,' she tried to push him away but the more she did, the more he tickled.

After five more sweaty minutes of tussles, wrestling and kisses, he finally pinned her to the bed, his long body pressed into the length of her. The feeling made her heart sing, and she wriggled sinuously and teasingly beneath him.

'Enough, woman. I can't take any more.' He kissed her nose. 'I should have known after today's performance in the pub that you'd be a demanding woman. You are in the wrong job. You could run the country. But I need to keep my strength up. I need sustenance.'

'Really?' Pretending to be disappointed she rubbed an idle hand across his chest, but even that was half-hearted. Tiredness had started to seep its way into her limbs.

'Down, woman.' He caught her hand and then brought it to his mouth peppering it with little kisses. 'I'm hungry.'

'Me too,' she purred.

'Enough. Behave.'

She grinned at him as he got out of bed and pulled on his robe.

'I need my robe.'

'I am not getting you that thing. I'll never concentrate.'

'I don't know what you mean.'

'Here,' he tossed her a shirt from his wardrobe. A soft blue chambray that she'd seen him wear a couple of times and noted because it brought out the blue in his eyes. 'Kitchen, woman.' She sashayed down the hall in front of him.

'And for God's sake, go put some pants on. I'm having trouble thinking straight here.'

Feeling all the power of a siren, she turned, flicking her semi-dried hair and looked over her shoulder and gave him a long slow sultry look. 'And there's a problem with that?'

He swatted her bottom and pushed her towards her bedroom door. 'Knickers. Now.'

'Oh my,' she paused in the doorway of the lounge, 'you've opened the other bottle of wine.'

Jason shrugged. 'Thought we deserved it after today.' A wicked light danced in his eyes. 'I'm sure Laurie won't mind.'

At the price of that bottle Laurie probably would, but Siena didn't care. Life was to be lived, wine to be drunk and there were too many bad things to be got through not to enjoy the good. One day she'd pay her back, although at this rate not at until she was thirty.

Jason handed her a glass of the rich ruby wine and sat down on the sofa, patting the seat next to him.

'You OK?'

'Yes, it's been quite a day.' She took a thoughtful sip as she sank down, nestling into the arm he'd put around her.

He touched his wine glass to hers. 'It has that. Regrets?'

'None, but if you,' she gestured around the room, 'you want to stop, it's OK. I mean I know you didn't plan on me staying here.'

Drinking his wine, he didn't say a word but she felt the tiniest tensing of a muscle in his arm.

'I can see that you might, we might, I might, what is it? We live in the same house. But sharing a bed doesn't make it living together. And if we were a couple not living together then we wouldn't share a bed every night or, of course, you might not want to share a bed again.'

Holding up a hand, he halted her flow.

'To be honest, the bed thing is definitely preferable. My field-with-horses-watching-days are over.'

She waited a second, hoping he might carry on, help her out here but he leaned back into the sofa, an ambivalent look on his face. Was he doing it deliberately?

'Right.' Heat seared her face, probably the same colour as the wine. She held the glass against her cheek to try and cool it down. This was turning out to be much harder than she thought. It had seemed so straightforward five minutes earlier when she'd been retrieving a clean pair of silk knickers from her drawer.

'So what were you saying?' he asked it as if he were asking after her health.

Gritting her teeth, she tried to phrase it better.

'It's … sort of … it might … you might not …' The more she tried to put it into words, the more they became mangled and useless.

'Siena.' He laid a finger on her lips. 'We can sleep in whichever

249

bed you want, whenever you want, alone or together. We share a house, that's inescapable. I'm attracted to you. You're attracted to me. We didn't plan this but we're grown adults, admittedly with a few side issues going on. You've got to sort things out with Yves and you know my main focus for the foreseeable future is getting the brewery into the black. You're only here for another two weeks. Anything could happen. Why don't we take each day as it comes? No promises.'

'OK.' She smiled.

Sometimes life was that simple. Tucked in the crook of his arm drinking one of the best wines in the world, Siena decided that it didn't get much better than this.

Chapter 23

'Sorry sir, can you repeat that?'

Working behind the bar and taking food orders wasn't as good as being in the restaurant where she could build up a bit of a rapport with the customers, but the bar area was busy today and the restaurant quieter.

'Whitaker?' The man spat the name out so quickly and in such a strong accent, he sounded like a part in an engine. Widddderrrrkerrr. No matter how hard she listened, she still couldn't get it and it was the third time he'd answered.

'Right,' her pleasant smile didn't soothe him, 'and which table?'

'Table six.' He spat and stomped off back to the table. 'Jesus the staff here, half-wits.'

'What?' she said beneath her breath. 'I don't know what his problem was.' Will with his back to her, shook visibly and Al sniggered into the palm of his hand.

'What?' she demanded as Jason sauntered up to the bar. He'd taken to coming in at lunchtimes to have his lunch.

'Did you see who that was?' Jason asked them all.

Will and Al nodded still acting like idiots and then Will said through wheezes, 'Yes, b-but Siena. Sh-she asked him. Three times what h-his n-name was.' He put his head on Al's shoulder and the two of them howled with laughter.

She scowled and looked back across the bar at the grouchy middle-aged man. He didn't look the least bit like a famous person. Scruffy. Cheap shoes.

Jason winced. 'He's John Whitaker, he was a big TV presenter for many years.'

'How was I supposed to know that? Besides, why should he get special treatment? It's his own fault I didn't get his name, he needs to learn not to mumble.' She tossed her head with disdain. Jason caught hold of her plait and gave it a tug before remembering where he was.

Will shot him an enquiring look, Jason flicked her plait back at her and she stuck her tongue out at him. They hadn't had the discussion about what they'd say to other people.

Far from being awkward, things in the house had worked out rather smoothly. They'd settled on Jason's bedroom, and fallen into an easy pattern of eating in, chatting, sex in the living room, sex before breakfast, after work and taking shared showers every morning.

As far as Siena was concerned, she didn't need to say anything to anyone because it was no one's business who she was sleeping with.

'So Jay, what's the plan for next week? You still going up north?'

'Yes. For a couple of days.' He turned to Ben. 'You're OK in charge aren't you?'

Ben nodded. 'Of course, boss.'

'So I can head off at the end of the week. I'm planning to call in and see Cam and Laurie.' He looked at Siena.

'It's fine, Hayley's going to take my shifts. I've cleared it with Will.'

'It was fine, General, until you upset Mr Whitaker, so I might have to review.' Since the Elmsley's wedding, that had become her nickname. She'd never had one before. She rather liked it.

'Oh but Will, I really want to—' She couldn't wait to see Laurie and she'd been bouncing with excitement since Jason had suggested the trip.

'Just joking, although you'd better not decide to stay up there.' Will grinned. 'Marcus couldn't survive without your input on tips.'

Marcus whipped at his boss with a damp tea-towel. 'Excuse me.'

Siena touched his arm with a reassuring squeeze. 'Ignore him. You know customers love you.'

'Love him, my arse. He knows how to flirt with all the old ladies.'

'I hope he doesn't,' said Al placing his hands on hips.

'See Siena, look at the chaos you're creating.'

'Me? I haven't done anything.' She giggled.

'Hey Siena. I'm glad you're here. Ben, Jason, Marcus, Al.' Lisa acknowledged them all, except Will, with a quick nod of her head.

'Lisa!' Siena darted to the other side of the bar, pleased to see her. 'I'm glad you popped in.' She heard Will grunt and didn't miss the wary, disdainful look Lisa endowed him with. 'Wait here, I've got something for you.'

She dashed out to the Land Rover and came back with a large Christmas gift bag.

'Here you go.' Her heart bounced in her chest as she waited for Lisa to open up the bag and peel the tissue paper back.

'It's not Christmas yet. Although funnily enough I've got something for you too. Two things. This one is from Nanna.' Lisa handed over a small cardboard box tied up with a rather tatty faded orange ribbon. 'And second, this ...' She dug in her purse and produced three ten pound notes.

'What's that for?'

'The black dress you altered. I showed to a friend at work and she wanted to buy it. I sold it for forty quid.'

'Thirty pounds? But you only paid ten for it.'

'Exactly, which is why these crisp notes are all yours. I'd rather wear my pink dress anyway. Even if I can't get shoes to match.'

'You'd better open your present quick then.'

Lisa squealed so loudly everyone in the pub turned round. 'OMG. Dolce & Gabbana!' She held a pink shoe aloft. 'And more. Siena!' She nearly knocked Siena off her feet with the force of her hug. 'These are amazing. Are you sure? This pair hasn't even been worn.' She promptly burst into tears. 'I love them. I love them. I love them.'

'I think they'll match.'

'Match? You're frigging kidding me! I'd wear them naked.'

'I'd stick with the dress,' chipped in Marcus.

'Siena, you are brilliant. I love them.' Lisa had already peeled her own shoes off and was putting the pink shoes on.

'Don't quite go with black opaque tights but,' she squealed again, 'they are gorgeous.' She walked up and down. 'Gorgeous. Gorgeous. Gorgeous.'

Marcus nudged Siena. 'I think she likes them.'

Siena smiled, grateful that everyone had been so focused on Lisa that they hadn't noticed her own tears. Every second of the sheer perspiration inducing terror she'd felt punching in the alarm code at the apartment had been worth it and at that moment she could burst with joy at Lisa's reaction. Definitely worth it.

'This is from Nanna. I don't think it can possibly match these bloody, fricking, gorgeous shoes. I can never thank you enough for helping her. She's so grateful.'

'Grateful, that old bat?' Will's voice held a note of outrage disbelief.

'Will!' admonished Siena. Did he know Alice? She wasn't so bad. A touch cantankerous perhaps. She unwrapped the box and pulled out a beautiful antique comb and brush set.

'Yes Will,' Lisa's voice dripped shards of ice, sharp and cutting. 'Some people are nice like that.'

'Now, now children,' said Marcus.

Siena turned her back on the whole lot of them. 'Thanks Lisa, can you thank your Nanna for me? It's a beautiful present. So nice of her.' She threw a glance at Will but he seemed totally unrepentant.

'So what did you do to help *Nanna*?' Will almost spat out her name.

Jason sat straighter on his bar stool. 'Actually Will, she did a lot. Siena put her handbag onto eBay and with the proceeds she's paid for a new boiler and the installation for Lisa's gran. I think that's pretty impressive.'

Will turned down his mouth. 'I'd say that's very impressive. Lisa's Nanna must tell one hell of an impressive sob story.' With that utterly mean sentence, he strode out of the bar, nose pointedly in the air.

'Lisa? What was that about?'

'Long story. Family feud. Boring. Will's being an arse. Nothing new there. I gotta go. Fancy getting together on Friday or Saturday? Katie's around. We thought we'd get a takeaway this time and attempt a film or maybe chill. And I wanted to talk to you about an idea.'

'Sorry, I'd love to but not this week. Jason's going to give me a lift up to Yorkshire to see my sister Laurie, so I really need to get a few extra shifts in.'

'Oh that'll be lovely. Didn't she use to go out with that bloke Robert? His mum lives a few doors up from Nanna.'

'I never met him. Cam's her boyfriend now; you wouldn't forget him.' The image of him, hovering protectively over her sister in the grand hall of the Chateau, the very first time she met him had imprinted itself on her brain. Sexy, gorgeous and utterly smitten with her sister, and her with him, although neither of them seemed to know it at the time. So romantic.

'When was the last time you saw her?'

'Two years ago,' said Siena without even thinking about it. Texts, Facebook, emails, that was all a lot more contact than she'd ever had before two years ago.

'Whoa! That's a long time.' Lisa looked appalled at what she'd said. 'Sorry. I forgot you lived in France, can't have been easy.'

'No, it should have been a lot easier. And I should have made the effort more. We don't really know each other that well.'

She couldn't wait for this weekend.

255

Chapter 24

'This must be it,' said Jason, as he hauled the Land Rover through the gap in an old lichen covered wall topped with a pair of carved stone pineapples. The tyres crunched on a short gravel drive.

Siena bit her lip; she'd never understood why Maman had been so cross but now she did. Merryview wasn't anywhere near as big or as grand as the Chateau but it was so pretty and English. Maman made a lot of her English heritage.

The façade of the house, no not a house, a mansion, had diamond lead lined windows, like sparkly eyes and an ancient gnarled climber covered most of the stone walls, tracking across the house and framing the lower windows. Not a single memory stirred. Apparently she'd visited as a child but there wasn't a flicker of recognition.

'No wonder Laurie would rather be here than back in the house,' observed Jason, looking curious. 'Ten times the size of our place.'

'It's lovely.' Romantic. She could imagine roaring fires and four-poster beds. For a minute her gaze lingered on the house before she turned back to face Jason.

'Bitch to heat in winter I would think.' Jason winked and her heart warmed, looking at him. 'Your home improvement company would have something to say about those draughty old windows. Whip 'em out and put nice double glazed units in.'

'Sacrilege,' said Siena.

'Until we get another snowfall.'

'I wouldn't know,' she teased him with a lazy smile and a shrug, 'I'm usually tucked up in a ski lodge in Verbier with a nice *vin chaud*.'

'See, there's the problem with shacking up with high maintenance women,' he gave her a mournful look, 'you have to keep them knee deep in thermal vests. Not that sexy.'

The narrowing of her eyes threatened retribution but he grinned.

'You didn't seem to find my thermal vest that off-putting two nights ago. Besides I've heard body heat is as effective.' She lifted a lazy brow and laughed when he shook his head and rolled his eyes.

He joined in, leaning over and smoothing back a strand of hair that had fallen over her face. 'I've created a monster.'

She turned her face and where his hand cupped her cheek, pressed a kiss into his palm.

He groaned, when she touched the tip of her tongue to his salty skin.

'Behave.'

The word turned husky as she took the tip of his thumb into her mouth, but the rest of his fingers caressed her face and he didn't put up much of a fight.

Warmth started to build and she knew she was teasing herself as much as him. Forcing herself to be good, she nipped the pad of his thumb with a promise and straightened up.

'You are a wicked, wicked woman.'

'I know.' Happiness danced low in her belly.

'And your sister got an eyeful of that.'

Siena's head shot up.

'You sod!'

'Five seconds earlier and she would have.'

Opening the door, relieved that Laurie must have only just appeared in the porch, Siena jumped down.

She launched herself at her sister and threw her arms around her, all the fear and uncertainty of the last few weeks poured into the hug that she gave Laurie.

Siena couldn't help herself, she burst into happy tears.

'It's so lovely to see you.'

'You too,' Laurie laughed, 'I don't normally make my guests cry before they've even crossed the threshold.'

Siena sniffed and laughed, giving her sister another hug. It really was so good to see her.

'Hey landlady.'

'Hey tenant, how you doing?'

'That bloody tap is still dripping and you should have warned me about the package you wanted storing.'

Siena felt Laurie stiffen.

'Joking!' Jason held out his hands towards both of them. 'Tell her Siena.'

'Ignore him. He's been the perfect host. Although he does get a bit territorial about the bathroom.'

Laurie had looped her arm through Siena and keeping a steady school-marmish gaze on Jason, guided them towards the front door.

'Territorial?' Me?' With an exaggerated, camp wipe of his brow and a naughty look her way, he said, 'I've been allocated a piece of shelf space less than a nano-millimetre square. I swear every product Clarins and Clinique make are represented, and Estée Lauder and Elizabeth Arden get quite a good look in, too.'

'Oh dear.' Laurie looked worried.

'He's joking.' Siena reassured her sister and couldn't resist adding. 'He likes to moan.' She shot him a wicked smile. 'Yes he's very good at moaning.'

Jason's eyes went wide and his mouth shut with a decided snap. She bit back a snigger. The dark look he sent her way, filled with the promise of retribution, sent a quiver shuddering through her belly. It didn't take a genius to work out that someone planned to make her pay later.

The door through the porch opened into a beautiful hallway with a high plasterwork ceiling. Siena's eye was drawn to what looked like William Morris wallpaper.

'Is that real?'

'Oh yes,' said Laurie with feeling. 'It is. It's taken me a while not to be terrified that I might inadvertently damage or recognise something that is old or valuable.'

'Pish,' Siena looked at the intricate botanical pattern of the rug beneath their feet, the rich greens and creams faded but still breathtakingly lovely. 'If they've lasted this long, they'll be fine.'

The large fireplace and its cast iron grate, the size of a small bed, would probably outlast the next ten generations of people living here.

'Easy for you to say,' said Laurie. 'You grew up with it all.'

Siena punched her arm. 'It's just stuff. Old stuff. Beautiful stuff, but still stuff. Seriously, what's the point of having it if you're so frightened you can't enjoy it? You might as well lock it away in a box.'

Jason caught her eye. With a flash of insight, she knew he understood in a way that she couldn't share with Laurie. A direct parallel of her life. She'd been so frightened of doing the wrong thing, that she'd shut herself away from experiences, from life.

How did you claim that your life had been wanting, when you'd grown up in a fairy-tale chateau, with designer clothes, millionaire playtime, mixing with celebrities and minor royalty? Especially not when she knew every last intimate corner of the two bedroom terraced house Laurie had grown up in, with their father.

Siena refused to feel guilty about the dad she'd never known. Despite his smiling photos in the house, she had no memory of him. No matter how hard she delved.

'Lovely house Laurie, I can see why you moved.' Jason moved in to give her a polite kiss on each cheek.

Laurie smiled. 'Wait until you've dusted and cleaned the place, especially since Norah's not been well. I'd swap for Brook Street.'

'For a few days,' Cam's voice came from a doorway to the right.

'Cam.' Jason strode forward and gave him a man-hug. Siena watched. He made up the third part of Will and Jason's university triumvirate. She was intrigued to see how he fitted with Jason. Definitely the most casual and laid back of them all. And even more at home in that double denim look.

'Good to see you. Nice place.'

'Belongs to the missus, but it's not bad.'

Laurie shook her head. 'I am not the missus and if you say that again, I'll make you dust every last book in the library.'

'See what I have to put up with?' It was obvious he absolutely adored her sister by the way that his eyes had never left her.

Siena's heart tripped. Jason looked at her like that sometimes.

'Tell me about it,' said Jason folding his arms and leaning up against a wall. 'Siena is known as the General at work. Obviously runs in the blood.'

'I am not' Siena pulled up short, narrowed her eyes at Jason and turned to Laurie. 'Yeah Ok I am, but I tell you. It's the only way to get anything done.'

Laurie nodded with great enthusiasm. 'Don't I know it?' She included Cam by hooking an arm around his shoulders and pulling him to stand beside her. 'Basically they'd be utterly lost without us.'

'Completely my darling.' Cam managed to look hen-pecked for all of two seconds, before he swooped down on Laurie and began tickling her.

Siena's mouth went dry and her eyes automatically sought Jason's. He grinned, clearly remembering the time he'd tickled her and moved to stand behind her, his breath warming her neck.

'Seems being ticklish runs in the family,' he muttered in her ear as if he'd made a great discovery. 'Useful to know.'

The small party made its way down the stone flagged corridor through a door on the right to a cosy drawing room, which was obviously where Laurie and Cam spent most of their time. The coffee table was littered with files and plastic wallets of papers, a couple of blueprint plans coiled loosely and a small fire crackled in the grate despite it only being three in the afternoon.

'Have a seat. I'll go and rustle up some drinks. Norah's out of hospital but she's still very wobbly on her pins. We've come to a loose arrangement. She's as stubborn as anything. She makes the tea and coffee and allows us to bring it through.'

'So who's in charge here?' asked Jason.

'Laurie is of course.' Cam's eyes danced, his lips quirking with suppressed laughter.

Laurie darted off to the kitchen and Siena settled back into the soft cushion of the old velvet sofa. Actually it was a touch too soft, a distinct dip hollowed out the rose velvet cushion of the seat and the back cushion sagged heavily, pushing its weight into her shoulders. Giving up the fight against it, she kicked off her shoes and curled up in the corner.

'There's still a heck of a lot of work to do,' explained Cam. 'We're concentrating on getting the—' he stopped, his mouth suddenly zipped shut. He continued awkwardly 'the rooms decorated. We come last. So you might have to rough it a bit, this weekend; the kitchen is being re-done. '

'Rough it?' Jason looked around the room. 'Looks a tough gig to me.'

'Not you. Siena's used to a bit more refinement. I've been to the Chateau. Very grand.'

Siena made a very thorough examination of her bare nails. Cam sounded slightly mocking.

'Yes, very refined.' Jason agreed deadpan. Too deadpan; if she dared look at him she might laugh. Jumping his bones and dragging him into a field for wild uninhibited sex hardly qualified.

Cam didn't seem to notice the undertone, although Siena wondered if it might be because they were such an unlikely couple, it wouldn't cross his mind.

'Remember that hideous student house we had?' He turned to Siena. 'That was when Jason and Will went into serious beer production. There were plastic bottles everywhere, and jeez, the spillages. Those carpets were rank.'

No, Cam had definitely pigeonholed them into two separate spheres.

'So what exactly are you doing?' asked Siena. She'd been so wrapped up in her new life, she'd been rather rubbish at asking Laurie about hers.

Cam's face shuttered. 'I'll leave Laurie to tell you about that.' He changed the subject none too subtly. 'How's it going with the brewery? I saw your beer in one of the Sunday supps.' Siena tuned out. Laurie had been quite cagey on the phone, lots of talk about builders and being busy but not much more. It was clear now that she'd been avoiding giving straight answers.

'Here we go, tea and coffee.' Laurie returned carrying a huge tray, rattling with delicate bone china cups and saucers.

'How gorgeous!' Siena jumped up to clear a space. 'You needn't have gone to this much trouble.' Not that Jason would be too appreciative; he liked his coffee long and strong. These pretty cups probably held no more than quarter of that of his favourite mug.

'Thank you. I've been going through Uncle Miles' cupboards. He had some beautiful things; it's a shame not to use them. Plus, I thought I'd start practising with you.'

As Laurie sorted everyone's drinks out, Siena caught a brief interchange between her and Cam. He shook his head and she put her finger up to his lips with a shake of her own.

'So what are you practising for?' asked Jason, snagging a second buttery biscuit from the floral china plate, having already drained his coffee. 'The national tea making championships? Yorkshire's quarter-finals of hostess with the mostess? WI membership?'

Cam and Laurie exchanged another one of those looks.

'Just being a good hostess,' said Laurie her voice a touch flat.

Siena wondered if they might have had a row. Maybe Cam

hadn't wanted guests. She didn't know him that well. Ha! She didn't know her own sister well.

'I hope Cam's not taking advantage. He's a lazy git. Remember that girl, what was her name, the one with the huge,' remembering where he was Jason hastily added, 'personality. You had her running up and down, waiting on you hand and foot.'

'I do remember that girl, thank you. Not sure Laurie really wants to hear.'

'Oh, I do.' She grinned at Jason. 'Always useful ammunition.'

Cam groaned. 'Remind me why I didn't kill you years ago?'

'Free beer, mate. Free beer.'

'Yeah, I don't get it free now. When you're finally making some decent stuff. Don't forget all the years I spent being your guinea pig, drinking all kinds of shit. Don't suppose you tell many people about the time you gave me alcohol poisoning?'

'Now there's no need for that. It was in the name of development. No major achievement's ever made without a few sacrifices along the way. Besides you're still here, what are you complaining about?' Jason jumped up. 'In fact, in remembrance of your historic services to drinking, I have brought you a couple of bottles. I'll go and get them.'

Siena started to rise but Jason waved her away. 'No, don't worry, I'll bring the bags in from the car.'

'Do you want a hand?' asked Cam.

'Yeah, that'd be good. You look like you could do with some exercise.'

Cam punched him in the arm, Jason retaliating with a headlock. Ribbing each other raucously as they went, the two men could still be heard from the corridor beyond.

Laurie smiled. 'God, I dread to think what those two were like as students. Probably had a full blown harem going. How's it going sharing the house with Jason? Is it a bit cramped?

'I feel mortified now.' Siena hid her face in her hand. 'Just assuming I could turn up. What a brat, eh? Jason's been really, erm,' she squirmed in her seat, 'good about it.'

'I did say you'd always be welcome and that the room was yours but—'

'You'd given up on me?'

Laurie crossed the room and sank down beside her on the sofa, their legs touching. 'No, I never gave up on you. You're my sister.'

'Real sister, not half-sister.'

Laurie's face became grave. 'I wondered when you'd figure that out. I was a bit cross, to be honest, that you hadn't. It seemed so obvious … but you were younger than me when it all happened.'

'Younger and stupider. I tackled Maman about it when you'd gone. She said it was easier when I was little to tell everyone that Georges was my father. When he left and she married Harry, I still assumed he was my father. I knew we'd lived in England and Maman had been married before. I was too dumb to question anything. I've been doing a bit more questioning recently.'

'So have you sorted a course out? Are you going home for Christmas? Will you come back in September to start?'

Siena took in a deep breath. 'Things,' shamefaced she turned to her sister; time to fess up, 'have sort of changed.'

Silence.

Laurie's level expression gave nothing away as she did the tipped head to one side, I'm-listening thing, which she was so good at.

'They didn't exactly go to plan.' Laurie's lips twitched, or at least Siena hoped they had. 'In fact you could say they haven't gone to plan at all.'

'So you had a plan?' Amusement twinkled in her sister's eyes.

Siena rolled her eyes and she drew her hair back into a ponytail which she knotted into a loose bun. 'No. No plan. None at all. Spur of the moment. I ran away. Left a note. Then you weren't there and I didn't want to go home.' She wrinkled her nose. 'Jason wasn't that happy at first.'

'Siena! That's naughty. You told me he was fine with you staying.'

'I know. I fibbed. But he is now, honestly.' She hugged the

secret of how fine he was to herself.

'How fine?' asked Laurie looking very suspicious.

Siena tried to study the fireplace without looking shifty but failed miserably.

'Siena! No, you and Jason?'

'Ssh, don't tell Cam. I don't think he approves of me.'

Laurie ignored the comment in a way that made Siena guess she was right. 'I hate to be a pessimist but isn't that slightly risky? It's all very quick and what about when you go back to France and then when you start your course?'

'Remember the plan that never was? Turns out I'm a fashion designer in my dreams but it's never going to happen. I'm not good enough.'

'No.' Laurie's sad cry made Siena smile but also grateful that she didn't try to offer up platitudes or solutions.

'It's OK. I'm over it. It was one of those, I want to be a fairy princess type dreams. Not terribly practical. I see it now.'

'So what are you going to do now? When do you go back to France?'

'Hmm, the big question. I've got to go back on the twenty-third for Christmas; it's Harry's sixtieth birthday party.' She bit back the sob that came from nowhere. For the last few weeks, she'd been so happy. Pretending everything was fine, not thinking of anything beyond Christmas.

'Siena!' Laurie scooted up beside her and put an arm round her. 'Don't cry.'

Now she'd started, she didn't seem to be able to stop. 'I can't b-bear the thought of going b-back. Everything's changed.'

'Hey, it's alright.' Laurie rubbed her back.

'I've got a job. I know it's temporary but I know I can do it. I've made friends. Real friends. Lisa, she's lovely. And Marcus and Al at the pub. My boss, Will.' She tugged at the skin at her neck. 'I can't go back. My other life *looks* wonderful. The houses. The holidays. The parties. The clothes. But it's all meaningless. I spend more time with Agnes the housekeeper because I'm lonely. Half the time I'm so bored I could scream and Maman is desperate for me to marry a man I don't love and who—'

'Look what Jason's done!' Cam entered the room carrying a cardboard tray of beer bottles, totally oblivious to the sudden atmosphere in the room. 'Made me my own beer. Look.' He lifted one of the bottles. 'Camshaft. Isn't that neat? We could sell it here to the … to people.'

Jason spotted her tear-stained face and leaving the bags crossed the room to crouch in front of her.

'Hey frog-face, what's the matter?'

'I'm telling Laurie what a waste of space I am.' She gulped back more tears.

He looped an arm around her pulling her close, resting his forehead on hers. 'That's crap and you know it. Look at you. Bloody brilliant. You were cut off without a penny but instead of crying and going home, you went out and got a job.' He gave her a mock punch on the arm. 'Bloody shit job but a job all the same. Then you got a job at the pub, which you'd run single-handed if you had to, all the while knocking up a couple of fabulous frocks on a sewing machine.' He kissed her on the lips. 'You're amazing.'

Siena sighed and touched his stubbled chin, aware of the astonished faces of Cam and Laurie who'd moved closer together. Her sister was giving Cam one of those, see-told-you-so looks.

'Oh sod this, let's get the wine out. I think Siena deserves a toast.' Cam said as he dumped the case of beer and disappeared, returning with four enormous balloon glasses, and a bottle tucked under his arm.

'Why didn't you tell me about not having any money?' Laurie asked. 'Did your mother, our mother, really cut you off? Why didn't you tell me? I would have helped.'

'You were already letting me stay. I thought I could get a job. Turns out I'm not qualified to do anything. Especially not a double glazing sales person, although,' she nodded at the beautiful lead lined windows in their deep bays, 'I could probably get you a good deal if you ever decided to rip those out.' Next to her, Jason's shoulders shook.

Cam sniggered. 'Seriously?'

'That didn't turn out so well.'

'No it didn't,' grumbled Jason suddenly tightening his grip on her hand.

'Actually I do have another confession. You know those bottles of Lafite …'

Laurie closed her eyes as if in pain.

Chapter 25

Jason couldn't remember when he'd enjoyed a happier afternoon, especially once Cam had got over his initial suspicion of Siena. He'd have to ask him about that. Something wasn't quite right there.

Laurie paused outside a door. 'I'd got two rooms ready. This one ...'

'This is Cam's idea of roughing it?' Jason's eyebrows almost disappeared into his hairline.

For some reason Laurie blushed. 'They're the first to be finished. Both have got en-suites.' She ushered them in.

'Wow, this is gorgeous,' exclaimed Siena and rushed in to touch the sheets on the king-size bed. 'I adore the bed. There's something so romantic about sleigh beds.' She ran a reverent hand over the chestnut coloured wood.

It looked like a nice big, comfortable bed to him. More than big enough to spark visions of what he'd like to do with her.

She'd darted to the window. 'Lovely view.'

Her slim figure was silhouetted by the light through the diamond-paned windows. It certainly was. His gazed lingered on her slender form.

Enthusiastic as ever, she moved again through to the open door of the bathroom. 'Look at the bath,' she said, looking over her shoulder at him, her eyes dancing with mischief. 'It's been a long while since I had a bath.' Which was a flat-out lie. Unless she meant it had been a long time since she'd taken one on her own. Feeling decided stirrings, and his jeans getting tighter, he peered past her at the old style Victorian bath.

'Or there's another room across the hall.' Laurie sounded repressive and for a moment Jason considered her. A lot more buttoned up than Siena, except when Cam touched her and then she softened. She wasn't at all like any of Cam's previous girl-friends. Now, *he* had been into high maintenance girlfriends. Jason closed his eyes recalling Cam's brief, train-wreck marriage. Sylvie had been a lot like Siena. In fact, in those days Siena would have been much more Cam's type, which was why Jason was so surprised that he seemed so wary around her.

'No, this is lovely. The bed looks extremely comfortable. I can see you've gone for high quality.' Rustling feather duvets on the beds and great big plump pillows. Had he developed a bed obsession?

Laurie laughed, a light gurgle, very different from Siena's infec-tious whole-hearted laughter. 'You're so like Cam. Is it comfort-able? Is the bed big enough? Do the curtains shut out enough light? Are the towels big ones, not scratchy? Does the shower have decent power? And yes to all of those things, because he made me write it all down and has tested,' she blushed a fiery red, 'most things.'

Siena giggled, not the least bit interested in sparing her sister's blushes. 'Men never notice the details. Like 1000 thread count Egyptian cotton. These sheets are divine.' She lifted the duvet, feeling the fabric in her hand. 'It's so soft but still lovely and crisp. I love good bed sheets. At home they're changed every couple of days, it's bliss.'

'Cam nearly had a heart attack when I told him how much they cost.'

'What are they? Frette?'

'Yes.'

'And the curtains, Designers Guild?

'You're like a walking luxury brand encyclopaedia,' commented Laurie.

Like a cloud scudding across the sun, a slight sense of unease rattled Jason. She'd written the book on luxury. Standing in the large, light room with all its expensive accoutrements, she looked utterly at home.

When Laurie finally left, he kicked the door shut, dropped his bag and rugby tackled Siena onto the bed, where they landed with a pfft in the deep feathered duvet.

After a prolonged few moments of kissing and tussling, she giggled up at him. 'Isn't this bed wonderful? I could get used to this.'

She'd have to wait a long while for this sort of luxury if she stuck with him. The thought punched him in the gut, like a physical blow. How long would it be before she decided she wanted her old life back? He'd been worried he might hurt her but it was more likely she'd be the one hurting him.

'Another bottle of amazing wine.' Siena's taste buds were ready to leap up and dance in gratitude as she cringed at the bottle of inexpensive New Zealand Sauvignon Blanc she'd brought with flowers for Laurie. A classic wine from the Marlborough region, but not quite in the same price bracket as this one.

'Uncle Miles' cellar. He had an incredible collection but obviously we don't drink wine like this every day, just in your honour.'

'I feel very honoured, this is lovely.'

'Tomorrow you'll be getting bog standard Sainsbury's Aussie Chardonnay,' chipped in Cam with an affectionate glance at Laurie, 'tempting as it is, we can't drink all the good stuff. We need it for the punters and our grand plan. Not,' he gave Siena a self-deprecating grin, 'that I can tell my Chablis from my Chardonnay. Your sister's the real expert.' He said the later with quiet pride.

'I'm not an expert, not yet. I'm working on it. Doing some wine qualifications so that we can keep the cellar topped up with lots of interesting wines.'

'That's great; you'll have to come out and visit Harry's vineyards.'

'Vineyards, plural?' Laurie looked very interested.

'Yes he comes from a very old French family and they own pockets of land all over the place. He has a vineyard in Epernay, one outside Bordeaux and another one. I can't remember exactly where.' Siena's smile faded with the realisation that Harry probably wouldn't want much more to do with her.

'I might take you up on that. Perhaps phase two if our business takes off. We decided, when I inherited Merryview—' she bit her lip and looked warily at Siena.

'Is that what you were worrying about earlier?' Siena could see Cam's grave face and the way he'd taken hold of Laurie's hand. 'Seriously?' She would have laughed but nausea rolled in the pit of her stomach. 'Look,' she said urgently, 'I know Maman made a huge fuss. Miles was her brother and she thought she should get something.' Siena snorted. 'Although it's hardly as if she would suffer financially. She has plenty. But me, I don't even remember Miles. Why shouldn't you have this house? Or the cars.' She stopped and then added in a small voice, 'Did you really think I'd come up here looking for a hand-out or a share?'

'No, not at all,' said Laurie briskly. 'You're always welcome, although once we've opened up our boutique bed and breakfast specialising in fine wine tastings and classic cars, you might have to sleep in the servant quarters. The aim is to attract real enthusiasts for private tastings down in Miles' cellar and offer viewings of the cars and a test drive on the track.'

'You've got your own track?'

'Track's a bit of a stretch,' said Cam. 'We're not talking Silverstone or anything. An old disused airfield. Miles bought it years ago. Private property, so we can drive there. He re-tarmacked the runway, so it's a lovely smooth ride.' Looking over at Jason, he added, 'If it wasn't for the snow I'd take you for a spin tomorrow. But you can come over to the garage to see the cars.'

'Ahem.' Laurie tapped her plate with a knife.

'You can see them anytime,' Cam said.

'I meant Siena. She might like to see them too.'

'Oh God, please don't tell me Miles had her driving the track when she was five or something?' He groaned. 'The first time I took Laurie, she didn't bother to mention that her uncle taught her to drive a two hundred horsepower car when she was only fourteen. Scared the bejesus out of me when she took off like a rocket.'

Laurie grinned unrepentantly. 'Served you right for being patronising, with your, "this is a very powerful car, nothing like anything you've driven before" blah, blah, blah.' She beamed at Jason and Siena. 'You should have seen his face when I floored it.'

'Took several years off my life.' Cam turned to Siena. 'Anything you want to tell me, now?'

'No, you're fine. The most exotic thing I've driven is my Mercedes coupé. It's only a two litre.'

'Nice car. Got plenty of poke.'

'I didn't know you had a Merc.' Jason sounded accusing.

Ignoring his tone, she said in a deliberately sultry voice. 'There's a lot you don't know about me.'

'Hell on petrol.' He scowled. 'Not like my Land Rover. Now there's a proper vehicle.'

'Nothing's like your Land Rover,' she teased. 'But now that I've cleaned it out, I think it's rather wonderful too.'

Her comment seemed to mollify him. 'Did you know seventy percent of all Land Rovers are still on the road?'

Cam nodded, chipping in with, 'Did you know the prototype Land Rover had its steering wheel in the middle?'

'Eyes glazing over to the left here,' said Laurie. 'Top Gear alert.'

'Sorry babe.'

As the evening progressed, Siena couldn't remember a night she'd enjoyed more. Not in company anyway. Recent evenings at the house in Brook Street held some very vivid memories. They retired from the lavish but slightly faded dining room with its heavy oak furniture and red flock wallpaper to a vast salon with cream sofas, pale walls and floral rugs in pastel hues. Elegant and formal, it contrasted starkly with the cosy drawing room where they'd spent the afternoon. Jason and Cam were deep in conversation, comparing notes on who they were still in touch with from university days.

'So, are you enjoying living in the house?' asked Laurie. 'It's very small after what you're used to.'

'Yes, it took a while. More for Jason than me. He didn't like having to share a bathroom at first.'

'He didn't? I thought you'd find it harder. Aren't there wall-to-wall en-suites at the Chateau?' Laurie frowned. 'I was quite surprised he'd agreed you could stay.'

Siena squirmed slightly in her seat, hoping Jason hadn't heard any of that. She hadn't reckoned on his bat-ears.

'I agreed you could stay?' He grabbed one of her feet and pulled it on to his lap and tickled.

She wriggled trying to pull away spluttering, 'I'm sure you did.'

'So what did you say to Siena?' asked Jason, holding her foot firmly between his hands.

Laurie laughed. 'Can't remember now.'

'Not, "you can stay rent free for as long as you like."'

'Not those precise words, no. They might have been along the lines of, 'if Jason doesn't mind then of course you can stay."

'Aha! So Sherlock Holmes here, deduces that young Siena has been telling porky pies,' he lifted her foot, 'and deserves to be punished.'

Five minutes of relentless tickling, leaving her begging for mercy ensured everyone forgot what had started it.

Waking up next to a warm body, a heavy arm snaked around your ribs anchoring you to them, had to be the best way in the world to wake up. She knew she wasn't at home because the light had a different quality, it bled around the edges of the heavy drapes, letting her know it was daylight outside and well enough to see.

Snuggled into the downy warmth of the bed in Laurie's beautiful house, she gradually surfaced. This quiet time of the morning where she could study Jason's face in repose, listen to his steady breathing and smell his musky scent, held pure magic.

Invariably as he came to, he'd pull her to him, open his sleepy eyes, give her a slow, sweet smile and then close them again. This morning, the unguarded exchange crept into her heart and with a missed breath of wonderment, the world tilted. A flash of aware-ness flooded her, a thunk in her chest. She'd only gone and fallen totally and utterly in love with him.

Dazed by the overwhelming feeling that had put out tentative roots and taken hold in seconds, she wriggled out of his hold and fled to the bathroom.

Looking in the mirror, she was very relieved to see that she didn't look any different. Love. That was big, grown up. Scary. Not part of the plan. In seven days' time she was supposed to be boarding a plane back to France.

Love wasn't part of the timetable.

Merde. Everything had been going perfectly. No promises. No commitments. No need to think of the future. Take each day as it came. No expectation on either side. Now she wanted something else. Promises. Forever. Things she and Jason had agreed were not part of the plan.

'Hey, you OK?' Startled, she saw his reflection in the mirror.

Sleep dazed, he stumbled towards the loo and unselfconsciously took a pee.

'Yeah, I'm fine. Woke up early that's all.' Mesmerised by his long lean back and the taut bum, she sighed. Even mundane as this, she couldn't imagine a life without him.

They showered together, made love and had to shower again. Jason rubbed her breasts with a towel, supposedly helping to dry her off. 'Sure you're OK? You seem a bit down.'

'Probably a bit emotional. Seeing Laurie. Family stuff.'

He looped the towel around her neck and pulled up against him, so that their noses almost touched.

'Sorry, I should have realised that. If you don't mind me saying, it's one dysfunctional family. Surprising that Laurie is,' he smiled and she could see the patterns in his iris, 'so normal.' It took a beat for the insult to sink in.

'You cheeky—'

'I'm joking.' He kissed her on the nose. 'Although you're not normal.'

Her face clouded but he still had that mischievous glint. 'You're phenomenal. Amazing. Brilliant and not normal, which I wouldn't want anyway.'

'We are definitely dysfunctional. I'd never thought of it like that before. A dad I never knew. Two step-dads. I think Laurie is disappointed that I don't want to know more about him but he isn't real to me. Three different dads, none of them real. That's weird isn't it? I feel I'm letting her down.'

'You're not letting anyone down. You're you. A good person.' He gave her bottom a gentle tap. 'Now go and get dressed before I forget myself and we have to start all over again. No,' he held up a hand and looked away, 'none of your feminine wiles trying to entice me. I know your game Siena Browne-Martin. Minx of the parish. Go strut your stuff elsewhere and let me shave.'

'You're no fun.' She grinned and left the bathroom. Time enough to worry about falling in love with him; for now she was going to savour these precious minutes out of normal time.

Maybe the weather contributed, the bright sunshine and blue sky was especially brilliant on the horizon against the snow covered fields, maybe it was the company, the idyllic setting or being in love, but the start of the day slid to the very top of the scale of perfection.

'Cam, will you let them finish breakfast?' Laurie rolled her eyes at his incessant tapping of a teaspoon against the sugar bowl. 'The cars aren't going anywhere, darling.'

Cam stopped tapping for a few minutes before flicking his fingers against the wood of the table. Siena could tell he was totally oblivious and that it wound Laurie up even more.

She nudged Jason, who was on his last mouthful of sausage. 'Bring your coffee. We need to avert World War Three or at the very least, potential divorce.'

'What?'

'Bring your coffee.' Siena nodded apologetically at Laurie, 'That's OK isn't it.'

'Yeah, it's fine. Just get Cam out of here. I'll tidy up and meet you over there.'

'Do you want some help?' Her half-hearted offer made Laurie raise an eyebrow.

'No, you carry on. I can tell you're itching to see the cars, probably more than Jason.'

'I'm keen.' Jason scraped up the last mushroom and wiped it in the egg yolk with relish. 'I like food too.'

With Cam leading the way, jangling a large set of keys, they crossed the paved courtyard to the hi-tech stable conversion.

Alarms beeped and lights flashed as they entered, quickly silenced. Siena stared across the hangar-like rooms which ran into each other. There must have been at least twenty cars in here. Glamorous two-seater little numbers, with high gloss paint-jobs and polished chrome trim, convertibles with hard and soft tops, classics and coupés.

Even Siena who knew very little about cars could tell this collection was something special.

Prouder than any new mother, Cam walked them through the collection, passion and enthusiasm in every word.

'That's my favourite,' said Siena pointing to a flashy E-Type Jag.

'Hmm.' Cam's dismissal told her she was a complete philistine.

'I like this one.' Jason pointed to a scarlet Ferrari, the stallion on the front stamping its brand. Cam shook his head. 'Stick with Siena, her taste is much better than yours.'

'But this is a Ferrari, you always said they were the best.' Jason looked disgruntled and Siena took the chance to poke her tongue out at him.

'In my opinion, they had a glitch during the Seventies. This one is too fur coat and no knickers. No finesse. Look at the GT 250 California Spyder.' He drew them over to the car which occupied centre stage in the room. 'Look at the curves on this. The sinuous design. That, my friend, is an orgasm on wheels.'

'I know this one. You drove it to the Chateau in. I recognise it.'

Cam seemed lost in thought for a minute. 'It's a very special car indeed.'

'Worth a fortune?' suggested Jason, walking round the car, admiring it from every angle.

'More than that.' Cam's eyes darkened as if he carried a secret. 'It's worth everything.'

Laurie had entered, at this she slipped her arms around his waist. The searing look they exchange was so intense, Siena had to look away.

With a hollow ache, she wondered if Jason might ever look at her that way one day.

Siena felt pleased for her sister and a little bit proud.

Laurie actually relented when they returned and let Siena help her bring the spread of cheeses, hams and bread through to the little sitting room, where they sat and ate lunch in happy accord.

A loud jangling bell interrupted Siena's second bite of the lovely cracker she'd just loaded up with cheddar. Laurie frowned. 'We're not expecting any builders or deliveries today are we?'

'No, the plumbers for the bathrooms in the east corridor aren't due until Tuesday. That's the only contractor booked in for the week.'

'It could be the sample roll of wallpaper,' Laurie rose to her feet and was already half way out of the door, as she threw over her shoulder, 'I ordered.'

The bell jangled again. Loud and peremptory. Siena's hairs rose on her arms. Foreboding rattling at the edge of her conscious.

A shrill complaint rent the air, carrying down the corridor. Shutting her eyes tight, as if that were going to help, she responded to the familiar voice by stupidly shrinking back into the chair, her breath bound tight in her lungs.

Jason placed a warm, firm hand on her knocking knee and she flicked open her eyes.

'You're OK. Safe.' He laced his fingers between hers and then cupped their hands with his other hand. In that moment, she believed him. And weak as it seemed, she was happy to take his protection.

Tip tap, tip tap. Fast, angry heels marched their way. Siena swallowed.

Like a miniature virago, her mother whirled into the room, her trademark Coco Chanel red lips thinned in icy fury, which flattened out into some semblance of a smile when she saw there were several people in the room.

'Siena, how lovely to see you. At last. I do wish you'd answer your phone when you go off on one of your little jaunts.'

'Maman,' she rose and went over to her mother to place dutiful kisses on either side of her face. 'Sorry I—' she bowed her head. 'I needed—' With every second under her mother's sharp-eyed assessment, she shrivelled inside, like an ugly prune. What was it about her mother than immediately managed to make her feel utterly ridiculous, stupid and lost?

'Next time you decide to have a holiday, it would be so much better, if you chose a less inconvenient time. But we can talk about that later.' Her mother turned and with her usual immaculate manners introduced herself.

'Cameron, we met in France. How are you? Still looking after the car? And Laurie?' She offered her cheek to him and to Siena's surprise, he obliged.

'Yes,' he answered. 'What brings you here?' He didn't bother with any false pleasantries.

Celeste didn't answer. 'And you are?'

'Jason, a friend of Siena's.'

Celeste raised an eyebrow. 'Indeed.'

Laurie had rustled up one of her amazing tea trays, which was bound to soothe Celeste. Although her mother would never make a scene in public, her temper simmered like a barely caged tiger.

'This is lovely. Both my daughters in my brother's house. A real family occasion.' She lifted a cup to her mouth giving it careful examination. 'The best china too. Miles always did like the finer things. The house must be full of priceless glass and cutlery. You need to make sure you take very good care of it.'

Siena thought she heard Cam snort, which turned into some coughing fit.

For half an hour, which seemed like ten times longer, Celeste held court making general pronouncements and observations. With her awareness of Jason so finely tuned, Siena found it hard to hide her smiles at the gamut of expressions that crossed his face.

'The weather in France has been atrocious. What about here?'

Polite disinterest.

'You missed a very good party at the Le Floche's.'

Boredom.

'Did you hear Claudine Valmont has finally got herself engaged? Not to the best family but he'll do.'

Amused disbelief.

'Yves is very much looking forward to seeing you next week.' She gave Siena a very pointed look. 'And to the party.'

Jason's face clouded.

Siena sucked in a breath but didn't manage to interrupt her mother, who rattled on.

'So, Laurie. I hear you've been very busy with building work.'
With poise and elegance, Celeste balanced her saucer on her knee.
'But not applied for planning permission for change of use. I'm
glad. I'd hate to think that you were thinking of turning our
ancestral home into a hotel or anything.'

Laurie gave her mother a very level look. 'Gosh, you can hear all
that all the way from France? Impressive. And no I'm not turning
the house into a hotel.' With a deliberate pause, she smiled at
Cam. 'We are going to offer bespoke bed and breakfast packages.'

'Bed and breakfast? Here?' Celeste didn't bat an eyelid. 'Oh, no.
You can't possibly do that. I won't allow it.'

Cam raised an eyebrow and was about to speak but Laurie
shook her head. 'I'm afraid you don't have any say.'

'That's where you're wrong. This is family business. I've
consulted my solicitors—'

'Miles bought this house forty years ago. It wasn't and never
was a family legacy. If anyone has more right to it than me, it
would be Penny or one of the other ex-wives.' Laurie sounded
so in control.

'I meant more immediate than that. Your sister.'

Celeste shot a triumphant smile at Siena. What was her mother
talking about?

'Siena has a rightful claim to this house and the cars. I've
talked it through with my solicitors and they think she has a
viable interest.'

Siena shot to her feet. 'But I don't—'

'You don't know what you want at the moment. It's about time
you stood up for yourself.'

Siena almost laughed; wasn't that what she was trying to do?

'Laurie got your father's house and now your uncle's. Are you
going to sit back and let your sister take everything?'

Siena's skin felt tight and her face burned. She didn't even dare
look at Jason, Cam or Laurie. What must they all be thinking?

'I think you should leave,' said Laurie, her jaw tight and stiff.

How she kept her voice so level and calm, Siena couldn't imagine.

Regal and self-possessed, Celeste's smooth, impassive face didn't give away a single emotion.

'Very well but I would like a private word with Siena before I go. Siena, you can walk me to the front door.'

Jason started and rose to his feet.

Celeste swept her along before she could think and they were walking along the flagstone hallway to the front porch. Siena hated herself for being so weak.

'I really am quite angry. It's very inconsiderate of you.' Celeste sighed heavily. 'I don't know what the problem is.'

'Maman, I don't want to marry Yves.'

'Darling, I want you to be happy. I know about these things. I married your father believing in love and all that rubbish. Passion is fine but it doesn't pay the bills and it doesn't make for long-term stability. Yves and you make the perfect couple. He will give you the life you are used to. The life you deserve.'

'I don't—'

'Siena, I've been very patient. You've had your way. Now it's time to come home and settle down. I appreciate young people want to,' her mouth pursed as if she could barely bring herself to say it, '*have their fun*, but it's getting tedious. You can't up and leave every time Yves has to do business and you are bored. He is a successful businessman; if you are kept in the lap of luxury, you have to do your bit.'

'That's not—'

'Siena, I'm your mother. I know you. It's always been the same since you were a small child. Easily bored. Wanting something different. I see you've found yourself another nice toy. A pleasant distraction.' Celeste folded her lips into a moue of distaste. 'By all means, have some fun if you must but don't let it jeopardise your future.'

'I'm sorry Maman. I can't marry Yves.'

Her mother shrugged, not a single emotion crossing her face. 'And when were you going to mention this to him? I take it you haven't spoken to the poor man.'

'I will.' Siena did feel bad that she hadn't spoken to Yves but he wasn't in love with her. 'I said I'd be home for Harry's party. I'll tell him then.'

'May I suggest,' Celeste's hissed words sounded more like a threat, 'that you use the next few days to think very carefully about what you say to Yves. Refusing to marry him will close an awful lot of doors to you. Life could become quite uncomfortable.'

Like a queen strolling out to greet her subjects, Celeste glided out of the house leaving Siena speechless with impotent fury, clenching her fists until she thought her knuckles might burst through the skin.

Rooted to the spot, she waited until she heard a car engine start and the crunch of gravel as it pulled away.

'Aaaargh,' she ground through gritted teeth.

'You OK?' The impassive voice made her jump.

She closed her eyes, feeling sick.

'No,' she said in a low voice. Everything felt claustrophobic. She had to get out here. Grabbing an ancient waxed jacket from the rack in the porch and pushing her feet into the nearest wellington boots, she rushed out of the front door and strode furiously to the side gate which opened out to a paddock. Throwing herself over the wooden bars, she hit the ground and began to run, her feet dragging through the snow, up the hill towards the poplars on the horizon, the boundary of Laurie's land.

Only when she got the top, breath torn out of her in painful bursts, did she stop and burst into tears. The wind iced them to her face with vicious bites. Her mother was never going to understand.

Siena wasn't going to waste any more time trying to convince her. From here on in, she was on her own. She wasn't going back.

Pulling the waxed jacket down over her bottom, she plonked

herself resolutely down on the ground and took the time to savour the view and breathe.

'That was interesting.' Cam helped Laurie stack the tray as Jason walked back into the room.

'Is Siena OK?' asked Laurie. 'Where is she? You didn't let her go with Celeste did you?'

'No, she's taken herself off. She needs time to rant in private. Your mother's quite a cold fish.'

'Tell me about it. Poor Siena. It's easy for me. I don't have the emotional attachment, or the sense of guilt that I should feel something for her.'

Cam's face was guarded and he stood, arms folded, watching Laurie like a silent sentinel. Jason saw that he had Laurie's back. A team. After three years he'd never have described him and Stacey as a team.

'Where is she?'

'At the top of the field,' said Jason. 'She's had a bit of time but I think I'll go up and see her.'

'Actually Jason, do you mind if I do? We haven't had much sister time and I do know what Celeste is like.'

'That's probably a better idea,' he said. 'I'm so pissed off with Celeste I'll pour boiling oil on already troubled water.'

'I could do with a hand out in the courtyard.' Cam suggested. 'The terracotta pots should have been brought in for the winter. Laurie's been nagging for weeks to do it.'

'Weeks? I mentioned them this morning for the first time,' said Laurie indignantly

'Second.' Cam's immediate response made Laurie crow in triumph.

'OK, second! That's not nagging for weeks.'

With a rueful grin, Cam nodded at Jason. 'Henpecked I am, completely henpecked.'

'And don't you forget it,' called Laurie over her shoulder as she left in pursuit of her sister.

Sunbeams flooded out from behind a big grey cloud like enormous grey spotlights, focusing on the untouched white fields of the opposite hillside. Siena stared at them, fascinated, already feeling soothed by the size of nature. It seemed unnaturally quiet, all sound deadened by the heavy blanket of snow. The hugeness of the landscape made her problems all seem quite puny. Leaning back against a tree trunk, her bottom numbing from the cold, she watched as the small figure of her sister got bigger and bigger.

'This space taken?' Laurie plonked herself down next to her before she could answer. 'You OK?'

'Getting there.' Siena didn't look at her sister. Instead, she carried on gazing at the view.

'If it helps, I didn't think for a minute you'd come looking for your share of anything.'

'I didn't.' Siena wrinkled her nose. Nothing but honesty would suit. 'But then I didn't exactly come out of an altruistic desire to see my sister. I came to England and to your house because I couldn't think of anywhere else to go.'

'And what's wrong with that?'

Siena looked at her sister in surprise at her calm acceptance. 'It doesn't exactly make me a very nice person.'

Laurie put an arm round her and pulled her towards her. Siena closed her eyes as tears pricked. Laurie's gentle acceptance floored her.

'Sorry,' she sniffed, wiping away at the annoying tell-tale trails as if she might be able to push them back into her eyes and pretend they'd never been there. 'I hate people who cry all the time.'

'It's hardly all the time.' Laurie squeezed her.

They sat together, both of them looking out over the view.

'You know, I feel terrible,' Laurie said.

'Why?' Siena put a hand on her sister's arm.

Laurie's deep and heartfelt sigh echoed with regret. 'If I'd been a better sister, you might not have had to run away. I could have helped you a long time ago.' Laurie shifted and dropped her arm. 'When I came out to France, I felt really envious of you at first.' A rueful smile shadowed her eyes. 'I didn't even want to like you. You were Celeste's. She chose you. Not me.'

Siena stiffened. 'Oh God, I'd never thought of it like that. You must have hated me.'

Laurie shook her head. 'No, I never hated you, but I avoided getting in touch with you. You had everything and it felt as if I had nothing. But then I realised that I'd had Dad. I'm really sorry you never knew him. He was an amazing dad. Actually,' she laughed, 'he was a bit crap at some things.' She rubbed at her jeans absently. 'A lot crap, but then a bit average at other things and brilliant a lot of the time. He never remembered I needed new clothes as I grew up, so everything was always too short. At school, the other girls would always ask if someone had died because my trousers were half-mast. I got to see a lot of action films rather than romances. We went on walking holidays rather than to the beach and he'd often turn up at parents' evening in his gardening clothes but,' she paused, her eyes brimming with memories, 'I knew he loved me. I came first. He was always there for me. Never ever let me down.'

'He sounds lovely.' Siena couldn't imagine it at all, especially not Celeste ever turning up anywhere less than perfectly dressed.

'You missed out. I felt really bad for you. I'm sure Celeste loves you.'

Siena hunched her shoulders. 'You think?'

'Of course she does. Her wanting you to marry Yves, that's her wanting to make sure you're looked after. She—'

'Er, Laurie? Why have you got your fingers crossed?'

'Aw, busted! OK, she's a skanky old control freak.'

Siena let out a tiny giggle and Laurie pulled a face, laughing.

'Look, she's not skanky, a control freak perhaps, but she does want the best for you.'

Siena lifted her shoulders and pushed them back feeling the tension knotted in the muscles there. 'Why doesn't if feel like that?'

'Because she's very formal. It's all about appearance and doing the right thing. She wants you to do the right thing. Not make mistakes.' Laurie turned so that she faced Siena. 'The thing is, the mistakes are yours to make. How do you know something is a mistake until you've made it? How you can you learn to do the right thing if you don't know what the wrong thing is?'

'But how do I tell her that? She won't listen and when she says all those things, she sounds so reasonable and I sound like a spoilt, stupid kid who doesn't know anything. You did it brilliantly.'

'It's different for me. You've been brought up to do what she tells you. You've never had the chance to grow up and be yourself. How long have you been here? A month? That's not exactly a long time to break a lifetime's conditioning. And that's why I said, and I meant it, in France that you always had a room. What I should have said is, you'll always have a home. You are my sister.'

Siena hugged her. 'Thank you.'

They sat in silence for a while.

'Jason's going to think I'm such a wimp.'

'I don't think so.' Laurie smiled. 'All his protective instincts were out in force.'

'I've made a terrible mistake with him.' Sadness filled her voice.

'Seriously? Oh no! I really like him. He seems lovely.'

'He is.' Siena's face crumpled. 'That's the problem. I've fallen in love with him.'

'Why don't you take her a hot drink and some shortbread biscuits?' suggested Laurie, when Jason declined pudding and she caught him looking at the clock in the dining room for the fifth time. The emotional charge of the day had made Siena subdued and she'd gone to bed early before dinner. Cam had entertained him playing billiards, or rather the bugger had entertained himself by trouncing Jason royally.

When he pushed open the bedroom door, the bedside lamp on his side of the bed was lit and Siena was a lump in the bed. He kicked off his shoes and padded around the end of the bed. She'd snuggled right into the bed so that all he could see were her over-bright eyes and nose peeking out.

'Hey, I brought you a hot chocolate and some of Norah's special shortbread. Scoot over.'

He lifted the duvet and squeezed on to the bed next to her.

Her fingers when she took the mug of hot chocolate from him were icy cold.

'You must think I'm rubbish.'

'Yeah,' he slipped an arm around her shoulders, 'but what's new there? You pinch my razors. Hog the duvet. Snore—'

'I do not.' Her head whipped round and he was pleased to see that near normal service was resuming.

'I meant not standing up to my mother.'

'Christ, I'm not sure I'd want to stand up to her. She makes a glacier look inviting. Is she always like that?'

Siena gave the question due consideration. 'I guess.'

'She obviously really rates this Yves guy.' And he could also see that Celeste wasn't the type of mother you could confide in. Certainly not tell intimate details of your sex life.

Siena shrugged. 'I told you, he's Mr Super Eligible. I'm surprised he's not given up yet and decided to go for someone else.'

Celeste's assumption that he was a temporary diversion rankled and Jason couldn't work out why. He and Siena had agreed at the outset that this wasn't forever, only for as long as they were both happy. He remembered the conversation clearly, the relief at Siena's easy acceptance of the proposed status quo. What he hadn't anticipated was that being with her made him the happiest he'd ever been.

'There's just over another week before you go back. Maybe she'll get the message.'

When she finished her drink, he got up, undressed and slipped into bed, putting an arm around her and kissing the top of her head.

'Jason?'

He tensed, still caught up in his thoughts and answered warily, 'Yes?'

'Can we go home tomorrow?

Something in the words *we* and *home*, settled the swirling thoughts. Pulling her against him, feeling her body soften, he kissed her forehead. 'Of course we can.'

'We need to get a Christmas tree.'

Chapter 26

'Thank God, you're here,' shouted Al across the kitchen. 'The bloody freezer packed up overnight.'

'Yes,' said Will, from his position lying on the floor in front of the freezer, his shirt sleeves rolled up to his elbows. 'Go and work your magic. Al's about to have a nervous breakdown, trying to work out what he's going to do with three legs of lamb and five tons of prawns. And I'm trying to put in a new fuse.'

'Simple,' said Siena, pulling on an apron, rolling up her sleeves and washing her hands.

By eleven, she and Al had sorted out three different prawn specials and the legs of lamb were cooking slowly in cast iron pans, each in a bottle of wine, which could be served up later in the week or refrozen if necessary.

The morning passed quickly and by three, as the lunchtime crowd had melted away, she enjoyed catching up with Marcus and Will over a coffee in the bar.

'Siena,' Lisa bounded in, said a universal hello to everyone, with her usual scowl for Will and hopped up on a bar stool next to her. 'I've got news for you.'

Will's mouth flattened in a mutinous line. 'It may have escaped your notice, but this is actually Siena's place of work and not a social centre. People usually come here and pay for food and or

289

drinks. I don't see you doing either.'

'Marcus,' said Lisa sweetly, 'what's the cheapest drink you have here?'

Marcus looked uncertainly between her and his boss. Will's lip curled and he stomped off into the kitchen. Siena wondered anew at the history between the two.

'Lime and soda.'

'I'll have a cup of coffee, now that Prince Charming's buggered off.' Lisa beamed but there was a definite sadness in her eyes.

'So,' she fidgeted on the stool and got out her phone. 'I went back to River Island on Saturday. The manageress grabbed me and said the day you were in the changing rooms doing your Gok Wan act, they doubled their takings.'

'What? Is that some kind of feng shui?'

'You haven't heard of Gok Wan?'

Marcus laughed. 'She hasn't heard of John Whitaker. Not likely to have heard of Gok Wan.'

'Seriously?' Lisa leaned back on her stool, almost falling off.

'I'm foreign, remember,' said Siena with a giggle at their mutually horrified faces.

'Gok Wan is a fashion presenter. I can't believe you haven't heard of him. Anyway no matter, when you were doling out fashion advice in the changing rooms, it turns out the store had its best takings ever. She wants you to go back and do the same again. How cool is that? And she's going to pay you. I thought you could go into business, position it as,' Lisa lifted her fingers in quote marks, '*Shopping with Siena*.'

'Really?' Ever since she'd been to the fashion school, she'd been thinking about an idea. On the long car journey back with Jason yesterday, she'd talked about it and he'd come up with lots of marketing suggestions. Which she guessed was why he ran his own business. She'd since phoned Ruth back to ask about other courses.

'That's brilliant and I've been thinking too. You know that dress, the one you sold? The lady at the fashion school loved my coat. I thought we could maybe go shopping again. Pick up some more pieces and sell them, online.'

'You could do more!' Lisa hopped up and down on her stool. 'You could set up a website, offering fashion advice, select outfits from different shops, be a personal shopper. Sell things online.'

'Or get a stall on the market? I was wondering about setting up a pop up fashion stall.'

Bubbling with ideas and enthusiasm, half an hour elapsed before Will stormed through the bar.

'If it isn't too much trouble, I'd be ever so grateful, if you could perhaps consider gracing us with your presence in the restaurant. You know, perhaps lay up the tables for service tonight, as we're paying you for the privilege.'

'Ooer,' whispered Lisa, hopping down from her seat and pushing a fiver towards Marcus as payment for her coffee. 'Better dash.' She winked at Siena and scuttled out of the pub.

Funnily enough Will's mood improved almost as soon as Lisa had departed.

By the time Jason came to ask if she was ready to go, Will was back to his usual self.

'Want a pint before you head off?'

'I'd love to but … can we do it tomorrow. All that driving over the weekend: I'm pretty knackered.'

'You didn't seem too knackered this morning,' whispered Siena in his ear as he unlocked the Land Rover.

He slapped her bottom and opened the door for her. 'That's why I'm knackered. Your insatiable demands on my poor broken body.'

'Pish,' dismissed Siena feeling decidedly pleased with herself. 'You weren't complaining when,' she leaned over and whispered the rest in his ear, grinning when he blushed.

'I'm a shadow of my former self. Wasting away, I am.'

'I'd better feed you up then. Seafood linguine tonight?' She lifted up a freezer bag. 'Al had to give everyone some seafood to take home.'

'Wonder if your sister has got a nice wine to go with it.'

Siena laughed. 'You really had no idea how expensive that wine was, did you?'

'No, I bloody didn't. Who in their right mind pays over three hundred quid for a bottle of wine?'

'Lots of people. You have to agree it was delicious. Worth every penny.'

'Hmm,' Jason didn't look convinced, 'as long as they're not my pennies.'

'Sadly it's back to supermarket plonk tonight. There's one bottle of Lafite left but I think we'd need a really good excuse to open it.' She sighed. 'I do love good wine.'

It was only as she was cooking and Jason was scanning the local paper that she suddenly remembered her friend's visit.

'Lisa dropped by the pub today.'

'Bet that thrilled Will,' he said his voice dry, not looking up from the entertainment page.

'What is it with those two? They clearly fancy the pants off each other but both pretend to hate each other.'

'I don't honestly know. He's a player and any woman who doesn't realise that is going to get her fingers burned. Maybe that's what happened, although it doesn't explain why *he's* so anti-her.'

'His loss, she's lovely. Anyway.' Siena proceeded to tell him her news.

'Lisa and I are going over to see the store manager tomorrow afternoon. She's going to pick me up from the pub.'

'Siena?' There was a questioning tone to his voice. 'It's the sixteenth of December today. A week before you go home.'

She stilled. 'Just for a chat with the manageress. About fashion.' She crossed her fingers under the table. Until she'd got things arranged, there was no point rocking the boat and suggesting that she might come back after Christmas.

Over dinner, Jason asked if she fancied going out on Saturday night to see some live music.

'What, like a concert?' She brightened, 'Do you know I've never been to one?'

'More of a gig in a pub. We'll start small, build up.'

'Sounds fun.' A thought suddenly occurred to her. 'Do you know something?'

He shook his head.

'That's the first time you've asked me out. That will be our first official date.'

He smiled. 'Better late than never, I guess.'

Who knew that domestic bliss could be so blissful? The quiet evening was the end to a pretty good day. If this was normal life, she could take it quite happily.

'Man, you are in so deep.'

'Don't talk out of your arse Will.' They were sitting at Jason's desk. 'Now what about the name for our spring seasonal?'

'Siena's Fancy. Under the Thumb. Married by May?' Will put his feet up on the table and leaned back on two legs of the chair, his hands behind his head.

'Piss off. I'm serious.' He pushed the new label designs over to Will's side of the table.

'I'm not surprised. She's a babe. Smart. Capable and puts a smile on your grumpy face. She's good for you.'

'And she's going home next week.' Why didn't that sound so great?

'She doesn't have to. She could come back after Christmas. I'll keep her on. She's a bloody good waitress.'

Jason's jaw tightened.

'Will, shut the fuck up.' He pushed Will's converse off the desk and tapped the A3 sheets insistently. 'Concentrate.'

'Ooooh. Touched a nerve.'

Jason sighed, Will really wasn't letting go of this. He sat back and folded his arms.

'Look mate, if you're so bloody insistent on knowing, Siena and I having been having a good time, probably because we knew it was finite. OK? That's all there is to it. Circumstances mean we're sharing a house but we're not living together.'

'Just having wild monkey sex on tap until then?'

'That's about the size of it.'

'By the way, that's a very defensive pose. Negative body language.'

'That's to stop me decking you. Now if we could get down to business instead of discussing my wild monkey sex life, which is nothing to do with you.'

Will narrowed his eyes.

'Jeez. You really believe that don't you? You poor deluded bastard.'

Jason clenched his teeth and counted to ten. Will leaned forward, not realising quite how much danger he was putting his ugly mug in.

'You could do much worse. I like her a lot. Like I said, she could stay on. You're punching well above your weight, but one day the brewery will take off and you'll make enough to keep her in Prada handbags and Mercedes.'

He winced. Siena used to drive a Mercedes. She once had a Prada handbag. She drank three-hundred pound bottles of wine without a second thought. It might be years before the brewery made proper money. At the moment they made enough to pay Ben and for Jason's own living expenses.

'I still think Married in May is a good name.'

'And I still think you're an arse, so shall we agree to disagree?'

'Fine by me.' Unrepentant Will smirked.

A top of the range BMW had parked in his space, which didn't improve his mood. Will's needling had got him thinking and his thoughts weren't encouraging.

No promises. They'd agreed. In five days' time she'd be gone.

Christmas Day. New Year's Eve. All without Siena. Now it had taken root, the thought wouldn't leave him alone. Like ivy, it pushed itself into every nook and cranny of his brain.

This had been a pleasant interlude for both of them. A brief novelty before going back to the champagne lifestyle she'd enjoyed all her life. He couldn't ask her to give that up, it would be Stacey all over again. Dooming someone to disappointment.

He'd topped off a bottle of lager when the doorbell went. They had nearly a week.

'Hi, is Siena in?' An urbane, business-suited man in his early forties stood on the doorstep. It took Jason a second to twig the French accent.

'Sorry, no she's out.'

The guy's face radiated supercilious amusement, reminding Jason of a particularly snooty cat. 'Shopping, knowing Siena.'

Yves. The suit said it all, along with the regal tilt of his head, suggesting an over-inflated awareness of his place in the world.

Jason shrugged, aware and amused by the contrast between his own faded jeans, bare feet and the obviously, tailored cut of Yves' suit and Italian leather shoes. 'I don't know. Do you want me to tell her you called?'

'Actually, I've come a long way to see her. I'd like to come in and wait, if I may?'

Not if he had anything to do with it. The bastard could go to hell.

'I've no idea how long she'll be. Haven't you got her mobile number?'

'I wanted to surprise her. She loves surprises.'

Did she? Should he have known that? 'So who are you?' Petty, but satisfying when he saw the expression on Yves' haughty face.

'I'm Yves. Her fiancé.'

Jason glared. 'Really? I should have guessed.'

'Yes,' the other man sighed. 'I'm the big bad wolf.' He held up his hands and grinned showing perfect white teeth. 'She's been telling fairy tales again about how awful I am. Mistreating her.

Taking her out to dinner against her will. Buying her expensive jewellery she doesn't need. You're not the first, you know.'

'Not the first what?' Jason felt as if he'd made the wrong move, left his queen in danger, enticed into it by a chess master.

'First lover she's taken. She's very impetuous. Impulsive. Acts on the spur of the moment.'

An image of her face laughing up at him, like a fallen snow angel, the day she dragged him into the field, filled his head.

'I've come to take her home. You probably think I'm mad.'

'Why would I think you're mad?'

'Because I'm so stupidly besotted, I forgive her every time she does this.'

Jason felt acutely uncomfortable discussing this on the door-step. Yves was supposed to be intimidating and authoritative. A heartless bully. Not understanding and lovesick, unafraid to declare his feelings.

'Why don't you come in? Have a drink. She shouldn't be too long. She's out with a friend.'

'Thank you.' When they reached the kitchen, the other man's eyes were round with fascination.

'Siena lives here? *Nom d'un chien*! I can't believe it.' His accent thickened and he laughed delightedly. 'My poor girl. Oh, she really will be ready to come home this time.'

'I wouldn't be too sure about that.' Siena didn't seem to mind the cosiness of the kitchen and the tiny lounge and certainly didn't complain about the size of the bathroom or having to share it any more.

'Would you like a drink? I've got lager or English beer.'

'Do you have any wine?'

'Yeah, some white.' He removed the open bottle from the fridge.

'*Actuellement*, no. Don't worry. It looks a bit—' He pulled a face. 'Poor Siena, is that what she's reduced to drinking now? We'll have to sort that out.' He placed his hands on the back of one of the chairs, like the foreman of a jury delivering important news. 'I think I need to explain. This is not the first time Siena has decided to have a little adventure. You have only heard her side of the story, which I'm sure was very sad.'

'Adventure?' Rather damning terminology.

'I know I'm an idiot. But I love her. However, I have responsibilities. She can't seem to understand that. Last time I had to go to the estate to manage some business and I couldn't take her to the Paris shows, so she went to Canada. A month's skiing. A fling with an instructor. Decided she was going to be a ski teacher. Then in January, I had to cancel our trip to London. She flew to New York. I think he was a photographer and that's what she was going to be.' He smiled sadly. 'It's a pattern I'm afraid. But she always comes back. This time, she wants to be a fashion designer and there's you. She's very impetuous, led by her passions, *non*?'

A flush heated Jason's body. Her hands on him. He had to turn away.

'She seems happy enough to me. Enjoying the independence.' Jason tried to reconcile what Yves was saying with everything he knew about Siena.

Yves laughed. 'You're not thinking of asking her to stay? With you, in this,' his eyes ranged dismissively around the room, 'love nest? Look around you. This is novelty. How long before she misses her designer clothes, shopping trips, the skiing – she loves skiing. You know that? Can you afford to take her to Zermatt?'

At the moment Jason couldn't afford to take her to Tesco, not until the next pay check.

Who knew how long it would be before his finances looked healthier? How long would it be before Siena's relentless optimism was ground down by disappointment? Stacey who had lived with him for three years hadn't been prepared to take the risk; why would Siena? And when had he started thinking of Siena with any permanence? Hell, Will was right. He was in too deep. They'd agreed this was never supposed to be forever. But he wanted her to be happy.

'Do you have a bathroom I could use?'

Of course they had a flipping bathroom, what did he think this was? 'Up the stairs, second door.'

When Yves didn't reappear, Jason started to mount the stairs and saw him coming out of Siena's bedroom, his hand inside his suit jacket pocket.

The other man gave him a dejected smile. 'Sorry I couldn't resist. Seeing where she's been all this time.'

Something didn't quite ring true but Jason couldn't put a finger on it.

'Hi Jason,' Siena's voice called as the front door opened.

'Hi, you've—'

'Siena,' Yves stumbled down the last stairs in his haste to get to her, enfolding her in a film star style heartfelt hug. He even threw in an expression of heart-rending pain.

Jason itched to shove him out of the way. Siena should be in his arms. For good. But it wouldn't be fair. He could never give her what she needed.

'Yves.' Her voice sounded choked. Jason couldn't bear to look. Retreating to the kitchen he took a long swallow of beer.

Siena walked in as he was pulling a second bottle out of the fridge, her eyes bright, as if close to tears.

'Yves wants to talk.'

Four simple words. Who knew four words could rip your heart out?

Yves held all the aces. He'd described himself as her fiancé. He could give Siena everything. What could Jason offer?

'He wants me to fly back with him but I've said I'd just go out to dinner with him. He's waiting in the car. It was the only way I could agree to get him to go.' She crossed over to touch his arm and he flinched. 'I won't be long.'

'Are you going to tell him that you're not going to marry him? He seems to think it's a done deal.' It felt as if he was grasping at the unravelling string of a kite inevitably pulling through his grasp. Illogical. She was going next week anyway. Why should a few days more make any difference? 'Tell him now.'

She sighed. 'I've tried. He wants to talk. It's only fair.'

'It wasn't fair when he punched you.' And being a jerk, making it harder for her, was fair? He couldn't help himself.

'No but I'm a different person now. Stronger. I can stand up to him.'

Typical sunshine princess, convinced she could take on the world and win.

'I owe it to him.'

'You owe him nothing.'

She gave him a disapproving look as if to say, you're better than this.

'He's a long-standing family friend. He says he feels humili-ated and wants us to discuss what we'll say to people. I owe him that much.'

'I don't trust him.'

'Jason. We'll be in a restaurant in public. I'll have my phone on me. What can possibly go wrong?'

Jason could think of lots of things. Yves, silver-tongued, prom-ising her skiing trips, sailing in the Bahamas, convertible Mercedes and next season's Prada handbag. All the things impossibly out of his reach.

Swallowing hard, he pulled her to him. 'Please don't go.'

The words hung between them.

Her face softened and with a tender smile, she put both arms around his neck and kissed him.

'I won't be long. And then,' she nipped at his lips, 'we can pick up where we left off. Maybe discuss things. I'm not sure I want to live in France. Do you think Will would keep me on? I could come back in the New Year. What do you think?'

With a heavy sigh, he let go of her, moving away to the other side of the kitchen. He hadn't planned to have this conversation.

'I'm being unfair. This is good timing. You're going home anyway. Why not now? Not back to him. But home. It's been nice. We've had a great time. I will miss you but you were always going to leave. I can't look after you.' And he sounded like a knob. A prize top-dog top-knob. 'You need someone, not Yves, of course, but someone who can buy you decent wine, fly you to Paris to see the Christmas tree at Galeries Lafayette every year, get tickets for a box at the rugby. Give you the things you're used to.' He tried hard not to look at her. 'The things you deserve.' Jeez, why did trying to do the right thing sound so wanky?

'What if that's not what I want any more?' Her chin lifted in the familiar Warrior Princess stance. 'What if I want to stay?'

Longing, stealthy and beguiling like a serpent gliding through water, wound its way around him. Easy to ask her to stay. But wrong.

'Siena,' his sigh sizzled with frustration, 'I'm in debt up to my eyeballs. What can I offer? I like you, a lot.' A vice closed around his heart, tightening with each word. 'But it's never going to be long-term. I can't look after you, not like you're used to. There will be someone right for you one day.'

'Who says,' she shot at him bitterly, 'I need someone to look after me?'

He raised an eyebrow.

'OK. You rescued me but I would have … I would have done something.' Her voice hardened. 'What's changed, Jason?'

'Nothing, we always knew there was an end. It's a few days earlier, that's all.'

Siena stared at him, still in combat mode. Glorious, proud. Not going down without a fight. She stormed over to stand nose to nose with him.

'Do you know what I think? This isn't about me at all. This is about you. Running scared. Not wanting to commit. Scared of what you might feel.'

'No it's not. This was always temporary. We agreed. You agreed

300

to that. Fun. Sex. Day to day.' He wasn't lying, so why did he feel so bad?

'Bullshit Jason. We've got more than that and if you're too cowardly to admit it, that's your problem but don't make it mine. If you want me to leave, say so.'

'Yeah, I want you to leave.' The lie slipped out to the soundtrack of another voice roaring denial in his head

With a slam of the door, an explosive bang that disturbed each piece of china on the dresser from somnolent slumber, she flounced out of the kitchen. A whirlwind of hair and defiant, furious attitude. He heard the second slam of the front door.

Christ, he was a pillock.

The quiet of the house throbbed with portent, as if punctuating the seismic mistake he'd made. A blanket of silence so empty he immediately wanted to fill it again with the sounds of her awful singing, the funny little noise she made in the shower when the first cascade of water hit and her tuneless humming as she applied her mascara.

Of course he'd miss her. The company. Her cooking. The sex. He was only human. But it was for the best, wasn't it? There was tons of stuff he wouldn't miss, like the softness of her bottom squashed up against his groin every morning or the fact that no matter what position they fell asleep in, when he woke he'd pull her to him.

Siena fumed. So cross with Jason that she barely heard Yves.

'I have to say,' Yves looked over his menu at her, 'you're looking well. What happened to the Prada?'

Jason was an idiot.

'Sorry, what did you say?'

Yves glanced at his phone before tutting and repeated his question.

'I sold it.' Satisfaction for that still hummed in her belly and it had been worth being admonished by a pint-sized, foot-stamping bundle of outrage and indignation. Nanna had insisted she kept the sewing machine. Jason had laughed when he realised what she'd done with the money. That was the first time they made love.

'Are you listening to me?' Yves caught her wrist.

'Yes.' She had no idea what he'd said. 'How did you find me?'

'Celeste had private detectives keeping an eye on your sister's house. You took your time getting there. I was beginning to give up hope. They followed you back here. Back to my question. How did you manage to find someone to look after you so quickly?' He snorted. 'I guess it's easier for women. A bit Neanderthal for you though, darling. If I'd realised you liked rough,' the ice blue eyes dropped to her cleavage and then further down, 'I'd have upped my game.' Again he picked up his phone, his finger tapping the screen.

Mustering every ounce of loathing, she levelled a scathing look at him. She wasn't scared of him, although she had to clench her back teeth quite hard to stop herself shaking.

'We share a house. It's Laurie's house. She let me stay and I got a job. No one is looking after me.'

Although despite his grumpy, unwelcoming denials, Jason did make her feel looked after. It was the little things he did. Handing her up into the Land Rover. Drying her off after a shower together. Stepping in front of Will.

The one thing that he said he couldn't do and he did it all the time without realising it.

'A job? Doing what?'

'Waitressing.'

'You. Waitressing?' Yves let out a guffaw of laughter that caught the attention of the other diners, their heads turning like curious meerkats.

With quiet dignity she ignored the staring faces. 'Yes.'

'I never thought I'd live to see the day that the ninth Comtesse was a waitress. Grand mère would spin in her grave.'

'Yves. I'm not going to marry you. It's over. I'm not coming back to France.' As soon as she said it, she knew it was true. She couldn't go back. Not now. 'Why do you even want me? You said yourself I'm …'

'Frigid? Cold? Ungrateful?' He arched a sardonic eyebrow.

'Maybe we're not compatible.'

'So *you've* decided. Like that,' he flicked his fingers, 'that it's over.'

'It never started. You and Maman assumed. I'm not ready to get married. I want to do something with my life.'

'So what is it you are doing that is so wonderful?' He looked genuinely bemused. 'Working? Serving people.'

With a rueful smile, she picked up the glass of red wine Yves had insisted she had. It seemed easier to agree to the small request when she knew she had a far greater battle ahead. 'Doesn't sound great, but I like it.'

The lines in Yves' face had deepened, contorted by disbelief and disgust.

'Be honest, Yves. Do you even love me?'

Yves considered the question, his head tilting to one side, before answering with surprising gentleness. 'People in our position do not "love". We have traditions and values to uphold. Land to preserve. Legacies to honour.' His glance returned to his phone and suddenly animated, he tapped the screen.

'Have you ever been in love?'

He swallowed and looked over her shoulder. Eventually, he brought his gaze back to her face and said with a self-deprecating laugh. 'Once. A long time ago.'

They lapsed into silence. His phone beeped and he grabbed it. Siena rolled her eyes as he read a message before looking back at her. Suddenly, she warranted his full attention.

'Do you love him?' Yves' question startled her.

'Yes.' She held his piercing gaze. 'Yes. I do.'

'Enough to make sacrifices?'

The question warranted serious thought but she knew the answer.

'Yes,' she admitted, with a steady calmness. Conviction

strengthened and grounded her.

Yves nodded. She could hardly believe this uncharacteristic sympathy. It had never occurred to her that he'd once loved someone.

'And does he love you?'

She shrugged. 'I don't know.'

'If he doesn't, where does that leave you?'

She shrugged again, ignoring the numb emptiness in her chest.

'Don't give it all up, Siena. Love hurts. Leaving your life behind on a whim. Sexual attraction. It's a mistake. I'm older and wiser. I know, I promise you.'

This was a side of Yves she'd not seen before.

'At least come back to Paris and make peace with your mother and Harry. You said you'd come back for the party. You mother wants you home. Come home for Christmas. Like you said you would. I've got tickets for the last flight to Paris.'

She shook her sadly. Jason might not want her but she couldn't leave, not without saying goodbye to him properly.

'No, I can't Yves.'

They finished their meal in virtual silence until Yves looked at his watch. 'I've got time to run you home before my flight. You could still come back with me.'

Siena looked at him. He held up his hands in a gesture of surrender.

'I give up; the girl of my dreams doesn't want me. I get it.'

Her withering glance made no impression on him. 'Don't give me that. I was never the girl of your dreams.'

In the darkness of the car with the engine running smoothly, she relaxed into the leather seat. The darkness outside raced by and Yves kept up an almost incessant stream of chat, about everyone they knew, although her mind kept straying.

Picturing Jason in the kitchen. It didn't have to be over. She needed to reassure him that she didn't need anything from her.

He was panicking. Thinking about Stacey. Not learning from the past. Not moving forward. She was different. He'd laid out the rules from the outset. She'd accepted them. There had to be a way to make him see that. If he didn't love her, he did care. Or was that wishful thinking?

Yves interrupted her chain of thought again. He was positively verbose and the journey seemed to be taking forever.

'Where are we?' she asked. They were on a much busier road, with three lanes and lots of lights.

Yves didn't say anything; he was too intent on the road, which had an awful lot of traffic. Blue signs over the road flashed by so quickly she couldn't read them.

Alarm bells started to ring.

'Yves. Where are we?'

'*Ne t'en fais pas*. I didn't programme the navigational system properly. It's taking us rather a circuitous route.'

But she did worry.

'Yves! This is the airport.'

He ignored her, concentrating on the unfamiliar lanes of traffic.

'Yves. Stop the car. Yves!'

'Stop being ridiculous, Siena. I can't stop here.'

'I'm not going with you.'

'Let's have the discussion when we get to the terminal.'

'I've already told you.'

'Give me one more chance, Siena.'

She shook her head and mutinously folded her arms. He couldn't force her to get on the plane.

They pulled up and Yves handed the keys to a valet before coming round to open her door.

'I'm not getting out.'

Yves face hardened. 'Do you know what?' he spat. 'I've tried playing Mr Nice and now I'm going to furnish you with a few facts. I suggest you get out of the car right now otherwise you will be extremely sorry.'

Siena swallowed hard, a rushing in her ears. He couldn't force her onto a plane. And! He didn't have her passport. Of course he didn't. It was in the top drawer beside her bed in the house. She was perfectly safe.

The minute she got out of the car, he gripped her arm and almost frog-marched her into the terminal and straight over to the Air France check-in. The girl on the desk wore a jaunty elf hat, green felt with a black buckle, holly poking out of the top. Down the check-in line, there were Santa hats and tinsel halos. She smiled. Yves couldn't do anything. Festive spirit withstanding, they had their jobs to do. Procedures to follow.

'You don't have my passport,' she hissed.

'Siena. Siena. Siena. What do you take me for?' With a slow triumphant smile, he withdrew a passport from his inside breast pocket.

Fear skittered up her spine. 'I'm not getting on a plane with you.' She raised her voice.

His grip on her arm tightened painfully and he whispered in her ear, his voice full of menace. 'Do as I say, otherwise you will be very, very sorry. And so will your new boyfriend. Has he mentioned Stacey to you?'

Breath whooshed out of her lungs and she gave him a wide-eyed stare.

'I rather thought that might capture your attention. We'll check in and I can explain.'

'But there's no point.'

'Hear me out. I think you'll find there's every point.'

Glancing around the airport, she was reassured by the sight of a British policeman. There were quite a few of them. She couldn't come to any harm, she hoped…

Once checked in, Yves relaxed his pincer like hold on her arm. Absently, she rubbed at the pinch mark he left. Jason would be furious when he saw them.

306

'Are you going to tell me what this is about?'

Yves had insisted on them going to a coffee bar, where a half-hearted attempt had been made to remind customers that it was December. The staff wore flashing, glitter encrusted badges and earrings along with late-night faded smiles. Tinsel had been draped along framed pictures of cities of Europe on the walls. One of Paris. Taken from Sacré-Coeur. Siena smiled.

'It's quite simple. You have one choice. You get on the flight with me and I do you a favour.'

Frustration knotted her stomach. Why wouldn't he listen? 'Yves, I am not going back with you.' She tapped her phone to emphasise the point.

'Did you not wonder why I didn't come knocking at the door, the day after you returned from your sister's house?'

Siena stared mutinously at him. In the background, she could hear *Silent Night* playing. She hadn't got Jason a Christmas present yet. Her eyes went back to the picture of Paris and the droopy loop of gold tinsel that obscured the Eiffel Tower. Her photo was much better.

'I was busy. Gathering information. Information makes you a king. I don't know who said that first, but it's true.'

A Hollywood blockbuster would be her guess.

'Stacey. His ex. It would be a simple matter to persuade her to make a claim against him. Half the proceeds of his flat in London. Did you know about it?'

'Yes. And she hasn't got a leg to stand on.'

'Not without a very good lawyer. *Non.*'

She went very still.

'Of course, with a good lawyer she could make a case. Even if she didn't win. It would cost a lot of money. So I suggest that if you want to spare him a nasty, protracted court case, you get on the plane with me.'

'You bastard,' she snarled at him.

'*Ma mère* would disagree.' His mouth curved in self-satisfied smirk.

He leaned over and before she realised what he was doing he'd snatched her phone from her.

'Give that back.'

'You don't need it. We're talking. You can have it back when we're on the plane.'

With a firm hand balled in the small of her back, threatening a punch, Yves guided her towards the security gate. Resolve stiffened her. She refused to let him win. As they passed an armed uniformed officer standing guard, she pulled away from Yves, let her legs go limp and collapsed at the policeman's feet.

'Up you come, young lady.'

Before she'd had chance to thank him, Yves intercepted. 'So sorry officer, she's a bit tipsy.'

The policeman's face darkened. 'I hope you've got time to pour plenty of coffee into her. If she's drunk they won't let her on the plane.'

'I'm not drunk,' protested Siena her heart pounding. 'Smell my breath.'

The policeman backed away.

'Darling, leave the poor man alone. Let's go find you a coffee.'

'No,' she grabbed the officer's arm. 'I don't want to catch the flight. He's making me.'

The man's eyes narrowed and he looked at Yves more carefully.

'Siena, stop making a scene. You're drunk. Flying is perfectly safe. We've been through this before.'

As if someone had said, 'at ease,' the policeman's expression returned to bored resignation.

'I'm not afraid of flying,' she said resolutely.

'Coffee,' the policeman nodded across the terminal towards the Costa coffee they'd left minutes before.

Refusing to give in, a stab of adrenaline, fired by panic shot through her. Without thinking, she kicked the policeman hard on the shin.

'What the?' he exclaimed. 'Madam, you need to sober up before I arrest you for assaulting a police officer'

All Siena heard was 'arrest you'. She kicked him again even harder.

'I've warned you.'

Yves tugged at her. 'Sorry officer, I'll sober her up. Once we're on the flight to Paris, she'll be fine. I promise,' he entreated. 'She's never done this before. Please don't arrest her.'

Siena did the only thing she could think of; she kicked the poor man for a third time.

Chapter 27

The whispered debate raged at the custody sergeant's desk, with lots of glances her way. Maybe they were going to let her go.

There'd been a rather depressing attempt at decoration comprising a lacklustre piece of silver tinsel looped along the front of the desk, which was falling off at one end and a plastic holly wreath hooked onto the coat stand in the corner. Enough to remind you that Christmas was coming, in case you'd forgotten and sparse enough to let you ignore it. Christmas was only days away and she had no idea where she'd be spending it. Not in France, that was for sure. Or with Jason. She was so mad at him. And terrified that he really believed what he said, *espèce d'imbécile.*

She screwed up her eyes as if that might shield her from the bleak ache in her chest.

Her bottom had almost welded itself to the hard grey plastic seat, she'd been here so long. They'd taken all her things from her. Watch, jewellery, handbag.

'Miss Browne-Martin. I'm afraid we're going to have to keep you here overnight.'

She got the impression that Sergeant Franks had been bullied into coming over to tell her, as if none of them wanted to break the news to her.

'Really? Can't you let me go and I'll come back tomorrow.'

'Sorry. I'm afraid it doesn't work like that. You've committed a serious offence.' She could see the struggle on his face between being professional and fatherly.

'But I did apologise to the police constable and explained why I did it.' Surely they could see she wasn't a real criminal. 'I was desperate and it was spur of the moment. It wasn't assault, not proper assault. In fact he saved me from a probable assault of my own.'

'Sorry Miss,' Franks shot a look over his shoulder at the two officers, staying put behind the desk. 'I have to follow procedure. What you say to me doesn't count. I can't make those decisions and as we can't get hold of a duty solicitor for you tonight, you're going to have to spend a night in one of our cells. Unless,' he looked hopeful, 'you have your own legal representation.'

The irony blossomed, brilliant and beautiful. 'I do, unfortunately the same man is also Yves' uncle. I don't think he would be prepared to help.'

The policeman winced. 'No one else?'

She could call Jason and ask him except his number was in her phone in Yves pocket probably half way across the Channel by now. Bloody phones, everything was in them. 'Not really.'

'We'll do our best to make you as comfortable as possible.'

Siena closed her eyes vacillating between the urge to laugh or cry. With a glass of Prosecco in hand with Lisa, or at the pub, Will leaning at the bar and Marcus perched on a stool, the retelling of her night in the cells would go down well.

But what about Jason right now? She tried to haul back the soft sob that broke. What was he thinking? That she'd left?

'Is there any way I can get a message to someone to let them know I'm safe?'

'Do you have a number?'

'It's in my phone.' She sighed. Which had been palmed by Yves in the coffee shop.

'If you have an address, I could phone the local police station.

See if someone could drop in.' His face concertinaed into lines. 'But there's a strong chance they're not going to have the manpower. Not this time of night.'

The alarm buzzed, ejecting him with a jump from the type of sleep extreme climbers on the edge of a mountain enjoy.

Balefully he looked at clock. At some time around three, he'd given up listening for her to come home. Given up trying to shape any sort of apology. Five was the last time he remembered looking at the digital numbers.

Groggy and hopeful, he reached for his phone.

Nothing.

He rolled off the bed still fully dressed and looked out into the hallway. Her bedroom door framed the sunlight pouring in through open curtains.

Nausea, a riptide of acid, curled low in his stomach. What had he done?

What an arse, telling her to go home. She'd done what he told her to. So now why did he have this hollow feeling in his chest? He shook his head and caught sight of himself in the mirror.

'You fucking dickhead.' Last night's clothes looked worse this morning. He looked like shit.

Shoving two indigestion tablets into his mouth, he stripped and got into the shower. As punishment, he turned the tap to cold halfway through. It cleared the fug residing in his head and he was able to face himself in the mirror with slightly more equanimity.

In the reflection behind him, he could see the rank and file of the red and white jars and tubes of her lotions and potions. Arranged in little trios of this and that, an order to them quite beyond him. Knowing it wouldn't help, he picked up the moisturiser she smoothed on her face and neck every morning, despite the fact she looked perfect already. Opened it, and like a dumb masochist, took in a deep smell.

As if he'd conjured up a ghost, she flitted through the bathroom, her ridiculous wisp of a robe floating after her during their ritual dance between sink and shower, the intimate mix of her scent riding like a shadow behind her.

He closed his eyes, almost felled by the ache hollowing out his chest. Had he made a terrible mistake?

'You bloody know you have,' he told his reflection in the mirror.

Coffee and toast did nothing to settle his stomach. His phone sat on the table, idle and utterly fucking useless. He wanted to shake the damn thing, make it work, make it ring. For the tenth time, he scrolled through the roll call of inadequate texts he'd sent last night.

Let me know you're safe.

Are you coming back tonight?

Can you ring me? I'm worried about you. Are you safe?

He understood why she hadn't texted him back. But what if Yves had hurt her? Not in public, surely. Christ, he didn't even know which restaurant they'd gone to last night. Where were they now? In a hotel? He could call all the hotels in the area. What sort of reaction would he get if he asked if they had a Frenchman staying with them called Yves?

He put his elbows on his knees, his head sinking into his hands. She'd gone. And he'd sent her packing.

He stared down at the floor, still covered in glitter despite Siena's blithe assurance she'd tidy up every 'last smidge'. A memory of her cheeky assurance and optimism that she could do a good job pierced him.

He jumped to his feet. Fuck it. Siena wouldn't sit here being maudlin. She'd be doing something about it. They could sort the details out later, but he had to get her back here where she belonged.

He'd call her on the hour, every hour until she answered and he could tell her ... His heart kicked in his chest, a bloom of sensation that radiated out to every nerve ending.

Tell her that he loved her.

Suddenly it was that simple. With a surge of hope, his fingertips tingling, he called her number, his foot tapping under the table as he listened to the beeps connecting the call. It began to ring. Snapping to attention he sat up. Held the phone away, looked at it and then put it back to his ear to listen again.

With a bitter groan, he slapped the phone on the table. Nothing could have broadcast her return to France more authoritatively than the alien long flat intermittent beep of an overseas dialling tone.

Chapter 28

Bright light forced her eyelids shut again as Siena came to. With a groan she unpeeled herself from the horrible blue plastic mattress, which squeaked as she moved. Shifting her weight and gaining purchase on the slippery surface whilst wrapped in a blanket with the texture of fibreglass, took some effort, but eventually she managed to get to a sitting position. Daylight poured in from glass bricks high above her head, glinting off the glossy glaze of the tiled walls.

The surfeit of man-made materials had left her in a cocoon of damp sweat, making her shiver slightly. She felt grubby, her skin soiled to the absolute bone, although the cell gleamed with the clinical spotlessness of an operating theatre. The first thing she'd do when she got out of here was wash around the back of her neck. Let clean water trickle down her neck under her clothes.

Worse still was the sense of being watched. For most of the night, she'd tucked herself into the wall, her back to the black half sphere in the ceiling. The slot in the door shot home, as it had done numerous times during the long dark hours of the night, and a face appeared.

'Drink? Tea? Coffee?'

'Coffee please.'

She closed her eyes, and tipped her head back. Thank God, it was morning and she could get out of here. Unfortunately getting out wasn't anywhere near as easy as getting in.

'Bloody hell Siena, you know how to get yourself to trouble. Assaulting a police officer! The old bill take that sort of thing very seriously.' Despite his wide-eyed amazement, Will looked reluctantly impressed. 'Can I ask the obvious question?' He led her out of the magistrate's court towards his battered Golf.

'What, why did I kick him?' she asked getting into the front seat.

'I think that was probably quite a smart move. I can see why you did it, although I'm not sure how Yves thought he'd force you to get on the plane.'

'He had a few aces up his sleeve.'

She told Will what Yves had been planning.

'Wow, he did his homework. Could he still go through with it?'

'Yes. I guess. But the threat would have been worse than reality and once you know someone is behind the threat, it undermines the case. I doubt Stacey would have gone through with it, especially not if she thought the police had been involved.'

'No, she wouldn't have liked that at all,' said Will with a cynical laugh. 'Reputation and money was very important to her. Jason was alright when he had a fancy job in the City but she didn't like the loss of status when he quit.'

'She doesn't sound very nice. No wonder he thinks that I won't stick around for too long. He's convinced that I'll get bored, get fed up with not being rich and go home.'

'You can't blame him, really, Stacey wasn't the best example of the female species. I don't think Jason was so in love with her that he was heart-broken, more disappointed she wasn't prepared to work with him as a team. He wanted a partner, support; not financial but someone who would say, 'I understand your dreams and I'll be there to help you get there." Will slapped his forehead. 'And if you repeat that I will have to kill you because he will fucking kill me.'

'So what about you? What are your dreams?'

'Me? I don't go in for that new age crap.'

Siena didn't believe a word he said.

'What I really want to know,' Will gave a coy look, 'is why you didn't call Jason?'

Siena's lips tightened. 'Because we had a bit of a row last night.'

Her head hurt like crazy and she felt like she'd been through an emotional tornado that had picked her up, given her a maximum spin and then spat her out, leaving her like a limp doll tossed over an old fence.

Thank goodness the magistrate had been prepared to listen. Will's character reference had also helped. She couldn't leave the country now even if she wanted to and there was the small matter of community service. There might be extenuating circumstances, but no matter what, you could not kick a policeman.

'I don't want to see Jason at the moment.' She fiddled with her watch, remembering how good it had been to get her things back.

She'd lain awake for a long time on that hard narrow bench bed in the small hours of this morning thinking about home. Wishing she was lying across Jason's warm, hard body, her leg crooked into his. That was home, except he couldn't see that. Would he ever? Tough, she had no intention of wasting any more time waiting for him to catch up.

He might be running scared of commitment and convinced that she needed more from him than he could give, but she was going to show him she didn't need him or any other man telling her what she did or didn't want from life.

Yves, Maman and Jason, even Laurie to an extent, all had views on how she should live her life. It was time she took charge and decided for herself.

She still had a lot to prove to herself. She had a life to live and she wasn't exactly desperate to tie herself to one man. She was going to start over. By herself.

'Now are we all done?' Will started the engine. 'Back to Brook

Street?'

'No, I can't go back. Jason doesn't want me. Can I ask you a massive favour?'

He suddenly hunched over the steering wheel, wariness bouncing from his body language.

'Perhaps? Please don't tell me you want me to take you back to Heathrow.'

Chapter 29

The combined rattles of the Land Rover were so loud, it felt likely something might shake loose at any moment and fall off, and his own teeth were in danger of being shaken from their sockets. Jason ignored the noise and kept his foot flat to the floor. As long as it wasn't the engine, he wasn't stopping. He had exactly fifty-five minutes before the flight left. If he didn't catch this one, he had no idea how to track Siena down. Neither Laurie nor Cam were answering their phones.

He floored the car up the hill to Luton Airport. Thank God for online check-in. He'd snagged the last seat on the twelve o'clock flight. He was due to land at two o'clock and the game at the Stade de France – where Siena's stepfather was spending his birthday – was set to kick off at two thirty.

Now he had just twenty-five minutes to park, get through security and to the gate. Fuck, he was cutting it fine. The tension in his shoulders was wound so tightly he could barely unclamp his hands from the steering wheel.

'Good afternoon sir, is this your first time with us? Can I take your registration number?'

Sweat ran down his back. Twenty minutes. He rattled off the number.

'Thank you, Sir. Can I ask you to—'

'No you can't.' He flung the keys at her through the window, opened his door, and squeezed the through the gap between the car and the kiosk, taking off at a run towards the terminal, patting his pockets as he went. Passport, wallet; he had them both.

Weaving through people, he jumped over a couple of pull along cases that threatened to derail his determined trajectory, any minute expecting to be rugby tackled to the floor by a gun toting police officer.

Bursting through the doors, he took a sharp left racing towards the escalator at the far end.

'Excuse me. Excuse me,' he panted, pushing through dumb-ass people who'd decided that the centre of the escalator was a good place to stand.

At the top, there was a small queue waiting to go through passport control. Shit. He rubbed his calf with his other foot like a demented stork. What was wrong with these people? The family in front of him hadn't even got their passports ready.

'Hurry up,' he muttered under his breath as they eventually began to root through an enormous holdall, saying to the man on the desk, all jokey and relaxed. 'They're in here somewhere.'

When he finally got the desk, the Border Force officer took his time giving Jason a careful look before studying his photo.

Jason attempted a smile, trying to hide his mounting impatience, knowing how easy it would be for this guy to make life difficult if he pissed him off.

At last he was waved through, to find an endless line of people snaking back and forth between tape barriers as far as the eye could see. The security barriers and detectors seemed impossibly distant. He looked at his watch. Ten minutes to boarding.

He had to get the plane.

'Are you OK, sir?' He'd missed the approach of the uniformed lady. She probably thought he was a bit suspicious, all sweaty and wide-eyed with panic.

'No, my flight leaves in ten minutes.'

'Have you got luggage on board?'

For a second he hesitated. Luggage on board meant they wouldn't take off without you. Delays while they waited for you. 'Yes,' he lied.

'Come with me.' She guided him straight through, ducking under the barriers, leading him straight to security. 'Have a good flight.'

'Thank you. Thank you.'

For once the metal detector arch didn't beep and he ran through to the crowded concourse till he spotted a departure board. Gate 27. A ten minute walk. Jeez. Couldn't someone give him a break?

He took off at a run, careering along the travellator, skipping over luggage. In the distance he could see the yellow illuminated sign for the gate.

Jumping down three stairs at a time, he tore down the two flights of stairs emerging at the bottom into an almost deserted waiting area.

'In the nick of time,' said the girl at the desk, her grave expression giving way to a sympathetic smile. With a quick look at his passport she waved him through. 'Have a good flight.'

Now, he'd caught the damn thing, it couldn't fail to be good. All he had to do during the next seventy-five minutes was work out what he was going to say when he got to the other end.

Jason pushed his way through the crowds of good-natured fans reeling with bonhomie, feeling a little punch-drunk himself. Operating on adrenaline after hardly any sleep couldn't be good for you. The tall, grey-walled sides of the stadium stretched up and he searched anxiously for the small door that led to the admin office suite.

With the place full of fans, security was much tighter. Fingers crossed Georges was there and could help. If not he'd have to blag it.

The unobtrusive door was unmanned. He slipped inside and ran lightly up the flight of stairs.

'Monsieur!' The startled girl, sitting in the big empty office, shot a barrage of impossible to understand French at him, with enough *ne* and *pas* in there to make it clear, this was out of bounds.

'*Je vuex vois.*' What was the blessed conjunction of *to see*? '*Je veux Georges. C'est très important.*'

'Georges Bouthillier?'

Jason nodded. 'Oui, il.' He had no idea if it was the right Georges or not.

'I can page him for you.' See, why did French people always do that? Let you make an arse of yourself with dodgy French and then speak in perfect effing English.

She picked up a phone and gabbled with high speed velocity down the line.

'Your name.'

'Jason, I was here with Siena Browne-Martin two weeks ago. He'll remember me.'

'Monsieur Jason.' Georges greeted him like an old friend. 'How can I help you? I trust you are not seeking tickets for the match today? They are completely sold out.'

'No. Not at all. I need to speak to Monsieur Harvieu, Siena's stepfather. It is very urgent.'

'This is most unusual. I'm not sure if I can accommodate your request. He has many guests with him.'

'Please. I need your help. I need to find Siena and I've no idea where she lives.'

Georges smiled. 'It is an affair of the heart?'

'Yes, yes, yes.' Jason nodded furiously. The French were famous romantics.

Georges pursed his lips. 'And it can't wait until after the game?'

Jason shook his head.

'I'll see what I can do. Wait here.' The older man opened the door to a small office. 'Take a seat and I will be back directly.' He closed the door behind him.

322

Calendars and wall charts filled every space on the walls, blocked off in elaborate colour coded lines. Far, far in the distance he could hear the muted hum of the crowd.

Alone in the room it felt as if he was awaiting a sentence. It took him back to the Place de la Concorde and the conversation with Siena. At least he wasn't about to face the guillotine. And she'd been right. History didn't have to repeat itself; you could learn. He'd made mistakes with Stacey. Not been honest with her at the outset. Never told her how important the brewery was to him. Let her assume too many things. Drifted into the relationship. Looked for the wrong things.

He picked up his phone. He should have rung Will, let him know he hadn't gone AWOL. Shit! He'd bloody done it again. Not set up his phone for roaming. The damn thing was useless.

With a loud crash, the door flew open and bounced back against the wall.

Like a hawk seizing its prey, the man burst into the room and almost dragged Jason to his feet by the scruff of his neck.

'Where's Siena? What have you done to her? Is she alright?'

Chapter 30

'Blimey General, can't I stop for a minute?' wailed Al. 'We've been at this for three hours.'

'Nope,' said Siena, wiping a dusty hand across her face and putting down the vacuum cleaner hose. 'Only two more boxes to go downstairs and then I'll make you a cup of tea.'

'I've finished the kitchen, I've put the kettle on,' said Lisa coming through into the tiny lounge, her tiny figure lost in the over-sized dungarees she'd donned. She'd got into the spirit of things by bundling her hair up in a spotted scarf, which she assured Siena, was very fifties cleaning lady. 'This place is really nice, although it's a shame you'll be in such close proximity to his Lordship all the time.'

'Lisa, I know you don't like Will for whatever reason, but he's been very good to me. Bailed me out and is letting me live here.' She tried to soften her face; she didn't want to offend her friend. 'I hope you'll still visit me.'

Lisa gave her a hug. 'Course I will. Anyway I promised to help you with the new job. Tea?'

'Yes please.' Al dropped to his knees clutching his hands together in prayer.

'You wee drama queen,' said Marcus coming into the room carrying a bulging black sack. 'What's this new job? You're not leaving us already.'

'No. I'll still be at the pub but I'm going to be a personal shopper.'
It had been a busy few days since Will had picked her up.

'Shopping with Siena,' Lisa bellowed from the kitchen. 'Fresh
from Paris, the leading expert on fashion.'

'Ooh, that sounds fun,' said Al getting to his feet.

Lisa appeared with a tray of mugs and they all took the variety
of seats in the room. Al and Marcus squashed together on the two-
seater sofa, Lisa curled into a beanbag and Siena took an eighties
style wicker backed dining chair.

As they drank their tea, Siena gave the small room a satisfied
smile, her eyes resting on her very own Christmas tree. She could
decorate it any way she wanted.

'It's looking a bit sad,' observed Al, following her gaze.

'It's better than nothing,' said Lisa stoutly. 'It's got lights and
tinsel and I can filch a couple of the cones from the tree downstairs.
It's easy to knock up a fairy for the top. A doily, old fashioned
clothes peg, pipe cleaner and gold spray and hey presto.'

Siena laughed. Apparently those were the sort of things teaching
assistants had on tap.

'I don't care. It's all mine.'

Since returning from her night in 'prison' as Al insisted on refer-
ring to it, all sorts of people had rallied round. Lisa had turned up
with a hoover and a mop. The Elmsleys had brought an old sofa
and table and chairs. Will had lent her plates and cutlery from
the restaurant, Marcus and Al had provided her with an old kettle
and an iron, and all of them had pitched in to clean the place up,
except Will who turned tail when he spotted Lisa.

'Aren't you going to be isolated here?' asked Lisa. 'You don't
have any transport.'

'Yes I do.' Siena beamed. 'Mrs Elmsley has offered me the loan of
her bicycle. It's got a basket on the front. So I can go to Sainsbury's
and get food and stuff. How cool is that?'

'Hmm, rather you than me,' muttered Al. 'Have you seen the

weather in England?'

'Shut up.' Marcus nudged him. 'She's going to be fine.'

'Yes,' Siena stuck her tongue out at him. 'Mrs Elmsley gave me her waterproofs.' She shuddered. 'They're hideous but practical.' She laughed. 'I wouldn't have been seen dead in them in Paris but do you know what? I don't mind now.'

'But what are you going to do here? On your own.' Al looked worried.

'I'm used to being on my own and I've joined the library. I've got Nanna's sewing machine and a stack of stuff from the charity shop to alter.' She and Lisa had reinvested the thirty pounds profit they'd made on the black dress. 'Lisa and I are going to try out a, what is it?' she looked at Lisa.

'Zumba class.'

'Yes that's the one.'

'I'll come.' Marcus sat up straighter. 'I've always wanted a go at that.'

'Oh lordy, spare me from the sight of you in Lycra.' Al fanned himself. 'Not sure I can cope.'

As Siena sipped her tea, she smiled. This was enough. For the time being. Until she saw Jason again. He'd not been at the house when she'd slipped in to pack up her stuff. It had been tempting to leave him a note but she'd assumed he'd be coming in to work and she'd see him then. It would be easier to talk face-to-face except, he hadn't turned up. And she didn't have her phone. So where was he? Sulking? That didn't seem like Jason but not even Will had heard from him, even after he'd phoned Jason's mobile to let him know Siena was safe.

Maybe he'd changed his mind and gone home for Christmas after all.

She knew he'd worry, or rather she thought she knew. There'd been no word from him. So maybe he didn't care. And she was. Not. Going. To. Think. About. Him.

The others had all been remarkably restrained about asking

about him.

'Right, what's next?' asked Lisa.

'Bathroom. Fifty million spiders have taken up residence in there.'

Al rolled his sleeves up. 'I'm your man. Marcus is terrified of the wee beasties.'

Marcus nodded, slightly shame-faced.

Lisa rolled her eyes. 'But you're ten feet tall …'

By the end of the day, after a Chinese take-away which Lisa had gone to collect, several bottles of beer had been drunk and everything had been tidied away, Marcus and Al said their goodbyes. Lisa curled her legs into the corner of the sofa and looked at the lamp-lit lounge.

'We've done a good job.'

Siena smiled. 'Yeah, it looks really homely. Thanks so much. I couldn't have done it without your help.'

Lisa leaned over and gave her hug. 'My pleasure. I had a great day. I hope you'll be happy here.' She paused. 'Are you going to tell me what happened with Jason?'

Siena pasted a bright expression on her face. 'It ran its course. It was only temporary. We never made any commitment to each other.'

Lisa raised a disbelieving eyebrow and tucked her legs in tighter. 'Pull the other one, it's got bells on.'

'Seriously. We said at the start. We agreed.' Siena tried not to let the memory of their last conversation back into her head. She'd revisited the words too many times already.

'Everyone says that kind of crap at the beginning. It's like a get-out clause in case it goes wrong. Nothing went wrong with you and Jason, not as far as I could see. Claire gave up pretty quickly when she saw the way he looked at you. And she'd been as tenacious as a tic before that. '

'He's all hers now.'

327

'You don't mean that. I can tell. You two were good together. He'd even started smiling again.'

Siena shrugged, feeling the lump in her throat lodge fast. She could think of plenty of times he'd smiled at her. The dopey grin when he woke in the mornings when his sleepy eyes focused on her.

'Jason doesn't need any responsibilities at the moment. He has the brewery, he doesn't have room for anything else.'

'Is that what he said, the bastard?'

'He didn't have to. Don't worry, I'm going to be fine.'

'You will. Look at what you've achieved since you've come to England. You've really established yourself. It feels like we've been friends forever and you've always been here. The fashion thing could be great.'

'Yes, I phoned Ruth back. She suggested I do a part-time course on Fashion, Media and Communication, given all my contacts in Paris. And the manager at the Milton Keynes store wants me to do a monthly slot and will pay me for the day. And the journalist who did a piece on it has asked if I might do a regular column.'

'And we're going to do a pop up stall,' added Lisa. 'Are you sure you've got time to work here?'

'I need to, I've swapped my wages in lieu of rent.'

'Yeah, Will doesn't do charity.'

'Actually, he did offer but I refused.'

'I know he can be nice.' Lisa's head dipped. 'One day I'll tell you but it's still a bit too raw.' Siena scooted along the sofa and gave her a hug. Lisa's ribs moved as she let out a long soft sigh.

'No hurry.'

Siena took a deep breath and looked around the room, a quiet sense of satisfaction settling. Such a lot had happened in the space of a few short weeks, since that panicked flight from Paris. A warm glow burned inside her. This was living and she was doing it on her terms.

'And Nanna and me would love it if you came for Christmas Day. I'm sure my aunt and cousins wouldn't mind. You might have to kip on the floor but we can squeeze you in.'

'That's really kind of you but I'm going to work. We're open for drinks and nibbles. Regulars only. It's double time. Marcus says the tips are great and it'll be fun. Afterwards, we'll have Christmas dinner in the dining room.'

Even though she'd be on her own waking up on Christmas morning, she was really looking forward to it, already planning to buy in her favourite goodies for breakfast and treat herself to a bottle of champagne. She couldn't wait to give her presents to Will, Al and Marcus or see the Elmsleys and other regulars on Christmas Day in the pub. It *would* be a wonderful Christmas.

'We're nearly there.'

Harry's voice roused him from the doze induced by gentle motion of the car. With its leather seats and smooth suspension, it was a hell of a far cry from the Land Rover. His heart started pumping. Siena. He'd stopped worrying about what he was going to say. Kissing the living daylights out of her would be enough to start with. Then he'd tell her he was an idiot, which no doubt she'd agree with.

Once Harry had stopped throttling him and let Jason explain that he was looking for Siena, the older man had swung into action, the rugby matched abandoned. It had been a long journey across France, first class all the way, requiring a chauffeur driven car from the stadium to the Gare de Lyon, a two hour train trip across France and now another chauffeur to the Chateau. They'd done a lot of talking and Harry's face had become grimmer and grimmer.

A slow, long turn and the car wheels crunched on gravel.

Holy hell. Jason swallowed. This was where Siena lived? The apartment in Paris had been swanky, but this was something else. Stone lions flanked the doors on either side of a flight of stairs in pale stone. Jeez, this place was enormous.

Harry didn't wait for the chauffeur to open the car door, he was halfway out even before the car stopped. 'Come!' he called over his shoulder.

Jason followed as Harry took the steps two at a time.

'Celeste? Celeste!'

Harry barged past a startled looking butler. '*Où est ma femme?*'

Jason followed and stopped. Two staircases on either side of the entrance hall, bordered with an elaborate tracery of wrought iron and gilt, curved up to meet each other. To the left a twenty foot Christmas tree almost touched the top of the domed ceiling. Blue and silver glass baubles criss-crossed the fir branches in a perfect symmetry of cold uniformity, nothing like Siena's cheery, glittery pine cones haphazardly cosying up with tiny white fairy lights.

'Darling, *qu'est-ce il y a?*' Immaculate as before, Siena's mother tapped down the marble tiled floor from a side room. She shot Jason a questioning glance, but maintained her calm expression.

Harry let loose a flood of French from which Jason could pick out Siena's name.

Celeste shook her head as Harry grasped her elbows and responded in sharp, staccato sentences. The smooth lines of her face creased and she flashed an unfriendly scowl towards Jason, tossing her head in angry denial and a torrent of fierce words.

'Excuse me.' Jason pushed between the couple. 'Is she here?'

Celeste's lips firmed in a mutinous line, her cheekbones flushed with a line of red. Harry slipped his arm around her shoulders and pulled her to him. Celeste softened and she opened her mouth to say, 'No, she isn't. Yves was supposed to bring her home. He said she refused to come.'

'No, that's not right. She left with him. I rang her phone. She's in France.' If she wasn't, where the hell was she? 'Yves must be lying.'

'Yves comes from a very good family. He came by this morning. To return Siena's phone.' Celeste drew herself up. 'I hope that you're pleased with yourself, young man. You've ruined her chances. What can you offer her? He has a long and illustrious lineage, impeccable pedigree.' She looked down her nose, making it clear

330

that she considered him to be no more than a jumped up mangy mongrel.

'That includes a history of wife beating?' snarled Jason.

Celeste looked up at Harry, her expression slipping.

Harry shook his head. 'I'm afraid Yves has perhaps not behaved as he should.'

Her face paled, her hands clenching into tiny fists. With a small incline of her head, her eyes flitted to where the butler stood. 'Perhaps we should take this into the drawing room. Jackson, can we have some tea please?'

Sitting in the drawing room was like taking tea in a doll's house. The spindly chairs just about allowed you to perch on them and the ornate occasional tables were more like well-placed trip hazards. Harry, on the other hand, seemed to be able to arrange his long rangy limbs to manage the elegant terrain.

The conversation had been equally uncomfortable, but Celeste had finally agreed to détente, if not cordiale, after which she swept out of the room, reminding them that dinner would be at seven.

'I think we're finished here,' said Harry. 'It would appear Siena is still in England.'

'Yes.' Jason sighed. 'I need to get back.'

'I will see to travel arrangements for you tomorrow. There's a train back to Paris. The chauffeur can drop you at the station in the morning.'

'Thank you. And sorry for the wild goose chase.' Jason nodded at Siena's phone on the table.

'Don't apologise. I'm sorry that you had to be the one to tell me what has been going on. I will be calling on Yves tomorrow.'

Jason wasn't fooled by his calm delivery. 'I'd like to come with you.'

'That won't be necessary.' Implacable steel flashed in Harry's eyes and Jason knew better than to argue. 'I'm sure you don't want to delay your return.'

'No.' Jason gave a rueful smile. He'd wasted a lot of time with

Siena because he'd gone charging off, but he'd got Yves off her back for good. So something had come of it.

'Would you like a drink?' asked Harry, rising from one of the silk and wood chairs. 'In my study? It's a little more,' he glanced around the room, his expression not giving anything away, 'masculine. There's a game of rugby I'd like to catch up on.'

Jason had to admire his loyalty to his wife, no matter how misplaced it might be.

'*Bonjour*, can I help you, *monsieur*?'

Jason smiled. 'I took a wrong turn. I'm trying to find my way to dinner. I followed the smell.'

'Bonne, however this is the kitchen.' To his surprise the woman spoke fluent English with a slight Birmingham accent. 'The dining room is down this corridor, take the second door on the right and follow that corridor to the left and it's the third door on the right.'

'Does anyone ever get hot food?' asked Jason, he took a look around the room. Half of it looked like a professional kitchen with stainless steel tops and counters, the other half was more cosy with a sofa in the corner, a dresser piled with papers, a bag of knitting and assorted boxes and bags.

Her faded blue eyes twinkled. 'We walk fast.'

The whippet-thin build under the simple denim dress belied her easy statement.

'Sorry, I'm Jason. A friend of Siena's.' The half-finished jigsaw on a low table under the window between two shabby armchairs caught his interest. One of the chairs held a pile of dog-eared fashion magazines.

'Siena?' The woman clasped bony hands together, knuckles white as she turned her intense gaze to his face. 'How is she? Is she alright? There's been such a fuss and commotion but is she safe?'

'You must be Agnes.'

She straightened in surprise.

'Siena talks about you.' He nodded towards the puzzle. 'She's fine. Staying at her sister's in England.' It was easy to picture Siena here in the kitchen, curled up in the chair, her feet tucked underneath her, reading one of the magazines. 'In fact,' he was sure Siena wouldn't mind, 'she bought you a puzzle. One of London, a thousand pieces.'

'God bless her. She's a good girl.' Agnes eyes sharpened. 'Make sure you look after her; Lord knows, someone should.'

'Don't worry I intend to.' The words came out as a promise, not to Agnes but to himself.

Chapter 31

Waking up was the worst. The view from the dormer window in Siena's new bedroom was beautiful but it didn't stop her thinking of all the mornings she'd woken next to Jason. Her subconscious couldn't seem to grasp that there would be no warm body to stretch out and touch. For two mornings in a row, she'd blindly reached out for him. Then their last conversation would fill her head. '*I want you to leave.*' '*This was always going to be temporary.*'

And she'd signed up to the whole temporary, day by day thing; never dreaming she'd fall in love with him. He'd made no promises. He'd been totally honest with her. She had no one to blame but herself.

And she was going to get over it.

After that, she focused on the day ahead. What she needed to do. Getting used to her new routine.

There was an awful lot to be said for being so close to work. It gave her an extra couple of hours in the morning to work on the clothes she and Lisa had bought. The midnight blue shift dress in a size eighteen had been altered to a size twelve and she'd removed the ugly, cheap beading around the neck, replacing it with a satin trim. Concentrating so hard on the detailed work also stopped her thinking about other things.

Tripping down the stairs, she greeted Marcus with a deliberately cheery smile.

'Morning. Why are you looking so pleased with yourself?'

'No reason.' The smile on her face hurt, it was so forced. Christmas Eve.

Her stomach flipped over. How would she react seeing his face again? How hard would it be to resist throwing herself into his arms?

'Come on then, lets getting cracking. Al's very excited about today's specials. Been muttering about knocking up an aubergine and goats' cheese timbale. I always thought a timbale was a musical instrument.'

'I think you might mean timpani.'

'Possibly. But local aubergines? He's having a laugh.'

Siena tutted and shook her head. 'The aubergines have been sourced from the orangery at Stainglass Manor, under the personal care of Lady Drinkwater's favourite gardener, sexy Spaniard Luis Mendoza. Have you not heard of Luis' prize aubergines?'

'Is that what they're calling them these days?' Will's dry voice quipped.

'There's a gentleman at table five asking for a word with you, Siena,' announced Marcus as she took a break at the bar mid-afternoon.

Will straightened, shooting Siena a concerned look before asking, 'What does he look like?'

'Oldish. Grey hair. Quite distinguished. Well dressed.'

'Not Yves,' she said to Will.

'Who's Yves?' Marcus quivered with curiosity.

'Long story.'

'Do you want me to go find out who he is?' asked Will.

'No. I'm on home turf this time. If he tries to make me leave I'll scream very loudly.' She started towards the restaurant.

'I'll check on you every five minutes.'

'Thanks Will.' It was such a shame Lisa couldn't see this side of him.

Rounding the corner to the restaurant, her eyes sought out table five. It was the one in the corner which Marcus usually looked after.

'Harry!'

Her stepfather rose to greet her, kissing her on both cheeks.

'Shouldn't you be at the Chateau? Your birthday party?'

'That's what private helicopters are for,' he said with a wry smile. He stepped out from behind the table and took her in an embrace. 'I'm very pleased to see you.' His voice sounded choked. 'I've been so worried about you.'

She buried her head in his tweedy chest, smelling his familiar Ralph Lauren Polo aftershave.

He took a step back, his hands still on both of her arms and gave her an assessing look.

'All things considered, you look as if you've survived. Can you sit down for a minute?' He glanced back and Siena grinned as she saw Will's head bob around the corner.

'Yes, that's my boss. He's checking I'm safe.'

A look of distaste crossed Harry's face and anger flashed in his eyes.

Siena pulled back. Harry never got angry. He'd been her stepfather for ten years and she'd never once seen him lose his temper.

'Safe. An interesting word. I thought you were safe with the son of my oldest friend. I thought his age and experience would protect you.'

She ducked her head.

'I had no idea that you weren't happy. Your mother and I have had words. Although,' his expression softened. For some reason he really did adore his wife, 'I do believe she had your best interests at heart and she had no idea what Yves was really like.'

'I don't understand.' How on earth did Harry know all this?

'Yves won't be bothering you again.' Harry laid a hand on hers. 'Siena, I am extremely angry with him. Needless to say he will not be welcome at the house. You can rest assured of that. I have made it quite clear that he is not to come anywhere near you. It is up to him, how he explains himself to his parents. I do wish you could have come to me.'

'It's OK, Harry.' She patted his hand, trying to reassure him. Her stepfather looked older and greyer than she remembered. He'd lost a little weight too. 'But how do you know? Did Maman tell you?'

He smiled sadly. 'I thought you were happy.'

Harry was a consummate negotiator and a smart businessman. He chose his words carefully. He'd dodged her question neatly. But why?

'No, no. I was happy. You've given me everything. I have no complaints. Honestly, please don't think I'm not grateful, it's just I've realised that I wasn't really living. It sounds awful, I didn't even realise how bored I was.'

'You were unfulfilled I think.' He straightened up the cutlery on the table. 'Everyone needs a purpose. Your mother's is organising and bossing me, but you? We should have seen that. I feel I've been remiss. I haven't looked after you properly.'

'Please don't think that.'

'Siena, you had to run away from the people who love you to feel safe. I have not looked after you properly. Anything could have happened to you. No money. No home.' He shuddered. 'No, I did not look after you properly.'

'You did. You always did but now I realise I need more. I've got a job. I like it. I'm living on my own. Cooking.' She pulled a face. 'Not so sure about the cleaning and stuff. I'm not saying I like being poor but there's something quite good about knowing what something costs and that you can afford it because you earned it.'

Harry's eyes shone and he blinked. 'I'm so proud of you. You've shown yourself to be resourceful.' Shaking his head, Harry took out one of the pristine linen handkerchiefs he always carried and dabbed his eyes. 'You do know that I've always considered you to be my daughter, don't you? Which brings me to another matter. Another young man has been to see me about you.'

The silence and stillness of the house told him no one was home. As soon as Jason opened the front door, he could hear and feel it, as if the dust settled the minute the key went in the lock and the shadows stopped jostling each other in dark corners.

He'd half hoped to hear Siena singing as she was getting ready for work. Smell her perfume. See her clothes draped across the newel post.

It was early and he itched with the grubbiness that came from all night travel. He'd come straight from the airport, after travelling for over twenty hours from the other side of France. He moved from the kitchen to the lounge. No shoes, no scarves, no leather jacket dumped on the back of a wooden chair. Unable to stop himself he took the stairs two at a time. Pushed open the bathroom door … the shelf, cleared.

She'd gone. It didn't seem possible. All those hours on the train. On the plane imagining her being here. And she wasn't.

Where was she? He couldn't even contact her, as her phone was nestled in his jacket pocket along with his.

He walked back through to the lounge. Under the tree was a solitary present, wrapped in the red, white and gold wrapping paper that she'd chosen to co-ordinate with her ribbons and gift tags. Typical Siena, the present wrapping had been painstaking. Every tag and ribbon had to match. Each present for Will, Marcus and Al had to be perfect. The more ornate bows were reserved for Lisa, Nanna and Agnes. He'd teased her. Laughed at her concentration as the tip of her tongue touched her top lip each time she focused on each perfect parcel. As instructed, he'd helped by placing his fingers on the seams of paper for her to Sellotape and almost had the tips of them guillotined when she pulled the ribbons in tight knots.

He hadn't helped with this particular parcel. He pulled it out from under the tree.

To Jason, with love, Siena x

It was Christmas Eve. In France they opened their presents

today. He weighed the present in his hands. Did he even deserve this?

The paper slid off as he tugged at the ribbon and slid a finger along the perfect taped edge. In a nest of tissue paper lay a photo frame. From the picture Siena laughed up at him, the city of Paris spread out behind them both. The picture from Sacré-Coeur. Taken moments after he'd made his first mistake and not kissed her as he'd wanted to.

He cleared a space and put picture in the centre of the mantelpiece where it belonged. Hope and happiness shone in her eyes, almost teasing as if to say, 'you might be a coward but I've got enough bravery for both of us.' He'd made an absolute mess of things but she'd left him this, a moment of joy. That was her all over and he'd seriously underestimated her. This was the real Siena.

Siena didn't belong in a fancy chateau; she wanted friendships, relationships, love.

He knew exactly where she'd be. With the people that mattered to her. He grinned and grabbed his car keys.

She cycled up the lane feeling the sun on her face and the satisfying twinge of hard labour in every muscle. With the basket on the front crammed full of mince pies, a bottle of red wine, smoked salmon, bagels and other Christmas delights, the additional weight made the slow climb even harder. Her thigh muscles screamed in protest but it would be worth it. She couldn't help the smile that had taken over her lips ever since Harry's visit.

She sighed and pedalled harder, pushing herself. Butterflies danced in her stomach. She hadn't slept last night. She'd tried to keep herself busy. Found extra to do. Put on a front. Chatty, friendly, helpful but if she was completely honest, all her energy went into not thinking about when Jason would finally get here.

Harry had been a bit naughty abandoning him in France. After taking Jason to the Chateau thinking that Siena had gone there with Yves, Harry had left him to make his own way home, while he commissioned a private helicopter.

For a minute, she stopped and hopped off the pedals, giving in to the almost physical pain slicing through her chest. She wanted to see him. Where was he? Why hadn't he been back to the brewery? It was hopeless; she couldn't stop thinking about him. Their first tumultuous, clumsy, crazy field sex. Sharing his bed, her leg hooked over his, head on his chest, watching the lift and fall of his breathing as he slept.

Wincing as she sighed and took a breath, she gripped the bike ready to push herself off again. Before she could move, she heard the roar of a car engine and the crash of gears. Someone was going far too fast, speeding round the bend. Frantically trying to hop onto the pedal and get out of the way, she wobbled precariously.

Like a rhino bursting out of the undergrowth, the car roared around the corner. She threw herself out the way as it came to an emergency stop, tyres squealing and burnt rubber skinning the road.

She and the bike landed in a heap on the verge, her nose planted in a thick clump of mud and grass, as she registered that it was a Land Rover.

A door slammed. Running feet.

'What the fuck do you think you were doing in the middle of the road and where the fuck have you been?'

Rolling over, she disentangled herself from the bike. Of course he'd be cross. Of course it would be her fault. Typical Jason.

'Where have you been? And what the fuck were you doing driving like a crazy person?' She laughed up at his cross face, her heart dancing at the very sight of him.

'Where have I been? I've been travelling across France for bloody days trying to catch up with you.' He seized her arms, eyes blazing. 'Where were you?'

'If I said in a police cell, would you believe me?'

He pulled her to him. 'With you, anything is possible. I think that's what I love about you.'

Her knees threatened to buckle as she looked into his hand-some, fierce face.

And then his mouth was on hers kissing her furiously and she was kissing him back, winding her arms around his neck, her heart thudding at a million miles an hour. He held her, pressing her length up against his, in demanding possession as if he might never loosen his hold. Melting into him, her last coherent thought was that she was happy with that.

He broke off the kiss to suck in a breath, whispered, 'Oh God, I missed you.' He kissed her again before stopping to run his fingers along her cheekbones. 'I'm sorry.' And then reapplied his lips again. She was much too dazed to say a thing. With her heart singing inside she contented herself with savouring the deliciously possessive kisses.

An outraged tooting came from behind the Land Rover.

'Shit.' He gazed into her eyes. 'Don't go anywhere.'

She laughed. 'Like where? Paris?'

'That's so not funny.' He glared and ran back to the car, acknowledging the distinctly pissed off driver of the other car, who was making very rude gestures. Jason waved cheerily and hopped up into his driver's seat to move the car over to the side of the road.

Shy all of a sudden, she started to pick her bike up, collecting the spilled groceries. As she went to pick up a bruised apple, his hand appeared on hers.

Crouched next to her he lifted her chin to look into her face. 'Siena, I'm so sorry. Can you forgive me?'

She sighed. 'For what?' For her falling in love with him when he'd made it clear he wasn't in the market for permanency?

He took her hand. 'For being a complete and utter knob.'

'Oh, you can't help that.' She tried for a light smile but she could feel the sadness etched on her face. It was OK for him to miss her, she missed him too, but it didn't really make that much difference to her. She wanted more and it wasn't fair to expect it from him. She was the one who now wanted to change the rules.

'Besides you were right.'

'I was right.' There was a panicked look on his face. 'I'm a bloke. We're never right.'

She smiled gently at him. 'It was temporary. That's all we agreed.' She felt a tad guilty at the sudden blaze of expression that filled his face.

He hauled her into his arms, his nose almost touching hers. 'I've changed my mind.'

'Don't I have any say?' She gave him an arch look.

'No, you bloody don't. I'm not letting you go. I was a complete idiot, not able to see what was right under my nose.'

He looked down into her face, his eyes shining. 'I love you. I don't want you to leave. Please stay. You were right. We have more and I want more, much, much more.'

She reached up and touched his face hardly daring to believe what she was hearing. Her eyes brimming with tears, she gave him a tremulous smile. 'I love you Jason.'

He hugged her to him and she relaxed into his chest, hearing his heart pounding in time with hers.

'You know I have to get up for work soon,' she said regretfully, stroking his naked chest.

'At least neither of us has far to go.' Jason nuzzled her neck and his hand swept across her breast. 'In fact I can see my office from this window.' He craned his neck to look out the window of the flat above the pub. 'We can both be at work within thirty seconds.'

'I think Will might have something to say if I turn up to work like this.' Siena giggled.

'I think I might too,' growled Jason, suddenly rolling on top of her, crushing her to him.

'I can't believe you went all the way to Paris.' She settled her head back in the crook of his arm, sighing with happiness.

'I can't believe it took me so sodding long to get home again. Harry's a devious sod. Dumping me the other side of France and leaving me to travel back when he hops over in a bloody helicopter. I might have got here in time to stop you moving in here. I should have known you'd marshal your troops to get moved in record time.'

'I had a good incentive. I wanted to show you I don't need you to support me. I'm not going to be like Stacey. Moving in and staying by default.'

He stiffened. 'What do you mean?'

She sighed. 'Jason, it would be so easy for me to move back to Laurie's house but I need to prove that I can do this. Prove that if everything at the brewery goes "tits up" to coin a Will expression, you don't have to worry about me.'

'But what if I want to worry about you?' He took her face in both hands. 'I love you. It's my prerogative.'

'I love you too but proving I can be independent is my prerogative too.'

'I knew you'd be the stubborn type.'

'I knew you'd be the possessive type.'

He stopped the argument with a kiss.

'I'm always going to worry that you're going to miss out. I've seen your home.' Jason's face sobered. 'That's one hell of a house. The fountain is bigger than the one in the Place de la Concorde.' With worried eyes he kissed her. 'I hate the thought of you not enjoying the things you're used to. I know you're not that shallow and you've demonstrated you can stand on your own two feet, but one day you might miss having a nice home, nice clothes.' He pulled a face. 'I'll never be able to keep you in the style—'

She put her hand over his mouth. 'Shh, I already told you. '

'Although your stepfather wants to put a cash injection into the business.' He pulled an embarrassed face. 'Of course, I refused.'

'Jason. That would be silly. He's a very successful businessman, with interests in drinks companies all over France. Remember Monsieur LeFoute and how quickly he changed his tune?'

'I wondered if it might be something like that at the time.'

'Whether you take up Harry's offer or not, it's entirely up to you. Whatever you do, it won't change my feelings. But I think you would be crazy to turn it down, not because of the money but because he can give you so much help and expertise. He's a good guy to have on side.'

'I'll think about it … on one condition.'

'Which is?'

'You come home for Christmas. After your shift tonight we go back, drink that last bottle of Lafite, light a fire and wake up together tomorrow morning.'

'Sounds like the perfect Christmas to me.'

'I'm not sure about that. No turkey. No Christmas pud. No sprouts.' Jason winced. 'Good job you're not some high maintenance chick, I don't even have a present for you. I found yours by the way. I love it. That makes even worse that I don't have anything for you.'

She gave a throaty purr and looped her arms around his neck. 'I think you do.' She kissed him, her tongue delving in with explicit invitation. 'And who needs sprouts?'

With a wicked grin, he kissed her. 'Not us, but now you come to mention it, I do have something rather special to offer.'

As she sank back into the bed, weighted by his body, his lips tracing their way down her body, she gave a shiver of pleasure and smiled to herself. It was shaping up to be the best Christmas ever.

Acknowledgements

Some days, writing a book is like pulling teeth, blinking hard work, but the goodwill of readers, reviewers and bloggers, who take the time and trouble to say lovely things, make it all worthwhile. Thank you to all those who have been so supportive.

There are a few people who are endlessly generous with their time and help, so I would like to thank Annie Cooper for beta reading this manuscript at a very early stage and her helpful comments, Donna, my writing soul mate, it is quite possible that I might write books without her constant backing but it wouldn't be half as much fun and Queen of Twitter, Anita Chapman aka @neetswriting, a fabulous friend and a wonder on social media.

Last but not least, heartfelt gratitude goes to my fabulous super agent, Broo Doherty and the team at HarperImpulse, especially Charlotte and Grace, who have done so much to put the shine into my work.